T0031949

THE NEW EMPIRE

award-winning author of *The Rose Queen*

Alison McBain

THE NEW EMPIRE

Alison McBain

woodhall press

Woodhall Press | Norwalk, CT

woodhall press

Woodhall Press, 81 Old Saugatuck Road, Norwalk, CT 06855
WoodhallPress.com
Copyright © 2022 Alison McBain

All rights reserved. No part of this book may be reproduced in any form or by any electronic or mechanical means, including information storage and retrieval systems, without written permission from the publisher, except by a reviewer who may quote passages for review.

Cover design: Alison McBain
Layout artist: LJ Mucci

Library of Congress Cataloging-in-Publication Data available
ISBN 978-1-954907-42-3 (paper)
ISBN 978-1-954907-43-0 (electronic)

First Edition

Distributed by Independent Publishers Group
(800) 888-4741

Printed in the United States of America

The New Empire is a work of fiction. Names, characters, places, incidents, and dialogue are products of the author's imagination or are used fictitiously. Where actual institutions or locations and real-life historical or public figures appear, the situations, incidents, and dialogues concerning those entities, places, and persons are entirely fictional and are not intended to describe actual events. In all other respects, any resemblance to actual events, locales, or persons, living or dead, is entirely coincidental.

Note on the Mutsun Language

Capitalizations of letters in a word changes the pronunciation, so standard English capitalizations were not used for several Mutsun honorific titles, including at the beginning of sentences. This is intentional.

To everyone who straddles more than one world,
who dances between cultures and traditions,
beliefs and languages,
the *hapa* and the halfs,
and most especially to those who realize
being half makes you whole—
this story is for you.

PR⬤LOGUE

Jiangxi was furiously buttoning his jacket when a familiar voice from the doorway stilled his fingers.

"Leave be. They have come here for you." After a pause, "You could not have waited for me to die?"

The tone of the words was lethargic. His master was an old man when Jiangxi had come to him and an even older man now, but his deep voice was slowed by sorrow, not age. The shadows of the room seemed to darken, despite the sliver of moonlight streaming in from the next room and the passage leading outside. The passage that should have led to freedom.

Jiangxi made no reply, but raised his head high. He stepped forward to face the stooped man waiting in the doorway. He met Onas's eyes, which were weighed down with the burden of mortality. There were a thousand answers Jiangxi could have given his master, but he made none of them. Onas nodded in defeat. After a moment, Jiangxi stepped past him.

Outside the door, he saw a row of rifles sticking into the air like the traditional spears of war. When the warriors saw his silhouette darken the doorway, they lowered the rifles and took aim.

Behind him, the old man sighed. Jiangxi walked towards the fate awaiting him.

They had come here to kill him. It was over.

CHAPTER 1

Twenty years earlier

Most of what Jiangxi could recall of his life before the ship were a few blurred images of golden rooms and soft-spoken women. Echoes of his past sometimes came to him at odd times, like in the folds of a dream, but most of it was seared from his mind with the pain of the slave brand.

He was a child when he received the mark, barely six years old. He'd struggled as the metal was heated in the brazier, cried out as it came close to his face. Trying to free himself was a futile effort, and he could do nothing but scream as the metal came down upon his forehead and cheeks in a caress as light as death.

After that, the memories became blurred again. He'd been thrown into the hold of the ship, tumbling head over heels while the laughter of the crew burned in his ears. Hell's Descent, the slaves called the passage. He had left his earthly life behind when he was taken below decks and learned a new reality, a reality of shit and vomit, starvation and thirst. The golden rooms and beautiful Chinese women were so far away by the end of the trip that they seemed like a dream, a serene image of a heaven from which he had been cast out. That life had never existed.

Jiangxi was one of only a handful of children who survived the passage. Many fell sick. More of them died. Those who perished early in the voyage were the lucky ones, tipped overboard to a spurious liberty, free from the months of pain and misery that the living had to endure.

He was ill, but not for long, and the fat of his youth saved his life in the end. There was little to eat, less to drink. The world became a pinpoint of gnawing aches, legs pinned in chains and unmoving, skin rotting from his body with sores, the stench so overwhelming that his nose quit in disgust. There was no light, no air, and most of those who survived were beaten into submission without a blow being struck. They emerged, he didn't know how long after being chained in, pitiful wrecks of humanity with empty, staring eyes and empty souls. The chains were unnecessary, since all resistance had left them. Their spirits had died.

After so long in the dark, being aboveboard was terrifying. Sunlight was a new pain to add to the old. Jiangxi's eyes watered fiercely, blurring the mishmash city into a stir fry of colors and odors. He barely glanced at the buildings that might have made his heart ache for home, built in the many-tiered style of the Imperial city of Beijing. Other homes were small and round, like overgrown mushrooms. From the waterfront below, the city looked like a puzzle of chopped-up shapes and colors, although his vision of the landscape morphed into a colorful stain as he blinked and squinted against the glare of the light.

Prodded from behind, Jiangxi stumbled and nearly lost his balance. The man in front of him was not so lucky, and fell to his knees on the pier. One of the ship's crew ran forward and kicked at the thin man's sides, and Jiangxi could hear the sickening crunch of the slaver's boot against bone, the hoarse screaming as the slave tried to get his legs back under him.

Eventually, the other crew intervened, and the slave was pulled back upright, but without the strength to keep his feet. Without thinking, Jiangxi leaned forward. On the other side, a woman did the same, and the beaten man gripped both of their shoulders. The man's thin fingers were brutally strong, his mouth pulled tight in pain. Unspoken: another fall would mean the end.

After that, Jiangxi did not falter or stumble. A purpose, however tenuous or brief: he would save this man. This tall, thin man hunched over the dual crutches of a skinny woman under one arm and a drooping child under the other. He limped along, and Jiangxi endured.

The walk from the pier and through the streets of the city seemed endless. Each footfall hurt, with the counterpoint of his fellow slave's fingers digging deeply into his bony shoulder. But Jiangxi's eyes were beginning to focus; either that, or his body's moisture had run dry, and his tears no longer had a source. Jiangxi panted and scraped his dry tongue across his lips.

A wooden platform appeared ahead of them, with five steep steps leading up to it. At the edge of the stairs, the man hesitated—perhaps gathering his strength, or perhaps only exhausted at the idea of the pain that would grind through his broken ribs when he lifted his foot.

A fist from the crewman remedied the situation. The man's head hit the stairs with a thud, and he bounced back to lie in the dirt, unmoving. Jiangxi nearly fell at the loss of pressure from the slave's hand, only catching himself on the rough wooden boards of the plank stairs.

"Get up," growled one of the crew behind him in passable *Guānhuà*, and Jiangxi didn't hesitate or look back. Sympathy was ephemeral; lives were ephemeral. The man lying in the dirt was nothing to him anymore, not even a burden.

5

When the survivors had all ascended, the same crewmember said another word, but this time Jiangxi couldn't understand him. The crew from the slave ship, like others native to this foreign land, seemed to misplace the intonations for some words common to many Chinese dialects. But when the men and women around him began to unfasten worn ties and shiver out of their clothes, he understood what the crewman's command had been. After he undressed and dropped the rags of his clothes to the ground, there was a brief moment of shock from the chill morning air.

The first shout below the platform wasn't a surprise, since any type of surprise had died below decks on the ship. Numbly, his eyes scanned the gathered crowd, noting the differences of their faces and clothes from his own countrymen and fellow slaves, listening with a shiver of fear to the harsh tone of their jeering, even if he didn't understand their words. Jiangxi tried to huddle in on himself against the chill and barely noticed when an old man in the crowd, a native of this new land, pointed at him and called out in their strange language.

Jiangxi's captors called back. The old man walked up to the platform and handed something to the slavers—it was long, like a belt, with purple and white beads formed into a simple pattern. He heard the word "wampum" as it exchanged hands. Jiangxi caught no more than a glimpse of his purchaser before he was being prodded ungently from behind.

"Go, boy," growled the same cruel crewmate whose impatience had killed his fellow slave. The man spoke in a twisted imitation of the Beijing dialect. When Jiangxi didn't move quickly enough, a shove from behind sent him stumbling to the edge of the platform. With his ankles and wrists hobbled together, he barely caught his balance before he would've tumbled down the stairs.

The lead rope around his neck was thrown down to the thin man, who had a dark, wrinkled face and deep lines around his mouth. When Jiangxi reached the bottom of the stairs, a crewman approached him with a hammer and chisel, and he cowered. Fear had not died, after all. But the tools were only to strike the chains around his ankles.

To Jiangxi, the old man holding the rope had a chilling gaze, his countenance alien in the bright sunlight. His eyes were spaced too closely together, his nose short and prominent, rather than wide and flat like Jiangxi's.

The man tugged on the rope and Jiangxi followed, unresisting. He did not care that he was still naked and shivering with cold. These details seemed unimportant. They walked through the crowded streets, the old man leading and Jiangxi putting one foot in front of the other and no longer looking up from the packed earth of the dirt road. He concentrated on movement, on keeping moving. Stopping would mean an end, like the slave from the ship who had never reached the auction platform.

Foot up. Foot down. Tug of rope.

Eventually, Jiangxi noticed the babble of strange voices had faded away, and he glanced up. They had left the settlement behind. The old man lived in a small dwelling outside of town that looked like two brown and feathery mushrooms leaning together, one bigger than the other. While each "mushroom" was built in the traditional Amah Mutsun conical style, instead of the sides of the building being constructed of bundled tule, they had layered bark like a Haudenosaunee longhouse. The walls inside and out contained painted symbols and pictures in bright yellows, blues, reds, and whites.

Inside were stacks of plain wooden boxes piled on shelves built into the walls. Woven mats of reeds covered the floor, overlaid with brightly patterned rugs, with a large space in the middle for a fire, with a covered smoke hole in the ceiling above. Baskets hung from hooks attached to the interwoven branches that formed the curve of the ceiling, but no furniture. An open doorway led to one other room.

The man's thick fingers worked patiently at the knots in the rope around the boy's neck as Jiangxi stood where he had stopped, too tired to move farther. When the rope fell, the man stared at the boy for a space of seconds.

"I am the *kuksui*," the man said. Jiangxi started as the man spoke in a Beijing dialect, Jiangxi's native tongue. All except the word "*kuksui*," which he had never heard before. "You labor for me. You obey and is well. You disobey and is bad."

He paused. Jiangxi felt an answer was expected, so he nodded.

"Good," the man continued. "You on long journey. There is stream, you bathe. Then sleep. You wake, we begin."

The first morning after arriving, Jiangxi opened his eyes, convinced something was terribly wrong. The room spun around him, and he nearly fell over as he tried to stand. The ground seemed to be lurching under his feet, and he barely made it out the door as the dizziness turned to nausea. However, there wasn't anything to expel from his system except bile, since they hadn't fed them on the ship that last day into port. "Why waste supplies?" he'd overheard one of the crew explaining to a newer shipmate as they were shepherded onto the wharf. "They're their masters' problem now."

That's how the old man found him, naked and curled up in the dirt just outside the door. The boy stared at the man's long, brown toes, but had no energy to look up to his face.

The man said something in that other language and, although Jiangxi didn't understand, it had the universal sound of an impatient exclamation. The toes disappeared back into the house only to be replaced moments later with a dark hand that turned his head upright and pulled him into a sitting position that he was almost too weak to maintain.

The man offered him something that his nostrils told him was food—sweet, savory, and completely undesirable to him. The fresh smell turned his stomach, so that it was only by biting his dirty lip that he prevented himself from heaving again.

The man said something, holding the rounded bowl towards him. He knelt in the dust next to Jiangxi, and shoved the bowl into the boy's smaller hands. Almost in self-defense, he took the offering. But when Jiangxi did nothing afterward, the *kuksui* held out a flat hand, palm up, and mimed moving food from the bowl to his mouth. Jiangxi shook his head.

"Eat," the man said in Jiangxi's dialect, eyes rolled back as if to search inwards for the correct words. He spoke slowly, his heavy accent garbling several of the intonations. "You not eat, you not can learn." When no action resulted from the statement, the old man turned his head slightly to nod in the direction of the port. "You not eat, you go back to ship."

The food was in his mouth before he realized his hand had moved. He would never survive another ship ride. He swallowed down the beans and squash, then swallowed them down again as they rose up, protesting, in his throat. He didn't understand why the food didn't appeal to him, but the very smell of it, the texture on his tongue, seemed repellent. But the tastes were not complex, and he managed to scrape the plate clean with his tongue and keep the food in his belly.

"Good," the *kuksui* smiled. He handed over a cup that Jiangxi hadn't seen him fetch. The boy swallowed down all of it before realizing it was water. If it had been piss, he'd have drunk it as quickly to prevent a return to that place of pain and suffering.

"To start," the man said as the cup was handed back. "The Mutsun not use names. Bad luck, bring bad spirits. But you should know how to say, help you learn." He paused, put his hand on his chest. "My name Onas," he began. Then he followed the simple sentence with a garble of sounds. "Repeat," he said sternly.

Jiangxi quoted him verbatim. The sounds were not hard, only strange. "No, no!" his teacher scolded. "*My* name Onas. Repeat, add *your* name."

Jiangxi said the expected syllables. "Again," said the man. Jiangxi repeated them.

"Again," said Onas.

When the sun was high, Onas directed him to sit under a tree near the hut. In the cool shade, they both ate this time, another simple meal of rolled flat cakes filled with vegetables.

Jiangxi remembered red-clothed women with softly tinkling jewelry bending over him and smiling. He remembered abundance, asking for and receiving food filled with savory meats and spices. His stomach filled with the sour taste of the vegetable roll and he coughed.

"Outside," the old man said as Jiangxi coughed and coughed. He made it as far as the edge of the clearing before he dropped to his knees and vomited the meal onto the brown earth.

He didn't bother to return to the man's home, but lay in the dirt next to his sickness and stared up into the sky. He remembered his mother, with her beautiful almond-colored eyes ringed with kohl, gently singing a lullaby. Now, when it was too late, he couldn't remember the exact words, only the feeling that it was a sad song. He'd never bothered to learn the words, but he would lie against her with his head pressed against her chest as she sang.

The melody lingered in his dreams on the ship's passage across the endless waters. And he would wake up from the dreams of gentle peace and cry for her, his cries lost among the torment of the other lost souls crying for release.

Onas found him there in the dirt when some time had passed, tears trickling down his cheeks. Jiangxi was humming a tune endlessly while his lips trembled with the effort to remember the words.

Too late.

CHAPTER 2

Twenty years later

Jiangxi started awake. His fingers curled in the dirt floor as he remembered where he was. *When* he was. He'd been dreaming of the hellish passage on the ship as a child. Back in that hold filled with the dead and dying, the cries and moans of the sick echoing through his head. On the ship, people had at first tried to talk and reassure one another. With little food and water, no one had any energy after the days spread out and became months.

He had thought he would die there, in Hell's Descent. He couldn't have pictured anything worse as a child.

This prison was certainly not worse—at least, he was unchained, if caged. And now he was an adult, and no longer filled with a child's fears. There was no window and no light, only the four dark walls of his prison. The door was to his right. He had already searched the cell when daylight seeped in through the cracks between the wooden logs, but found no way of escape. The door was barred from outside and the wooden logs of the walls were thick and unyielding, sunk many feet into the ground. His fingernails were broken and bloody from trying to dig under the wall, but he had only made a small hole. The corners of the room stank with human waste from previous tenants. The air was stale and close, the ground cold.

His captors had searched him when they took him from his master's home, leaving Jiangxi only the shirt and jacket he'd slept in. After the search, they'd beaten him until his vision started to blacken around the edges and then thrown him in here.

"Tomorrow," one man tossed scornfully over his shoulder as he stood in the doorway, outlined against the rising sun. The door closed on the word.

Slaves weren't people. Even if they'd been freed, they would always be looked down upon. The man didn't mean that, tomorrow, he would be granted a fair hearing where he could explain his side of the matter. He could tell no one that he was a man and he deserved to live. No, tomorrow, they would hang him publicly, as an example to any other insurrectionists. Tomorrow, he would die.

Death wasn't a new idea to a slave. It was the first lesson they learned from the moment they were shackled. They worked or they died. A slave marked the days by temperature and length, for seasons meant little in the ebb and flow of work. There were no holidays to celebrate, no days of rest and meditation. There was only hot and cold and work, work, work.

Warm days meant longer hours, but they were better for all that, despite the heat of the work and the infrequent breaks for water or rest. Spurred by a fellow-feeling of sympathy as they remembered their own harsh beginnings, they'd learned long ago to shuffle together to cover the lack of someone who was sick. The overseer was indiscriminate with his bamboo whip, and no excuse would spare him punishing the offender.

Winter had its own whips to wield that were no match for human punishment. Even though some of the newer ones would fall prone to the dirt from exhaustion or thirst during the summers, they mostly had the chance of recovery. But though the season was milder here than in Beijing, winter gave no second chances; it killed.

After their day working in the fields, workers returned to the only home they were allowed. Several neighboring fields combined into a shantytown in the center, like the connecting spoke of a wheel. Their shared home was a longhouse, and it was for all the slaves belonging to the multiple owners of the surrounding fields. There, the men and women slept, had sex, gave birth and died, packed together like they'd been in the hold of the slave ships.

The hard sun of this land beat like war drums on his skin. After the one year he'd spent working in the fields, Jiangxi would glance at his sun-burned, dusky arms and feel the childhood memories he carried were only the whispering of unreal dreams. But he needed something of his own to lead him through each day, even if the presence of his dreams had no substance.

He was not alone. The overseas slaves all had some secret from their previous life that kept them going. He could see it in their eyes, in the sideways shift of pupils as they looked around them and saw... something else. Something that cushioned them from madness in the first few months after they arrived, something that kept them alive when it would be so much easier, so much less painful, to let go. To fall under the whip and make a choice for the first time in their servitude—the choice to never get up again.

CHAPTER 3

Twenty years earlier

Fresh off the ship, he had no idea of his future, except that his master took a special interest in him. Jiangxi had no idea what to expect after Onas came outside to find him. He said nothing to the tears on Jiangxi's face or the pitiful vomit in the dirt. Instead, he said, "Wash—stream. Then back. Back here."

Jiangxi visited the stream. The lullaby had died in his throat, and he did not try to resurrect it. Onas waited for him outside the hut's door, and language lessons resumed. Jiangxi repeated the strange sounds by rote, and didn't even realize when the days of repetition became months, and some of the words began to stick.

Onas never raised his voice, never beat him, never withheld food. But his eyes stayed cool to Jiangxi's efforts, even if they never were completely cold and indifferent. The shadows of Hell's Descent continued to haunt Jiangxi's sleep, but slowly started to fade during the day.

Unexpectedly, written language was borrowed, and this was to Jiangxi's advantage. The first time he saw the old man putting paintbrush to paper, Jiangxi moved to stand behind him and was surprised to see familiar characters forming across the page. Jiangxi knew only the fundamentals of Chinese writing, but seeing the figures on paper, he was forcibly reminded of the dry-voiced tutor who had schooled the children of the Imperial nursery. The swish and scrape of calligraphy brushes on paper. The infrequent times of encouragement, and the more common punishments for failure.

The old man noticed his interest. "Here," he said and handed Jiangxi the brush. "You know to write?"

In response, Jiangxi nodded shyly. For the first time, the old man's eyes flared with interest. "Show!"

Slowly, the boy bent over the paper. The sheet was a tally—a list of the crops of the field, dates, and numbers. He saw where Onas had left off and he glanced up, questioning.

"Four hundred of corn," said his master.

The brush felt strange in his shaky hand, and Jiangxi's first character ran with ink. However, it was legible, and the next one had only one blotch to mar it.

Jiangxi did not know the character for "corn." He had eaten corn in the Imperial Palace, but it was a luxury imported from overseas, and the Imperial tutor had only had time to teach them the fundamental characters—proper foods native to China. Onas showed him the new word by sketching it in the dirt with his finger, and Jiangxi copied the figure perfectly onto the tally sheet.

"Good!" said Onas. The first praise, after the slow silences that hinted at disapproval during his attempts at the spoken language. "Here," his master pointed. "Five hundred of squash." Jiangxi wrote, only stopping to ask for the words for unfamiliar items as Onas's voice droned on with items and numbers. When the list was complete, the old man nodded at him and Jiangxi smiled. His first for months.

"Reward," said his master. "You go out. Return for eating time. No work now."

Jiangxi's mouth flattened. Would he not face trouble if he roamed free...? What if he were caught? He didn't know enough words to ask the questions of Onas, or to explain himself to a stranger if they stopped him.

Onas nodded to the door when he didn't move. "There, by stream. Place to think. To play."

Jiangxi didn't want to think. Thoughts led to the past, to the future, to hopes that were impossible now. And play? *Play?* How could he return to that time before, a time surrounded by the endless toys available to him and the other children? Those days had ended with his eldest brother's entrance to the nursery in a monsoon of violence and pain. The last toy he'd seen had ended up covered in his nurse's blood after they were discovered.

Women screaming and running in a flash of silks. His caretaker's hand over his mouth. The blunt-fingered hand choked him, and Jiangxi bit hard at her palm, until it disappeared and he could breathe again. Her tears, the terrified screaming outside, and her frantic attempts to shush him—

Discovery. A face, recognizable as the faces of all his brothers were by the man's long features and drooping eyes. It was their father's features stamped upon him that proved them kin, their father who had ruled the household and its gentle women. Their father, who had died in the night.

Their father ruled his household, but he controlled more than that. He controlled the city and the countryside around it, all the cities up and down the coast and over the mountains. An empire stretching back millennia.

But with his death, there were too many sons for a clear succession. For one who would seize power, now had to be a time of cleansing, of purification.

Jiangxi was pulled from the arms of the girl holding him and he remembered the look on her face. It was despair, hopelessness. There was no fear, only a resignation, a recognition of defeat. She was dragged away by the collar of her dress, and he watched it happen like a shadow play put on for a special performance. It couldn't be real.

He tried to resist the hands on him, squirming like a snake. He was stopped by the shock of his brother's face as the man bent over him. There were lines cut into that indifferent face, furrows and ridges from the long passage of time. His brother belonged to that world Jiangxi sometimes glimpsed, but in which he never participated—the adult world, where everyone was the same unreachable age and distant as history. Jiangxi knew enough to recognize him from palace social events, but that was all.

"Fat," his older brother grunted. Jiangxi yelled when the man poked a finger into his side, and his brother half-turned away from him. Jiangxi thought he meant to leave him here, alone without his nursemaid. He had never been alone before. He drew in a deep breath to scream louder.

Instead, a shape whipped across his vision and bounced him to the floor. His brother's hand. Spread-eagled, Jiangxi struggled to move, to get up. But it was as if his limbs had become disconnected at the impact, shattering like porcelain into a thousand breakable pieces.

"All to market," his brother announced to the room. The loud voice wobbled in Jiangxi's ears, which seemed as broken as the rest of him. His vision faded, and he blinked and attempted to breathe. The blow had had enough force to stop a man, let alone a child. His brother's face loomed over him again, close enough to see hairs sprouting like straw from nose, ears, and brows. The odor of his brother this close was unpleasant, strong with musk.

"And you, little prince," his brother grinned. "The first wife's favorite. Remember me in the time to come, and how I spared your life."

So Jiangxi remembered. It was all he had, all he could hold onto of the good life that had been his. It was not overshadowed by the evil that had ended the good and brought him here, but he held onto the earlier time and remembered.

But play? No. There would never be play again.

Instead of voicing these whirling thoughts and memories, Jiangxi just nodded to his master. Onas had already turned to something else and didn't say anything further.

Jiangxi walked out the door and sat by the stream on a grey, rounded rock. He stared into the water and thought about how he had smiled at the old man's praise of his writing, as if it mattered.

But it didn't. It didn't matter at all. Nothing in this new land mattered to him.

He didn't know what name to give to the flame he carried inside his heart. Someday, he would return to his home, the emotion told him. One day in the future, he would see his brother suffer.

"My writing. Not good," said the old man when Jiangxi came back to the house for the meal. The extra food Jiangxi had been given at the beginning when he was fresh from the ship had helped replace some flesh on his bones, and so now that he was starting to fill out, the master had returned to the Haudenosaunee tradition of one large meal near midday. "I dreamed you come here," Onas continued. "Write for me. Learn from me."

Jiangxi said nothing. He had no curiosity about his master's dreams.

"Now, you cook. It is this and this and this." Onas held out a small sack of mealy golden flour and several covered baskets balanced in a stack. Jiangxi automatically took them, but hesitated until Onas said, "Outside is fire. Mix together."

When he still didn't move, Onas sighed. "Here, I show you." He led the way outside and Jiangxi watched his master put in a clay bowl some flour, water from the stream, and a handful each of corn kernels, seeds, and nuts. Water boiled in a black pot over the open flame and Onas kneaded the mixture he had made into small round balls and dropped them into the water. When Onas fished them out with a wooden spoon, they were burning hot and dense as rocks.

Jiangxi couldn't manage to eat more than two, and he burned his tongue on the first one. The rest of the small loaves were wrapped tightly in oiled cloth and removed to one of the many baskets that hung from the ceiling of the old man's hut, which helped guard against pests on the ground.

Jiangxi was just beginning to learn about the hundreds of tribes that made up this coastal area, and to which Onas traded his goods from the fields—the endless lists that were tallied regularly by Jiangxi. Amah Mutsun was a tribe native to the west coast—Onas was half-Amah Mutsun. But there were many more tribes in the interior of this great and expansive land, too many for Jiangxi to grasp when Onas attempted to explain. It was an intricate network like a spider's web, and Jiangxi was just starting to realize that Onas was one of many spiders who helped maintain it.

Onas had storage on the farm, but the overflow trade goods came to his hut. There was too much to keep in his one-cone dwelling, so a second, larger hut had been attached to the first with an open doorway. Each cone had a second doorway that led outside, blocked off by weathered and faded blankets that could be tied down in a storm, but no blanket closed off the interior opening. One room was for sleeping, one for storage.

Between the hut and the stream was another structure, which was half-buried in the ground, with a log-reinforced, tiny opening to enter that would require a person to crawl in on their hands and knees. Every day before the midday meal, Onas would spend part of the morning there, entering and exiting the structure completely naked. Once he was inside, smoke could be seen twisting its way from the door and from a smoke hole over the roof—when the *kuksui* exited a short time later, he would be flushed and covered in sweat, then immediately splash in the stream afterward.

While Jiangxi wasn't very curious about the structure, when he tried to enter it one time, Onas told him a sharp, "No. That is not for you, boy." Jiangxi did not try to venture inside again.

The days passed, and Onas spoke to him frequently in the Mutsun tongue, the language of the local tribes. Jiangxi's original indifference began to fade as he learned more and more words. He was called from his rest every morning to begin his work with the command "*Haayi!*"—"Come here!" Jiangxi learned about the *taacin*, a small rodent that leaped like a rabbit with its powerful hind legs, that they caught in traps and slow-roasted over the fire. The bushy trees that grew in copses around the settlement were called *porpor*, and the low-growing plant with jagged leaves and a flowering stalk was *hamatay*. While it grew wild in abundance, it was also cultivated in Onas's garden, and could be used for almost anything—medicine, making soap and flour, in addition to just cooking the leaves and shoots as part of a meal.

Without realizing it, each word was a stone dropped into the still waters of Jiangxi's mind. The narrow confines of his thoughts slowly stretched and expanded to encompass the language and the new things he was learning of cooking, household tasks, and traditions many *li* distant from his birthplace.

Some of the lessons were many *li* distant from this place too. "I was born not far from here," Onas said as Jiangxi prepared corn for their meal. The old man worked on a different task, his fingers busy with one of the colored belts. Jiangxi was not allowed to touch the belts, and any questions he directed about them were met with cold silence.

However, Onas seemed in a mellow mood this morning and had been humming quietly to himself, until the buzz of the melody became gentle words. "Amah Mutsun do not speak of those who are no longer here. It brings the anger of the spirits upon those who mention them. It is also ill luck to use the names of people still living, because it draws attention to them from the evil spirits.

"But in Haudenosaunee tradition, the dead are revered, and their spirits are protective. I walk both paths, and speak when I need to speak and stay silent when I must be silent."

Jiangxi glanced up, pausing in his work, then turned his eyes back down.

"My mother traveled from the Haudenosaunee tribes in the east, where another ocean meets the land. She knew no western languages when she arrived with her family, but they had come here to speak for the eastern tribes in trade negotiations. She learned Mutsun from a young man in the Amah Mutsun tribe, whom she married. She died in birthing me, and he was gone in the hunt before I was born. Their two deaths marked me, since I had both protective and destructive spirits that had become a part of me. The Haudenosaunee Elders dreamed a message from my parents, and so both tribes knew I would walk a different path."

The silence was expectant. Haltingly, Jiangxi asked in the language, "What is 'different path?' "

"My people here—the Amah Mutsun—have ones who are chosen by the *kuksui*—the spiritual leader of the *Kuksun* religion—to be guides in this life. To hold counsel with the tribes. To lead our mourning rites when they are needed, the dances for the people in celebration and loss, and to ensure that our land stays bountiful and protected from our enemies." The old man nodded to him. "You, I have dreamed of many times. There is something in your future. You are here to help, to bridge two tribes, like I do."

Jiangxi resisted the surprised laugh that threatened to escape. Help? *Who* was he here to help? He was forever reminded of his position every time that he looked at his scarred wrists and ankles poking out from the deer hide tunic he had been given to wear. The chains had rubbed the skin off his arms on Hell's Descent, and the wounds had become infected. While the chains had been struck off and time had healed the open sores, his mutilated flesh had reformed in rippled and shiny ridges. Like his slave brand, he would carry the marks for life. He absently rubbed the scars as his master continued to speak.

"I dream, too, of your home." Onas's long fingers caressed the nubby surface of the half-finished belt like a lover's touch. "It is burning in conflict, a war to come. You," and Onas looked at him directly, so there was no avoiding his black eyes, "were created in war and are a part of it. You are not like the others."

Jiangxi bit his tongue to avoid any response. Onas didn't seem to expect any and returned to his beadwork. "Maybe, someday, I will see your land," Onas finally said. The next words froze Jiangxi's heart. "But you will never return there again."

CHAPTER 4

"kuksui," a voice spoke from behind them. Onas glanced up from his beadwork towards the speaker. Three middle-aged men were walking up the path from the town.

Jiangxi was behind Onas's back to the side of the hut, working in the garden. While the farms produced crops on a large enough scale to have a complicated array of irrigation channels maintained by the slaves, Onas's garden required a more basic system. To the side of the hut was a water storage tank that was filled both by rainwater runoff collected from the roof during storms and by water ported by bucket and handcart from the nearby stream. Jiangxi's job was to fill the water tank when needed, keep the ridged rows of dirt from crumbling and blocking the water flow, and also trim and water the plants as they grew.

He watched the men out of the sides of his eyes. The largest man looked like a bear—shaggy eyebrows slashed over a thick face, with darker features than Onas. He wore the traditional Haudenosaunee loincloth and a sash slung over his shoulder. The two shorter men flanking him had faces shaped like apples, with a sharply-defined widow's peak of hair forming the fruit's stem. One wore no clothes in the Amah Mutsun style and the other wore a tunic similar to Jiangxi's.

"It is the same," said the largest man in accented Mutsun, coming to a halt in front of the old man. His tone was aggressive, but he spoke clearly enough for Jiangxi, even with his rudimentary grasp of the new language, to understand. "We need your help."

"Yes," said Onas calmly. He stood and disappeared into his home, carrying the wampum belt, only to return moments later with a different object in his hands. It was held at an angle from Jiangxi and covered with a cloth, so that the boy couldn't see what it was. By the size, it was no bigger or thicker than a turtle shell.

"Go," Onas said to Jiangxi, switching to the Chinese language, to the *Guānhuà* dialect that Jiangxi spoke. "Go to stream. I come for you later. Do not stay near. Bad for you."

Jiangxi left without speaking or looking back, but once beyond the initial screen of bushes that circled the clearing, he stopped and crouched down. Why, he didn't know. He had no fear. Not even curiosity—it just seemed that Onas telling him "don't" challenged him to find out why.

From the distance he had to maintain, the words spoken between the four men were unintelligible. Jiangxi wasn't sure he would even understand rapidly-spoken Mutsun if he were closer, so missing what they said didn't bother him. But the object his master had hidden from him... Onas dropped the cloth covering it and brought up the secret item to cover his face.

It was a mask, wooden and carved at sharp angles. Bulging rounds for eyes seemed to pierce through Jiangxi, even as distant as he was, and an open, full-lipped mouth screamed in fury. The mask fastened behind the old man's face and Onas suddenly dropped to his hands and knees as abruptly as if he were struck down from behind.

Jiangxi was afraid that this was exactly what had happened—that the visitors had attacked Onas through some sort of treachery. Jiangxi had barely gotten accustomed to this life, and a tiny needle of terror pinched at his heartbeat. He wondered what would happen to him if the old man died here and now. Would he be taken by this man-bear and sent to the fields like the other slaves?

But, no—Onas was shaking himself back to his feet. A thread of sound came to Jiangxi's ears, but it was like no voice he had ever heard come from Onas before. It was a wolf's whine—thin, with the undertone of a growl behind it, and the sound carried to Jiangxi, where the men's voices had not.

The sound raised the hairs on the back of the boy's neck. It was a sound no human could make.

The shaking of Onas's limbs was pronounced, even from this distance. Jiangxi flattened farther down behind the tree trunk he had chosen for his hiding place, instinct to become small and unnoticeable, but no one was looking at him. Instead, the three men stood before the Elder, who raised his hands up and down in a patterned dance of sinuous movement. His feet followed, step by step, and the sound coming from him grew in intensity. If the men flinched before it, Jiangxi could not see—but the boy flinched, crouched behind his cover. He had never seen the like and tried to compare this wailing creature with the soft-spoken man who had taught him a new language and the skills of cooking. This creature with the wooden face was different and unknowable.

Jiangxi had seen enough. His shoulder blades itched with the reluctance to turn his back on the quartet. He didn't know what was happening, nor did he want to know—but he was still oddly hesitant to leave. Backing away, he kept them in sight as long as possible, until he nearly tripped over a root he didn't see. When the leaves closed over his vision, he turned and ran—ran as fast as he could, his limbs pumping with effort, his breath trapped in his throat.

He splashed through the stream and sprinted over the softened dirt covered in the debris of foliage that seasonally rained down from the forest. Careening off the tree trunks in his terror, he gasped and grasped, scraping his bare arms and legs as he fell and then picked himself up, and then fell again. One final time, his legs failed him, and he dropped into the shade of the forest, the dirt rising up to meet his hands and face as he caught himself.

The earth was cool against his flushed cheek, and he panted through his mouth, catching the odd grit of dirt on his tongue as he struggled to breathe. Time unwound and his lungs relaxed, until he was able to close his mouth and inhale deeply through his nose. His fingers dug into the damp soil, which smelled rich and thick, like steamed mushrooms. There was a peace here that had been lacking before, the calm of calling birds and the breeze through the needles of the trees creating a sound like trickling water.

Hush, said the trees to his spirit. He listened, with his eyes closed to hear better. From his homeland, he knew about the spirits of place. He wondered what spirit dwelled here in this forest, with the tree trunks colored red, an omen that would mean good luck in Beijing.

Time passed, but he was unaware of how long he lay there, soaking in the cool and quiet. Perhaps he fell asleep. When he next opened his eyes, they were gritty. The shadows had lengthened into twilight-sized pockets of darkness under the enshrouding branches of the forest.

Jiangxi pushed himself up to his hands and knees, and then all the way to his feet. Mud smeared across his hands and dried blood speckled his limbs and tunic. When running, he had felt no pain. He touched his cheeks with his palms, and they were scratchy with dirt and snot. Rubbing his face as best as possible to clean it, he turned a slow circle in an effort to discover a direction. *There*, he thought—a trail of snapped branches and footsteps in the soft mud that showed him where to go.

Each step back along his own path, retracing his steps, he thought of what he had seen. The mask had created a monster, a devil. It was power, he knew. Here, they were called... he tried to remember what the man had named Onas. *kuksui.*

At the stream, he knelt and splashed water along his body. Finally, shivering in disgust, he stripped off his tunic and rubbed his skin clean. Water dripped from the long ends of his hair. Onas never seemed to cut or treat his own hair, which was long and lanky down his back, but it was always kept clean from his daily routine in the sweat lodge and stream.

Jiangxi had unaccountably followed the example of keeping his hair untrimmed, mainly because there had been no way to control his queue on the ship and he had not taken any pains in the new land to tame his hair. It was growing out in front in relaxed spikes, shorter than the longer tail at the back. When working, he tied it back, but it was loose from his flight and smelled of the mud he had rolled in. He rinsed it in the stream and then braided it back with a twist of grass. The ends, too short to braid, flopped over his eyes as he crossed the stream and climbed the slight hill back to the hut.

He'd been told to wait at the stream, but it was long past the hour when his master must have come looking for him. The three men had gone, and the cleared land around the house was empty. There was no sound other than the harsh caw of a distant bird and the throaty purr of quail wandering into the cover of the bushes. Onas could be in the house or he could be absent on some errand. Sometimes, Onas would stand up abruptly from a task and walk away, gone for hours at a time with no explanation. After all, what explanation did he owe his slave?

Pushing aside the blanket at the door, Jiangxi entered a room as close and dark as a cave after his time in the forest. The lanterns hanging from the ceiling were unlit, and it was like stepping into a bowl of ink. Even the central fire was out, or as near to it as could be.

It was his job to maintain it throughout the day and night, and so this was something he could fix. A thin thread of hope—perhaps it would garner some appreciation in the midst of whatever reaction he would face from disobeying.

More by feel than sight, he patted the floor in front of him as he crawled forward until he reached the circle of stones marking the boundary of the firepit. He moved his hands along the circle until he fastened upon a stout branch and used it to scrape away at the central mound of the firepit. Wood was outside, but he needed hope of a coal first.

Red pulsed under the stick's touch and he sighed with relief. Two trips brought back enough wood to continue and he used the fire stick forcefully as he manipulated the coal he had found. A few wisps of dried grass and a little bit of patience rewarded him with a thin trickle of flame.

He was so intent on his task that when the voice tapped at his back, his breath huffed out in a yelp as he spun around. "We talk," the old man said from the far shadows where he sat cross-legged on the ground.

It was hard to imagine the man he faced was the same as the masked creature that had frightened him. Onas seemed perfectly human in the wan light, a thin old man with nothing dangerous about his small smile or his rudimentary *Guānhuà*. It was hard to picture that he held any sort of power other than the respect age conferred.

"Y-yes." Jiangxi bowed low. "I am sorry—"

"No," Onas replied, stopping him before he got much further. "I said go, but you stay. Tribe gives death for outsiders who see Haudenosaunee magic."

Jiangxi dropped his head as fear raced through him.

"But I need eyes," the old man said in laborious *Guānhuà*. "Ears. Mouth to speak for me. Where I go, I am known. Some things need to be done, but not known by tribe.

"You have seen magic," Onas continued. "If you were from the true people, you would become our clan. You are not us. You are slave. Slaves die when rules break."

"I am sorry," Jiangxi repeated. Head bowed, but the fear had receded. Onas still spoke calmly and had not risen to his feet to threaten him. Perhaps he was not meant to die. If Onas meant harm, he would have had men waiting here. That he was alone and talking to Jiangxi must mean he had something else in mind.

"If you were our clan, you could not be slave. No slaves in tribe. Only slaves out tribe. You to be punished. You not forget again."

The darkness inside the hut was darkness no longer. The space filled with the gentle radiance of the growing flames Jiangxi had coaxed from the firepit's coals. In the light, he could see a man had appeared from the second doorway. The man was tall and round, wearing a loincloth and Chinese *zao* boots—black leather boots with calf-high tops and a cloth-wrapped wooden sole. The boots reminded Jiangxi of the numerous, faceless officials from Beijing who would hover around the throne during state business, shuffling and exchanging papers back and forth in endless succession.

Another person here showed why Onas had spoken in *Guānhuà* —so he would not be understood by anyone but Jiangxi. Was death to come for him after all? His body tensed on the edge of flight, but the fear he felt before was largely absent. This man also didn't move in a threatening manner towards him, but remained standing next to Onas.

Onas said, "This is my overseer, Cosso," before he switched to Mutsun and repeated the words slowly, but without Cosso's name, which would be considered bad luck. "This is overseer for my lands. He will bring punishment to you."

The man bulged with muscled arms crossed over a rounded stomach that knew too much of abundance. At Onas's words, Cosso brushed past Jiangxi, heading for the outside door without looking behind him. An expectation that he would be obeyed. The temptation to ask for clemency was strong, but how could Jiangxi appeal to the one who had set the punishment? Or to the one who carried it out? He might as well ask the sun to heal the scar of his slave brand. He turned and followed.

Jiangxi hadn't noticed it when he returned to the hut, but leaning against the cooking rock outside was a long-handled and jagged fan-shape: an arm-length stick of bamboo, split on the end into what looked like a many-fingered hand. Cosso grabbed it and tapped the end against his leg. He nodded his head towards the cooking rock. Jiangxi swallowed and placed his palms upon the block of stone when he knelt down. He bowed his head, ignoring the whistle of the split bamboo as it sang through the air. The slap of impact was painless at first, and he wondered at the mistake—it had missed.

And then the pain hit.

It doubled him over, sucking all the air from his lungs and the tears from his eyes. As his face smashed against the flat rock in surprise, already his ears rang with the thin sound of the bamboo through the air, prepared to strike him again.

"No, wait!" he cried, not lifting his face up from the stone. Forgetting that he spoke in *Guānhuà* and would not be understood. Although, looking back later, he realized it would not have made a difference if he had spoken in Mutsun or a Haudenosaunee language or any other tribal tongue—it would have caused no change and no mercy. "I have learned. I have! Please, do not do this. Please stop."

Smack! went the whip, loud as a mountain breaking in two. He flinched, too late, and the burn raced up his back, down his buttocks, and through the soles of his feet. Then a third time.

The sudden silence made no impression on him at first. But the whip had fallen silent.

"Come," said Cosso when Jiangxi looked up. Spoken in Mutsun, but the words were clear enough for the boy to follow. "I will return you to the *kuksui*." He added as an afterthought, seeming to grudgingly remember something outside of his normal routine, "You have done well."

The man lifted him to his feet as if he weighed nothing; maybe, to this giant man, it was true. Onas was still seated in the same place, same position, as if he had frozen while they were gone. But, instead, he dipped his head towards his overseer. "Thank you, overseer. You may go." Onas turned towards Jiangxi and switched back to *Guānhuà*. "Now, listen. I give order, you obey. Haudenosaunee magic dangerous. Not for you. Yes?"

"Y-yes," said Jiangxi, angry at the hitch in his own voice.

"You do again, I give you to the people. They will judge by old laws. Yes?"

Jiangxi shuddered as the streamers of pain still raced up and down his body, and did not see the flicker in the old man's eyes as Onas looked away from him. Even if Jiangxi had, he might not have realized what it meant. He also didn't notice the quavering in his master's voice or the trembling of his hands that marked out that Onas was lying and had no intention of following through on his threat. Jiangxi saw nothing but his own misery, his own pain and fear and hatred of this man who had so casually ordered his punishment and listened to him begging and pleading for the pain to stop.

Even so, after the initial lesson of Hell's Descent, one whipping was enough to complete Jiangxi's education. He nodded. He would not disobey again.

CHAPTER 5

The change of the season wasn't marked by a severe difference in the weather like it would be in Beijing, but instead by a gradual chill. Jiangxi guessed that it was autumn less by the turning of the leaves, since most of the trees were evergreen and they did not change, and more by the shift of plants in the field and the behavior of the wild creatures who were preparing for winter. Harvest came and went, and then the master handed him a fur coat one evening after the sun had set.

"The people will be coming here for our rituals, and so you must leave," Onas told him. "Take branches into the forest for a fire, and stay next to the stream. Return in the first light of morning."

Onas spoke almost exclusively in Mutsun, only switching to *Guānhuà* when others were nearby and he didn't wish for them to overhear. But those circumstances were rare, since there were seldom visitors. Without any other guidance, Jiangxi had adapted. One day, he had simply woken up with the bits and pieces of words and sentences and sounds from Mutsun as natural to his brain as his native tongue. His mind had stretched to finally encompass the newness of this place, which was no longer strange.

"Yes," he replied now, and shrugged on the fur coat. He tried to not think about what being sent away meant; about if the mask would make an appearance, or if the wild whine of Onas's voice when he wore it would fly above the trees like murderous black crows. Onas had called the mask Haudenosaunee magic, which meant his mother's people from the east, but he also was a spiritual leader for the Mutsun who lived here in the west. But whether it was one tribal magic or another, both were forbidden to Jiangxi, and he had no interest in trying to discover more.

Jiangxi bent over the woodpile to take an armful of branches, and his back twitched, remembering the cruel singing of the whip as he bent over the cooking stone and the handclap as the bamboo tails stroked his back. He straightened and walked away, each footstep putting distance between him and the memories.

While nighttime could be brisk, it was never bitter. Still, sleeping on the ground next to the dampness of running water was not warm, despite the fire which toasted his front. After the comfortable heat of the summer, it was hard to imagine such a cool night. The fur coat and the flickering fire soothed him to sleep, but he woke several times, shivering, and threw more branches on the fire until the blaze of new flames warmed him enough to sleep again. If this land was anything like his homeland, it would turn colder yet before the end of winter.

But it did not. He expected snow in the days following his night by the stream, but it never materialized. For a double handful of days, it grew cold enough to see his breath, but the temperature never dipped below freezing. Afterward, the days and nights grew more tolerable again.

His bare feet never ached in the mornings, although he was not too proud to jump back and forth to warm them up. Onas would watch Jiangxi's morning ritual of hopping around outside before fetching water from the stream, and he could see the smile in his master's eyes. Just like the colder weather, Onas's smile rarely materialized, and it was slight when it did so.

Jiangxi woke one of these winter mornings and uncurled himself from his rug at the foot of Onas's bed, hopping as he scooped up the bucket on his way to the stream. Jiangxi thought about the quail cooing in the bushes and how funny they looked with their tiny bob of a feather stuck onto their foreheads and tilted in front of their faces. It wasn't until he crouched at the stream and dipped the bucket in the water that he realized his thoughts about the bird made use of the Mutsun word for them rather than thinking of it in *Guānhuà*.

He dropped the bucket on the stones of the stream bank and said aloud, "*Ānchún*." He noticed that the word tasted strange on his tongue after all this time speaking little but Mutsun.

He picked up the bucket and refilled it and brought it back to his master. But his head remained bowed as he worked throughout the morning, doing the simple tasks he did every day. As his fingers and body moved in familiar patterns of labor, Jiangxi struggled to remember different patterns: all the words of his childhood, the sing-song intonation and the beauty of his homeland's language. This new world, with its guttural syllables and changeable words as complex as a sentence—they were foreign to him. They would always remain at a distance, and he had to remember that this land meant nothing to him. He would learn what he needed to survive, but it would never be a part of him. His mission was to return home. To face his brother.

Over the passing days, though, his thoughts continued to spiral into new patterns. By spring, it was hard to remember certain words he had spoken when young. They were fading from his mind, unused. He saw only Onas and his master's guests, although infrequently. The other slaves lived and worked separately from Onas's home, and so Jiangxi had no chance to speak and be spoken to in *Guānhuà*. The overseer, Cosso, was the only contact between Onas and the slaves of the field, and his eyes became blank anytime Onas spoke anything other than Mutsun. The punishment still filled Jiangxi's head and marked his back with phantom pain every time he saw Cosso. And the giant man knew it too, and seemed to take some small amusement whenever he flinched from out of his way.

Spring woke him from the endless patterns of winter, and made him realize that he had been sleeping through the days. The first he knew of it was when he walked outside one morning and left behind his fur coat. Or, even before that, when he noticed the summer monsoon season was absent from this new land because the seasons ran backwards—winter storms and a dry summer. So, when the rain dried up and there were a handful of days with water-blue skies and a sun determined to shine, he put aside the hibernation that had overcome him and his thoughts for months.

That morning, he did not do his morning dance to warm up, for there was no need. The temperate day greeted him as he stepped outside, and he felt the accompanying growth in his heartbeat. The sun's heat on his scarred face was a promise of new things, even to him.

From the quickly turning seasons, a year passed, and then two. Sometimes he was told to sleep by the stream when the tribe turned to the *kuksui* for advice and magic, and Jiangxi did so without question. He tended the garden, marked in the supply ledgers, and received his food daily, with never a stint on it. When winter brought sickness and he grew weak with fevers and chills, Onas tended to him and fed him broth and water, wiping fever-sweat from his forehead when needed. By contrast, Onas never seemed to become sick, not even when he practiced healing on the townsfolk. Visitors from the tribes began to recognize Jiangxi as a background presence at the hut, although only Onas ever used his name. Jiangxi wasn't sure if it was the Mutsun taboo against using names to endanger the person with evil spirits, or the simpler idea that the names of slaves were unimportant.

Without meaning to, Jiangxi's fear waned and broke against the tides of familiarity. Two years became three. His limbs stretched and his appetite grew fierce. Without asking for more, and without words being spoken, the daily helpings served in Jiangxi's bowl doubled. At night, before sleep, Onas started a new ritual. He would stretch to reach a hanging basket and retrieve a gift. Sometimes, it was the dense, ball-like loaves that Jiangxi favored, sometimes strips of fire-dried jerky, or perhaps even a rare wedge of honeycomb. As the year stretched like Jiangxi's body, he found that he became tall enough to reach the baskets himself. At a nod from Onas, he would retrieve one of these treats before he rolled himself into his sleeping mat. It wasn't every night, but enough so that it didn't feel as if his ribs were caving in when the world turned dark.

Although he never saw the mask in this time, he knew it existed and shared space in the hut with him. The stacked boxes in the secondary room came and went as the fields were harvested and Onas acted as go-between in trade deals between the tribes. But Jiangxi was always aware that one of those baskets hid the terrifying object that had begun his punishment and obedience, the mask he had dared so much to glimpse.

But the Haudenosaunee artifact didn't surface, and so he could keep the idea of the terror it engendered in the back of his head. Instead, he ate and worked and grew, the hands and eyes of Onas. Now, when the Amah Mutsun men came, they inclined their heads to him in greeting before requesting his master. He listened to them speak while he catered to them, and reported the conversations back to Onas when his master wasn't around. Sometimes, he was sent into town for supplies, and no one questioned him—they knew who he served and didn't bother him as he carried out his errands.

Ignored for the most part by the townsfolk, he overheard conversations at the marketplace, the idle chitchat of merchants and customers, and he brought the information back to Onas in vivid detail. So-and-so was unhappy with the latest trade deal for the price of tobacco. This trader worried about a shortage of ammunition for the eastern war effort. A fur trader complained about an overabundance of game in the interior and too much competition, which was driving down the prices for his products. Another one, just arrived from the south, talked about new Spanish settlements along the trade routes, and the fierce response by local tribes in retaliation against the encroachment. If the Dutch/English/French war at the mountains in the far east was not settled soon, it might come to a double or triple war front, with the English and French to the north, the eastern Dutch, and those devious Spaniards heading up from the south.

The words he parroted to the *kuksui* held little meaning or interest to Jiangxi, but Onas would tighten his lips whenever he heard news about the invaders, especially the Spanish. The tribes in the Confederacy that tried to make "peace" with them were often thrown into an indentured servitude, enslaved, or even killed. Retaliation would mean venturing farther outside the Confederacy's territory—being offensive rather than defensive. There was little support for this idea because of the eastern war.

Some of these things, Onas explained to Jiangxi over meals or during the odd moments of rest at the end of the day as they drank tea together at the cookfire before retiring for the night. Most of it made little impression on him—what did he care if two tribes killed each other? Or were killed? They were all the same to him.

But time passed and the established routines of Jiangxi's life became familiar and habitual. Even the bamboo whip of Cosso seemed like a nightmare from the past. While Jiangxi didn't aspire to grow to the same impressive size as the overseer (and probably would have been disappointed if he had), he was not so much shorter anymore. He no longer cowered when the overseer stomped up the path and demanded to speak with Onas. Instead, Jiangxi met the other man's eyes head-on, the only defiance he was allowed, and went to fetch

Onas with slow steps that caused Cosso to have to wait impatiently for his meetings.

In all this time in the new country, Jiangxi had seldom seen another man or woman of his race except in town, and his visits there were rare. When surrounded by others, he didn't speak to his fellow slaves, although he filled his eyes with their familiar appearance—they were owned by others, and he had no cause or permission to approach them that wouldn't garner punishment in some form or another. Usually, Onas would go into town and leave Jiangxi with a list of tasks to accomplish back at the hut, and so he wouldn't even get that opportunity.

The Amah Mutsun townsfolk and plantation-owning neighbors of Onas acknowledged Jiangxi, but they rarely spoke to him. If any slaves accompanied visitors to Onas, they stayed in the background and said nothing, either to their Amah Mutsun owners or to each other or to Jiangxi.

Once in a while, Jiangxi would be given some time to himself as a reward, and he would run through the woods as he had on that day when he had seen the *kuksui*'s mask and fled in fear. But instead of fear, he tasted anticipation—his speed had purpose now. He had found two important things.

First was the unfettered ocean.

From Onas's hut, removed from town and farm and set in a clearing in the woods, the waters were invisible. Even when traveling through the nearby town, it wasn't until Jiangxi reached the actual marketplace that he could see the choppy waves that splashed against the wooden and stone wharfs. Some of the structures were built out over the edge of the waters, so that the coastline of the trading city's littoral zone was a series of flat lines and unnatural angles that sharply divided the water from the land. He never went near the actual wharfs, but he came close enough when going to the marketplace that the brine of sea and sand created a spicy tickle against the back of his nose.

Much of the coastline was marshland—it required careful navigation to get to the ocean proper. Teeming with fish and fowl, it had the stagnant smell of sitting water and was sometimes hazardous to navigate without knowing the safe paths to walk. But he had found several sandy beaches away from inhabited areas, not at all close to the town. He had originally been sent there by Onas, but he returned again and again on his own.

Seaweed was a common ingredient to many dishes—salty and herbaceous, it added the wild flavor of the ocean to the domesticated stock foods and gathered ingredients that were the basis of most cooking. When dried, it could be sprinkled over soups and stews and meats to bring the flavors to the forefront. One of the first tasks Jiangxi had learned was how to dry seaweed and crush it into the flakes they added to nearly every dish.

Near to town, the beaches were generally picked clean of seaweed. So, on occasion when their supplies were running low, Onas would direct Jiangxi to a beach several miles up the coast. It was far enough from town or any other settlements that he had the space to himself. He would cut through the forest until he hit the marshes, and then turn north until he reached the dryer expanse of sand dunes. Out near the beach, the ground would soften and the trees begin to thin. The branches grew shorter and twisted as he came near his preferred beach, bent by the sea wind he could smell from miles distant. When he finally emerged onto the blowing sand, he would be close enough to see the city's harbor, but far enough north to be invisible to the people of the town from the curve of the shore. He had arrived at his final destination when he saw the half-rotted old hut that had been abandoned a season or two before his time. In the abandoned thatch hut was stored a wooden boat.

When he first found the boat, he had thought of escape. Of course, how could he not? But as soon as he dragged it down to the ocean to check its seaworthiness, the hull had filled with water and he had barely saved it from sinking. After that, he had come to this distant location as often as he could—whether through the pretext of gathering seaweed or on his rare moments of rewarded idle time—and he had spent long hours repairing the small boat through trial and error. The first time he had dragged the vessel to the water and it had remained afloat, he had shouted loud enough in celebration to cause the seagulls to veer away from him in sudden terror; they were used to his quiet and lack of threat.

Now, when he came this way, he would sometimes venture the boat out onto the waves. Never too far and never for any great length of time. Dragging the boat over the sand from where it was hidden in the hut, he would walk it past the first foam of waves, until he could safely step into it and steer it with the paddle stored in its bottom. He had learned the knack of keeping himself afloat despite the rise and fall of the swells, but would never dare take the boat out farther than he did. It still leaked a little and any large wave or nasty weather would overturn it. He had no supplies to sustain him, and no idea of where to go if he were to run away. But every time he rode the waves, he pictured a different outcome for himself other than slavery, and plans built up in his thoughts like stacked bricks. He never felt so free and at peace as when he was on the ocean or resting on its shore dreaming of how he would get away someday. Soon, he would leave.

But the boat was only one discovery. The second was the fields.

The fields were separated from Onas's small hut and immediate gardens by a long stand of old trees that grew on a shallow incline. They were enclosed by a palisade to prevent comings and goings except through a guarded opening that faced the main road. Eventually, beyond the woods, the land turned to gently rolling hills and, farther away, mountains purple with distance.

There were roads that crossed those mountains, he knew—roads traveled by caravans bringing the trade goods from the middle country and even from the far east, where Onas's mother's people came from.

Some of the caravaners were from the various tribes and some were even from his homeland. It was dangerous, though, for the men from his home to travel freely. Even with the brand that marked slaves, the features of his countrymen carried their own prejudice in the interior. It was far easier to let the native tribesmen travel the far distances and bring the goods to the coast rather than risk the interior themselves. The largest population of free Chinese were located right in the city nearby, although Jiangxi had never visited their enclave. When Onas was forced to travel there for supplies or medicines imported from overseas, he left the boy at home.

Today, though, was a day of freedom. As soon as his master made his slow way over the rise on the path that led to the city, Jiangxi turned and sped away. The bottoms of his feet were like rock—no soft shoes for him here, no boots in the wintertime. Just his bare feet, darkened by exposure and the unavoidable dirt of work. He ducked into the woods and ran through the stream, barely wetting his hard feet. He did not feel the rocks of the stream beneath them, but merely moved through the water like the leaping of a deer. There was a faint trail through the woods, a path he had taken before, although it was not so well-worn from his infrequent use. Even without a path, he had committed the route to memory.

That long-ago day when he had run from the *kuksui* and his fearsome mask, what he thought of as his boyhood, he had almost stumbled upon the palisade that guarded the fields. He would have reached it too, if he hadn't fallen and given up. If he'd only known, he might have looked through the thin cover of trees and been able to see the cleared area where the slaves lived and worked.

However, he hadn't known, and he had left that day unaware of how close he was to his own people. It wasn't until the next time he'd had a free day that he had returned to the spot and been drawn towards the sound of voices. Not the long, stilted language which now occupied his waking thoughts, but the softer, sibilant tongue of home.

The song of the words coaxed him past the redwood trees and he had crept closer, as if in a dream. Afraid it was unreal, he had tried to be as silent as possible. Perhaps due to his stealth, he wasn't discovered.

He discovered others, though. He reached the palisade wall, which was composed of a series of posts with cross-posts woven around and through them like a giant basket. Although secure from animals and attacks, there were small gaps that allowed for him to peek through. Screened by a cover of trees and underbrush, he put his eye to an opening and saw his people—slaves, like him. A wave of longing washed over him so strongly that he felt dizzy.

Burned brown in the sun, skin dark as their overseers, the men and women worked in the fields without surcease. They wore no shirts, both sexes, although the women had longer skirts than the men, who wore loincloths. They held simple hoes, with which they were attacking the ground along a row of obviously cultivated plants. What the plants were, he had no idea, but they had broad, veiny leaves and would probably be chest-heigh on him. It was mid-spring, so he guessed they might become taller before the end of the growing season.

Jiangxi stared, fascinated. Both sexes had short hair, although some of the women had theirs braided back. No queues, though, not on the men. Their cheeks and foreheads shone with the round shape of their brands, which were lighter in color than their sun-burnt skin and gave them an exaggerated appearance, as if they were part of a theater play. He wondered which, if any, had started out peasant-dark and which ones, like him, had grown up shaded from the sun. Could there be any from his home city? From the palace? From... his family?

Back home, he had never thought about slavery. It existed and slaves served him. There were the eunuchs of the palace, and some of them could rise quite high in the ranks with the right connections. Look at Zheng He, the hero of China. Over three hundred years ago, he had set out with his fleet of junks—large Chinese ships that were seaworthy enough to cross oceans—and discovered this land of opportunity. He had been a highly celebrated favorite of Emperor Zhu Di, but Zheng He had also been a eunuch.

Jiangxi had never thought about slaves or the tribal Confederacy in this new country when he was a boy. There was no need for him to concern himself with it—it existed in the realm of adults. Now, it was too late to learn more. All he could learn was through observation.

But it was good to see his countrymen and women. He crouched in the bushes, motionless and barely breathing, his eyes hungry at the sight. How could he meet them? Did he dare call out from behind this wall? Would it instead bring the attention of guards down upon him? The men, women, and children looked so busy, so absorbed in their work. He wondered if they would get in trouble—or he would—if he tried to make contact with them.

In the end, he held back. Aside from the conundrum of how to overcome the palisade guarding the fields, his recent whipping was still too fresh for him to commit to risky actions. His back burned from the punishment, and he wasn't eager for a repetition. But he heard the gentle murmur of voices as he walked away, and each step he took was as if he drove a spike through his heart.

That was the most unnatural aspect of his slavery. Onas, deliberately he was sure, kept him from others from his homeland. He had spoken of taking the boy to the capital city of this region of the empire, but had not yet done so. He spoke also of visiting the fields together, but, if he ever ventured to the slave quarters, it was on his own—one of the many times he simply stood up and walked through the door and did not return for hours.

Today, Jiangxi had been granted a reprieve. Nearly four years older and larger than when he had arrived by ship, he was swift in his run through the forest. Perhaps today he would overcome his reticence and the palisade and find a way to talk to one of his countrymen. Maybe today was the day.

He had never plucked up the courage before. He went, he watched, and he returned to the space he shared with Onas. The punishment which had so cowed him as a younger boy was years in the past, and the stripes—even the memory of the stripes—had faded from his mind. He obeyed out of habit, rather than in some true fear of punishment. He perhaps did not believe in the *kuksui*'s power, although some small part of him was still wary.

But, that day of freedom, things changed without any effort of his part. For, when he was crossing the last few lengths of forest to his usual vantage point and plucking up the courage to approach the fields, he was stopped quite abruptly when a person unfolded themself from one of the trees and stepped into his path.

CHAPTER 6

It was a girl. She was older than Jiangxi's nearly ten years, but probably by no more than a couple more. Enough so that she seemed vastly strange and alien to a boy whose only contact with others was in the realm of men. Like the other slaves of the field, she wore a long, woven skirt but nothing above it. Changes in her body, her bare chest, marked the difference between a girl and a woman. Her face was smudged by dirt and the tracks of tears and she spoke in a soft hiss almost before he noticed her.

The words were strange to his ears after speaking almost exclusively tribal languages for the past three years, almost four. Although he spied as often as possible on other slaves like him, there was a difference between idly hearing a language every few months, even the language of his birth, and using it on a daily basis. It was only sheer luck that she was not using one of the many dialects of his home that would render her words incomprehensible. No, she spoke with the accent and intonations of Beijing, and her words eventually became clear.

49

"What are you doing here?" she repeated when he didn't answer the first time she asked it. "Are you escaping?"

He stared, fascinated, before he shook his head. He had to listen intently as she spoke and focus his concentration on the words in order to make sense of them, for she spoke rapidly. His tongue remembered better than his head, for he was able to answer her in the same language, "No, I am coming to look." He waved a hand half-heartedly behind her back.

She turned, as if noticing the field for the first time, but then glanced back at him. "It is dangerous," she said and sniffed. Her slave brand was ugly against her skin, circles marking her as property. Although he had seldom been aware of his own mark, a dull anger bloomed in his chest that she had been marked also and would carry the scar for the entirety of her life. "I am running away," she said, as if he couldn't have figured that out from her earlier words.

He looked at her—involuntarily, his eyes moved over her young body, ropy with muscle from her work in the fields. "Where are you going?" he asked.

She scrubbed at her cheeks. "I don't know. Away. Anywhere but here."

Her eyes looked dark under the shade of the trees, but an errant gleam of sun turned them amber. There was pain there, a pain he could not touch or comprehend. "How did you escape the compound?" he asked softly. The palisade fence loomed large in his thoughts, but he also thought of the guards at the entrance and patrolling the fields.

"It doesn't matter," she said. She shook her head. "I shouldn't have come out of hiding. I shouldn't have talked to you." Suddenly, she leaned forward until her face was near to his. He breathed in the musk of her sweat, amazed at the physical closeness of another person from his home. Her eyes were wide and filled with meaning. "You won't tell, will you?" she whispered, and he could taste her breath across his tongue.

50

He was both tempted to lean forward as she was doing, and flinch back at the close contact. In the end, he held his ground and did neither. "No," he responded quietly. "I will not."

"Good," she said. She brushed past him and he felt drunk with the contact. Not since before his journey had he encountered such a casual touch, almost an animal touch, like fur brushing fur. It was unconscious and unintended and it made his head swim with longing for the previous life of unnoticed and unappreciated human contact. The *kuksui* never touched him. He had no contact at all except with the inanimate objects of his work.

"Wait!" he called out, only too late realizing that his voice would travel. She turned on him, the fear in her eyes tangible. She said something that he didn't understand and then grabbed his hand tightly in hers and tugged on it. He followed her without thought or intent, his long legs matching hers as they ran.

There were no voices behind them, but the girl didn't slow down. When they finally stopped, Jiangxi was gasping in great mouthfuls of air and the girl was in no better condition. Still, she turned on him and hit him across the face, a blow that rocked him backwards. He could have blocked the move if he had anticipated it, but he had not.

"You useless *èrbï*!" she shouted. "How could you give me away like that?"

"Hunh," he wheezed, still unable to speak. She paced away from him, then came closer, as if she would hit him again. He held up his hands defensively and she dropped hers. "I'm sorry," he finally gasped. "I wanted to help."

"Help!" she snorted. She collapsed on the ground, her legs sticking straight out from her skirt, and then flopped back so her sweaty back flattened the earth. Her eyes focused upwards, but not as if she were looking at anything specific.

"I'm sorry," he repeated. Then, when there was no response, he said, "I don't think they heard. That anyone heard, that is."

"Lucky if that's true," she said without looking at him. "But unlucky if we were found. Why, oh, why did you shout like that?"

In a smaller voice, he said, "I didn't mean to."

"This is useless." She turned dark eyes to him. "Where are you from, anyhow? What farm? And how did you get out here?"

He shook his head and dropped cross-legged down into the dirt next to her. He picked up a small stick and scratched at the dirt as he spoke instead of looking at her. "I'm not from a farm. I live at the *kuksui*'s house."

"The *kuksui*?" she echoed incredulously.

Although it didn't sound much like an actual question, he clarified, "Onas."

"The bastard!" she said with emphasis. At his glance, she said, "Yes, he is my master too. The terrible and ferocious *kuksui*."

"What do you mean?" he asked. When she didn't answer, "Is he the reason you're running away?"

She raised her brows at that. "Why? Do I need more of a reason than freedom?"

He thought about it and remembered the deep pain in her eyes when they first met. "Yes," he answered slowly. "I think you do have more of a reason." She moved her hand and he tensed himself against another blow. When she noticed his reaction, she laughed involuntarily.

"Don't be such a baby," she said, but her voice held an easy affection and he relaxed again. Then, quick as lighting, she closed her lids and her smile faded.

He wanted to ask what was wrong, but lacked the courage. Instead, he said, "Is there some way I can help?"

"Lot of good that would do me, your kind of help." At his fallen eyes, she relented, "But, yes, I could use help. I just don't know what."

"Dogs," he said. When she looked at him, he raised his eyebrows. "They will track you and find you. One of the men who visits Onas brings his dogs with him and talks about how he hires them out to find runaways."

She groaned and flung one hand over her face. "I didn't think about that. But I can't go back. I *can't*. I'd do anything, even—even kill myself before I let them take me back."

The pressure of wanting to ask her again why she needed to run so badly beat against his skull. But he hadn't stayed with the old man for so long without learning restraint. "Dogs can track you anywhere. Except maybe in a city, where there might be too many people. But it would be hard for you to go there and not be caught by the guards."

"It's hopeless then," she said in a brittle tone of voice, as if she might break apart at any second.

"No. Not quite," he said. Her eyes were closed and he wanted her to look at him again, to see how much he was about to risk. For her. He struggled for a moment with the choice—his freedom or hers. But was it really a choice? "Do you know how to swim?"

She obliged his wish and turned her fierce gaze on him. "No. When would I learn such a thing?" Her words lacked the biting tone of before, though, and that gave him hope.

"Doesn't matter," he said. "If you can't swim, you can paddle. Just don't fall out of the boat." He stood up and, shyly, offered his hand. She stared at it, then at him, before meeting him palm to palm and allowing him to pull her upright.

"Dogs can't track in water," he said. "Come on. This way."

He took a moment at a rise of hill to make sure that he had his bearings before continuing down the far side. "Where are we going?" she asked.

"Not far. We will reach it before you are missed," he said.

"What about you?" she asked after a space of footsteps. "They will have your scent too."

"But they are not looking for me," he replied.

"They will be, if they find out you helped me," she muttered. "He would do anything—" Then she bit her lip and held back the words.

The ground became gritty with blown sand. The evergreens, bent by the breath of the sea, beckoned them with curled branches towards the saltwater they could smell from the forest, even if they couldn't yet see it. When they finally emerged from the cover of the foliage, the sun was bright overhead and the crying of the seagulls welcomed them out onto the white-yellow expanse of beach.

"Wait here," he said. "Just under the trees. I'll be back."

The girl nodded and crouched under one of the small, twisted trees for cover. Jiangxi walked north to his abandoned hut and patchwork boat. It was a quick jog up the beach, and he counted each passing moment with unease.

When he finally arrived at the hut, he quickly dragged the boat from its hiding place and pulled it into the water. He climbed in and sent it south with the paddle stored in its bottom. When he reached the original stretch of beach where the girl and he had come from the forest, he pulled the boat up to shore and glanced at the trees. His heart skipped when he saw nobody there, but he breathed a sigh of relief when he finally saw movement: the slight girl stepped from her hiding place and made her way down the incline of the beach towards him.

"What... is *that*?" she asked, equal parts scorn and disbelief in her voice.

"That," he said, grinning despite her tone. "Is how we will leave here."

"We?" she asked. He wasn't sure what emotion she showed, but it wasn't relief at including him.

"For now." He was disappointed at her reaction. "I will take you up the coast a distance so you will be safe. Then I will return here. No suspicion will be put on you, and it will be thought you drowned yourself."

"I see," she said. She looked at the boat, her chin wobbling. He saw her eyes were wet and was afraid she would cry. Instead, she said, "Let's get going, then. Before they start looking."

He could have responded, but thoughts raced through his head too quickly for him to choose one. In the end, he nodded and pushed the boat out into the waves again. He turned to her, who still stood just out of reach of the water.

"You need to come in," he said. "Don't worry, the water is shallow here. It will not hurt you."

"The waves?" she asked, and he knew what she meant.

"They do not go so high. See? It is low tide here. That means the water is gentle. We must go, though, before that changes."

She nodded and he saw her swallow. But she put her feet forward, holding her long skirt above her knees. When the first small wave washed up and splashed over her ankles, she gave a little shriek. He rolled his eyes.

"They're coming, remember?" he said to prod her. And he saw her swallow again, but she walked towards him steadily. He held the boat for her when she reached him, the water above her waist now, and boosted her up into it. It rocked with her motion and he could hear the involuntary sound she made as she held onto its sides. He could see her visibly trying to be brave, and he felt his throat thicken with sympathy. Gently as he could, he pulled the craft farther out to sea, then heaved himself in behind her and picked up the paddle.

"Relax," he said. "I will propel the boat, but don't make any sudden movements. Hold onto the sides as you are doing, and it will all be fine."

She held so still as he paddled the boat that he worried she was holding her breath and would pass out. But, no—she was breathing shallowly through her mouth, he could see when she turned her head to glance back at him. "How far?" she whispered, but had to repeat herself more loudly when he didn't hear her the first time over the sounds of the ocean and cries of the gulls.

"Some ways." His paddle dipped first one side, then the other. The waves tried to push him closer to shore, so it took some concentration to stay parallel to the coast and also to not drift farther out to sea. There were tides that could pull the boat out, and he kept his eye on the sandy strip of beach to make sure that they didn't stray too far. He remembered that she had asked a question and tried to elaborate. "There aren't many people here. The fishermen go out with the early morning and would not be so close to the land, anyway. The rest of the tribes stay inland, where the land is good for farming. The nearest coastal city is where we came from."

"I see," she said quietly. Then, "How do you know so much? And why are you out here?" Her gaze flicked upwards and he knew she was eyeing his slave brand.

"I am given a certain freedom," he replied.

"Is that why you go back?" she asked scornfully.

He hesitated. Anything he said seemed to bring on her ire. Would he never know how to interact with other people? He felt the lack from the past few years. This was the most he had spoken to any one person in one sitting. Onas seldom spoke more than was necessary, and sometimes days would pass where Jiangxi performed his tasks with no conversation, knowing what was expected of him.

"No." His voice was quiet. "I go back for your sake."

"Me?" She laughed harshly. "What does it matter to me?" she asked.

He realized then—or thought he realized—she attacked him because she was scared. Scared of running away, scared of being by herself. Scared of the wilds that might mean death to her. Despite her brave words about killing herself rather than facing slavery, she was frightened of death too. She was so full of fear that she lashed out, and he was the only one around to receive it.

So he answered the unspoken words. "I will come back and bring you what I can," he said. "But it might be some time. I cannot leave easily, only when the master is gone. Until then, I will show you what I know so that you can survive."

Her eyes met his, and the amber was warmer than before. She nodded to him, as if not trusting her mouth not to say something mean, and turned back to face the waters. They completed the rest of the ride in silence.

Aside from any fear of what punishment he would receive if caught, Jiangxi enjoyed the ride. By himself, he never dared to venture so far up the coast. He worried about the leaking boat and what he would do if stranded. He had taught himself to swim, but was still unsure of his skill, since he used it so seldom. If the boat turned over in the cold water, he thought he could probably swim to safety but he wasn't sure, having never tested it. Hopefully, he would never have to, either.

The day was beautiful, despite the earliness of the spring season. The air warmed quickly in this gently rolling land, even if the nights remained cold until the summer. On the water, the wind carried its own chill and he looked forward to returning to land for more than one reason.

He eyed the sun as he rowed, and when it had moved a handspan in the sky, he turned the boat to shore. He saw the girl's white-knuckled grip on the sides of the boat relax as they moved closer and closer to the sandy beach. Finally, he jumped over the side and pulled the boat up on the beach with the girl riding in it. When the sand finally stopped him, he held a hand out to her, which she grasped with cold fingers and allowed herself to be drawn free of the boat.

"Thank you," she said quietly. He smiled at her and she looked away. "What... where are we?"

"I don't know," he replied, to intercept her scornful look with quick words. "I've not been here before, but I figured it would be a good place to stop. See, the water is curving inwards, so there must be a river nearby, but it's not too marshy to go through. There are still only small hills farther inland, so it won't be hard to hunt and forage for food. Now, let's pull the boat up and I'll let you know what I can."

Together, they tugged the boat ashore, hiding it behind a small hump of rocks that were half-buried in some wet sand so that it wouldn't be directly visible from the ocean. They slogged through the marshy outlet until the ground firmed, and then followed a stream inland until the twisted sea trees gave way to copses of evergreens and deciduous. While she knew some of the plants for gathering because of her time on the farm, he pointed out the water plants, such as cattails and tule, that were good for weaving and constructing temporary shelters. They headed for the nearest grouping of trees and found a dense thicket of bushes underneath.

"This would be a good place to stay. If you add some layers of cover, it will be relatively waterproof and warm at night if you weave some mats to cover the ground."

While everyone knew how to prepare acorns for food, it wasn't yet the season for them. He gave her some rudimentary instruction on spearing fish from the stream, hitting a target with a sling, and making snares. She listened gravely, only nodding her head occasionally.

After a final warning about bears and coyotes and what to do if she encountered them ("Don't run—the first thing they will do is chase you"), he squinted at the sun, and was a bit alarmed at how much it had moved across the sky. "I must head back before I am missed."

In another lightning-quick change of mood, she grabbed his hand as he turned away and tugged him back around. She met his eyes. "Thank you," she repeated. "I owe you my life."

He shrugged, more uncomfortable with her gratitude than he had been with her constant anger. "I will be back to help," he said, blushing. "But, first, you must help yourself." She released his hand, but still smiled.

He turned to hurry back to the boat, although he couldn't resist one last glance over his shoulder before topping the ridge that led to the beach. But the only sight that met his eyes was the gently gurgling stream and the waving leaves of the bushes and trees. She was already gone.

CHAPTER 7

It was late afternoon when Jiangxi returned, and Onas was already in the hut. Although the old man eyed him, he didn't say a word. Not even when the overseer came through near twilight with reports of a missing slave. Jiangxi didn't dare look up from his writing as Cosso spoke to Onas. Instead, he bent his head and filled his thoughts with the tallies he was recording.

It wasn't until the next day as the *kuksui* and he were eating the midday meal that Onas spoke. "A girl from the farm," he said, the first words he had spoken to Jiangxi since before he left for the city. "She was about your age. The overseer's son was particularly concerned about her disappearance."

Ah, thought Jiangxi. That explained the tears and running away. He had met Cosso's son. Cosso looked like a brute and had no qualms about wielding the bamboo whip, but he did what he was told to do by Onas—nothing more, nothing less. But his son had a vicious temper and took it out on easy targets—Jiangxi had been on the receiving end of it more than once. His nickname, even among his

61

own people, was *hasseSte-k*—"He's angry." That slight girl Jiangxi had met would have had no chance against someone like him.

It was then that he realized he had never asked the girl's name. Nor had he told her his.

Onas said, "Her mother died recently from the winter sickness. So it is a double loss to the farm."

Jiangxi nodded, but stuffed his mouth full of squash without answering. He could not quite meet his master's sharp, black eyes. The old man saw more than what was on the surface, and Jiangxi was afraid Amah Mutsun magic would seek him out to reveal the truth of the girl.

He wouldn't give her up, though. He would never give her into the hands of Cosso's terrible punishment or, even worse, the cruelty of his son.

"They tracked her to the beach," Onas said. "The trail ended at the water, with no other trace.

"Too bad," Onas added, subsiding back to his meal. "But I guess she decided to join her mother."

Now was Jiangxi's first day of freedom since he had met the girl. In the two months since, summer had faded to fall. With only one thing on his mind, he sprinted through the cool shade of the forest to reach the beach. He had shown the girl all he knew about surviving, but it was little enough. He would not have run away with such scant knowledge, but he didn't have as much of an impetus as she did. He had been planning his eventual escape because he had time to plan.

The boat was still in the hut, and he dragged it along the sandy beach to the waves. This day was not so beautiful as that other one two months previous when he had helped the girl to escape. The water was choppy with a stiff wind, and the sky loomed with grey. Still, he pushed his watercraft out into the waves and struggled into it. As he paddled up the coast, he thought that it was probably too far for him to travel and not be tardy coming back. The *kuksui* had not said anything, but it was much later in the day now than when Onas usually left to go to the city. The old man never stayed out for the night, and so he would be back fairly soon. But it was the first chance Jiangxi had had to return, and he had thought about little else except the girl with amber eyes and no name.

Some time had passed out on the water, and the day was not so bright. He was afraid he would miss the right spot. Much of the beach and marshland looked alike, stretches of sand and reeds interrupted by rocks and streams. The paddle dipped the water, but his progress was slow against the wind and waves. The flowing of time seemed interminable, and the coastline stretched on and on. Finally, when he had nearly given up and was battling against the voice in the back of his head insisting he turn around, he spotted the gentle curve of the beach heading inland.

It was a struggle to return to land, a struggle to pull the boat up onto the sands. When he had done so, he sat down for a moment, catching his breath. The clouds were an angrier grey now and the winds carried the spume of the water with them. It would be hard to return via the sea. He might have to walk back or risk his life in the thin and easily tippable boat.

He finally pulled himself to his feet and headed inland, following the same stream from before. He remembered the split oak, there, and the stand of three pines growing closely together. Near enough to the beach, he had told her, was a good place to stay. There were plenty of things to eat off the beach, such as the crabs that scuttled away from his feet, the birds that dipped their beaks in the shallows, and the mussels that lined the rocks.

When he reached the thicket where he had suggested she stay, he could see what work she had done to make it habitable. The branches of the bushes were woven together and draped with thatch made from pine needles and tule to form a fairly secure barrier against weather. He searched for an opening and found it on the far side away from the beach. Hesitating, he finally called out, "Girl? It is the boy who brought you here."

There was no answer. It was day, so she might be elsewhere. He knelt and crawled through the opening.

Inside, it was dark from the thatch, but he didn't need to see with more than the light from the opening. It was empty. From the looks of the webs from enterprising spiders, it had been abandoned for some time. He patted down the area, but found nothing, no trace of her.

Crawling back out, he knelt for a moment just outside the entrance with his hands on his knees and his backside propped up on his heels. His head hung down, and all the hope he had felt on the journey north—despite the fear of being caught—dissipated beneath the reality of what he had found. She had disappeared, perhaps for a while. Maybe she hadn't trusted him to come back—maybe she hadn't trusted him at all, and just stayed long enough to gather some supplies for a journey. Or maybe—worse thought—maybe she had been captured.

Whatever had happened, he might never know. She was gone, and he was a long way from home.

CHAPTER 8

Jiangxi was unsurprised to see Onas waiting for him and, beside him, Cosso. He nodded and walked over to the rock and bent over. This time, the overseer did not stop with three lashes. He did not stop until Jiangxi's back was bleeding and he was hoarse from crying out. When his vision started to grey, he heard Onas's quiet word to halt the punishment, but he was too weak to stand on his own. Perhaps it was part of his punishment, but Onas walked away from him and left him there. It wasn't until the night had turned cold and the stars stared down at him from their unblinking distance that he regained the strength to drag himself forward and crawl inside.

The next morning, the old man did not speak a word to him. It was as if he didn't exist. The *kuksui* went about his daily tasks as Jiangxi lay wrapped in his rug inside, burning up with pain. The noon meal came and went and the boy lay there, smelling the good food cooking outside. His stomach rebelled against his control, and he lay in his own stink for the remainder of the day, unable to move. His tongue felt woolen by the time night fell, and he was raging with thirst.

When Onas returned to the hut, Jiangxi thought that he would be ignored again. He wondered if he would die there—if that was his punishment this time. A death for a life. Haunted by pain and weakness, he didn't at first realize what was happening as the man lifted him, filth and all, and carried him out of the hut. Onas brought him down to the stream, his strength belying his age, and dropped him carelessly beside it. Jiangxi screamed, but it was nothing compared to when Onas rolled him into the water.

He struggled against the weakness that held him. The water, shallow, swirled past his closed mouth and nose, over his head lying prone against the stones of the bottom of the stream. Finally, he managed to flop his hands beneath him and push his face the smallest fraction out of the water to gasp the air. By this time, Onas was sitting on the stream bank, watching him as he crawled halfway out of the water.

"You have learned nothing," he said to Jiangxi. "So you will take the girl's place."

After that, Onas nursed him as he used to do when Jiangxi was sick with the usual ailments of children. The old man fed him, cleaned him, and bandaged his wounds. Only when the stripes had healed to faint pinkish lines criss-crossing his back was Jiangxi led away from the hut by the *kuksui*'s overseer and passed, for the first time, through the palisade gateway and into the slave compound.

From the gateway, it wasn't too long a distance before they came to the four-farm crossroads that marked the dividing line between Onas's fields and those of his nearest neighbors. The slave longhouse was right next to the road and shared by all four of the owners. It lessoned the number of guards each individual owner needed to put up to keep the slaves from running away, and probably decreased the costs of maintenance. The two of them pushed through the longhouse's doorway of hanging blankets, and then Jiangxi arrived at another type of hell.

Or at least, that was what it reminded him of. It was like Hell's Descent, the ship's passage—packed full of people, squalid with poverty, and a place where no one wanted to be. When the overseer walked into the slave's longhouse with no warning, the soft babble of voices paused and died as all eyes turned to him. Cosso marched inside, followed by Jiangxi. Eyes flickered towards the boy and away again, mostly focused on the overseer.

"Listen," Cosso barked. "This here is a new one. I don't want special treatment for him. Treat him as you would me." He grinned at his own witticism and walked away.

Eyes watched the big man go, and then turned to the boy he left behind. Unlike the ship ride, none of the slaves were chained, but the longhouse was crowded with humanity and the accompanying odor of close bodies in a small space.

The layout was similar to other traditional longhouses—two sets of built-in platforms jutted from the outer walls, one near the ground for sleeping, one above their heads for storage. Each uninterrupted section of platform was a little bit longer than a person lying down, with the regularly spaced posts that held up the roof forming a natural barrier, which separated each sleeping area from the one next to it. They had also reinforced the separation between each family's section by tacking handwoven mats between the posts to allow for a small amount of privacy. The walls were lined with handwoven mats for insulation, as was the ground, except for the rock-lined fires in the center of the aisles. Rows of hooks from the second platform had woven baskets hanging from them, much like in Onas's house.

The cookfires were in the center aisles of the house, so there was a permanent haze that hung in the higher reaches, and the sound of chronic coughing. Mostly, the smoke was drawn through the covered openings in the peak of the building's roof, but some of it lingered in little eddies and swirls and scented everything with the perfume of burning wood.

A soft round of muttered greetings welcomed him little, and many averted their eyes as he stood in their midst, and returned to their business as if he was no more than a mosquito flying by. Marked with disfavor because of the overseer, he could see them turning their shoulders towards him. Or maybe he was too sensitive to his own importance, for he saw meals being cooked and babies nursed, and the minutiae of daily life. With the absence of the overseer, maybe he was of no importance at all to them.

He wondered how often a new slave was brought and if he would stay here long enough to find out. For, once he had been whipped, he had decided that if he survived it, he would run away. He would go up the coast as he had shown the girl and make his way inland. Maybe he could even find her again, take the same trail she had.

It was a hope, but something to keep him going. So, when he was ignored, he simply sat down on the ground by one of the cookfires and listened to the conversation.

Next to him, in a hard dialect to follow: "Twenty of them too. Lost from the sickness."

The woman beside him was speaking to a man about the same age as her as she nursed a baby. The long skirt became a cushion for the baby, who was covered in a woven blanket that looked clean enough but was undyed, and so resembled the different colors of dirt. There was a pattern of stripes on the blanket.

"I don't know why they don't learn. Put us in pigsties, we die like pigs." The man spat into the fire, which sizzled at the gift from his mouth.

Food was served. It looked like each cookfire fed the people sitting around it. They looked at him when they ladled out the meager stew and he swallowed at the smell of it surrounded by the odor of the house. There were latrines outside, for they had passed them on the way here, but with young children and old people inside, the place had a smell of urine and less wholesome things. So, when a none-so-clean bowl was scrounged up and handed to him, he shook his head. At their heated look, he realized his rudeness and tried to cover it by saying, "I have eaten already today. Give it to someone who needs it more."

The wrinkled old woman shrugged at his refusal and took the bowl for herself. The flames glared over the faces around the fire and he watched as they ate. Some wolfed the food down; some took each mouthful as if it were gold. There were no utensils—no spoons, no chopsticks—and they ate by shoveling food from the bowls to their mouths with their hands.

Afterward, the bowls were scoured outside with sand and water and stacked in a wooden box on a shelf near the door. That corner was sectioned off with crude boards and seemed to house daily supplies used by all of them—he saw more hanging baskets filled with dried foods, rolled blankets that looked the worse for wear and needed mending, and some undifferentiated wooden crates filled with saved odds and ends, such as scraps of cloth and hide, coiled lengths of handmade rope, and large and small tools, such as pestles for pounding acorns and needles for repair work. These would be put to use when needed. There were more shelves built against the boards that held other, less distinct items that were hard to see with the distant light of the flickering flames.

At an unspoken signal, the people stood up and gathered their blankets rolled up on far edge of each platform—the sleeping platforms were shared by families and friends, for he saw a group involving a man, woman, and two children lie down on one, and two women on another. There seemed to be some order in the proximity to the fires, and Jiangxi found himself ignored as people set up their blankets and sleeping mats.

Finally, he found an empty section of platform near the entrance to the longhouse and sank down on it. While there were blankets hanging from the doorway to prevent the worst drafts, the breezes still drifted in around the edges, diluting the heat from the fires. He had been sent with nothing from the *kuksui*'s house, only the tunic and loincloth he wore, and he tried his best to curl into a ball to stay warm.

"Here," he heard once he had closed his eyes for a moment. He opened them to see the woman who had been nursing the baby at the cookfire. She held one of those beige-striped blankets in her hand, but this one was larger than the one swaddling her baby. It had one or two holes in it that required patching, but it was sturdy enough and certainly better than nothing.

"Thank you," he said. She nodded and turned away to settle some distance away from him on a platform that contained a girl probably half his age and also the still figure of a man. Jiangxi lay on his side with his back to the wall and watched the fire dance its way to exhaustion over the bodies of the slaves. Several people snored, and most of the people seemed asleep as soon as they lay down.

Since he had done no work today or several days past, his thoughts wouldn't rest. After having come from the quiet and relative peace of the old man's home and into the stench and noise of this crammed-together group, he could not close his eyes at all without feeling as if he were in danger of... something unnamed. It did no good to hear his native tongue and see familiar faces up close. Familiar to him, both because he had watched them in the field and because they were his own face many times over, the brands of their slave scars prominent on their cheeks and forehead.

No, these were strangers who looked at him and saw one more mouth to feed on stingy rations, one more threat to their daughters, already at the mercy of the overseers. They saw how he was different from them—well-fed, unpatched clothing, and shiny with cleanliness. His belly grumbled miserably as he lay on his side and tried to think of other things so that he could gather together enough bravery to close his eyes on this nightmare.

Before much time had passed, a woman began moaning on a pallet next to him. He was afraid to look and see why. He placed his hands over his ears and turned his back to her to face the wall. He didn't want to know what was happening—if it was pain, sickness, or some other cause.

Finally, he closed his eyes with defeat and slept.

The next morning, he was roughly shaken awake. He blinked, confused at the hairy face hovering over him, and rubbed his eyes. He was surprised—he never overslept. He was always the first out of bed. Where was Onas...?

The same man smacked his hands away from his face. "Hurry," he said harshly. "If we're not out before the overseer, there'll be hell to pay." The man grabbed his wrists and pulled him to his feet.

He remembered everything that had happened yesterday in a rush, and his footsteps slowed as he exited the building. It only resulted in a smack on his buttocks as he dragged his feet. The man hissed, "Who do you think you are? Get us into trouble, and we'll show *you* trouble."

At that, Jiangxi picked up his step and followed the figure in front of him. Looking around, he saw children probably half his age marching out with them. Only the youngest stayed at the longhouse, watched over by those too old to pick and tend the crops. The rest of them spread out their meager rations to feed the ones who couldn't work from youth, age, or infirmity. Only those who worked got a ration. A slave stopped working, he stopped existing to the masters.

Was it worth it, what he had done? He wondered it often, over the next days and months. He'd done little enough, but it was considered a crime deeper than murder. Helping a fellow slave escape. He never spoke of it, and no one ever asked. Although at one point, about a month after he had arrived, he dared to ask the mother who had given him a blanket if she knew of a girl who had escaped. A girl with no mother.

She stared at him so long that he thought that she must have frozen in place. Finally, she shook her head.

He wondered if he was too new for them to trust. Or if the girl had never come from here. But the girl had said she was from Onas's fields, and he believed her. What reason would she have to lie?

He wished now, in hindsight, that he had insisted he come with her. Or that he had overcome his fears and left. Instead, he'd taken the easy route, the safe route, and returned to his regular meals and temperate life. She had been right, not he, when she condemned him for going back. He should have taken the same leap, no matter the cost. He was weak and soft.

But no longer. Now, he was under guard and couldn't run no matter what. They were sent to the fields under the sun or rain, with the palisade encircling them and preventing any escape. They planted, hoed, watered, harvested. When those tasks were finished, they would often leave the compound in small groups under guard—to level the roads for carts after the rain had cut deep and unsafe channels in them, to cut down trees and strip their bark for use in construction, to harvest mussels at the shore. Always, there was work from sunup to sundown.

In the evenings, there was time to cook a meal and eat it and sleep, with maybe a bit of conversation or stories to end the day. Often, they played music—although they had no bamboo in this land, those who were versed in instruments were able to make do with native reeds and create pan pipes and simple flutes. The children enjoyed playing on small drums in accompaniment, and one skilled artisan had created several *xun*, an egg-shaped ocarina flute, and had taught others how to play them. Men and women would sing traditional folk songs, ones that were unfamiliar to Jiangxi. He had only known *yayue*, the court ceremonial musical and poetry performances. They were as unlike the music and stories told in the slave compound as the ocean was to land.

For Jiangxi, despite the camaraderie shared in the longhouse, he felt like an outsider. Perhaps he ignored overtures made to him; perhaps there were few made. He didn't reach out to others, but did the bare minimum to get by—do his work, eat his food, sleep. Each day was the same. The summer passed in a blaze of heat, and autumn harvest came and went. The season turned and the cold deepened, but, here, there was no master looking out for him. Here, he had no warm fur coat to keep him through the winter. No matter that it was not so bitter as the city of his youth. No matter that snow didn't fall. The temperatures were barely above freezing. Once they left the warmth of the longhouse and walked into the ripping winds of winter, there was nothing standing between him and the cold, nothing except another day of hard labor.

He lost weight. The constant physical work and meager food eroded his reserves of fat, little though they were. He began to take on the half-starved appearance of his fellow slaves, covered in stringy muscle and little else. His mind grew dull and he found days passing with barely a thought to his condition.

He had seen the numbers flow by when he was Onas's personal slave, but never seen the application firsthand until he'd been forced to become just another number. He now knew from conversations he heard that Onas was unusual, even for a *kuksui*. No one knew what he did with the money he earned from this plantation. The other owners—he'd heard stories about their elaborate Chinese houses and servants and the banquets they gave for their fellow tribesmen. Sometimes, the largesse translated to extra food for the slaves, the leftovers from one of these feasts.

Only Onas's slaves never received any extras from their master, although the slaves from the other farms shared what they could. Only Onas's slaves struggled with the meager allotment they were given each day and never had more except what others gave them.

At first, he had planned and plotted for escape. Some way to run away, as the girl had run away. When he worked near the enclosing walls, he would poke at them with his hoe when the guards turned their backs or relaxed their attention, trying to find a weakness or opening.

But either the girl had had a lucky escape or they had tightened the watch after she had gone. Now, the slaves were in sight of at least one Amah Mutsun guard at all times. The men were blank-faced giants who towered over their slight and starved bodies, patrolling the edge of the fields with muskets propped on their shoulders, watching and waiting for any resistance.

As the rains tapered off and the days lengthened again, Jiangxi found his head fuzzy with fatigue and hunger. The moon grew and shrank, and the month passed in a blur of discomfort. He was always too tired to plan much of anything. It wasn't until the heat came on in earnest that Cosso singled him out again.

It was midday and the field was muddy from a recent rain. A contingent of slaves had been separated and sent outside the fence to chop wood to enlarge the field and dig up the massive roots of the old trees they were cutting down. Jiangxi was digging in the soil, covered in mud, when the overseer hauled him to his feet from behind with a hand on his shoulder.

"Come with me," he growled. Without curiosity, Jiangxi dropped his axe with the other tools and followed him.

They walked away from the outside wall rather than towards, down the leveled road that had taken them days to complete. He noted with a sinking feeling that the rain had cut tiny runnels into the newly smoothed surface. They'd be sent back out there in a month or two to do the work over again.

Cosso and Jiangxi came to the crossroads that marked the dividing line between the edge of the farms and the long road that traveled up and down the coast. Cosso made a sharp right and Jiangxi stopped walking. This way led to... this way led to the *kuksui*'s house.

Finally, when the overseer was several lengths ahead, he realized that the boy had stopped. He barked at Jiangxi, "Come on, then! Come now or..."

Jiangxi hadn't realized his feet had stopped moving in the dull horror of his position. He ducked his head and hurried to catch up. Cosso gave him a suspicious glare, then resumed walking, this time at the boy's side so he wouldn't lose him again.

For some reason, Jiangxi felt humiliated at Onas seeing him as he currently was. There was anger, true, but he felt panic at being seen in his threadbare garments, all skin and bones, as if he had done something dishonorable. He couldn't help it that his heart raced as the well-known hut came into view. He didn't see the *kuksui*, so he trained his eyes on the ground when they reached the door. Cosso stepped through, and there was the low murmur of voices before someone emerged from inside. Someone who could only be Onas, but Jiangxi still refused to raise his head.

"Boy," said a voice familiar to him. Below the surge of anger was a fresh wave of shame. And then a new flame of anger on top of that, that he would feel any shame at all in front of the person who had done this to him. "Are you ready to return here?" asked the old man.

"Yes," he replied faintly. Tears leaked from the corners of his eyes and his skin burned.

"Very well. Go inside, take the items from your rug, and bathe in the stream. Then we will begin again."

With that, he was back. Onas walked over to the cookfire and sat cross-legged in front of it without any more words. From the hut, the overseer strode towards him and Jiangxi automatically cowered. But Cosso walked by, his eyes passing over Jiangxi as if he didn't exist anymore. With the overseer's job of delivering the slave to Onas completed, perhaps Jiangxi no longer did exist, as far as he was concerned.

Jiangxi shook his head at himself and went inside. This abrupt change after a year of deprivation—it would take a long time to get used to being here again, although in some ways it was as if he'd never left. The hut was exactly the same as before, the garden the same, even his few meager possessions from the year before seemed intact and stored where he'd left them. He found a new tunic and loincloth laid out on his old sleeping mat and rug from last year, the rug neatly folded next to the old man's bedding as if Jiangxi had stepped out yesterday. Just the storage boxes in the second room of the hut were different from the last time he'd been there, although they appeared neatly stacked and ordered, as they had previously been.

It felt like a fever dream as he mindlessly obeyed what Onas had told him and took his new clothes down to the stream. He felt human again after he had washed off the mud and the filth from his tenure in the fields, and dressed in an unpatched tunic that had a smooth and unfrayed hem. As he looked at the pitiful heap of his worn-out clothes that he'd worn for a year, it was then that he felt something more than anger and shame. It was the first stirrings of a rage that was more than a match for what had burned in him at his brother's cruelty when he'd been sold into slavery.

Here Jiangxi was again at Onas's hut, as if nothing had happened. When *everything* had happened to him—the work in the fields, the deprivation, the scorn and whippings. He had never had it made so clear to him that he was nothing to this stranger, no matter the old man's superficial kindnesses towards Jiangxi compared to how his other slaves were treated. Jiangxi had no connection to the *kuksui*—how could he? They were not blood. And blood itself—Jiangxi's brother—had first betrayed him. Even the girl he had helped had departed without waiting for him to return, and he had been made to pay many times over for what he had done to help her escape.

No one—*no one*—was to be trusted.

He hoped the lesson was not learned too late. He carried his old clothes to the far side of the stream and made a hole in the ground with a sharp stick. There, he laid them down as gently as if he held a baby, and covered them over with the muddy earth.

He dipped his hands in the water, after. The dirt staining his hands loosened its hold and flowed away downstream. The stain on his soul remained.

CHAPTER 9

He lost an exact count of years that were passing—maybe four or five—and, only later, wondered how much time had gone by. Sometime between when he was returned to the *kuksui's* house as a boy and when he was considered a young man, he was able to exist and learn and grow. Time erased many of his first memories from the palace in Beijing, leaving behind only isolated images and worn-out emotions that no longer resembled anger or fear. Until he realized he'd forgotten how many years he'd been a slave, and how many years before that when he hadn't been. He stretched in body and mind, his voice deepened, and he learned to scrape the stubble growing from his chin with a knife. He never reached the same height as Cosso, nor became as bulky. But he was as tall as Onas, or perhaps a little taller.

While Jiangxi grew up, the old man seemed to stay the same. Perhaps the years were lighter the more one accumulated, but his master never slowed the pace of his work or seemed at all affected by the hardship of living in what many of his countrymen would consider primitive conditions. Many of them had abandoned some

79

of the older ways of their ancestors, although they still held with the rituals and festivities that marked the turning of the seasons and the major events in life, such as birth, puberty, and death. Many of them lived in Chinese-style houses and wore Chinese-style clothes. Longhouses were built for storage, rather than for residences; Mutsun huts were too small and not ostentatious enough for the owners of the grander plantations.

Jiangxi wouldn't have asked why his master lived in the old way, in a hut with no amenities, but he didn't have to. One of the *kuksui's* visitors did so within the boy's hearing.

It was an overcast day in the winter after he had been returned to the relative luxury of the *kuksui's* house. The anger still burned brightly within him, but he was wary too. He dared nothing to jeopardize his standing. In the back of his head was still the option of running away and never coming back. But he was not allowed the freedoms he was before. He was kept to the house and garden and the stream. So far, the *kuksui* had not left him alone for more than a few moments.

But Onas still received visitors. The first time it happened, the old man had looked a long time at him as Jiangxi weeded the garden, since he refused to glance up without a direct command ordering him to do so. When it came, the *kuksui* said, "Go into the house and stay there until I summon you."

He had immediately dropped his tools and said, "Yes, *kuksui*," and gone into the house. The fire smoldered in the center of the hut, but it was cold inside without a proper blaze of new wood to stoke it. With nothing better to do, he lay down under his rug for warmth. Without meaning to, he dozed off, hearing nothing outside except the angry wind.

When he woke, it was dark and the *kuksui* was sitting in the doorway with the blankets tied back to let in the cool air. He was outlined by the twilit sky. When Onas heard movement, he said, "It is done," and no more.

The next time, the three men came—the original three men who had asked help from the *kuksui* on the day Jiangxi had been punished for spying on the sacred rituals. Jiangxi knew enough to recognize they were Onas's three neighbors, who owned the slaves on the nearby fields and whose slaves shared the longhouse with those of the *kuksui*. Their names were Sirak, Hö:ga:k and Yuure—names that Jiangxi didn't know how he knew, since no one ever used names. Or perhaps they were their place-names, the ones they used instead of their birth-names, the ones to avoid ill-luck. They seldom spoke directly to him, so it was unlikely he would ever find out.

Jiangxi was writing figures with the old man when Hö:ga:k's voice crept through the open doorway. It was morning and he had not yet started cooking the day's meal.

"Prepare the food," said Onas. Jiangxi walked by the three men and heard his master saying behind him, "What is the problem?"

"The same problem," said the leader of the three. And the men walked indoors while the meat sizzled in the wok and Jiangxi boiled bread. Without direction, he made enough food for the three men too. They came out of the hut just as he was putting the bowls together, and he handed out the meal. No one made eye contact with him; no one thanked him. But he didn't expect it.

"Worse weather is predicted this season," said Hö:ga:k after he used a long-handled spoon to take a bite of food. He spoke around the food in his mouth, the meat of deer cooked in long strips and seasoned with spices. "Why do you live in *kuutYiSmin rukka*, this hut? You need a big home like mine—like ours." And he waved an expansive hand at his companions.

Onas smiled and chewed his bread. "There is no need for material goods in the spiritual world," he replied. "I live by our traditions. Food and shelter—that is all that is needed. I have enough to live by, and can use the surplus to benefit our people."

"We live in the physical world," argued Hö:ga:k, highlighting his point by taking a large mouthful of the deer. "In the past, we did not know about what the world had to offer. But now that we do, it is good to enjoy the physical and be generous with what we have, even if the spiritual is different."

"You are known to be a generous benefactor to our people," Onas said. "But there is also an old story about what you are saying, a story that has been told and retold for many generations and been passed down from one family to another."

Onas's voice held a tone that Jiangxi had never heard before. It bore a sing-song quality and rhythm that quickened his heart, for it reminded him of the language of his home, the speech of the slave compound. It carried a musicality that was normally foreign to the harsh intonations of this land. For once, he saw a beauty he had never seen before in Mutsun, even though he had spoken and thought in the language for years. This was the first time he heard something that confused him because it was so different, almost like a song—but unlike the songs he had witnessed from afar during feast days. He sat up straighter and listened.

"You are Amah Mutsun, so you don't know this story. This is a story of my mother's people.

"Once, long ago, there was a girl who was never satisfied with anything she was given. She wanted the best of everything. Her parents saw how she was when young men came to court her and their hearts were sore with the fear she would never marry. She would mock her suitors and criticize them. This one she would call too fat, that one too thin; this one she would call slow of speech, that one talked too much; this one had too long a face, that one had sharp eyes. She was never satisfied with the men and so she did not take a husband.

"One night, when the moon was absent from the sky, a strange man came to their fire. He was beautiful in the flickering light from the lowering flames, his eyes wide and hair long and black as midnight. 'I am here to take your daughter as my wife,' he told the girl's parents.

"The girl and her father rejoiced at the man's richly beaded clothes and handsome jewelry and pretty face, but her mother worried and said to her daughter, 'None of the men of our tribe were good enough for you. Why would you marry a man you don't know?'

" 'Mother,' said the girl without listening. 'I have found the man I will marry.' And she took all her things, the best the village could offer, and packed them up to take with her. They left the village that night, the girl walking behind her new husband into the darkness."

Jiangxi was captivated by the story. The three other men had finished their meal and had to prod him to take their bowls to clean them. Onas caught Jiangxi's eye and nodded slightly towards the ground when he saw him hesitating by the fire. He sat again, just outside the circle of men.

"And so," Onas continued in his mellifluous storyteller's voice, "the girl followed her husband into the dark. But she realized as she walked that her mother's voice was in her head. Her mother's voice that said her husband was someone who she didn't know. And so her steps lagged and she started to fall behind. Noticing this, the man turned to her and pulled her close.

" 'Wife of mine,' he told her. 'Worry not, for my home and people are waiting for us. Soon, we will be amongst them.'

"In the distance, she heard the rushing of the river and thought that her husband's people must be fishermen. And so, her heart was relieved, at least until they reached the edge of the river and the lodge house there. For over the door was a pair of long horns, the strangest sight she had ever seen. Seeing her fear, her husband said, 'It is late. We will sleep and, in the morning, I will show you to my people.'

"That night, the girl could not sleep because she was so afraid. She thought about all she had left behind her—the good people of her village, the warm and caring lodge of her family. Her husband's house smelled like the river, a rancid odor like dead fish.

"The next morning, the girl greeted the day with black-ringed eyes, so tired was she. And the day seemed tired, for the skies were grey and the land covered in fog. Her husband greeted her and his beauty failed to raise her heart today, unlike the night before when she had first seen him. In the light of day, it seemed as if his eyes were cold and reflected nothing.

" 'Hello, wife,' he said. 'Here is a dress for you to meet my people in.'

"It was a beautiful dress. It was covered in wampum, but new and supple. Instead of being grateful, the girl felt only fear. It had the rotten smell of the river about it.

" 'No, husband,' she said. 'I will not wear the dress.'

"The man was angry as he took the dress away, but he did not force her to it. Instead, he said, 'You cannot leave here until you wear the dress.'

" 'I will not wear it,' she repeated. He put it down and left her after that, walking away over the foggy landscape until he was lost to her eyes.

"Her mother's words echoed in her head. She had chosen material goods and beauty over the good advice of her family. If she had only been content with the simple things of her village, she would not be stuck here, alone and afraid.

"At that moment, there was a sound at the door. Thinking her husband had relented and returned to her, she rushed to greet him. Instead of the beautiful man she had married, there was a horned snake waiting on the threshold. After it looked at her for a long time, it turned and slithered off.

"The girl followed it. Outside there were many more serpents and she realized that her husband had lied to her. He had disguised himself as a man, but he was nothing more than a cold and ferocious snake.

"She knew that she needed to escape, but could think of no way to accomplish it while guarded by so many fierce serpents. She returned to the lodge and wept at her own foolishness. Finally, exhausted, she fell into a deep sleep.

"In her sleep, she dreamed. An old man came to her and looked her in the eyes and she saw pity and love in his gaze. 'Granddaughter,' he greeted her. 'You are not without courage, but this is a trap of your own making. In order to escape, you must do exactly as I say. Will you do it?'

" 'Oh, yes!' she cried.

" 'Then listen to me,' he said. 'From out the door of the lodge is a tall mountain. You must run directly to this mountain and climb it without stopping or speaking, no matter what cries you hear in pursuit. If you hesitate, you will be lost. When you reach the top, I can help you escape.'

" 'I will do it,' she vowed in the dream, and then she woke up.

"She jumped to her feet and rushed out the door. Standing there was her beautiful husband and he cried out to her, 'Wife, where are you going?'

"She bit her tongue and said nothing in return, just ran past him. His cries followed her.

"As she ran, she went by an old woman who called to her, 'Help me, I am sick.' Although the girl's heart broke at the cries, she heeded the old man's advice and did not stop.

"Last, she ran past a child trapped by a circle of snakes. 'Help, they will bite me!' he cried. Although her heart was torn to shreds, she did not heed him and ran past with tears streaming from her eyes.

"She came to the mountain's edge and began to climb. She climbed and climbed as the sun set and rose and set again. Her hands were torn to shreds and her dress became tattered and she was pummeled by wind and rain. She felt hunger, but she grabbed weeds as she climbed and gnawed on them and they sustained her. She felt thirst, but she opened her mouth to the rain and her thirst was quenched. Finally, she reached the top of the mountain and had just enough strength remaining to pull herself up. Waiting for her was the old man of her dream.

"Looking back, she saw that the snakes had followed her and she was afraid. But the old man at her side pulled back his hand and threw something at the serpents—something that flashed and burned them as they followed. It was lightning. Now she knew the old man was Heno, which means Thunderer.

"Heno threw lightning after lightning and the sky played drums of thunder. The snakes tried to flee, but they were all caught and burned.

"When the last serpent lay dead, the old man turned to her and said gently, 'Thank you, my granddaughter. These creatures were a plague upon this earth, bringing much ruin to the true people. You have saved them.'

"The girl was brought back to her village by Heno, who told the people of her bravery. There was much rejoicing and, when the first good man came to ask her to wife, she went with him and was happy for the rest of her days. As the years passed, she often said the same thing to her children, and then her grandchildren and great-grandchildren.

" 'Happiness is found in simple things.' "

The fire popped as Onas subsided and the spell of the story that held his visitors captive was released. Jiangxi re-gathered the bowls from supper as the men sat thinking. He turned and walked away.

As he cleaned the bowls, he thought about the *kuksui*'s story. And it was then that he had a plan on how to carry out his revenge. The girl in the story was spoiled, and he felt no sympathy with how she made her own unpleasant fate. In fact, he had wanted her harmed for her willfulness, for having the best of everything and being contented with none. It reminded him of the slaveholders, overflowing with abundance and giving the slaves nothing in return.

86

Jiangxi's plan was simple. He would be the beautiful serpent in their midst. He would smile and nod and be agreeable, and he would lull them into following him into the dark.

He would find a way to free the slaves. All of them, not just himself. He would find a way, some way—any way he could—to lead his people to freedom.

CHAPTER 10

As the next two years rolled by, the *kuksui* fell into his old patterns of trust and left on his mysterious errands again, leaving Jiangxi with free time on his hands. He tamped down the rage in his breast and listened and learned as much as he could. He worked diligently at all that was set before him. He didn't waste this time in idle pursuit, but began to implement his plans.

First part? Build boats.

With only rudimentary tools to aid him, the learning process was slow. He studied the pattern of the one long, narrow boat he had found on the beach. Without the proper tools, even being able to use the original boat as a guide didn't help him to progress much. He gave up the task after multiple tries of trying to lash together a wooden frame by himself only ended in failure.

But there was a simpler way, even if the product was temporary. While he couldn't construct a wooden boat or anything that would remain seaworthy for long, tule boats were often created by the Amah Mutsun villagers for short-term and seasonal fishing, and were particularly light and flexible to use. Through trial and error from his observation of the village fishing fleets sent out from previous years, he managed to fasten together three large bundles of tule reeds—one larger and fatter bundle for the bottom of the boat, and one bundle for each side, tied tightly together with braided rope. The watercraft could transport two or three people at a time. The crafts were waterproof for a few days of use—enough to send someone or several someones up the coast.

Second part—penetrate the slave compound.

From his year of being in the fields, he was intimately aware of the inside layout of the palisade fence. Now, he crept around the exterior, keeping to the cover of bushes and trees to avoid any chance of being spotted. When he was far from the central compound and gate, he found what he was looking for: the location he remembered, where there were a series of boulders half-buried in the ground near the edge of the wall. Close to the bottom was a gap where one of the cross-posts showed signs of rot and had begun to crumble.

Over the course of several days, he worked at the location—quietly cutting away at the rotting wood and enlarging the hole underneath. He had peeked through the hole as he initially began making it—the opening he created was hidden by the tip of the boulder protruding from the ground on the other side. So, unless one knew where to look—or unless someone was very observant while doing a close search of the wall—it would be invisible.

Then he made contact.

It was harder than he thought, but also easier than it would have been when he was working the field. Years had passed since he had helped the amber-eyed girl get away, and the guard shift had relaxed as no new slaves had attempted (or, if they had attempted, had not succeeded) at escape. The workers were minimally supervised, par-tially because the palisade was a sufficient deterrent, and also maybe because Cosso was spending more time in his own pursuits while his son, who had replaced him for several guard shifts, was not nearly so concerned about security as his father. hasseSte-k was lazy and inclined to take what fell into his lap. That included the slave girls, willing or no.

Jiangxi spent added days perched in the branches of a nearby (but not *too* nearby) tree, observing the guard shifts from above. One problem he'd been trying to solve: the longhouse quarters were in the middle of the fields, well away from the walls. While nighttime might be the easiest time to reach out to one of the slaves while they were at their meal or sleeping, it would also be the hardest time to get close enough to talk to them, since he would have to traverse the entire farm to get there. The likelihood of capture went up exponentially. And how would he explain why he was there—and how he got into the compound—if he were caught?

But he wouldn't have to, it appeared. The guards had a vulnerability, and that was the midday meal. While the slaves still labored in the fields, the guards gathered together near the entrance of the compound, where a lean-to and benches had been set up against the wall. For those who were married, their wives would arrive to cook a meal for the group. They would spend time talking and eating together, secure in the knowledge that the slaves were busy, and any attempt to leave the compound would have to go through the front gateway.

On a burning hot day, Jiangxi dropped down from his observation perch in the tree once he saw the guards congregating at the front gateway. Their wives had just arrived with baskets filled with foods to cook, so it would be some time that they would be occupied. On hotter days, the guards tended to take more time under the shade of the lean-to before returning to the fields to excoriate the sweating and suffering workers. Jiangxi had been waiting for this opportunity for months, planned and plotted, and now it had come about.

Jiangxi shimmied through the hole he had made in the wall and walked right up to a woman he recognized from years before. It was the one woman who had shown him kindness amongst the indifference: the woman who had given him a blanket the first night he had been taken to the longhouse, and whose nursing baby back then was now a child working the fields beside her.

"Mother," he said respectfully. She turned to him, her lean features stretched taut with hard living. "Do you remember me?"

She squinted. He knew the moment she recognized him because her eyes widened and her mouth dropped open. "Boy," she said. "Jiangxi. I never would have guessed. I thought they took you to sell at the market. But you look," her eyes shifted over him, "you look well."

"Yes, Mother," he said. He held out the package he had put together and she took it automatically. "That is food. I have more stored away. I thought of your kindness and I wanted to offer you and any who cared for it an opportunity."

Her squint this time was suspicious. "An opportunity?" She looked over her shoulder, and he knew she was checking to see if any guards were nearby. "What opportunity?"

He took a deep breath. "To be free."

She turned back to her hoe, dropping the package next to her in the dirt. "I don't listen to talk like that," she said.

"It is true," he said. "That girl who ran away. Years ago. I helped her escape, and that is why I was punished and brought to live as a field worker for a year. I am back with Master Onas now, but I vowed I would not be afraid to help others escape too. That girl is free—somewhere. I don't know where. But I brought her up the coast and she kept on traveling. She made it. She is free."

"She had no children," said the woman. "Nothing to lose. I'm older now and not reckless. I am past the days of running away."

"You aren't old," he argued. "And you can bring your children with you." He gestured at the fields. "This is what you want for them? I see you have a girl there. She is young still, but what happens when she is older? What happens when hasseSte-k decides to do with her what he is now doing to another girl?"

The woman turned on him and shoved the hoe in his face, barely managing to avoid his eyes with the sharp blade. "You shut your mouth! What do you know, with your fat stomach and charity and promises of better? There is no better! I stopped hoping for better years ago." And her face crumpled.

He held her while she cried. She let him. He was taller than her now, a young man capable of doing more than living in fear.

"Fine," she said when it was over, as if he had just asked her a simple question. "We will go. Now, what do we have to do?"

He told her. He explained the hole in the fence, the route through the woods, and how to tell direction amongst the trees. Over the last two years, he had created markers that looked natural by now—a split branch leaning like the written character for tree, a pile of stones shaped like the two dashes in the character for the number eight—a simple list that he showed her in the dirt for, like many slaves, she couldn't read or write.

"I will come back two more times before you go," he told her. "And I will test you each time to make sure that you remember what I have told you, and so that nothing will go wrong when you are ready for the journey. After the second time I return, you are to wait two days and then go as close to midday as possible, once the guards have gone to their meal. That will give you enough time to get to the beach, take the boat up the coast, and arrive to make camp before nightfall. That is your best chance to not get caught. And, hopefully, they won't notice you're missing until evening, so they won't know when you left."

The woman looked him in the face for a long time after he had finished speaking. She searched the contours of his features and stared deeply into his eyes, as if trying to discover the secrets of the Buddha. Finally, she said simply, "You are a blessing, *xiǎo huángdì*."

93

Jiangxi caught his breath at her nickname for him. *Little emperor.* "Why do you call me that?" he whispered.

She tilted her head at his reaction. "You always carried yourself like royalty. It set you apart, back then." She shrugged. "I felt pity for you. You seemed so stiff that, if a wind blew around your body, you would break into pieces like a dropped teacup."

"Oh. You do not know—" He caught himself in time, but he saw a sudden curiosity on her face at his careless words. Quickly, before she connected his words to his background, he added, "Very well. That is a good name for me. Tell them—one or two people you absolutely trust here. Tell them *xiǎo huángdì* will help them, if they are brave and can keep the secret."

"Thank you." She looked down at her hoe, stabbed it into the ground in disgust. "I have been here for many years. I... I had stopped hoping."

He blushed, still uncomfortable with praise. "Do not thank me yet. It is a long and dangerous road for you, and it may not end well."

She smiled, but her eyes were still inclined to film over. "It will. There is luck coming with you today, and you have passed it on to me. I feel it. Now, go. You have been here too long."

It was true, he had been here too long. He bowed to her and she smiled. Then he turned and hurried away.

Jiangxi had returned twice more to go over the directions with her, just as he had promised. Two days after his last visit to the compound, he was sitting outside in the sun with Onas, eating the meal he had prepared. He tried to stay calm, but his heart began racing and stopping, racing and stopping, the farther the sun crossed the sky.

A little before nightfall, the overseer appeared. He gestured Onas inside and Jiangxi heard little of their conversation, only the hum of murmured voices in the distance. When the overseer left, he glared darkly at Jiangxi, but stalked by the boy without a word.

"Jiangxi," Onas called from the hut. It was one of the few times he had ever said the boy's name. Jiangxi hurried inside.

"Yes, *kuksui*," he replied. The inside of the hut was already fairly dark, only the glow of the snapping fire providing any illumination.

"What do you know of the missing slaves?" Onas asked him, and his eyes glittered in the dim light.

Jiangxi remembered Onas's story of the serpent people and found himself relaxing. This was his plan. He had carried it out. Now was the time to believe in it.

"Missing slaves?" he said. When his tongue ached to continue, to blurt out something, anything, he bit down on it in reproach.

There was silence. He held the old man's eyes, but he felt the calm of the Buddha overcome him. He was a statue, living and breathing, but made out of wood and impermeable to outside influence. He was a tree, with all the calm of centuries behind him. Nothing could harm him.

"Very well," said Onas finally. "Go, now."

He went. Out into the growing dark and the knowledge that he had just begun his true purpose in life.

The first time was the worst. So many things could have gone wrong. They searched for days, he knew from what he overheard from Onas and Cosso. They found nothing. Just the dogs traveling to the beach and stopping at the waters, like the girl before.

Onas eyed him, though, and curtailed his trips to town and therefore also Jiangxi's freedom. But the young man was buoyed up on his accomplishment and showed nothing to the *kuksui*. Or... he *thought* he showed nothing. It was hard to tell, with those beady black eyes following him around all day. It was hard to tell what Onas knew, and if his magic would tell him anything.

But nothing came to pass from that incident. Or—one thing.

"Boy," said Onas one evening as they sat by the fire. "Did you have anything to do with that girl going?"

He knew what the *kuksui* referred to, but he said, "What girl?"

The black eyes watched him, and he wondered if he had overplayed his hand. "Years ago," said Onas. "A slave girl was lost to my farm. The same day that I was in the city. Then, when you disappeared for so long that day. That was when Cosso whipped you and I sent you away."

Jiangxi paused before speaking again, his eyes lowered and his mind racing to find the right level of humility without overdoing the lie. "I did not know why you did that," he murmured. "Or why you took me back."

"Hmm," said Onas. His tone was gruff, as if he begrudged the words that followed. "I might have been mistaken. It is someone else who is helping these slaves run away. It was bad luck that my suspicion fell on you."

Surprised, the boy looked up at Onas. The old man seemed ancient, his dark eyes housed in a sea of weathered skin pulled tightly over his bones. Jiangxi barely hesitated before he said, "Thank you for telling me this." He knew it was the closest he would get to an apology from the old man, an apology he didn't deserve—at least, not for this. He had earned each one of those scars across his back, if the *kuksui* only knew.

"Go, now." The old man waved him away. "Take a day and go."

He stood up. It was his original inclination to hesitate, but he was striving and second-guessing what would seem natural and normal, if he truly had been innocent. "Thank you, *kuksui*," he repeated and then walked away.

If he had been stupid, he would have gone straight to the beach and begun building another tule boat. But Onas's sudden turnabout was suspicious in more ways than one. If they were looking for a culprit, he wouldn't oblige them. So, he headed in the opposite direction, towards town.

It wasn't far. He stopped on the last rise before he reached the buildings and sat by the side of the dusty road so that he could see the activity of the market just below. He wasn't the only person on the road, but no one seemed to pay him much attention as they came and went, bought and sold goods, talked and laughed and yelled. Just a quiet shadow under a tree, he sat with his elbows propped up on his knees, only his eyes moving and watching.

A man walked into the town, giving him a quick glance as he passed by. Jiangxi wouldn't have noticed, except there was something familiar about him. Then, when he saw the same man moving around the fringes of the market closest to the hill where Jiangxi rested, he remembered him. He was a servant of Sirak's house, an upper servant from the man's family—a distant cousin, if he remembered correctly.

It was hard for Jiangxi not to smile when he stood and saw the other man look up, like a dog scenting a trail. Jiangxi was the target, and he had been smart enough to fool them.

He dawdled on the way back. Stopped at a stream larger than the one by Onas's house to have a drink and watch the fish float through the water. Without spear or hook, he had no way to catch the fish, although it might have been pleasant to come back with such a gift for the *kuksui*, the further to throw him off. The fish were not large, anyway, and would be little more than a mouthful. Jiangxi continued on his way, empty-handed.

Every so often, he would glimpse the man behind him, but there were several people on the road leaving the market and the man wasn't so obvious about his activities that he would attract suspicion if Jiangxi hadn't recognized him. The funny thing was, his own slavery worked for him now. A servant and cousin of a master wouldn't remember yet another slave and would have no reason to think that Jiangxi would remember *him*. To the masters, he was just one more *hikTiSmin*, one of the "scarred," just one more back to labor for them.

The late summer day burned with the heat of the sun. He was glad enough for the shade of the trees when he reached them, after the lack of shade in the cleared land around the city. The trees had been used to create the buildings and for defense against attack; the original stockade was still in place, and it was repaired as it got damaged from age and weather. But it had lost its original purpose as a deterrent for attack, since this was a trading city above all else. It merely served as a reminder of the people who built it, who had originally welcomed the men from China in their grand ships over three hundred years before. Little did they know then that the ships brought more than men. They brought disease that spread like wildfire through the peoples here and wiped out entire tribes. Three hundred fifty years ago, the people of the coast had been decimated, and this beautiful place had been a wasteland.

A wasteland no longer. The survivors, hardier, had recovered. And a new empire had been born.

Old history for his people and for the natives here. It was still looked back on as a holocaust, albeit unintentional. The bitterness of the generations who followed had been woven into the myths and stories of the Amah Mutsun, and intermarriage between the Chinese and the natives carried a stigma that went beyond a breaking of tribal traditions. Sometimes, it still happened, but it was rare.

The sun was lower in the sky, although he couldn't see it from the woods. But the light dimmed fast under the trees, creating a dusk before real twilight. The man would have nothing significant to report about Jiangxi's activities for the day, just ennui from following a wandering slave who was drunk with the freedom of an unexpected day of leisure.

Distraction accomplished; it was time for Jiangxi to go back home.

CHAPTER 11

Jiangxi wondered how long it would take before things returned to what passed for normal. Onas pretended friendliness. Jiangxi pretended ignorance. They both eyed each other and circled like dancers, or fighters. In the end, it became a test of wills. Who was more patient? Who had the most to lose?

Apparently, the slave masters. Jiangxi witnessed them convening time after time, but was always sent into the woods out of hearing. He didn't dare linger to eavesdrop, and so would sit for hours beneath a tree or watching a stream or doing an endless number of busywork tasks. He didn't always see his watcher, but he did not doubt that someone was there to observe him and report back. As he sat and thought about how next to free more slaves once his watchers tired of their job, he hoped that the men who followed him were as bored as he was. He wished upon them all the irksomeness in the world, and was rewarded with some satisfaction when he was able to stay particularly idle for hours, even if the inaction grated on his own nerves.

Other than the breaks he was granted as he was put to the test, Jiangxi wrote figures, cleaned and patched clothes, cooked meals and fixed the garden. When shipments of boxes arrived, he put them where he was directed to and never once opened them. He knew what was inside them, though, from his endless lists and tallies—or thought he did. Usually within a day or two, a cart or several carts would arrive for the boxes and then Jiangxi would haul them out again, load them up, and then sweep the room clean of debris to make it ready for the next shipment. In all that time, he had no reason to question the boxes.

Until, one day at the normal routine, he tripped over a bit of rough dirt and fell forward with nothing to catch him but the box. He dropped it and put his hands out, hitting his chin hard as he landed on top of the crate. His weight, or perhaps the drop, had fractured it. When he was recovered enough to push himself upwards, brushing off the splinters from the rough wood, he was able to see its contents, which were spilled out onto the ground.

The carter came up behind him and yelled. Automatically, he squatted down and shoveled the items back into the damaged corner of the crate. He took a strip of cloth and tied it around the crate to seal it, all while the carter swore about stupid and lazy slaves.

Muskets. Neatly stacked and packed around with cotton to prevent rattling about. He recognized them when he worked on the plantation and saw the weapons of the overseers. They carried the guns slung across their backs as they walked.

Guns weren't much good in terms of quick firing, but they were meant to intimidate, nothing more. An overseer who made a habit of shooting valuable slaves would no longer have a job. The slaves eyed the muskets as much as the men who carried them, and there were seldom any problems. The workers were too tired, anyway, to do much.

But Onas must be a supplier, a stopover for munitions. Jiangxi wondered where they were going—they were obviously coming from his homeland. More importantly, why were there so many? These same boxes passed through Onas's home nearly every full and half-moon, and had been doing so since he first came. Who needed—and was paying for—so many guns?

"Boy," said Onas the next day. Jiangxi was trimming the plants in the garden, and he sat back on his haunches with his hands on his thighs but didn't bother standing. When the old man used that tone of voice, he wanted to talk.

"Yes, *kuksui*?" he said.

"I want to take you with me the next time I travel," he said. Jiangxi tamped down frustration—if he were traveling, he wouldn't be able to free more from the slave compound.

However, the old man's eyes were soft and mellow; it was a good mood for asking questions, so perhaps he could get more information out of him that would end up being useful in the future.

"Where are we going?"

Onas fingered the belt he wore and then said, "I go to meet some men from my mother's people. Like my mother, some of their parents traveled with her when she came this way, but they stopped before they reached this place. We will meet their sons."

"How long will it take to go there?"

"A handful of days," said the *kuksui*. "Maybe longer, if the weather stalls us."

"How long will we stay there?" he asked his last question.

"I do not know." The old man absently rubbed his chin, as if thinking. "It depends on the news."

He didn't dare ask, but the master answered him anyways. "Something has happened, you see," he said. "Something that might mean war for us here. We have been lucky up until this point that the Confederacy fights in the east and war does not bother us here. Now, times might be changing."

Jiangxi said nothing. He had felt the tension recently in the men who came to see the *kuksui*, but it had never occurred to him that it could be something that was important to him too. He thought it was the normal bad dreams and spirit magic it had always been.

He realized he had been quiet for too long and that Onas was watching him. He wanted to ask what this meant for him, but he didn't quite dare. If war came to this city, to this hut in the woods, what would he do? He knew nothing about who would bring fighting or who opposed the tribes here. But he felt that he would throw his lot in with the enemy, no matter what. It couldn't be worse than what slaves faced at the hands of an indifferent master. He longed to be free, to bring freedom to everyone.

"*If* war came here," said the *kuksui*, still watching him with eyes sunk deep beneath his brows. He seemed to read Jiangxi's thoughts by the tangible weight of his gaze. He didn't say anything more, just turned and walked away.

Jiangxi sank his fingers back into the soil and tended the plants of the garden, but his first thought was, *guns*. So that was what they were for.

It scattered all his plans to the winds. Should he stop playing this game and simply run and save himself? He knew it could be done and how to do it.

He dithered as he worked, arguing with himself and fearing that he would wait too long, again. The questions boiled through his head, his thoughts, and he was no closer to an answer when he was packing for their trip to go. He placed the rolls of their tent and bundles of supplies on the back of their packhorse when the day dawned for their journey. Onas was straightening the saddle on his own mount, and Jiangxi wondered at the old man's fortitude. How could he get into the saddle, let alone make a journey of so many *li*?

But, though the old man's bones creaked as he heaved himself upwards, he managed to swing his leg around and settle himself on top of the horse's back. He took up the reins in his hands and glanced down.

Jiangxi would admit to no nervousness. He had never ridden a horse before and knew the basics only vaguely. He had watched the old man get up, so...

He put his hands where he thought they should be. The creature was stamping as he hesitated, obviously eager to go. The beasts were loans from Onas's nearest neighbor, glossy coats shining with sleekness. But their feet were large, their backs more so. This distance from ground to back was... intimidating.

Jiangxi placed the ball of his foot into the stirrup and pushed himself off from the ground with his other foot. As he pivoted to bring his knee up and over the creature's back, he had an awkward landing and found himself grunting in pain due to an unwelcome, but hopefully temporary, injury to himself. The horse shifted under him minutely and he adjusted as well, until he found as sturdy a position as he was bound to find, with his legs split at an uncomfortable angle over the animal's wide back.

The *kuksui* appeared undisturbed by Jiangxi's obvious nervousness and signaled his horse to move by digging his heels into its sides. The boy watched, then tapped his own heels gently against his mount.

Nothing happened. His horse sidled towards the pack horse, whose lead was attached to his saddle. He must not have hit hard enough with his feet. So he spread his legs and brought them in with a good amount of force, his heels bouncing off the animal's round belly.

The beast leapt forward. The sudden acceleration snapped back his neck, and he nearly fell off. His hands were already clutching the pommel and automatically clutched tighter, which saved him from plummeting to the ground. A yell was ripped from his throat without his own volition, and Onas turned his head as beast and slave passed him.

Jiangxi heard the master's distant voice wobble in his ears, "Puuuulllll baaaacckkk!" before they were out of earshot.

The horse caromed down the path and so, by default, did the packhorse, caught on the lead. *Pull back on what?* he thought. He tried pulling on the pommel, but nothing happened. Then he saw the reins flapping against the horse's neck. It took an added moment of bouncing up and down before he convinced his one hand to unclench from its death grip on the pommel and grab the flapping bit of string. *With this, he will stop?* Jiangxi thought incredulously, but, with no better option, he pulled.

And stop the horse did. Rather abruptly. The boy found himself rucked up on the beast's neck, his hands full of mane, and the horse snorting and pawing at the pain of Jiangxi's full weight forced upon its shoulders and neck.

"You're a pain in my neck too," Jiangxi said, rubbing his sore... everything. Then he waited for Onas, who was moving at a more reasonable pace, to catch up to them.

After that, the day was mostly uneventful. He received a chastising look from his master, but no words of reproach, and he relaxed. Onas himself did not appear so skilled and comfortable at riding, but that could have been the stiffness in his limbs from his age. Although Jiangxi felt uncomfortable, a discomfort that only worsened as the hours passed, it must have been many times worse for Onas. But neither of them said anything about it.

That first day, they rode into the hills on a path wide enough for them to ride abreast, with the pack beast trailing on a long lead behind them. The trees provided a cool and dappled shade, broken in intervals by clearings in which farms sat. Jiangxi turned to look at the small figures working in the distance—not all the farms were large, and not all of them were worked by slaves or enclosed by tall fences, although most had at least a rudimentary enclosure to keep out wild animals. The higher they climbed, the fewer farms they saw, until eventually it was just forest and small, natural clearings. They could not move at a fast pace, not only because of Onas's age-frail bones, but also because of the steepness of the trail.

They stopped at midday for a meal and to rest the horses. After they ate, Jiangxi watched over the old man as he unrolled a mat under the shade of the trees and lay down to take a nap during the hottest part of the day. The boy had never seen his master sleep during the day, since he had never once gotten sick, although Jiangxi himself had been ill on more than one occasion. The dappled light of the sun through the branches of the trees speckled his master's skin with odd patches of white and made him look like the bone was showing through his skin. Although he was vigorous when awake, Onas looked nothing so much like a sun-dried fruit when asleep, his skin stretched taut over ancient bones. His chest barely rose and fell, and his eyes were sunken deep within their sockets.

It was hard to imagine the *kuksui* as being the perpetrator of such horrors as what had been visited upon Jiangxi. He looked simply... dead. Jiangxi felt uncomfortable watching him sleep, as if he witnessed something he should not, a secret meant for someone else.

When Onas woke after the sun had moved a handspan in the sky, they got back in their saddles and continued.

The path for the most part stuck to the lowest part of the hills, and wound and twisted along the route of dry streambeds and around the larger mountains rather than up and over them. As they came out of the nearby hills, the sun crept lower in the sky behind them and eventually disappeared over the mountains they had already passed by. Jiangxi glanced at the drawn eyes and pursed lips of Onas as the shadows deepened, but the old man said nothing. The hills fell away behind them, and they rode over the last ridge to see a wide valley before them. It was flat and stretched out in all directions for many *li*. In the distance, Jiangxi could see a glimpse of water that looked big enough to be an ocean. From their vantage point, he could not see the far side of the water and wondered at if it was a sea or a lake.

"There is a camp at the bottom, there," said Onas, pointing, the first words they had spoken since the meal. "You will start a fire and then set up the tent."

"Yes, *kuksui*," he said.

They reached the camp within a matter of minutes and, this time, Jiangxi had to help the old man down. There were logs set around the perimeter that were waist-high, and he settled Onas to rest on one of these while he unsaddled and tethered the horses, gathered deadwood and grasses, and set the materials in the firepit in the center of the clearing. Jiangxi struck together two *huŏchái*, Chinese matches that Onas had packed for their trip, to spark the flames and ward off the growing chill of the night. After the flames caught, he struggled with lashing together the tent frame, knowing that the old man would be unable to help. However, just as he had never ridden a horse, he had never had the opportunity or need to use a tent, and so much of it was a mystery to him.

A voice called out tiredly behind him, "Drive those stakes into the ground in a circle, then tie them together at the top with cordage. Wrap the hides around them." With these and other verbal cues from

Onas, he finally managed it and unrolled the mats and blankets inside for when they slept.

"I will... I think I will rest now," the *kuksui* said when Jiangxi returned to the fire. "It should be safe here. We are surrounded by Amah Mutsun tribes and allies. No strangers could penetrate so far into this land, and the animals will not trouble us with the fire."

Jiangxi had never even thought about that—about the added dangers of travel away from their hut. He nodded as the *kuksui* passed him, but stayed sitting by the fire. The tent was just on the far side of the firepit. It was too small to have been built over the pit, as was traditional.

He was not yet ready to sleep. If anything, he was too tired—the fire captivated him, and he sat in a half-dream state, exhausted to the bone, but not ready to close his eyes on the flickering light.

He did not know how long he sat there, watching the fire, but he felt like he fell into a trance. The leaping flames twisted into pictures, and he saw in the flames the face of the girl he had helped save from slavery. But, in the vision, she was older, as much older as he was now. She was beautiful, as she had been, with eyes the color of firelight.

With a jerk, he straightened. His chin had fallen to his chest, and he had been dreaming. The fire was lower, the sullen glow like a deep orange sunrise. He added another pile of deadwood to the fire, to keep it burning in the night, then stood and stretched. Yawning, he made his way over to the tent. Tomorrow would be another long day of travel.

Onas was completely still, wrapped chin to feet in his blankets. Jiangxi crawled over to his own blankets and wrapped himself up. It was much colder away from the fire, despite the other occupant of the tent. And it would be morning before he knew it.

Jiangxi closed his eyes and slept.

CHAPTER 12

The next day when Jiangxi woke, he lay still for one moment, listening. When he heard nothing, he propped himself up on one elbow to look at the other side of the tent. Onas's blankets were in a sullen heap, but their owner had disappeared.

Strange, he thought. He never slept longer than Onas. He never overslept, in general.

He struggled out of his blankets, groaning at sore muscles, and crawled through the small flap of the tent. Outside, the fire was dead and cold, and there was no one in sight.

Jiangxi, with nothing better to do, ambled over to the horses grazing in the long-topped field of grass. They paid him no attention as he wandered by them, simply tearing off mouthfuls of the long vegetation and chewing contentedly.

He heard the footsteps long before he saw him. Jiangxi turned and there was Onas walking towards him, his stride a little short. He didn't quite limp, but there was a definite slowness to his progress.

Jiangxi, feeling little better, did not envy the older man his stiffness piled on top of age.

"There is a stream just over that ridge," Onas said by way of greeting when he had closed the distance between the two of them. He pointed. "It is not as cleansing as a sweat lodge, but it will do. We will leave when you are done."

Jiangxi replied absently and went in the direction indicated. He felt dusty and sore from yesterday's ride and was able to splash some of his fatigue away when he reached the stream. In fact, he felt so much better, so much like his old self, that he was humming his nurse's lullaby from childhood when he returned to camp.

Onas said nothing. Jiangxi unfurled the tent and packed it up, then saddled the horses. Onas's mouth was pinched tight as he accepted Jiangxi's offer of help into the saddle.

Today was not so far a ride, though, and not such rough terrain as the day before. The way was, for the most part, over even ground, and the path was large and sure. The sun shone, but the ferocious heat of yesterday was absent.

It was well before noon when the road widened and they could see the outline of a walled compound in the distance. Farms began to appear, dotting the side of the road, and they passed several people who greeted them in the traditional manner. By the time they reached the open gates of the town, they had exchanged greetings with a score of folk. These farms looked smaller than the ones to the south. Smaller, certainly, than Onas's plantation.

At the gates, two men stepped in their paths. "Elder, forgive me, but you are not from this tribe," the taller man told Onas. "Please tell us your business."

"I am known to the one who runs the boats," said Onas. It had become second nature to Jiangxi to refrain from using names, in the Amah Mutsun way, and he barely noticed that Onas kept to the tradition here. "An Elder like myself. He has been notified that I am passing this way. Tell him that the *kuksui* from Wacharon is here. We will not stop for long, but ask for crossing over the water for us and our animals."

"Very well, *kuksui*," said the taller guard again. "I will fetch him. Please come rest in the shade while you wait."

Jiangxi dismounted and helped Onas do so too. In *Guānhuà*, Onas murmured, "My friend's name is Maayit. Keep your ears open."

While the remaining gate guard probably heard nothing of Onas's quiet request, he watched the two of them steadily as Jiangxi helped the old man down.

Before Onas even sat down under the guards' lean-to near the gate, a voice called out, "*kuksui!*" Jiangxi, holding the horses' bridles, turned to look. He was unsurprised to see a man approaching who looked of a similar age to his master, maybe a little younger. The man's hair, though seeded with white, was tied neatly back in a braid, unlike Onas's loose and unkempt locks. He looked Amah Mutsun through and through.

"Good friend," Onas said, his face breaking open in a smile. "It has been a long time since I have pulled these bones over your vicious mountains. And a long time since you have done the same and visited me." He glanced at the two young guards. "I have much to tell you."

When Maayit followed the direction of Onas's gaze, his eyes were canny with understanding. "Come, I invite you to take the meal at my home. I insist that you do so before you continue your journey." He clapped Onas on the back and began to lead him away, still talking. Jiangxi shadowed them, leading the three horses.

Maayit's house was a modest structure situated near the water. The tall wall extended in a crescent moon around the town, with the mouth of the moon opening into a low fence near the harbor. If attacked from the water, the half-wall would provide good defense for archers, Jiangxi noted. Otherwise, it allowed people to come and go freely. Most of the boats were away from the harbor, and he could see several of them in the near distance.

He hadn't been paying much attention to the two men's conversation, mostly because they walked ahead and spoke quietly, so he only caught an odd word or two. They reached Maayit's house, but the old man had no stable, having no horses of his own. "I will ask my neighbor," said Maayit. "Please, enter my home," this to Onas, "and rest." Jiangxi remained standing outside, holding the horses, until Maayit returned.

His neighbor had a slave boy of about ten who took the horses and said he would put them to pasture just outside town. When they were ready to leave, he would bring them to the harbor.

"You will have to wait, though, for my son to return," said Maayit. "He is out with his boat, but will be back by the meal. After you have eaten, he will take you across the water."

Jiangxi sat against the wall, ignored for the most part. Onas's friend had his own slave, who served the two old men tea in the Chinese manner. However, no tea was brought for Jiangxi, and he fidgeted.

Onas and Maayit bent their heads together and talked. Jiangxi listened for a bit—it was a recounting of their uneventful journey so far, and the word "war" came up more than once—but his mind had the inclination to wander. He kept on trying to focus, but would then find himself thinking of the undertakings ahead, or about how they would cross the water, or even about the slaves back on the farm. The soft murmur of voices fell into the quiet spaces of the house with the cadence of trickling water.

A loud voice woke him. He was still leaning against the wall, his chin on his chest. The voice came from the door and Jiangxi straightened up quickly, so he would not be caught out in sleeping.

First the oversleeping this morning, and now falling asleep here! He wondered if anything was wrong with him other than tiredness from the journey.

"Father!" called the deep male voice, belonging to a figure who came into view. He brought the smell of the sea and fish with him, but he carried nothing but his own self. He must have just returned from the water. "And Elder! I welcome you back to our village."

"Thank you," Onas said with dignity, awkwardly wobbling to his feet to greet the new arrival. "I am told that you have taken over as headman of this village. I congratulate you."

"Thank you," said the loud man seriously. Then he let loose with a booming laugh, probably the same sound which had woken Jiangxi in the first place. "But I must know what brings you here! When I saw you many years ago, you spoke of not returning. I see your bones aren't as old as you claimed."

Onas laughed—a sound that startled Jiangxi immensely. In all the time they had been together, he couldn't remember the old man ever laughing aloud. Jiangxi stared in astonishment as Onas said, "Ah, but they are even older now. What needs to be done is more important than what should be done. And so, I find what I bring myself to do is not so different than what I need to do."

"Riddler!" roared Maayit's son. "Always, you speak in circles. Too much for a simple fisherman like me. But I see you are perishing of hunger. My wife and daughters have made a feast worthy of a *kuksui*, so it is lucky we have one here."

Again, Onas laughed. "If I am a riddler, then you are a flatterer. But I agree—we are both dying from hunger faster than old age."

The son's eyes flashed past Jiangxi, but didn't linger, as he clapped Onas on the shoulder, his father with his other hand, and ushered them out. "I'll see someone feeds your slave," he said. "Tell me of this journey..."

The absence of sound after they left rang louder in Jiangxi's ears than the noise of the son's voice. He stood up, stretched, and absently walked around the confines of the circular room. He had no doubt he was meant to remain here, waiting. A feast was not for the likes of him.

115

At a soft sound behind him, he turned abruptly to see the same slave who had served the Elders tea. It was a man about ten years older than him. The slave's behavior seemed odd to Jiangxi—the man's eyes didn't focus on Jiangxi when he spoke. Instead, they moved past his left shoulder, as if he were speaking to an empty room.

"There is food for us. Come." His voice was neither friendly nor upset. It was neutral, like his absent gaze. The man turned and walked away. Jiangxi followed a few paces behind.

The house was built in the Chinese style, with two stories and several rooms, but the panels on the walls had no paper screens to let in light. Instead, they were wooden panels that swung open and closed at a touch. Right now, they were fastened open to let in light and air.

The two of them did not go upstairs, but only to the next room, a small space containing a simple wooden table with a surface scarred by knife blades. On it was a covered pot and bowls. The other man ladled a portion into a bowl and handed it to Jiangxi.

It was simple fare, a fish stew with many vegetables. He ate it quickly and was surprised when the other man filled his bowl again. "Thank you," he said and ate that portion too.

"I've heard," said the man abruptly, after Jiangxi had grown used to the silence as he ate, "your master say there will be war."

"Yes," replied Jiangxi. "That is what he says."

"There have been men visiting," said the other slave. He still did not look at Jiangxi, but fingered the scars on the table. "They have come to the harbor and spoken to my master. They did not know our language, and they did not speak in any language he knew. They went away again, afterward."

"What did they look like?" Jiangxi asked, curious.

The man tapped the table with one finger. "Dark skin and hair, like the masters. But the strangers had skin more creamy than red, and they were not so tall. They stank with no washing."

"A long journey?"

116

"Perhaps. Their ship was small, so maybe not so far." The man looked up, finally, but his eyes were shifty and restless and did not linger long. He wore only the loincloth most slaves wore, not a tunic like Jiangxi. But the boy had learned that the tunic he'd been given was also more of an eastern tribal custom and was a mark of difference for Onas too. Few Amah Mutsun wore them—when the winter grew cold, they wore cloaks or the more common Chinese jackets and pants.

Jiangxi had never caught Onas wearing anything Chinese, not even to his shoes. If pressed into covering his feet, Onas would wear deerskin boots or moccasins from the northern tribes, which were often traded to the coastal towns and sometimes sent overseas to Beijing as a novelty fashion item.

There seemed nothing more to say. Jiangxi cleaned the bowls with the other man and then sat back in the central room when the man pointed to it. He thought about strangers on ships coming here. Explorers? Conquerors? Who had sent them and why?

Onas was aware of these things and probably knew some of the answers. But for something so important, maybe Jiangxi would not learn the details until it was too late.

Not for the first time, he thought of the girl he had saved. Where was she now? What would happen to her if war came?

He hoped she was safe.

It was mid-afternoon by the time Jiangxi heard voices approaching again. He remained sitting cross-legged in his corner as the *kuksui* came into the room, still talking to his friends.

"It is late," Maayit was saying. "It will be dark soon. You are old, like me. Stay here for the night and then set out fresh in the morning. After the mountains, it will rejuvenate you for the long journey ahead."

"Who am I to argue against such persistence? If I did not give in, you would probably follow me across the river, still trying to convince me. I thank you for your hospitality."

"We will put our heads together and ask the spirits for guidance," said Maayit, "after the moon has risen. For now, I must attend to those who need me. Will you rest here until tonight?"

"Thank you," replied Onas, and Maayit and his son went out.

The old man glanced at the cushioned seats, but instead came and sat down beside Jiangxi and leaned against the wall with him. Almost conversationally he said, "What did the slave say to you?"

Jiangxi hissed out his breath in surprise. Then he admitted, "There was a ship that came with strangers who did not look like Amah Mutsun. They stank."

Onas smiled, but it was his usual small curving of lips, not the raucous response he had exhibited with his compatriots today. "I see," he said. "And what did you think of our hosts?"

Jiangxi glanced at the door through which the two men had left, the ones whom Onas had called friends. "I have no thoughts," he finally said.

"It is not good to have no thoughts," said the old man. "But it is a wise move to keep one's own counsel. Come, we will take a walk to the harbor."

Outside, there was a fair amount of activity. They passed the smoke house, which was situated near the harbor and against the wall, some distance from the other buildings. The ceiling was hung with strings of fish that were in a half-moon loop, fastened at the far end of each side of the building and hanging low over the fire in the middle. The burnt smell of wood and fish combined to a delicious aroma that made Jiangxi hungry, even though he had eaten well earlier.

118

They passed many houses in the Chinese style, with only one or two more traditional Amah Mutsun houses that looked similar to Onas's home. These were mostly located near the harbor. At the docks, the boats were guarded by two young men near enough Jiangxi's age. They sat by the open gate, cross-legged, playing at *pupai*. It was a Chinese gambling game of double-sided tiles, but the two youth were using acorns as counters instead of something more serious, and laughing. They barely glanced up as the two outsiders walked by, and they said nothing to challenge them.

"I wonder what they would tell us if we asked about the ship?" asked Onas idly, but Jiangxi got the feeling that the question was anything but rhetorical.

"I can talk to them," he offered.

After a pause, Onas said, "No. Better we leave it alone." They strolled on.

The air smelled cool and damp, blown off of fresh water. The sun was already touching the near mountains that stood between this town and the ocean proper. The sunrise over the estuary would be glorious each morning, with the smell of the water and the freshness of the day. Jiangxi took a deep breath.

Some of the fishermen hadn't come in for the meal, but instead brought food with them, and Jiangxi could still see them out on their boats. No one walked nearby; effectively, they were alone.

"I made a mistake with you," Onas said. "Did you know that I originally purchased you in order to train you to help me in the mysteries? It was a dream I received that you would come. When I saw you at that market, I knew you were the one."

Jiangxi said nothing. He strove hard for no feeling, but he felt the tiny wiggle of what-if in his throat. He swallowed convulsively.

"But then, I saw your betrayal. And I thought—even the gods make mistakes. And so, I sent you to the farm." He paused. "It took me a year to realize it did not matter. But, by that time, it was too late. I had made you what you are today."

Onas did not look at him, did not even seem to direct his voice with any emotion. "Now," he said. "I cannot trust you. Just as you cannot trust me. We are at a stalemate. But I grow older and worry that I will leave an absence at my passing. I would like to give you your freedom. It is why we travel to my mother's people. They are the seat of the Haudenosaunee council in this region. I intend to make you my apprentice."

At that, Jiangxi did swing around the face the old man. He found his mouth was open and closed it. "They will think you crazy," he said baldly.

Onas laughed. Only the third time Jiangxi had witnessed it. Maybe the old man *was* going crazy, had finally snapped and let his mind wander. "Perhaps. But I am not considered the least important of our people, and some might think me more."

"If you give me your land, I will give all your slaves their freedom," Jiangxi said. It was more to test his master's resolve, because he did not believe these things he was being told.

"That is your decision to make once I am dead," said Onas calmly. "I will have no need for slaves in the afterlife."

"Why?" *Why now, why do it at all, why...?*

"It was meant for me to do," said Onas. His eyes were deep as the midnight skies. "It is I who made the mistake that set us on this path. I hope that you will learn to trust me, in time. At least before the end."

"I cannot trust when trust is not given," he heard himself say. He didn't know where the words came, or why he was being so bold to say these things. He wanted to stop talking, but his mouth seemed independent of his caution, and certainly had a will of its own. "You have told me nothing of what is going on, ever. I am a slave, nothing more."

The words were as bitter as acorns in his mouth and twice as poisonous, more bitter than he had intended them to be. He had been born more, he wanted to shout. He had been free, he had been a prince of his people! At one time, that had meant something, and his life was planned in beautiful detail.

Now, there was nothing ahead that he could see except his own machinations to help his people. People who had scorned him and ignored him when he lived among them. He had already helped the only one who had ever shown him any sympathy at the farm, the mother and child. And even she had not trusted him completely—maybe she did now, since he had helped her gain her freedom. But that part of it was bitter to him too. He helped them because he felt he must. He helped them because he hated his master and all the masters and wanted to find some way to exact revenge. It was a desire more burning in him than achieving his own freedom.

The thought was sobering, and brought him up short. Was that why he had never chosen to leave? Because revenge was more important to him than anything else?

Onas turned to him. He did not touch Jiangxi, although an abortive movement of his hands might have been the start of something. But they were in the open, in plain sight of all the people here. Onas, too, would be considered odd. Perhaps too much so.

"I have thought about this a long time," he told Jiangxi. "It is time we mend the past. I cannot fix it without your help. But... I will tell you what I can on this journey and when we return home. You must learn, if you are to take over the responsibilities that are mine."

"Your slaves," Jiangxi said. "You treat them worse than the dirt upon which you walk."

Onas looked surprised. "But I give them what they expect. What the other masters give."

"You do not," said Jiangxi fiercely. Then he turned his back on Onas, taking several deep breaths. "Because you live in the old way, they do not get the castoffs from a grand house. They have less, even, than the other slaves, who share with them. They live like animals. Worse than animals."

Onas was silent at his back. Jiangxi realized his voice had risen, but not high enough to travel to the nearest people who might observe them. Or... he hoped not. He bit his tongue in the effort to restrain it.

"We have much to talk about," said his master at his back. "This is not the place. I just wanted to tell you that much. I have been wrong. I was foolish in misinterpreting what I saw. I should know by now that the Trickster is in all things. I have told his story numerous times, and yet when it happened right in front of me, I was still unable to see it. Mistakes are what most often cause the gravest errors."

Jiangxi closed his eyes. He heard again the story of the maiden and the snake. He would be the snake, he had decided a long time ago. It still felt in his heart that this was right. But Onas was confusing things with his words and promises.

That was all they were—words. The whip—that was real. The chains—those were real.

"Yes, *kuksui*," he said as emotionlessly as he could.

At Jiangxi's tone, Onas sighed. Limping slightly, he walked past him and headed silently back towards Maayit's house.

After a moment of hesitation, Jiangxi followed. As he walked, he replayed Onas's words over and over in his head and still came up nonplussed.

Was this a trap to lure him? Or a trick—one more riddle to solve? Or... *could Onas be telling the truth?*

CHAPTER 13

Jiangxi slept almost immediately that night, although he figured his thoughts would keep him awake long past when he should be taking his rest. Instead, as he lay in the main room beside Onas and listened to the old man breathe, he felt soothed at the familiar sound among unfamiliar surroundings. He did not even hear when Onas woke and left the room at moonrise, to join Maayit in the promised ritual for the spirits. He slept on, oblivious.

In the morning, Maayit's son helped Jiangxi load the horses onto the wide, flat-bottomed barge. Several slaves were brought on board to power the boat across the water, and Jiangxi joined in the labor. When they reached the far side and the dock there, they stepped out. Maayit embraced the old man and murmured something quietly to him. Onas nodded and then made his way over to Jiangxi.

Once they were free of the shore, they mounted their horses and turned them north to follow the water. The ground was pounded down in a trail, but not as well-traveled as the one over the mountains, which they had crossed on their first day of travel.

As they rode, Onas spoke, stopping momentarily only when he became hoarse. He told Jiangxi about the Spanish who were creeping up from the south, hoping to seize what they could where they figured the Confederacy was weak. He explained the English were in a holding pattern in the east and unable to take new ground because of the fierce Haudenosaunee who had blocked their advancement past the mountains there, although keeping the tribes supplied with adequate ammunition was a never-ending problem that he and the other Elders were trying to solve.

When the sun was growing high and hot, he spoke about the promised help from the Chinese ambassador to hold off the Spanish. The guns that passed through his hut were headed in two directions—south to the outnumbered, Spanish-beleaguered tribes, and east to arm more groups against the Dutch, English, and French. The horse trains headed from the coast into the interior made their way from one tribe to the next, each section of the trade route then taken up by the next group to go to the next region, in a relay race that crossed the continent. He painted a complex picture of warfare, governance, trade, travel and bargaining, with the slaves owned by the coastal tribes as the link that held it all together.

"With slaves to farm, the men are free to fight, while women and Elders govern and trade," he said. "Take away one part of the balance, and each part will weaken and fall. In your homeland, you would have been executed. At least here, you are alive."

Jiangxi was silent. He didn't doubt the veracity of Onas's beliefs, nor did his memories show any alternative. The criminals and dissidents from China were sold into slavery.

He remembered his brother's face, but it was faded around the edges now. He couldn't quite recall exactly how his brother had looked and what he'd said. It was like woven cloth washed many times over a generation and dried in the sun—it became thinner and thinner with use, until eventually it tore away and was lost. So, too, his earliest memories were dissipating. But enough remained for him to realize that, yes, he probably would have been killed along with the others of the palace if he had not been sold into slavery.

As Onas continued to speak, Jiangxi, for the most part, was silent. He listened and, once in a while, asked a question for clarification.

When they stopped for the midday meal, Jiangxi prepared it silently over a campfire while the horses grazed and Onas rested. The land was composed of gentle and rolling hills, much easier than the mountains two days ago. The forest had been cleared near the path, although there were still small copses of trees, but they were spaced wide apart and provided scant shade. The sun was not too hot, though, but pleasant on their heads and shoulders. They had passed many small streams and had stopped for their meal beside one.

When they continued after a couple of hours, Onas lapsed into silence. Jiangxi watched the strain on the old man's face and knew the cost of this journey on him. If it truly was for himself that they went, so that Onas could set right what wrongs he felt he had committed... Jiangxi let the thought slide away. He would believe it when it happened. Now, it was too soon. They were still just words that he'd heard, that Onas was telling him. They could be lies or half-truths to mask what intentions his master truly had. Or to catch Jiangxi out in his own lies.

The afternoon light slanted over their shoulders, then melted into twilight. They found a place to camp next to a stream, and Jiangxi helped Onas down from his beast. He staggered and would have fallen except for the young man's arm around him.

There were no more structured campsites, so they had merely stopped when the sun was gone. Aside from the stream, they were stationed by one of the thickets of trees, and Jiangxi helped Onas sit down on a low branch that ran along the ground like a snake. It was an oak tree, the giver of life and bread. The *kuksui* rested in the sacred tree's shade, and Jiangxi set about gathering deadfall for a fire and setting up their tent. The horses wandered the length of their tethers, grazing desperately to make up for the long day's journey.

Onas was quiet that night and his eyes drooped as Jiangxi worked. Like before, he made straight for the tent after their campsite was set up.

For not the first time, Jiangxi worried at the strain on the old man. As things stood now—if it was to be believed—he would soon be free. However, if the old man died on the journey...

He would be a slave. A slave far from home with a dead master.

So, he worried. He was too tired to sleep again and spent some time gazing into the mysteries of the fire. It revealed no secrets to him, though, and eventually, he was able to drag himself to his feet and join Onas in the tent. He fell asleep instantly and, if he dreamed, he did not know it.

It felt like only moments later that he opened his eyes. There was light coming from under the edges of the tent and he saw that Onas was still deeply slumbering beside him. He checked the rise and fall of the old man's chest before unrolling himself from the blankets and creeping out of the tent.

Jiangxi fetched water from the stream in their kettle and poked at the embers of the fire to bring it back to life. He fed the tired flames a steady stream of smaller sticks and grass until it blazed up fiercely. After the water boiled, he added tea leaves.

The sun, which had been flirting with the sky, now took possession and rose over the land. They were near the crest of a small hill, and so the light stretched out like fingers to touch and explore the grass and trees. It caressed the horses, which were awake and cropping down the grasses. Although the air was chill, the sun lifted Jiangxi's heart and brought an imagined warmth with it. Soon, the day would heat up and they would be on their way again.

The boy heard a sound and, turning, saw Onas slowly crawling through the flap of the tent entrance on his hands and knees, looking a bit like a turtle. When he was out, it took him two tries to get to his feet.

"*kuksui*," said Jiangxi quietly and poured a cup of tea out of the pot. He brought it over to Onas, who had settled himself on the oak's snaky branch. The old man nodded his head in acknowledgement as he took the tea and sipped it. "Are you well enough to travel?" he asked the *kuksui*.

Onas grunted in response. Then he said stiffly, "It is only old age, boy. It happens to us all. I am not dead yet."

It surprised a laugh out of Jiangxi and his master looked up, smiling his slight smile. "I would not have willingly undertaken this journey, no. Not nearer to the end of my life than to the beginning. But we Haudenosaunee are not the least of the peoples. I am not sick, merely tired. And there is time enough to sleep later."

After the tea, Jiangxi packed up the site and covered the fire. Then they rode on.

Onas was quiet most of the day until they stopped for the meal at midday, when he talked about growing up as Haudenosaunee and Amah Mutsun, and feeling torn between the two traditions, which were vastly different. When they picked up the trail again, they followed it sometimes close to the water and sometimes farther away, but the land was fairly flat and easy to travel. When they ventured closer to the water, it was a marshy landscape of reeds and waterways, filled with flocks of waterbirds and the hungry hum of insects. Although the path was sturdy enough for the horses to travel, Jiangxi could see how it would become dangerous terrain during the winter rainy seasons.

To the east were more mountains, although not quite so high as the ones they had skirted nearer to home. Still, Jiangxi was glad, at least for the old man's sake, that they hadn't moved inland yet. However, his optimism proved unfounded, because shortly after they started again, they reached a large body of water and had to turn northeast. They were still in gently rolling hills, but Jiangxi could see the higher land up ahead. Not what he would label mountains, not quite so tall, but they looked as if they would be laborious to cross.

They stopped before the sun set, just shy of the taller hills that ran along the coast. Onas seemed less tired and sat by the fire for some time drinking tea, although he said nothing to Jiangxi. The next morning, they were back in the hills, climbing steadily. The water was to their left and they walked the horses all that day. When the ground leveled out, they continued for only a short space of time before camping for the night.

The weather stayed clear. One of the benefits of this land, a lack of the monsoons that characterized the weather in his homeland. Instead, most of the year stayed fair, with blue skies as far as the eye could see. Along the coast, the fog often rolled into the coastal valleys from the water in the mornings, but cleared before the midday meal, so that the weather was balmy.

Now that they were a bit inland, however, the temperature rose. The cooling fog of the coast was absent here. But no matter. It wasn't the hottest part of the season, and it was pleasant to sit by the fire in the evening and try and think about nothing at all—not their destination or where they had come from. Instead, Jiangxi tried to think only of the sound of the wind through the grasses and the creaking of branches as the trees shifted and moved. And, when he rolled himself in his blankets, he slept and did not dream.

The days had taken on a rhythm that had a life of its own. By this time, Jiangxi felt as if they had been riding forever. It was hard to imagine a time before this journey, before living in a portable tent, before his thighs chafed each time he moved. The pain must be so much worse for Onas, but neither of them complained.

The hills were tough on the old man, again. They slept in late the next day, both of them, and took a leisurely day's journey. By this time, Jiangxi counted back five days, this being the fifth day of travel, and wondered if Onas had spoken truly when he said before they started that they would reach their destination in just over a handful of days.

The land had flattened out once they passed the last of the hills along the coast and now stretched as flat as the ocean. They made good time that sixth day. The water opened out into a grand lake or series of lakes, then narrowed again to river-width by the time the sun set.

That night, Onas said, "By tomorrow, we will reach the city."

"What is the name of the city?" Jiangxi dared to ask.

"It is called Aguasto," said Onas. "It is where I was born and raised to become a *kuksui* and a healer. It is where I will convince them that you will be able to become a *kuksui* too."

Alison McBain

CHAPTER 14

The islands in the river were green and fertile, some just glorified sandbars barely large enough for a colony of birds, some widening into entire ecosystems of life. Although Jiangxi and Onas followed a trail, it had not been a well-marked one over the mountains, and so Jiangxi assumed that the city they came to would be the same size or smaller as the one near Onas's farm.

However, he was very mistaken. The majority of traffic here did not arrive by roads. This was a river city, and ships were its main transport. But now that the mountains were behind them, the road widened all that day until it was big enough for ten to ride abreast or for wagons to pass each other easily. From grasslands and wild sections of trees, there started to be buildings surrounded by ordered plants in rows. Workers in the fields did not look up as they passed, and Jiangxi studied their downturned heads and thought about his own time on the farm. The slaves here, though, did not look so pinched in face and form. He noticed more tunics and Chinese clothes among them rather than just the loincloths of the coastal slaves. One thing

131

he thought surprising was that when he saw the overseers, he noticed they did not carry bamboo whips strapped across their backs. Maybe they were not considered necessary here.

And there were ships. The water was on their left, although the road had wandered inland a bit. They could still see the ships—everything from the smaller, one-person hulls of the Amah Mutsun to the larger Chinese junks. The river was crowded by travelers. He wondered where all the ships went and why they hadn't seen them on the water before. Maybe he just hadn't been paying attention.

The roads, also, had travelers. Most of them were Amah Mutsun, some Haudenosaunee. They passed an entire contingent of Plains warriors with their braided hair, riding their horses as naturally as if the beasts were an extension of their bodies. Jiangxi was startled to see that among the warriors were several women who carried an assortment of weaponry and rode near the front of the band.

Many others they passed were walking on the road, but some had horses or carts. One traveler was a woman in a Chinese-style cart drawn by two slaves pulling it along. She glanced at them as they passed, but then looked away again without expression. Surprisingly, she wasn't native, but Chinese. It was the first woman he had seen from his homeland who did not bear the marks of slavery—her face was unblemished and strikingly beautiful.

Jiangxi stared at her until the cart passed and, strangely enough, was reminded of the amber-eyed girl whose face would always be scored by brands. They didn't resemble each other much, but he found that the girl invaded his thoughts frequently. He'd puzzled over why this would be so—why, after such a brief meeting, she lingered. But he had no answers.

In the distance, he could see a structure rising from the flat countryside. The road led towards it, and the traffic became much denser. Other roads branched from the path occasionally, and the foot traffic grew thick. Now, they sometimes had to move to the side of the road to allow some cart or other contrivance to pass.

Onas looked grim, but gave his slight smile once when he caught Jiangxi looking at him. Although it was meant to reassure, Jiangxi still felt uneasy among what felt like the crowds of people on the path surrounding them. His back itched with the exposure.

As their horses walked closer, Jiangxi could see the structure more clearly, and it drew his breath from his body in amazement. A bridge that stretched across the water, with flowing arches tall enough for the smaller ships to pass under it. The top of the bridge was covered with graceful, pointed pagoda roofs painted in colors of red and gold. Jiangxi couldn't remember ever seeing something so beautiful except in the hazy distances of his childhood. And it grew larger and larger, so that it towered over the flat land like a palace of the river gods.

There was a line of people waiting at the bridge. At least a dozen guards were at the wide entrance. The guards looked to be local tribesmen, but dressed in Chinese linked armor coats that must have been hot in the sun. They glittered from far away and carried muskets across their backs.

When Onas and Jiangxi reached the bridge, two of the guards moved over to them and the shorter one said, "Welcome to Aguasto. What is your business in the city, Elder?"

"We have traveled many days from the town of Wacharon, and I request to speak with the council of Haudenosaunee Elders. I am Onas, a *kuksui* of the Amah Mutsun, and Elder of the *Onödowá'ga* tribe of the Haudenosaunee. This is my apprentice, Jiangxi."

At the word "apprentice," both the boy and the two guards looked askance at him. But Onas sat his horse as if holding council in the grandest court in the land, and his face revealed nothing.

"Very well, *kuksui*," said the guard after a pause. "You may pass."

And the two of them rode on.

The piers of the bridge were stone, but the deck where they rode was composed of planks made smooth by decades of passing feet. The thunk of their and others' horses' hooves was loud against the wooden surface, after the relatively quiet passage for days on the hardened dirt paths over the hills. Jiangxi could see where planks had been replaced over the years, the newer wood less pitted than the old. The way was painted brown, but the center faded to a more scuffed and dirty grey, weathered by traffic and age.

From afar, they had seen the beautiful archways of the bridge as it crossed the water, but once riding over the river, it was much harder to see because of the number of people. It seemed as if this was a place for all the peddlers of the city to display their wares, and they harangued the travelers as they entered into the dark confusion. In the shade under the roofs, the myriad sounds and smells seemed like being transported to a nightmare scene of constant and chaotic movement. Although it couldn't have been long for them to push their way through, Jiangxi was sweating profusely by the time the horses put their feet once more on solid ground. The beasts themselves, long used to wide open spaces, sidled and fretted as they rode through the noisy mess of humanity that blocked their way into the city.

From the other side of the bridge, they had seen the bright colors of the buildings, but no details. Jiangxi himself had only been to the city near Onas's farm, and that was infrequently. So, the city of Aguasto was like a slap in the face, an abrupt transition to what seemed like a limitless supply of humanity.

There were the normal Chinese residences two to three stories tall, with curling square tile roofs and hung with lanterns at each corner. There were no traditional Amah Mutsun buildings where they were, but he saw modified longhouses and short, squat buildings made out of a mosaic of stones in beautiful shades of red, blue, green, and yellow. There were children running in the street, darting in and out of the adult pedestrians, and carts drawn by horses and oxen, people riding everything from short, squat ponies to large chargers that seemed to tremble the ground as they passed. There were as many women as men in the streets, although they tended to not be alone, but travel in groups or with men walking beside them.

And everywhere, the noises and smells. Shouting, screaming, talking, laughing—cooking meats, manure, perfumes, body odor— and the colors! All the hues imaginable in a mixed tableau that would give an artist a headache. The street was lined with temporary square booths and every imaginable ware was sold—and some unimaginable—and the hawkers shouted louder than anyone else.

Onas rode straight ahead, and people were magically not where the horse stepped, but seemed to effortlessly glide out of the way just in time. There was a slight incline as they moved farther inland, and they found that the crowds thinned a bit as they left the immediate area of the bridge. It was quite the gauntlet to enter the city by that way, and Jiangxi could see how it might repulse people who were used to the peace and quiet of the natural world. Onas, as usual, looked untroubled.

As they moved away from the market and there were fewer people, the clothes and equipages of the ones they passed grew fancier. There were handcarts pulled by slaves, carrying ladies covered in jewelry, with painted eyes and faces. Men rode horses sleek as silk, and they themselves were dressed in colorful jackets or in the ceremonial linked armor of high councilmen. As they rode past, the dressed-up men saw Onas and eyed him for a moment before tipping their heads in a respectful gesture. The old man nodded back.

The buildings in this section of town were Chinese more often than not, and grew taller as they rode. In the near distance, Jiangxi could see a stone block tower rising many stories high. It looked old, as if it had stood there for centuries. Maybe it had. It could, possibly, be one of the original buildings from when the Chinese first crossed the ocean and made contact with the tribes here. They had established a government post along the coast, but also expanded inland to establish and follow the trade routes. Although their welcome was friendly from the beginning, it didn't mean there hadn't been opposition. Some of the sturdiest buildings in the cities were from that uncertain time.

"There," said Onas suddenly and pointed up the street. The boy turned to follow the old man's hand and saw nothing but more buildings and houses lining the street.

"Where?" he began to say, but then realized what the master must be pointing at. It was one of the low longhouses, but the rough wood was plastered over and had been painted in scenes that came to life the closer they rode. There were figures both brown-skinned and white-skinned, some dressed and some wearing armor. One man bowed from the back of a horse and the naked natives in front of him were bowing also, their hands offering up gifts of fish and beads. The riding man, in turn, was handing them a musket that looked different from the modern guns Jiangxi had seen. It was longer and fatter, and he was handing it to them sideways, indicating a peaceful transition.

At each end of the building were doors in the Chinese panel style, but again made from solid wood. There were no windows that he could see in the building other than these openings, but smoke rose from the traditional peaked roof in the center.

Next to this longhouse was a secondary building, also large, but this was a stable. Jiangxi helped the old man down from his saddle and they brought the horses to the entrance, where a boy appeared in order to take their reins. When Jiangxi looked a question at Onas as he paused by their gear, the old man shook his head and spoke to the horse-boy. "Please watch our things," he said.

"Yes, Elder," said the boy and led the three beasts into the building.

That left them, travel-stained and grimy, with the building next door. Onas walked slowly, as if his legs pained him or were maybe only stiff; Jiangxi followed at the same pace. The door was open, and

Jiangxi looked into darkness as they approached it. He was, for some reason, afraid. But of what, he could not say.

Change was coming, he knew. He wondered if he would, when the time came, be brave enough to face it.

CHAPTER 15

There were the ubiquitous guards on either side of the door, but by their ceremonial fringed tunics and old-fashioned spears, they were for show only. Onas paused at the door and they greeted him in the traditional manner, then let him pass without too much questioning. It was obvious that Onas had traveled far, and it was even more obvious who and what Onas was.

Inside, there were voices laughing and talking. At their entrance, a man stood up from the tables that lined the walls and came forward to greet them. The tables, which in a proper longhouse would have been platforms for sleeping and storage, had instead been built higher than the normal sleeping areas. There were benches lining them so people could sit to eat and drink. Jiangxi had expected the group they were meeting would be all men, although he didn't know why; while there were men here and there, the majority were women.

The man who'd stood up from the table looked to be near in age to Onas. But unlike the soft-spoken *kuksui*, this man bellowed like a bull. "Can it be? Or do my eyes fail me after these long years?"

Onas's voice, thin and quiet, seemed to carry farther than it nor-mally would, since the other man's loud shout had caused a hush over the assemblage. "Your eyes are good yet, Dá:snye't. Maybe it is your courage to face me that fails you."

One seated young man drew in his breath sharply and audibly at Onas's words. Dá:snye't, so named, only laughed and strode over like a man half his age. "Onas, the years have taken all that was good from you and left only a stick! My courage is quite safe, I assure you." And with that, he embraced the smaller man and thumped him on the back. Jiangxi, who was the only one nearby, saw that though the greeting looked hearty, the other man was gentle and it seemed more show than vigorous greeting. In a softer tone that wouldn't carry beyond the three of them, Dá:snye't said, "And how are you?"

"Tolerable," replied Onas, but with a slight smile. "You are right about one thing—these bones are not meant for the abuse I have heaped upon them. To have a younger man's back! And legs and stomach, for that matter," he said slyly. Dá:snye't laughed.

"And woman, no doubt," Dá:snye't added. "It must be some import-ant business to bring you so far. But sit and eat, and you can tell me of it when you have rested."

"Yes. But first, let me introduce you. This is my apprentice, Jiangxi."

Dá:snye't looked at him and, to his credit, his face did not change expression. He merely said, "I see. Well, he is welcome too. I will seat you at my left, and he will sit beside you. Come, come!"

There was a muttering as Jiangxi sat beside Onas, but no one challenged his right to be there. He ate neatly but without much enthusiasm, for his stomach had shriveled beneath the stares of the Haudenosaunee in the tent. He kept his own eyes down upon his food and did not dare say a single word to anyone. Nor was he spoken to at all.

Onas was greeted by more than one member of the council by name, mostly from the older men and women. Jiangxi could see he was known and respected here. Or he was now. Tomorrow, maybe he wouldn't be. And, unexpectedly, Jiangxi felt a wash of emotion. He felt like a fraud sitting at that table, as if no matter what legal matters were settled, he would never belong.

He wanted to have what they had with an intensity that surprised him. All this time, his heart set on vengeance, and he found that his memories of his homeland were more distant than ever. He had grown up here from boy to a man, and he knew the land and the languages as he never would the place of his birth. He wondered when—if—he gained his freedom, would he ever set sail for China? If he did, would he be able to find a place there? He had never heard any story of a slave returning home. They carried the badge of servitude on their face, which could never be erased.

So, he ate and had these thoughts and remained sunken in his quiet despair at the realization that he probably would never belong anywhere. At least, not with the easy familiarity of Onas, who seemed to comfortably switch from group to group. Onas came from two distant tribes that had met here in his parents, but he was accepted wherever he went. Perhaps it was the *kuksui*'s age and spiritual connections, but Jiangxi felt it was more than that. When at home, Onas was perfectly content to silently keep his own company for hours, if not days. He was like an octopus—he had tentacles spread out in all directions, but could quickly change his exterior to adapt to whatever environment he approached.

The talk flowed over his head, and he listened idly, sunk in his misery. Just as Onas adapted easily to his environment, he also switched languages without any effort. While Jiangxi was fluent in Mutsun, he only knew smatterings of the many Haudenosaunee languages, Onödowá'ga being the most familiar to him. It was the most common because it was the largest tribe in the group. But Onas seemed versed in whatever talk that came up, and many of the words spoken were unfamiliar to Jiangxi. When he could understand what was being said, it was mostly news relayed by Onas about happenings on the coast, including marriages and births and trading.

Jiangxi had no idea that Onas was so involved in the community despite their many years together, but it made sense that he was present at important occasions—those days when he disappeared for hours at a time with no warning. In his dual spiritual roles, he could be respected as an ambassador between tribes.

There were some Haudenosaunee in the coastal town of Wacha-ron, but many more here in this city. Many of the tribesmen of the Plains also lived and traded here, and a few from the south had come up seeking aid or escape as the Spanish encroached on their land. Mostly, though, the Amah Mutsun made up the bulk of the peoples here, having become central to this trading hub between the Chinese empire and the tribal Confederacy.

The meal came to an end and farewells were exchanged. The younger people left after summoning the slaves to clear the meal, to go about whatever duties they had, but most of the older men and women lingered. "We can convene the council now, if you wish," said Dá:snye't. "But we need to summon several who were absent today, if you would prefer a full meeting."

"I would," said Onas calmly. "There are several matters to discuss."

"Then we will find lodging for you and your... apprentice for the night," said Dá:snye't. "And attend to our business in the morning. In the meantime, I would be happy to show you the changes to our fair city. It has been many years since you came this way."

"I would be honored to have you as my guide," said Onas, bowing his head slightly.

"Enough, old man," laughed Dá:snye't. "I am not so risen in this world that there is need for that. Come, we will walk." He clapped an arm around Onas's shoulders and led him from the building. Jiangxi, unsure, followed a pace behind.

"This wasn't here ten years ago, the last time you passed through," said Dá:snye't, gesturing expansively. The boy wasn't sure what the man was showing Onas, and so glanced around without much comprehension.

Onas, catching his apprentice's eye, nodded his head down the slight incline of the road to where the land met the water. "The stockade," he explained. Then, "When was it built?"

"Oh, shortly after you left that time. We began hearing the rumors then, and news of ships." He glanced questioningly at the boy who was listening, but received a sharp look from Onas, and so continued. "We were only one voice, of course, but the threat was deemed sufficient. It's why we haven't expanded much beyond here on the far banks, although the land has been opened for farming. Do you remember old Níá'a:h's son? Yes? He now has a farm on the far bank, fifty slaves too—" As if suddenly realizing who he was talking to—the second set of ears—he coughed and said, "Erm. He is doing well, at least."

"I noticed that the city has grown more... mixed."

"Ha, did you? Young ones, of course. We're having a lot of settlers coming from the east who are tired of the wars going on there. Or, at least, tired of the unstable peace that often becomes fighting. There are more and more of those English and French trying to push inland, and the Haudenosaunee are finding recruits from the tribes growing scarcer, especially as ammunition always seems scarce. No matter how many we are, it seems that there are always more who wish to fight against us. Some have even suggested taking an example from the ancient Chinese and building a wall to keep them out! But that is an undertaking for another day..."

They had reached the northern harbor by now. The stockade was only partial because, unlike the earlier town where they had rested at Maayit's house, this city was too large to block the harbor effectively. The wall formed two half-moons around the city, open in the middle for the northern and southern harbors. The northern harbor, explained Dá:snye't, was much larger, as more of the river traffic came that way. The city split the river, so that one portion came from the north, one from the east, and they joined together into one large river that flowed out towards the estuary and eventually met with the sea.

"Although we have temporary gates in case of attack," said Dá:snye't. "Stored in these warehouses here and by the southern harbor. With an hour or two of warning, we'd have a usable defense against river attack."

"Hmm," said Onas, looking out at the water. The afternoon light was slanting far away west and a number of boats were docked or returning to the harbor. "And what do the Amah Mutsun say?" At the hesitant look on Dá:snye't's face, Onas smiled apologetically. "Of course, time enough for that talk in council tomorrow."

Dá:snye't nodded. The sea birds screamed above, and the air was cool by the water. Finally, they turned and walked back to the main road.

"There must be work that needs tending to," said Onas, and Dá:snye't smiled.

"There is, but it is hard to say no to visiting with an old friend." He hesitated, then accepted Onas's wave to be on his way. "Very well. Meet me back at the longhouse when you are tired of wandering. Although I would warn you to stay away from the sections around the walls after dark. There have been some attacks in recent times on travelers here."

"Thank you," said Onas, and Dá:snye't nodded one last time before walking away.

"Boy," said his master and he startled, thinking about Dá:snye't and not expecting the voice addressing him. "There are some things I would buy before tomorrow. Let us go to the market now. I do not relish the idea of trying to find my way in the dark."

They wandered among the stalls, and Jiangxi drank in the different sights. What had frightened him before was now oddly exciting, and his heart beat faster when he caught sight of several girls standing idly by at the market. They didn't appear to be selling anything, but they waited together and watched the passerby with sharp eyes. Every once in a while, one would be collected and move off. He looked at their painted faces and black eyes and young bodies and thought some things he hadn't had much opportunity to think about before.

Onas stopped at a booth, bought several items, and piled his packages into Jiangxi's arms. A few booths down, he stopped again and gave more bundles to his apprentice. Then, for the most part, he seemed to stop and look at things, but did not purchase anything more.

Jiangxi was bored at this point and looked up and down the street. Some vendors were packing up their wares and even dismantling their small, open-sided tents. After the tents came down, they were left with several bundles that they put into hand-carts and pulled after them to an unknown destination. There seemed to be fewer people now too, as the light faded in the sky and the sun turned molten. The hawkers called out, but their voices were hoarse and had lost the intensity of the morning. The day was winding down, and business too.

"That is enough," said Onas finally. And Jiangxi carried the burdens, walking at Onas's side. It seemed much longer to return, and the old man moved slowly and paused occasionally. His look was fierce, though, when his apprentice opened his mouth to ask if he'd like to rest, and so Jiangxi said nothing.

When the building came into sight, Onas paused one last time. Expecting nothing except a rest, Jiangxi was startled when his master said, "One last thing before we enter."

"Yes, master?"

"Tomorrow, I will take on my power," he said. "What that means is that you will be witness to it. And to witness it, you must become a part of the tribe."

"Yes, *kuksui*," Jiangxi said instead of asking the questions pressing against his head.

"It will become clear tomorrow," said Onas, his sharp eyes not missing the unspoken questions. "But I would like you to trust that no harm will come to you, no matter what happens."

"Yes, *kuksui*," Jiangxi repeated. And, oddly enough, he had no fear. He had no doubt Onas would protect him from whatever hostility he received from the other men.

"Very well," Onas said. "Let us go on, then."

Dá:snye't was waiting inside—or, more correctly, he was with a group of men and women inside, bent over the tables that were covered by books and papers and maps. They glanced up at the interruption, then Dá:snye't tiredly rose to his feet to greet them again.

"Gaëni:yo:h will be happy to escort you," he said. "I am sorry that I cannot attend to guide you myself. But there are things that need to be settled before the morning."

"I understand, old friend," said Onas. "And I thank you."

They stopped at the stable next door and their young guide took their belongings upon his own back and led them away. Jiangxi still carried the packages from the market.

Thankfully, the way wasn't far. Down a not-so-narrow alley, they reached another intersection and a house on the corner. It was a block-shaped building two stories high, and lanterns shone from the open screens. A welcoming and friendly sight.

"This is Dá:snye't's home," said the young man, who was a few years older than Jiangxi. He had the look of Dá:snye't about him, and confirmed this by saying, "Please do not hesitate to ask me for anything. I am Dá:snye't's grandson, and well known here."

The door opened and a pleasant-looking older woman stood in the doorway. Her braids were thick with white hair, and her face carried the marks of her age. "Welcome to our home, *kuksui* Onas," she greeted his master by name, bowing in the traditional manner of Jiangxi's homeland. It startled Jiangxi, who was accustomed to the Amah Mutsun tradition of avoiding using a person's name to turn away the attention of malevolent spirits. But the Haudenosaunee had no such taboo.

Onas returned the greeting to Dá:snye't's wife. Gaëni:yo:h carried their belongings upstairs, reappearing empty-handed. Then he took the packages from Jiangxi and did the same.

"Please, may I interest you in some tea while you wait for Dá:snye't?" she asked.

"Thank you," said Onas. "But it was a long journey we have had, and I would ask for rest before tomorrow's council."

"Of course." She led them to their room, which overlooked the street. There were two side-by-side pallets, some scattered artwork panels gracing the walls, a small table, and lanterns on the table that she lit. The room matched the house, elegant but simple.

"Goodnight, Elder Onas," the woman said. "And Apprentice Jiangxi."

At first, he was too shocked to respond. Other than Onas, it was the first time in his memory that someone had said his name aloud. He had unknowingly grown accustomed to his name being something private, not to be shared. On top of that, she acknowledged him with the title of his apprenticeship, as if he were someone worthy of respect.

Jiangxi collected himself enough to belatedly return her gesture and bowed his head. The door slid shut behind her.

Onas blew out a long, rattling breath, then said, "Regardless of the council tomorrow, we will stay for several days here."

"*kuksui?*" said Jiangxi as Onas sank to his knees on a pallet. At the questioning tone, Onas looked back at him with raised eyebrows. "Why did we not take a ship here?"

At that, Onas seemed to relax and his lips turned up in a small smile. "It would be an easier journey, would it not? I must admit, I am not fond of boats. And I did not think you would appreciate riding in one, either."

Jiangxi just stared. The overland trip was, in part, for him? To avoid those memories of his first overseas voyage as a slave, rotting away in the hold like a piece of meat?

"Thank you," he said softly, his voice almost too quiet for his own ears to hear.

But Onas saw his mouth move—or maybe his master's hearing was better than he'd thought. Onas nodded, though said nothing more. Instead, he lay down on his pallet and pulled the covers over himself. He gave a long sigh and was asleep before Jiangxi doused the lanterns.

CHAPTER 16

When Jiangxi woke, it was to a clatter of noise from the street. It took him a moment to remember where they were, and he panicked at first, seeing the four neat walls enclosing him. He propped himself up on his elbows and looked over at Onas, still asleep. The shutters were closed over the windows, but light leaked through the edges and was enough to see the deep weariness etched into the master's face. As quietly as possible, Jiangxi rose, dressed, and then tiptoed out of the room.

He hesitated in the hall, hearing movement downstairs. The air still had the wet feel of morning, so he knew it was fairly early. Maybe it was only some servant. But no—he crept down the steps only to find Dá:snye't's wife. She had prepared tea and smiled as he entered the room. "Come, sit, young man," she said. He did, bemused at her deference. She handed him a cup and he warmed his hands, drinking in the aroma of the fragrant tea.

"Thank you," he said. She nodded, taking a cup and seating herself across from him.

"You are the Elder's apprentice?" she asked politely as he sipped from his cup. A bit uncertainly, he nodded. She smiled at him. "I am sorry, but I did not know that he had taken an apprentice. They write their letters, Dá:snye't and Onas, but my husband does not always pass on such news. It is a good thing for Onas. He is wise and has much to teach."

"Thank you," Jiangxi repeated. He had no idea what to say to this woman who saw him as a person and talked to him like a friend. Instead, he sipped his tea.

"But I am making you nervous," she guessed accurately and laughed at his expression. "I am like a mother hen, even though my children are all grown. I do not mean to pry."

"My apologies," he answered. "I am... unused to talking."

"About your apprenticeship?" she asked, but didn't wait for his answer. "I see. It must be new then. I congratulate you." She sipped her tea as he waited, tongue-tied. "Our people's ways are different from the Amah Mutsun. Although we respect all the people of the Confederacy, it is sometimes hard to be so far from home." She glanced away, her gaze moving beyond the open shutters to the courtyard of the house. But he did not think she was looking at the stone benches spaced there. "You are far from home too."

He didn't know what to say to that and found his mouth moving without his intention, voicing what he had been thinking yesterday. "This is my home," he declared. She looked back at him, eyebrows raised. "I have spent more of my life on these shores than anywhere else."

"Ah, that is true. But home is not necessarily where one rests. It may be the place that rests in one's heart." He had nothing to say to that, and she laughed again, but it sounded more forced this time. "An old woman's ramblings," she said dismissively. "And much too heavy of a thought for such a beautiful morning."

"It is never too hard a thought that is true," said a new voice, and they turned to see Onas standing in the doorway. "Good morning."

"The best of mornings to you, old friend," she said. She rose and fetched him tea while he settled himself down between the two of them.

"I fear we have not much time before we must go. Is Dá:snye't...?"

She smiled. "He left earlier this morning. He was here barely enough time to warm his blankets. You must have brought news."

"Hmm," said Onas noncommittally. "This is excellent tea."

So put in her place, she laughed again. "Scoundrel, I should call you," she said. "I will not try to speak of these matters again. Doubtless, I will find out in time."

Onas smiled.

When they entered the longhouse, the fire was banked in the middle of the building, but the council was grouped around it, seated on benches that had been pulled away from the tables against the walls. At their head sat Dá:snye't, who did not say anything as Onas and Jiangxi approached. Instead, he rose to his feet and silently gestured them forward.

They approached and stood to his right, and silence reigned for several moments before he drew air into the bellows of his lungs and began to sing. His voice rose and fell in a rhythm and words that Jiangxi did not know, and he was joined by others of the council, who also rose to their feet as they joined the song and moved to stand beside him.

When the song ended, the men and women resumed their seats. Dá:snye't announced, "This council of Elders is to hear the news of Elder Onas and his request. We will listen and find judgment in his actions and decide whether to accept his petition this morning. Elder Onas."

He nodded towards Onas and took his seat. The old man stepped forward to take his place and Jiangxi stood mute beside him. The pressure of all the eyes upon them was almost tangible, like a force pushing him back. He leaned against this unseen force to stand upright, the censure of their regard burning into him. Sweat sprang out on his forehead and under his arms, and he wondered why they had attempted this. They would get no sympathy here, no acceptance. It was a fool's quest and Onas was a fool for taking it.

"Elders," began Onas in his unmusical voice. It was almost startling to hear the quiet tone after the haunting song and then the loud noise of Dá:snye't's announcement. "I have come here today to present you with my apprentice. I also request that you accept the freedom I give him and gift him with the freedom brand."

At the word "brand," Jiangxi slanted his eyes at the *kuksui*. What was this? He was to be branded again? He remembered Onas's words about trust and gritted his teeth.

"And with this request, I bring news. The Spanish are moving. The have already contacted the Emperor and members of the Confederacy. They are attempting to make alliances as they go. But their plans are not for friendship, but for conquest. We must guard against them. War is coming to our peaceful settlements, and it may be a war involving tribe against tribe."

Murmurs, but none rose above a low hush of sound. And then they dropped down again to silence.

"That is all," Onas said.

Dá:snye't was back on his feet and facing the group. "We will take the request first, and then we will talk more on the news," he said. "Those who support the wisdom of Elder Onas, please stand."

Jiangxi dropped his gaze to the ground. He felt his heart thrumming in his chest as there was movement visible at the edges of his eyes. Rather than give into the temptation to look, he wriggled his toes. They were dirty, as all of him felt dirty. What he wouldn't give for a wash...

"Very well," said Dá:snye't. At that, Jiangxi looked up, but the council was already settled back in their seats. "Now, we will speak on the news."

"How do you know that the Spanish are moving?" said one woman.

"I have heard from several towns along the coast and inland. There is talk about ships and men, foreigners speaking to the headmen of the villages. So far, they have not offered violence. But the people to the south who have come here—I am sure they have tales that they tell, tales of torture and slaughter of their people. Is that not right?"

A murmur again, fading to silence. "How do you know the Spanish have contacted the Chinese?"

"The ambassador from the Empire has told me so. They have come to him, offering many rich gifts from the lands to the south, where they have enslaved and killed the people. Their gifts are marked by the blood of the land. He has pledged to aid us against their encroachment."

A louder whisper of conversation. In the midst of it, "What aid will they send?"

"Guns," said Onas. "Slaves. They have not promised soldiers yet, but we have spoken of it."

"Soldiers!" exclaimed one man. "We don't need their soldiers here. That would exchange one enemy for another, to put the yoke of slavery on us." At the swell of agreement following the man's words, Onas held up his hand.

"If the soldiers come, they will come to aid an ally. They do not come to stay, and that is not the only discussions we have had."

"Promises! How can we be sure of them?"

Onas shrugged nonchalantly. "If they had wanted this land, they could have taken it. Many times over. Their numbers are greater than the drops of rain or the leaves in the forest. If they sent a true force to take our home, we would be helpless before it."

Shocked silence at the *kuksui*'s plain speaking. Dá:snye't broke the ice of it with the hammer of his voice. "I think we can all agree to the wisdom of Elder Onas's words. We have nothing to fear from the Emperor at this time. They have worked long centuries with us, to help us stay the threats of the invaders to the east. There would be no need to break that covenant now, especially when they would face the double threat of the Spanish too. It is in their interests for us to fight back the invaders rather than for them to invest in fighting us, as well as the Europeans."

The man who had raised the protest muttered, but he said nothing else aloud.

Dá:snye't's gaze swept the assemblage. "If there is nothing further—"

"There is plenty further!" said a woman near the back. "What is the plan? The Spanish have not yet attacked us. Do we wait for them to do so? Or do we go after them first?"

"This is just a council, not a war-meeting. We gather to discuss the news that has been brought, but not to decide."

"Enough discussion! We have been discussing this for years as they creep closer and closer, never quite crossing the boundaries of our territory. But they have destroyed the tribes to the south who were never part of our Confederacy. They come here, and they will destroy us too. I say we bring the attack to them."

"Preposterous! Attack on their ground, on their strength? Let them come here, if they dare. We are safe with our walls and our guns."

"Our families are here. What about them? I have been in war. I have seen it in the east. The Spanish take their example from those murdering infidels, the English and French. You think they will not have short memories too?"

"Short memories of what? Of treaties? We have no treaties with them. I wouldn't trust them so far as to exchange the wampum."

"But all we do is sit here and send our young men to build settlements and go to war. We might be safe in our cities, but our farms, our fleet—all of it is outside these walls. If they burned them, they would burn us too."

Jiangxi let the voices wash over him. They were all the same, all arguing a moot point. Onas's black eyes were calm, although the light from the doors was dim in their depths. Dá:snye't stood with his feet braced apart and his arms crossed. He seemed like a statue, set in stone and immovable. It was hard to believe he and the *kuksui* shared an age, for Dá:snye't was so vital and seemed immeasurably strong, like a creature made from the earth.

After some time had passed, Dá:snye't turned to Onas and said in a quiet voice, "They will be shouting all day. Should we leave them to it and go discuss this somewhere more private?"

Onas smiled. Some of the arguing groups saw them going, but none raised an objection.

The topic that was brought up on the walk to Dá:snye't's house did not start with war. Instead, Onas said, "May we do the ceremony tonight? I find that I am anxious to get my business concluded so that I may return home."

"Tonight—unfortunately, no. Tonight is a full council of tribes, and you are invited. I am sorry, but your apprentice is not."

"Will there be slaves there, to serve refreshments?"

Dá:snye't gave Onas a sharp look, but the *kuksui* just shrugged. "Yes."

"Then he can attend. After all, without the ceremony, he is still a slave."

There was his answer, then. The council had agreed to free him. All it waited on was the ceremony, whatever happened there.

"Are you sure this is an issue that it behooves you to pursue? Especially now?"

155

"I am sure that I am a stubborn old man too set in his ways to bother listening to a younger man telling me no."

At that, Dá:snye't threw back his head and laughed. It was then that they arrived at his house and his wife. She had opened the door and was waiting for them. "I can hear you from a block away," she scolded affectionately. He patted her ample hip as they walked by.

"The council argues. We have come here to argue more quietly," he said. This time, it was his wife who laughed.

"The children are in the courtyard while their mothers are at work," she told them. "I will join them, but I beg you to remember that your women are here."

"It is hard to forget," said Dá:snye't, chuckling quietly. Jiangxi saw, though, that the man escorted his wife to the courtyard door and cupped her face briefly in one hand. There was real affection between the two of them, an affection that must have lasted decades. He wondered how it would feel to have known another person so long, someone to share a life with.

Dá:snye't caught Jiangxi looking wistfully at him as he came back up the hallway and, for the first time, acknowledged him with a grin. "Young man," he chuckled. "I see the questions in your eyes. Perhaps, as a free man, you will have some time to find answers." At Dá:snye't's raised eyebrows, Jiangxi blushed and looked away.

"Now, back to the business at hand. We could not have kept your coming hidden, nor would we have. But it is no secret that you have close ties to many communities and can give us more information about the situation we find ourselves in."

"I can give dates and ships and number of men," said Onas. "A list I have put together over the years. And then there is a compilation of information about the movements and tribesmen killed in the south. All of it combines to paint a very grim picture. The Spanish have stepped up their activity recently with the wealth they have stolen from the southern tribes. Based on the pattern, they will attack soon. They already made a wrong move by contacting the Emperor's ambassador here."

"And where does your young apprentice fit in?" It took Jiangxi a moment to realize they were speaking about him. He had been looking out the window at the courtyard, where Dá:snye't's wife was herding the children and laughing at their antics. He turned around and moved towards the two men who were watching him.

"I hope that he can be a bridge," said Onas.

"But is the bridge willing?" pressed Dá:snye't.

Jiangxi didn't know how to answer. He didn't even know what it meant, him being a bridge, or what Onas intended. For a moment, his anger burned. Here he was, being discussed as if he didn't exist, and the plans for his future being decided without his knowledge or say-so. But he pushed the anger back and stood before them, silently. He would learn nothing with his anger.

Onas said, "I have yet to explain to him what I hope for. I have just begun explaining the situation we find ourselves in. I worry, because not everyone will be on the same side anymore. I have good friends who have lived long lives, but still lack the wisdom of presenting a united front, despite what our history has shown us."

Jiangxi remembered the slave of Maayit at the town they had stopped in telling him about the Spanish, but nervously. He wondered if that was what Onas referred to or something else.

Onas continued, "What if the Haudenosaunee had not united the tribes of the east and north? By now, even the land where we are would have been overrun by these Europeans. As it is, it's a war that has been fought for lifetimes. They are greedy, these English and French and Spanish, and they try to take whatever they can. They have no qualms to make and break treaties from day to day. Even land, they use it up until it is like an old rag and good for nothing. I do not want to see that war come here, or a new war—here, where peace has reigned for centuries. Our common enemy has made us friends. It would be a pity if treachery could undermine our Confederacy and make us enemies again."

"We have lived a long time," agreed Dá:snye't. "Perhaps too long, if our days are marching towards war."

"Ah, but war is an old man's game," said Onas. "Only those who have lived a long time can judge how best to throw young men's lives away."

Dá:snye't laughed, but softly. "If anyone heard you, they would think you spoke seriously. You need to learn to curb your impulsive tongue."

Onas grinned. He looked younger for a moment, and Jiangxi could suddenly picture him as he must have been as a mischievous boy. "You are right. I speak too much. As young Jiangxi could probably tell you, I talk and talk endlessly."

Jiangxi, who had just been growing accustomed to Onas's new turn of humor, smiled ruefully at that.

"It is safe to speak here, at least," said Dá:snye't. There was a trace of bitterness in his voice. "Men I have lived with and grown with through the years in this city—I find them saying things behind my back. Saying I am too old to lead our western tribe, too old for the position I hold. That the young men need a chance to ascend in the hierarchy. But they have hot heads, even these old ones who are now calling for a change. I do not know where they get such energy. They tire me out. Even me!" And his laughter boomed in the small room. "It is a serious thing, where I see the split widening amongst us. But that is what is happening. We are divided, and a divided army is like having a person with two heads. They are so busy arguing that they will end up accomplishing nothing at all."

"How many are with you?"

Dá:snye't sighed and rubbed a hand over his head. "More than half. Perhaps three quarters. Enough to count, but enough people against us to matter."

"No decision is ever unanimous. It reminds me of a story..."

Dá:snye't laughed. "I love to hear the old stories, friend," he said. "But save them for tonight. We will need all the wisdom of our people's history then."

Onas didn't seem offended by Dá:snye't's interruption. "Very well. But I think that we need more than facts and figures to win our argument. I have a plan, but I know that you, old devil, have an idea of something too."

"Of course, I do." Dá:snye't grinned. "I don't know if now is the time to share it." His eyes darted, but Jiangxi knew where they would rest before he met Dá:snye't's flat, black gaze.

"There is no better time than now," said Onas. He did not bother to look at his apprentice. "I am holding little back from him. I would like you to do the same."

"I will trust you then, old friend. And the gods help you if you are wrong."

"If I am wrong, the gods will not be able to help anyone."

CHAPTER 17

After the noon meal, Jiangxi got his wish: a bath. It was sheerest luxury, a tub filled with steaming hot water carried in by hand. He had never had such an extravagance in his memory, and if he hadn't worried about taking too long and therefore making them late to the council meeting, he would have lingered until the water grew cold. So he scrubbed himself all over with a soap that Dá:snye't's wife gave him that was scented and soft. It reminded him of flowers in the springtime and, when he emerged, he held up his arm before his face and breathed deeply, smiling. He had never smelled of anything before, except himself.

Onas disappeared with Dá:snye't and, when they returned, their skin was flushed and their hair wet. Jiangxi guessed they had been to a sweat lodge nearby to cleanse themselves for the meeting.

Jiangxi now found out what was in the packages Onas had purchased. So, despite his words to Dá:snye't, Onas had known—or at least guessed—they would be taken before a united council. For he had bought suits, formal Chinese silk suits, with collars and frogged buttons that fastened in the front. Jiangxi wore black and his master wore red. The boy braided back his hair and felt, for the first time, a growing swell of confidence. Still, he chafed his scarred wrists and thought about the marks on his face as Dá:snye't hailed a rickshaw to carry them up to the tower.

For that's where they were headed—the large tower on the hill in the middle of the city. In his homeland, such a tower would have had a religious purpose, such as a temple. Here, it appeared, it served both a spiritual and temporal function as the seat of the united Confederacy. Each tribe except for the Amah Mutsun also had their own government buildings in the city, such as the Haudenosaunee's longhouse, but this was the western seat of the grand council.

The Amah Mutsun, alone of all the tribes, had no secondary building, but housed their regular meetings here. They were, after all, the largest group living in the city, since this was their territory. But Jiangxi was unsurprised when they reached the building to see the marks of many different tribes, such as the Plains, northern, and southern peoples. The marks and symbols were picked out in shiny, colored stones set into the building's walls around the large base of the tower. There were some marks he didn't recognize, but it was startling to him that he recognized any of them at all.

Jiangxi watched Onas's eyes pass over them and thought that the *kuksui* probably knew all of them. No, not probably—he *would* know all of them. Jiangxi was learning more and more what an important role this seemingly humble man at his side played in the international sphere. At the same time, he pictured the slave barracks back on Onas's farm. It was hard to reconcile the images of the man who had had him whipped and thrown into such a hell compared to the one who now stood by his side and explained in a quiet voice the meanings of the pictures and people they passed.

Why me? he thought. Why would Onas suddenly trust him and bring him here? What was the point? He *wasn't* trustworthy. He hated all his master stood for and believed. So why was he here?

His hatred had fractured, though, and become complicated. He closed his mind to the riotous mess of his emotions. His true purpose needed no confusion added to it.

Although he could still be impressed by the building. A distant red roof towered as a beacon over the apex of the city, visible for many *li*. There were steps leading to the tower. Onas walked up them slowly, and the two with him matched his pace. They arrived at the top, and Dá:snye't began explaining the number of tribes that would be represented. Without meaning to, Jiangxi lost part of what was being said as he stared in wonder at the imposing beauty of the architecture.

There were many people climbing the steps beside them and streaming into the building. All of the arrivals were dressed in different sorts of finery, from vests and belts made of wampum to full regalia with feathers and beads trailing behind them like a bird's crest. Some of them nodded at the two men and called them, "Elder." Most of them had eyes which slid past Jiangxi.

"Are you sure this is a wise idea?" said a voice behind them once they had gained the summit of steps. The three of them turned to see one of the women from the council that morning. It was she who had been one of the most vocal against Chinese troops entering their land.

"To what are you referring, Ëgadiyóhšö:'?" asked Dá:snye't politely.

The woman's lips thinned and her eyes were sharp as flint. "Do not play those games with me, Elder Dá:snye't."

"Then do not question the wisdom of your Elders," said Dá:snye't.

"Very well. But when they are at our doorstep and beating down the gates, do not say that I did not warn you." Ëgadiyóhšö:' moved quickly to walk past them.

"The young," said Onas loudly, "forget that the Elder was young once too."

Ëgadiyóhšö:' must have heard, but she did not slow her pace and soon disappeared in the building ahead of them.

"Just one small step," said the *kuksui*, matching action to words. "But there are many more steps behind it."

Inside, the space echoed. What looked like three levels from the outside was open-aired construction, dwarfing the people who walked into the hall. Only on the fourth story was the area closed off and, presumably, rooms situated above it for more private conferences. But this area had seats spaced around circular tables, so that each group of delegates were seated together. They were being served tea by a number of female slaves who were uniformly young, their faces painted white in the traditional style. When one woman walked by him in a drifting robe, Jiangxi couldn't help but watch her pass. He had never seen so many Chinese women all in one place since he'd left Bejing. It was a moment before he noticed anything else.

The walls were covered with tapestries, but the air was cold, like they were in a natural cavern. The hangings were in the Chinese style, depicting scenes from this land—what looked like a first meeting between the natives and the Chinese ships, the building of homes, trading silver and tobacco for horses and guns. No slaves were pictured anywhere in the artwork but they were omnipresent in the room, soft-soled girls pouring tea as more and more delegates entered and took their seats.

"Here we are." Jiangxi followed Dá:snye't's pointing hand and they made their way over to their own table, which was near the front. Jiangxi saw that the Haudenosaunee, even so far from home, were an influential group. Each of the separate tribes that made up the Haudenosaunee as a whole had their own table, although the location of the Onödowá'ga was central to their group, and the table where the three of them were directed to sit.

Jiangxi knew some of the history; how the Haudenosaunee had banded together the tribes on the eastern coast to form the first

164

Confederacy. Like other tribes, each area and peoples had stereotypes pinned onto them, whether true or not; if the Amah Mutsun people were long-regarded as traders and farmers because of their Chinese connections, the Haudenosaunee were seen as the leaders and diplomats because of their foundations of government.

And then there were the Plains peoples, who were seen as both nomadic hunters and excellent farmers. They owned small populations of slaves, although far less than the coastal tribes. Jiangxi eyed them as he passed, but didn't even know any of their languages or much about them. It wasn't often that they ventured all the way to the coast. Most often, the Amah Mutsun traveled to trade with them in the interior, not the other way around.

There was even a contingent from the far south, the Kumeyaay, although they were few and the farthest back from the Amah Mutsun table. They were darker-skinned, their features softer. While the tribes here from west to east all had their own religions and magics, some of the southern tribes had missionaries attempting to foist a different belief system upon them.

Jiangxi knew that religion was what made the Europeans so strange. He wondered what it would be like to have only one god, and it seemed ridiculous to him. What if something happened to their one god? There would be no one else to turn to, no other spirits of nature to help. It was like having a village with only one person in it. They would have to fulfill all the roles themselves and do all the tasks. There would be too much to do.

The noise of chatter echoed and bounced off the high ceiling, but some of it was absorbed by the wall hangings. When they finally reached their table, there was some shuffling and rearranging as it became understood that Jiangxi was supposed to have a seat. He ended up at the end, with Onas and Dá:snye't as a buffer between him and the others, as if his slavery was contagious and could be caught. The thought made him smile, however grimly.

The Amah Mutsun table was at this end of the room, and their seating was directly next to it. Their table was larger and it formed a half-moon facing the other delegates. When one man, about Onas's age, stood up and brought an elaborately carved stone down upon a curved brass bell, the sound was loud to Jiangxi's ears. The tone was repeated three times, each time seeming louder in the growing quiet as delegates shuffled into their seats.

"Thank you," said the man. He put down the carved stone, but remained standing. "As most of you know, we are gathered here today because of news brought to us by a Haudenosaunee Elder and *kuksui*." The man nodded his head towards their table and Jiangxi slouched down, afraid of being seen and singled out. There was a murmuring at the other tables, but it died down quickly as the man on dais continued to speak. "We have long feared that the Spanish were covetous of our land. They have sent their ships to scout our settlements, but they returned empty-handed these many years. It seems now we are to understand that they will not be content to return home again with nothing to show for their venture."

A louder murmur. The boy scanned the different tables; there must be several hundred men and women in the room. At their own group of tables, there must be fifty alone. He wondered how many tribes were here. He had tried counting the tables as he entered, but gotten lost somewhere in the middle.

The sound once again died down as the Elder continued. "We have come to hear the news from the Elder. And then we will proceed to determine what course of action we must take to face this threat."

Onas stood and shuffled towards the Amah Mutsun table at the man's gesture. He stopped right before it and turned to face the delegates, his back to the head table. He repeated his message, adding onto it his list of dates and numbers which Jiangxi hadn't heard before. Then he concluded by saying, "We don't have much time. Whatever is decided, we have help on our side. The vast might of the Empire is behind us. Whether we choose to be wise and accept the friend who has stood by us for centuries or be foolish and scorn them, that is for this council to decide." He didn't wait for a response, but returned to his seat amidst a loud wave of sound.

Hard to make his opinion clearer. Dá:snye't stood to assist Onas when he reached their table again, but Jiangxi knew that the *kuksui* needed no help. By the brightness of his eyes, Dá:snye't was no fool. He was showing the delegates where the Haudenosaunee, however divided, might stand in the end. And the Haudenosaunee were no idle member of the Confederacy.

"Thank you, Elder. Would anyone else from the Haudenosaunee delegation wish to speak before we turn the floor over to the next?"

There was a rustle of sound and Jiangxi turned just in time to see Ëgadiyóhšö:' begin to stand and the two women on either side of her pull on her arms and return her to her seat. Rather than indulge in a scuffle, she glared straight ahead. Others had noticed, though, and there was murmuring in the room. "We are content," said Dá:snye't.

"Very well. Now I would like to turn the floor over to our own tribe, the Amah Mutsun. I will remove myself in order for our Elder to speak."

Another man further down the table stood up as the Elder sat down. As he began to speak in a sonorous voice, Jiangxi found his mind wandering. He tried to yank it back, but he could only pay attention for a short time before he found himself looking around again. It probably didn't help that the man droned on in a monotone voice that had even Onas beside him looking glassy-eyed. And the chief spoke in circles, never touching too closely on the main reason they were all there.

Although he had no name for the chief's action, Jiangxi could plainly see he didn't want to commit to one opinion. It seemed as if the whole room was divided, or could be, and it wasn't tribe against tribe. When the chief sat down and delegates from the other regions spoke, some were passionate about each side. And the dissention was as much within each group as it was between groups. For a number of minutes, a very heated discussion occurred at a table far in the back. Jiangxi had a hard time catching the words, but it was two delegates from the Lakota. Onas murmured a quick translation to Jiangxi—one wanted to bring war to the Spanish and one advocated waiting.

"Our people would be safe. What could the Spanish do to us? We are never in one place. We travel with the buffalo while they are static."

"But they would seek us out. They would find us. Don't forget how it was in the south."

Always, it came back to the south and what had been happening to the tribes there. The few representatives from the Kumeyaay were so far back in the room that Jiangxi couldn't hear them speak—nor would he have understood them, even if he heard. But there was a wave of murmuring that passed back up to the front of the room, and it relayed a strong message.

In the end, the tribes stood up and took a vote. Jiangxi was not the only one to remain in his seat, but none of the other delegates had brought slaves. The others who abstained looked stubbornly away from the ones who spoke to them, trying to convince them not to waste their voice.

But the hard facts of history were not too hard to sway the delegates. In the end, they decided, and the decision of the Elders was final.

They were going to war.

CHAPTER 18

Onas was fairly quiet once the council broke up and the tribal Elders scattered into the city. Since there was such a demand on rickshaws, the two men decided to walk for a space and maybe get a cart later, away from the crush of people. Jiangxi trailed behind them.

"It's hard to imagine," said Dá:snye't finally when the loud voices were left behind and they had reached emptier streets. "Where we will be a year from now."

"Hopefully, the same place we were a year ago," said Onas. When Dá:snye't raised his eyebrows at his friend, Onas sighed. "I feel that more and more, my time is passing. The time of those like me, the ones who speak to the spirits. The young do not heed us, and even the Elders and chiefs are willing to argue us into the ground. I noticed that not one of the councilors asked for any talk from a *kuksui* or spirit-man other than myself."

"But this is a council of war, not of healing. When we are on the eve of battle, you will be remembered. The people need intermediaries with the gods to bless us. But you have less of a place, old friend, in a talk about war, especially when battle is far away." Dá:snye't looked into the distance. "I bless the Confederacy and would hate to return to the ways before, when we fought tribe against tribe, but I often think about what we have lost. What part of our people and our culture has been taken from us when we come together like this? There is no denying why we have done this, and I do not say that the Chinese have not given us many benefits, but our culture has changed. With every change, there is a loss."

"Yes," said Onas. "We have lost a part of our spirit."

Behind them, the boy struggled with a response to what they said. He didn't want to identify with them in any way. He saw them as hypocrites. They mourned the loss of their culture, but what culture did slaves have?

The two men fell silent. In the distance, the boy heard the call of a long horn and wondered what nighttime ritual it marked. Or perhaps it was nothing, just a note ascending to the heavens like a prayer.

At the next corner, they came upon a rickshaw with the two men drinking sake at the corner outside a tavern. They agreed to take the three of them back to Dá:snye't's house.

The men who drew the rickshaw were slaves by the scars on their faces. They did not seem to notice the difference between Jiangxi and the Elders; at least, they spent no time saying anything except agreeing on a price for their service. Noting the boy's look, Dá:snye't explained that each rickshaw pair were owned by a merchant, who gave the slaves a portion of their fares, with the eventual hope of the slaves that they could buy their freedom.

The concept of a slave buying his own freedom—and with the blessing of their master—was eye-opening to Jiangxi. "What happens when they are free?" he asked.

Dá:snye't shrugged. "Not much, I expect. They might continue pulling a rickshaw. Or they might become merchants themselves, with their former owner's help. Several of the hawkers at the front gates are former slaves."

Jiangxi hadn't noticed yesterday, tired and overwhelmed by the crowds of people. He wondered if the girls in the alleys ever had a chance to make the same bargain. If they were ever freed from their servitude.

He guessed that they probably were not, but it led him to think about the girls at the council. How he had known they were slaves under their white paint, he didn't know. Maybe by how they carried their bodies or just the casual way they were ignored.

At the house, Onas bade their host goodnight and was once again asleep before Jiangxi had shut up the lanterns in their room. Despite the long day, Jiangxi stared into the dark shadows of the room as he lay in his pallet, and he thought about slavery and war. The struggle wasn't with his conscience, which was clear, or yet with his loyalties. There was some lessoning of his hatred towards Onas, but not a clear liking, not something that would make him want to give up his dreams of vengeance against slaveowners. He was bitter, but with good reason, he thought.

When he finally fell asleep that night, he dreamed. Again, it was of the amber-eyed girl. In his dream, she was the same age as him, yet wearing her slave clothes. He stood by her, and something about her bare torso and amber eyes called to him as they hadn't when he was a boy. Then, he had been fascinated by her, knowing her for different. Now, he knew why he thought of her, and he wanted to be with her with a fierce longing.

When he next opened his eyes, he was alone. The pallet next to him was empty. The light didn't seem too bright, though, so it must still be early in the day.

He got up and opened the shutters, which overlooked the courtyard below. The quiet voices and laughter of women floated up to him. They were in the courtyard, and it looked like they were pounding out acorns for bread. Dá:snye't's wife was absent, and Jiangxi guessed she might be sharing tea with Onas. He wondered if he should go down the stairs or if he should just sit here and enjoy the sun shining in the window.

Travel was strange—now that they were here and had discharged their message and purpose, they had very little to do. Jiangxi understood that Onas needed rest before they returned to their home, and that there was still the ceremony concerning him, but the boy felt no inclination to do anything. He wanted to lie in the sun and drowse, even though he had just woken. He'd never felt so relaxed—never been given the opportunity to be so lazy, not since he was a child. And even then, there had been lessons to learn and nurses to obey and an endless schedule of duties, even for one so young as he.

But it wasn't his place or his nature to be lazy, not usually. There might be something to do, or more news, at least. He went downstairs, where he heard the familiar voices he expected. There was one additional voice, though, and it wasn't one that he had wanted to hear in this haven. It was Hö:ga:k's voice, Onas's neighbor.

When Jiangxi walked into the room, Hö:ga:k didn't even pause in his speaking to look at him, as if he were not worth noticing. "I will respect your wishes, Elder, but I would be negligent if I did not offer you passage back. My ship is small by trading standards, but plenty big enough to take you and the boy."

"Don't forget Sirak's horses," said Onas. "They must return with us also."

"There is enough room," said Hö:ga:k. "I am just coming back from a run up the river. My hold is not quite full."

"When are you planning on leaving?"

"I have some business to conduct in the city. Say, tomorrow morning?"

"Then I would be honored to accept." They bowed to each other and Hö:ga:k said farewells to his host and hostess and stood. He walked right by Jiangxi without acknowledging him in any way. Jiangxi resisted the urge to shuffle aside. When he didn't move, Hö:ga:k paused for a moment and then shouldered his way past him.

"Come, boy," Onas said. Maybe Jiangxi had opened his mouth to say something or maybe it was just how he looked at Hö:ga:k. Either way, whatever action he would have taken or inflammatory comment he would have made was halted. He sat and was served tea by Dá:snye't's wife, which he drank in sullen silence.

"Tonight is the ceremony," said Onas. "At twilight, the time of transition. It will be painful."

He could have asked for more details, but he didn't. Not knowing was easier than anticipating something he couldn't change.

The day passed without him noticing much. A steady stream of visitors came to speak with Onas and Dá:snye't, and the boy recognized some of them from the grand council the night before. It wasn't until the midday meal had passed that he began to get nervous. Then when Onas came to fetch him from the courtyard where he had been watching the children playing, his stomach dropped. He thought he would be sick. He didn't remember much from his first branding, but enough of the pain lingered. It had been like the whipping, which created another type of fire.

"I am sorry," said Onas quietly. Dá:snye't and Onas had visited the sweat lodge again that afternoon, but Dá:snye't had gone ahead in the previous hour to prepare for the ceremony. Onas had lingered to guide Jiangxi to the longhouse. "It is the only way to change the brands."

Jiangxi said nothing. There really was nothing to say. He had to go through this or remain a slave.

When they arrived at the longhouse, the council was inside, waiting. The words of the ritual passed in a daze. All Jiangxi could see at first was the fire in the center of the building and the handle of the tongs poking from the flames. Then Onas moved into view, and he was dressed in his terrible mask. But instead of causing surprise or upset, Jiangxi only felt distant from his former fear, apathetic.

Certain select council members came forward, including Dá:snye't, anointing Jiangxi's body with oils, then rubbing him with herbs that made his nose twitch. Onas held something in his hands—it was a wampum belt, one that Jiangxi had seen Onas working on before they came here. The *kuksui* laid it across Jiangxi's shoulders and intoned words in a tribal tongue that he didn't understand. The belt was removed and handed off to Dá:snye't, who accepted it.

When they told him to lie down, he lay down. When they explained he would be held down, he closed his eyes and nodded. Inside, his heart raced. He opened his eyes to watch them carry the red-hot iron from the fire and saw that it was cooled to black before the brought it before him.

"Ready?" he heard a voice say. They didn't give him a chance to answer, and it was that moment of tension that kept him still as they pushed the brand against his skin and held it for one long, indeterminate second. He felt nothing except a slight pressure against his forehead until it was pulled away and bits of his skin sizzled and stretched with it. Then the pain lanced through his skull, searing away bone and blood, and he screamed. His eyes leaked tears and he coughed and retched as he was held down and struggled against the hands. Finally, they let him lean to the side, where he vomited all the half-digested food in his stomach, retched until he was spitting out green slime in fitful wads. Sobbing still, he lay on his side, exhausted by the searing pain.

They had had to put a brand over each scar on his skin, so forehead, cheek and cheek. Where there had been circles before, now was etched the tribal symbol of the Haudenosaunee delegation, which was a simple figure like a leaf. Inside the leaf was the Chinese symbols for freedom.

They left him there, and he lay in a half-daze as people were busy around him. It seemed like hours but was probably only moments before something was touching his burns. He flinched back, but he saw it was Onas, still wearing the mask, putting a poultice on the wounds. The pain did not go away, but it dwindled until he felt he could bear it.

Onas knelt beside Jiangxi until he managed to stand up. He walked away but Jiangxi didn't watch him go, instead struggling with the nausea brought on by the pain. When the *kuksui* returned a few moments later, the mask was gone from his face.

The ritual was over. Together, the two of them made their slow, careful progress back to Dá:snye't's house to rest.

Before the sun rose the next day, they were at the harbor leading their borrowed horses. Hö:ga:k greeted Onas, still carefully ignoring Jiangxi. One of his men took the reins from the ex-slave and led the horses below decks. Jiangxi followed the two neighbors where they went; although Hö:ga:k scowled, he said nothing.

Jiangxi's face was bandaged in patches where Onas had changed the poultice and put wrappings on this morning to protect his burns. They were a constant ache he had grit his teeth against—or, at least, he *would* have gritted his teeth against them if clenching his jaw didn't sharpen the pain. Instead, he metaphorically did so and bore the raw ache without complaint. Of course, talking hurt too.

The men moved to the rear of the *chuán*, a mid-sized wooden cargo ship with the traditional three fan-like sails and colorful flags topping each mast. The sails were tied up, but the men were busy on the decks; their arrival had been the signal to depart.

"We should be back by tonight," said Hö:ga:k to Onas.

Jiangxi gazed out over the water. It was clearly a river and not an ocean, so maybe that was why he felt nothing being on board a smaller version of the ship that had carried him across the waters when he had become a slave. Maybe it was something else entirely—such as being older and knowing himself for a free man. Even if he inherited nothing from Onas, he had been given that. And his freedom couldn't be taken away from him again.

He wondered if this was one more test. If his master—now, former master—was watching him to see if he would continue his clandestine activities. He felt his purpose wavering behind the idea of his own freedom. Now that he was free, did he want to do anything to jeopardize it? He had helped several slaves escape already. Was it really so bad a thing to hold onto himself and his dreams—to see where his life could lead, now that it was *his* life, *his* choice to do with it as he wished? He couldn't save everybody. Maybe it was enough he had already saved a few.

He drew the air into his lungs that carried the scent of water, but not yet the salty tang of the sea. It was hard to picture a time other than the present, with his burning face that meant freedom. How could he picture what the future would hold?

Right now, the present held him in its jeweled grip and he felt rich with the marvel of his life. It didn't matter if he was ignored by one of the men who had only seen him as a slave, and seemed to continue to see him as such. Maybe Onas hadn't even told Hö:ga:k his plans for Jiangxi, but it really didn't matter.

He was alive, he was young, and he was free. Right now, it was enough.

CHAPTER 19

Jiangxi spent most of the voyage doing little except sitting in the foredeck and watching the water part before the hull of the vessel. At one point, one of the sailors attempted to put him to work, but he eyed them and said, "No," with such finality that the man simply looked at him for one long moment and then walked away. When he smelled food, he went and ate. If no one spoke to him, neither did they object to his presence. When the meal was finished, he resumed his vantage point and watched the water and land change around them.

The sun set before they were at their destination, but the moon was full in the sky. By its light, they approached the glow on the horizon that marked the city of Wacharon by their home. It was late by the time they arrived, though, and Onas looked stretched thin once again from travel. By the time they arrived back at the hut, Onas went directly to sleep, and Jiangxi unsaddled and tethered the horses before he was also able to get some rest.

In the morning, Onas seemed recovered, although his movements were still slow as he drank his morning tea and went about his day.

He asked Jiangxi quite politely to return the horses rather than telling him to do so; quite politely, Jiangxi agreed.

The main road was empty between the farms. Jiangxi rode along with not a little trepidation, Onas's borrowed mount and the pack-horse trailing behind him. He passed the slaves working in the fields, who did not bother to look up at a solitary rider.

The sight of the field slaves brought up a sudden strike of fear. While he still wore salve on his face that masked his burns, reapplied that morning, what would happen when his burns healed? When he returned to the farm, what would they think of him?

He neared Sirak's house, and he passed through the gates with a wave at the guards and on to the stable with no one questioning him. He spoke to the stable master to pass on Onas's message of thanks to Sirak, and the man agreed to do so even though he looked through him, as if the message were delivered by the breezes. Then Jiangxi made the slow walk back to the hut.

When he arrived, he saw Onas had prepared a simple meal. They sat down and ate with very few words between them, but when they were done, the old man sighed.

"You are free," he said. "And that means I can no longer make you do things, but I must ask as a master to his apprentice. But, as such, I expect you to obey me. You are young still, and I have promised you to follow in my footsteps."

Jiangxi was silent for a moment, toying with his spoon and bowl. "And what if I choose to leave?"

"Then I would be disappointed. But I would not stop you."

"Wouldn't you?" Jiangxi challenged. Onas's eyes were flat and he did not respond. "Why have you done this? You are wrong about me, you know. I am not to be trusted."

"Maybe not yet," said the old man. "But I do not think I am so far off. If you were not to be trusted, you would not have told me what the slave said in Maayit's house. You would not have returned after you were branded with your freedom. You could have left at any of the times when I gave you time and opportunity to wander, even if I had not yet given you the mark that made it legal." He paused. "You are angry, yes. Bitter towards me, yes, I can see that. But your heart is loyal. You have the potential for trust within you too, because you can see how much more you can accomplish if you are able to follow your heart."

"Ha!" shouted Jiangxi, jumping to his feet. "You are deluded if that is what you think."

"Maybe so." Onas smiled his little smile. "But I prefer to hope that I am right about you, rather than be proven without fail that *you* are right."

It took some time for the boy to puzzle through this. He stared at the *kuksui* in disbelief. "You are crazy."

Onas laughed. He seemed to be doing a lot of that recently. Maybe he really was crazy, Jiangxi thought with some alarm. Maybe he had gotten too old and his mind had gone wandering.

"Crazy is subjective," Onas replied. "I am content to have the title—as long as I end up being right, as well."

At that, Jiangxi laughed, it was so unexpected. But the laughter was cut off as abruptly as it had started. "You will regret this," he promised. Dared, almost.

"Then I will regret it. Not the first thing I have regretted in my long life. If it is the last..." Onas waved a hand in dismissal. "It won't be the worst of my offenses, either."

Jiangxi sat down again. He faced Onas. When the old man smiled again, the expression was strained. Jiangxi's first thought was that the *kuksui* was still fatigued from the trip, and to help him.

In a flash of insight, he realized he cared for this old man who had so scorned and punished him, and yet who'd also shown him some of the few kindnesses and compassion he'd ever received in his life. Onas was human and he had his weaknesses, and yet he was a strong person too. Strong enough to admit his mistakes. A man who could be respected because of it.

Jiangxi would betray Onas, he knew. He had already made his decision, and he couldn't imagine giving up on his revenge. There was only so much that respect could do when one lost all respect, when one was chained in soul as well as body. Any lingering effects of affection were a misplaced ghost from his former life. He knew this path would be hard, but he had chosen it—or it had chosen him.

He bowed his head. "Very well," Jiangxi said, the bitter lie twisting his tongue in his mouth. "Teach me, then. Tell me all that you know."

Although he hadn't understood it at the time, he had already begun the transition. When he was given his freedom, when Onas had donned his sacred mask and performed the ritual, he had been inducted into the family clan of his master's tribe. No man could witness the secrets of the False Faces and be an outsider.

But there was one more task to complete before he would truly be part of the Onödowá'ga. While he was now an adopted member of the confederation of Haudenosaunee tribes, he still had to complete a ceremony for his guardian spirit to arrive and to receive his sacred name from the Elders, something which usually happened much earlier in life for a youth born into the tribe. For Jiangxi, Onas told him this would happen in midwinter during Niskowǔkni ne''Sadē'goshä, a week-long festival of thanksgiving. They would return to the city then, and complete the ritual.

Onas's neighbor Hö:ga:k belonged to the Onödowá'ga too, he found out. "But did he know?" asked Jiangxi as he worked in the garden doing many of the same tasks as before, but now with Onas as constant companion as he coached Jiangxi in both the Onödowá'ga language and customs. "He pretended I didn't exist."

"He knew," said Onas. "As you might have guessed, he didn't approve."

"He is half-blood too," Jiangxi realized. It had never been spoken aloud.

"Like me, yes," said the old man. "But he shows more of his father's people in him. I take more after my mother's side."

"If you are training me to your ways," said Jiangxi, "does that mean I will hold a place of... of precedence in the clan? In the tribe?"

Onas paused at the question. Jiangxi, knowing the silence for thought, continued digging his hands into the soil. When the *kuksui* finally spoke, the boy had fallen into the half-daze of repeating his mindless task over and over, and was actually startled at the interruption.

"Perhaps," the old man said inconclusively. Then, "It has never happened before. There has been intermarriage, which is not uncommon. Some of the men, they have grown a preference for the women of your race. *hahmestap*, they are called, but it is not a good name. It means they take a woman who has no choice. But none of their children have been so marked as I have marked you."

"That is what I don't understand," said Jiangxi, finally sitting back on his heels with his hands propping him up on his knees. "How I have been marked."

"I know your story," said the old man carefully. He was not looking at the young man, but squinting into the sky against the light of the sun. "The death and blood that have changed you. Not so strange, considering the passage of slavery. But I know something more about you too. Your royal blood. You are from as noble a birth as any of us here. Just because you were the son of a foreign chief does not make you any less of a chief's son."

He just stared, not realizing that Onas would talk about his background so openly. The *kuksui* continued, "And I dreamed of you. Of your coming. I saw your face for months before I arrived at the marketplace. I knew you would be there that day, and I came for you." Onas contemplatively rubbed a bit of dirt between two fingers. "Dreams… they are brought to us by the gods. They are a warning and an instruction, and it is important not to ignore them. Death often waits for those who do."

Jiangxi saw no profit in pursuing the subject, and so went back to his planting. The garden was just for their own personal use, since the farm itself was for trade. They harvested a much wider variety of plants here than the stock crops that were overseen by Onas's hired hands. One of the main commercial crops now was tobacco, which had a wide demand in China. While it was still used in sacred rituals to the Haudenosaunee, it was also another of the links that Onas was teaching him in the web of trade, politics, and war that connected the Confederacy.

"You must learn to listen to your dreams too," said Onas finally, before he left Jiangxi to his task. "And I will tell you what they mean."

That night, he dreamed of the girl again. She was waiting for him, he saw, in the forest hut she had made. The girl beckoned him inside from where he had paused in the doorway, and he came towards her with joy in his heart. He felt a rising tide of something, some elemental feeling that he couldn't describe. But he found himself before her, grasping her arms in his hands and then moving closer, so that they stood chest to chest and cheek to cheek.

When he woke, he lay on his rug for a long time and stared at the thatched ceiling. Every so often, they would replace the outer thatch, a laborious job that took days to do properly. It was coming up on that cycle again, and he wondered idly if he would be required to do it or if he could tell Onas no. Perhaps it would be best not to argue until he was sure of the stability of his freedom.

It was hard to think that the majority of his life, he had been a slave. He had spent less time free than under bondage, and most of that time of freedom was too early for him to remember. And a lot of the years before he was sold into slavery, when he should have remembered something of his life, was composed of isolated images. He should have remembered more, but he felt that the ship's passage had burned something from him, some elemental part of him that was his past. So, when he stepped off the boat, he was a new creature, a baby again, learning the process of living. He was created anew in this land, and he didn't truly believe anymore that he would ever return to Beijing.

However, he didn't believe everything Onas said, either. He had lived with him for too long to believe that the powers he claimed were without fail. What the old man said did send shivers up the back of his neck, but that didn't mean he didn't make mistakes. He had admitted to several.

It was strange, though, that Jiangxi would dream of the girl again after Onas had told him to watch his dreams. While most of his dreams were nonsensical or unremembered, she often featured in the ones he could recall. But, of course, she was the one person he could never discuss with the *kuksui*.

When he went outside, Onas was sitting by the cookfire with his face turned to the sun. In his hands was a cup of tea. Jiangxi poured a cup for himself from the heated kettle and sat down opposite the *kuksui*, who opened his eyes and asked, "What do you remember?"

"About what?" said Jiangxi evasively, taking a sip from his cup. He looked in the direction of the stream rather than at Onas.

"Your dreams. Tell me about them."

Jiangxi paused too long, then said, "I don't remember what I dreamed." In his mind, though, was the image of himself and the girl pressed together, and he had to turn from the older man. "I am going to the stream," he said, putting down his cup and taking himself off without waiting for a reply.

When he came back, Onas was still drinking tea and looking contemplative. Jiangxi went to work in the garden. When that was done, he refilled the water tank and prepared the midday meal. They ate in relative quiet, but the lack of words from the old man, who had been explaining the ways of the tribes the past few days without surcease—it was uncanny for Jiangxi to sit and chew his food across from the old man, who said nothing. Nor did Onas look up at Jiangxi, either. Instead, it seemed obvious that he was thinking.

After the meal had been cleaned up, Onas said, "I think it is time we talked about slavery."

Jiangxi was standing, but his old master had not left his seat by the fire after the meal was finished, so the boy sat back down and waited.

"I will not free my slaves," said Onas. "Tell me, then, how to make their lives better. I have wealth enough."

"Why won't you free them?" asked Jiangxi. He tried to keep the bitterness from his tone, but even to his own ears, it still sounded angry.

"Boy," said Onas, finally meeting his eyes. Although set in a nest of wrinkles, Onas had large eyes, and they were warm now, as if there was pity or some other emotion that softened them. "If I did not make money on my land, I would not be able to be in the position I'm in or have the knowledge or contacts I need in order to aid in this coming war. But I have enough wealth that I can treat my slaves better, because of you. I am learning in my old age what it means when a change is coming. I may even be the harbinger of that change, through you. But my life is still set firmly in where we are today. I am no bridge between distant peoples over the sea. I am a bridge for the tribes on this land. I am sorry I cannot be more."

"What if more slaves run away?" he dared.

"Then they run," said Onas relentlessly. "And we will hunt them as best as we are able. And punish them—and anyone who has helped them—if they are caught."

Jiangxi drew in his breath sharply at the not-so-veiled threat. But he also thought about how much Onas had changed—was changing still—and wondered if it was only his own stubbornness that would harm the people he had the ability to help, through Onas. Did it really matter if the *kuksui* didn't understand completely? If Jiangxi couldn't free them all at once, as long as the men and women were treated better and given what they needed to survive, that would matter to them right now. He remembered the awful, stinking conditions they were forced to live in. He couldn't let his pride stand in the way of that.

"Clean up the longhouse," he said. "Or have the slaves do it—give them one day in eight to themselves, to do the things that are needed, and for them to rest. Give them blankets and clothes and..." He looked down at his own hard feet, "Shoes and jackets in the winter. They are barely fed as it is. Feed them well, and they will be able to work those long hours you give them and work faster if they are not starving. And by so little a thing, you could help with their loyalty too."

Onas was silent for so long that Jiangxi wondered if he should have said so much. Instead, the old man surprised him once again. "I will put you in charge of this," he said. "Order what you need. Work with the overseers to distribute it, or do it on your own terms. I cannot give them a full day, but I will give them a half-day off before the meal, once every eight days."

"Whippings," suggested Jiangxi, but no more. It was not a word that required much explanation.

185

"Unfortunately, they are necessary," replied Onas, his tone reluctant. "They are used seldom enough, so I don't think there could be something that can be substituted with the same effect."

"But maybe there is something else you can do," argued Jiangxi.

"I have done all that I will, for now," answered Onas. While his tone was neutral, the words were spoken sharply. Jiangxi bowed his head, knowing he had pushed too far. "Make up the orders, and I will sign them. Then take them to the overseer, and get started. Some of the goods can be taken from the farm's storage, some will need to be purchased in town. Go to the merchant Huupuspumsa and use my name. He will put the items on my account and have them brought here."

"Thank you, *kuksui*," replied Jiangxi.

As he carried out the new orders, he realized again there was a growing fear within him. And the fear was seeing his fellow slaves now and giving them Onas's bounty. Jiangxi was a part of that other class now—the class of the free and the privileged. And here he would be, distributing shoddy presents that meant nothing in the face of slavery, all on behalf of their master.

He worried about this as the day passed, busy with his errands, and into the next several days too. It wasn't until the supplies he'd ordered were delivered from town, and the time had come that he had to face the men and women of the farm, that he took a deep breath and forced the tightness in his chest to ease. He stacked the crates of supplies in the little handcart Onas occasionally used and pulled it up the road on the connecting path that passed through the palisade gates and snaked through the fields to the slave longhouse located in the central area.

It was midday, but the slaves didn't eat a meal until the end of the day, so the cleared space around the longhouse was empty except for the children and elderly. When they saw him pulling a wagon behind him, they said nothing. It wasn't until he unloaded the crates near the longhouse door, and began opening them up to reveal handfuls of items, that the children ran up to him and asked in excited voices, "What are these? What are these?" Then, the old men and women who had been hanging back at his appearance came up to him.

He explained to them, "These are for the men and women," with a quick look around, "and children on Onas's farm."

"Why?" asked one old woman, who had many more wrinkles than teeth.

Flummoxed, Jiangxi had no answer. He hadn't anticipated any discussion, merely looked ahead to the giving away of things and, maybe, their gratitude. Or, perhaps as a worst-case scenario, the condemnation of himself as the messenger. The one thing he had never expected was questions.

"He does it because of me," he finally blurted out. When they looked at him, he realized his answer explained nothing. He added, "Don't you remember? I was here on this farm for a year."

"I remember you," said an old man. He pulled absently at the cloth of one of the blankets, a brightly colored zig-zag pattern. "The quiet boy."

"Yes," he said. "I am free and now Onas's apprentice."

There was a bit of a silence. Even the children, who didn't understand because they were too young, paused in exchanging the gifts and stared at him. The word "free" popped up every so often in their parents' conversations, but it was hushed, as if it were a bad word. Maybe it was.

"Free?" asked the same old man. "Does that mean he will free us too?"

Several of the women cackled at the old man's audacity, or so it seemed to Jiangxi. The original woman who had asked the first question said, "We're not blind, lad. Or most of us aren't blind. We can see the marks on your face that mark your freedom. He made you his apprentice? And you trust that old bear?"

"He gave you these things," replied Jiangxi, feeling like a traitor. Why had it come to this, to the point where he was defending the man who had held him in bondage these many years against his own people, his fellow slaves and compatriots?

"Well, whatever you are doing to gain his approval, we thank you," said the same old man, with a significant look at the woman. She nodded her head and repeated the thanks, but her words were routine and insincere.

And that was all. He said, "I will visit the farm from time to time. Please let me know what you need when I come."

He paused, but no one said anything else. He took the empty cart back to Onas's house. The *kuksui* watched him carefully, knowing what errand he had been on, but let him alone to do his normal tasks around their home and said nothing.

Later that afternoon, a cart came and delivered the same crates as before, which he helped unload into the back storage room. When he raised his eyebrows at Onas, the old man nodded. More guns.

When the carter had left, Jiangxi asked, "Who do you get them from? And where do they go?"

Onas rubbed his square chin, and Jiangxi could see him gathering his thoughts. "I am an ambassador, of sorts, for our many tribes in the west. And I deal with the Chinese ambassador who lives here in the city. The guns come in on the same ships as the slaves. Our tobacco goes to pay for them, in addition to the silver we get from the southern tribes."

"The southern tribes? I thought the Spanish had overwhelmed many of them."

"Many, yes." Onas stroked his chin again. Jiangxi had noticed that the old man had picked up several nervous habits recently, but they were so gradual that he was hard-pressed to remember exactly when the implacable Onas had become so twitchy. He always seemed to be doing something with his hands, even when unnecessary. And his hands were thinner and sometimes shook even when it was not cold.

"But that is in the far south, which is a journey of many lunar months. What I meant was just south of there, less than a month's journey by horse. Where the Spanish are trying always to push closer to us, to our lands. These are not the tribes subjugated to the foreigners, but ones on the border we have drawn by wampum and word."

He squinted up in the sky again. "We... encourage those tribes to harass the Spanish. Steal from them, where possible. And then we trade them cheap guns. Although the Spanish haven't yet offered direct aggression to our Confederacy, they are attempting to explore our coasts in their ships. They make big promises to men who see only a small part of the trade of this rich land, and they give the young men something more to hope for than waiting years and years for their Elders to be gone. They promise them riches and power, and those are hard things for the young to turn down in a time of peace.

"One of the biggest drawbacks of our many alliances, I feel, is that the young men have no outlet. They are made old before their time, with the responsibilities of old men, and they chafe against the restrictions of our long-held peace."

Jiangxi looked away, uncomfortable. He felt the same burn in his chest, but he had no desire to reveal it to Onas, whose eyes saw too much. "What do you see of the future?" he asked instead.

The *kuksui* smiled. "Others may see better into the future than I. I fear that my eyes grow dim, and not just to see the birds against the clear blue sky. I have troubled dreams, but they are like smoke in the wind, and I cannot hold onto them. I am afraid that my time is nearly done. That is why I am passing it on to you. You will be needed. How, I cannot say. But I saw you, long ago, and I saw war coming here. Somehow, you will be involved in it and will help the people of this land."

How? Jiangxi thought. The only ones he wanted to help were the slaves and himself. Helping the tribes wasn't part of the burning desire in Jiangxi's chest. Instead, he wanted to hurt and destroy the ones who had put him here and kept him here. What Onas dreamed of, which prompted the opposite reaction from where Jiangxi's instincts lay—that was as hard a concept for him to grasp as the smoke that the *kuksui* spoke of.

"Very well," he said instead. Onas turned his eyes back to his apprentice, and this time it was Jiangxi who looked away. He knew he never would be worthy of trust by the *kuksui*, because his goals were so different. But, not for the first time, that lack of trust hurt him. If only he had been born someone else—Onas's son, perhaps—he would not have been conflicted in his loyalties. But he had not been. He had been born in a far-off land, a child of parents long dead. His life was no longer his own, but caught up in a grand struggle that pitted him against this man, however much he might wish otherwise in a moment of weakness.

So, he walked away. He knew that Onas would be watching him, wondering if he had been wrong about his dreams after all.

CHAPTER 20

Things went on much as normal. The only difference was, Jiangxi had made a choice.

Once per lunar month, he went to the slave quarters. He started to time his visits so that he arrived during one of the half-days that Onas's slaves were allowed to rest, so he could speak to more of the younger and able-bodied men and women.

The first time he did so, he went with his heart in his throat, deathly frightened to confront these same men and women who had so thoroughly ignored him and mistrusted him when he also lived in the longhouse. However, his reception the second time he arrived surprised even him. They had obviously heard and benefited from the previous month's deliveries he had made, and had been expecting his return. He received several pats on the back and arms as he passed out the new foodstuffs and goods.

Jiangxi had also been worried he would have to distinguish between the slaves of the *kuksui* and the slaves of the other three neighbors who worked their individual fields. However, the other slaves were not given the half-day off that Onas's were, and so they were never there. He was careful not to give anything to the wrong men and women, but he noticed that they often asked him for more items even when what he'd already given them should have still been perfectly good. And he saw when passing the fields that the other masters' slaves wore new coats and shirts. The blankets were scattered through the longhouse, not just where Onas's slaves slept. Like before, the slaves shared what bounty they received. At first, he ignored it, but one day, he said straightforwardly to one of the friendliest of the women, "I've noticed."

"What?" she asked warily.

"It's okay," he replied instead of answering. "There is enough for everyone."

She nodded and, for the first time since he had seen her, smiled back at him.

However, he wasn't the only person who noticed. Onas's neighbors came to call on him, and this time not for an interpretation of dreams. They came and they brought their overseers with them. And, this time, Jiangxi was not excluded from the meeting.

"It's not right, *kuksui,*" said the usual speaker, Hö:ga:k. The other two men sat slightly behind him, all of them warming their hands with the tea Jiangxi had served them. Onas did not sit alone, since Jiangxi sat beside him. "Now, they demand these things. They say that you are giving it to yours, and so they deserve it too. They want their day off, just like your slaves. We will be bankrupt before the season turns if we give in. I have already whipped three of my best, but for nothing. Still, they ask."

"What do you propose I do?" asked Onas quietly.

"Go back to the way it was," said Hö:ga:k. "What was wrong before? We fed them and clothed them. They did not complain. Although they wouldn't know it, we are actually much better to our slaves than almost anyone else. We do not whip them unnecessarily, and they live a long life. You know I travel a lot for my trade, and I've seen all kinds of things. In the north, they beat their slaves and starve them on a whim, just for amusement. We are benevolent to those on our farms, and they have a wonderful life."

Onas glanced at his apprentice. Jiangxi wasn't sure if he was supposed to speak or not, but since the old man said nothing, he cleared his throat. "They don't, though," he said.

Jiangxi could see the struggle on Hö:ga:k's face as he decided whether to ignore him or not. In the end, he said, "Don't what?"

"They don't have a wonderful life. They aren't treated well. In fact, they are half-starved and half-frozen in the winter. The babies grow sick from bad food, and our elders do not fare so well as yours. They are worked until they are too bent and broken to work more, and then they are considered dead long before they die. Animals are not treated half so evilly as a slave."

"You are biased," said Hö:ga:k through gritted teeth. "What do you know about how other slaves are treated? Things are worse elsewhere."

"I know how a human being is treated, or should be treated. I am one, even if you do not acknowledge it. A human is not property. What if you were out there in the field, working all day under the hot sun, shivering on the ground all night under a thin blanket? I bet you would sing a different tune then."

Onas held up his hand to stop Jiangxi, and he bit his tongue on all the extra words that wanted to be free. The old man turned to Hö:ga:k and said, "You have heard my apprentice. There are amends I must make before I die. The spirits are displeased, and you know the same things I do about the foreigners. We must draw together now, before it is too late."

"We have already drawn together," said Hö:ga:k, his voice rising. "It is only now that you are drawing apart, separating yourself from the true people. What madness is this that you pursue in your old age? Turning your back on clan and tribe—"

"Elder," interrupted Sirak, shooting a telling glance at Hö:ga:k to shut him up. It was enough to quell the man—temporarily. "I apologize for Hö:ga:k's hasty words, but he is not wrong in his meaning. It is anathema to be bringing in a foreigner and treating him as one of the tribe."

"He is less foreign than you might think," answered Onas. "Less so than, say, someone who would question their *kuksui*'s wisdom."

Even Sirak and Yuure drew back in shock at the plain words. Jiangxi found himself smiling, but quickly tamped the expression when he received Hö:ga:k's glare.

"Then there is nothing more to discuss," said Hö:ga:k stiffly. "I will be having words with the council."

"Do what you feel you must," said Onas calmly. "As will I."

Jiangxi was tired of feeling guilty for things he had no control over. But, as the three men walked away, he knew what it meant. "Are you sure?" he asked the *kuksui* without turning to look at him.

Onas patted his knee in reassurance. "We are divided if we cannot trust in clan and tribe. Even if we do not all agree, they will come around."

Jiangxi was not so sure. What he was sure of was that Hö:ga:k held no such regard for him, nor would he ever hold it. Instead, he had seen a killing rage in the neighbor's eyes. Given the chance, Jiangxi felt that Hö:ga:k would take care of what he perceived as a threat to his own domain, his own stability.

So it was not unexpected when he heard from the slaves that another longhouse was being built for slave quarters, out of sight of the one where the slaves of Yuure, Sirak, and Hö:ga:k currently lived. And it was only for the three neighbors to house their slaves—their guards would go with them.

Onas had a conference with his overseer. For the first time in Jiangxi's memory, Onas decided to visit the slave barracks. The other longhouse would be completed within two or three lunar months, and then Onas's slaves would have the old one to themselves.

Cosso, Onas, and Jiangxi made their slow way to the longhouse. It was the half-day off, intentionally so. The men and women, expecting only Jiangxi, drew back in shock at the three men. One bowed, uncertainly, and then the rest followed suit. It was mostly only Onas's slaves present, for the slaves of the other men were in the fields.

"And how do you like the new things that have been brought to you?" Onas asked one old man congenially, as if picking up a conversation he had let lag a few moments before.

"Very well, master," said the man, bobbing comically, frightened at being singled out. The overseer glared, but said nothing. He, too, did not like the changes, Jiangxi thought.

"Is there anything you lack, now?" dared Onas.

Freedom! thought Jiangxi, but knew no one would be so impertinent to say so.

A woman stepped forward. "We are well, master." Jiangxi saw it was the friendly one, Mei, who had smiled at him before. She was not much older than him, with a plain face that faded into the background. Her mother was a slave here, also, but he had never seen any father with the two of them. Maybe she didn't know her father.

Mei's gaze darted to Jiangxi, and then away.

"What do you think about the changes coming up? The second longhouse?"

There was silence. Onas met several eyes with his own, but the slaves flinched from the contact. "You," he finally said, pointing to a young boy who had not yet reached his teenage years. Certainly, puberty had not yet changed his voice.

The boy squeaked as he answered, "I don't know, *kuksui*. We are fine?"

The overseer laughed, but no one else did. At a reprimanding look from Onas, Cosso stopped and scowled again. "No, boy," he said. "What do you really think?"

"I can't tell you!" exclaimed the boy, about ready to faint.

"Anyone?" asked Onas into the silence, like a stone falling into a quiet pool. However, there were no ripples here, no indication that the stone of his voice had fallen except for the intense stillness of the slaves. "Very well."

He turned to go. At that moment, Mei called out, "Wait!"

All three of them turned. The overseer scowled, but the woman didn't back down. "Does this mean the separation of the slave quarters will be permanent?" she asked.

"There is no way to know," said Onas. "But I would like to hope that the better conditions I have instituted through my apprentice, here," with a casual wave of his hand at Jiangxi, "will last. The other masters are a lot of noise. They are confused by change, and fear it too. But change comes, whether we want it or not. I just hope that change can be seen as positive."

"Thank you, *kuksui*," said Mei. A wave of "thank yous" spread out from her. Onas and the overseer left beneath the undulating sea of bowing backs. Only Jiangxi lingered behind for one second. He smiled at Mei, and she smiled tentatively back.

Then he turned his back on them and followed Onas and Cosso out. The neighbors had made his job that much easier. He knew how he could continue to carry out his plan and be a part of Onas's vision too. He just hoped he could walk the fine line between the disaster that threatened and the success of his earlier ventures.

"Mei," he called to her the next month. She was mixing together a stewpot for the nightly meal, but she dropped her spoon at once. Smiling, she approached him. "I would like to speak with you privately," he said.

Her smile faltered a bit, but she nodded and followed where he led.

It had been over a year since he had first started coming with new goods for the slaves; this time, there was a great demand for items, since the other slaves had finally moved to their new quarters. Onas's people had given many of their belongings to the slaves who had left, so he had to make it up to them. It was summer, though, so they had not suffered too greatly at the lack. Jiangxi's only worry was that the overseers of the neighbor's slaves might confiscate the goods and sell them. But there was no help for it, and nothing he could do now.

But there was something the girl in front of him could do. Or, rather, young woman. He looked at her, at her plain face, and felt an affection towards her easy smile, despite her plain features. Although it was hard to know someone in the brief periods of time that he spent here, he felt that he knew enough about her to know that he liked her, as one person to another. Her beauty lay in her easy nature.

They moved outside, and he took the liberty of leading her down the farm road a ways, out of sight of the others. She twisted her hands together in front of her and wouldn't look at him as they walked, but he knew he couldn't speak when the other slaves were present. He felt he could trust her; he wasn't so sure of all the others.

"Do you remember a girl about your age?" he began. "Or a little older. A number of years ago. She ran away when the overseer's son molested her."

"Ha," she said, then, "No. I mean, I remember the girl, but nothing much more. We used to talk together. I remember she was very beautiful, and he was not the only man to notice. I think that his father would have come after her, even if he did not."

"Well, yes," he said, a bit taken aback at Mei's honesty. This was the hardest conversation he'd ever had. "Well, that was before I came to the farm. You see, I met her in the woods when she was running away, and I... I helped her escape."

Mei looked at him and her face went slack with disbelief. "But... how old are you? You must have been a boy then!"

"Yes," he said. "But not without resources, for all that. She got away. And then, a few years later, I helped the mother escape. The one with two children."

"That was you?" Mei's eyes flooded and she turned her face away. "We called her 'little mother,' she was so good to us. I cried and cried when she was gone. They—the overseers—told us that she and her children had been fed to the dogs for disobeying. I knew it wasn't true, but I didn't know what they had done to them. I thought they were... that they had died. The overseers were so angry with all of us."

"They are free," he said gently. His heart was sore at her reaction. He had not thought of how the other slaves would react to the woman leaving, only that she had been kind to him when he was alone and afraid. But, of course, it made sense that he was not the only one she had shown kindness to. "I knew how to help them escape. It is not easy to do, and it is not without risk. But I want to help others. I want to help the slaves of Yuure, Sirak and Hö:ga:k escape."

"What?" she asked. Her voice had risen and she wiped her eyes quickly, turning back to face him. "What about us? Why not help us?"

"Eventually," he said. "But I am Onas's successor. When he dies, I can free all of you. Until then, I will do all in my power to help you. He will not free you while he lives."

"Then kill him," she said coldly.

He was stunned at her reaction. "What?" he said in disbelief.

She glanced away. "I'm sorry. I should not have said that."

After a pause, he said, "I understand." But he couldn't quite reconcile that voice, that tone, from her mouth. Nor could he think about killing Onas, no matter their complicated past. "He is different, though. I think he knows that he made mistakes. And he is trying to make up for it."

"No, no," she said quickly. "I apologize. I should have said nothing."

"I want to free the other slaves," he continued after a pause. "Because I cannot free them legally, I am willing to do what is necessary. I want to start with these farms, but I don't want to end here. I don't know how many of our people are here, property of the tribes. But none of them should be. There are free Chinese—I am one, now. If there are enough of us, they won't be able to take us back."

"A dream," she said, but sadly.

"A dream worth having," he replied. "Isn't it?"

She was quiet, looking away. Her arms were crossed defensively against her stomach and she looked small there, as if she could be blown away at any second. The extra food rations were good, and many of the slaves were losing that half-starved look, but they were by no means fat. They were just starting to look healthy. With the half-day to themselves, the longhouse was kept cleaner and sickness had gone down.

"I will help," she said. "I have nothing to lose."

"I have everything to lose," he reminded her. "But it is still important to do."

Suddenly, she laughed and pushed him in the shoulder. Startled, he took a step back before he recovered. "You are nothing but a spoiled prince," she said, still laughing. He was stunned at first, before he realized that she didn't know his past. She *couldn't* know, she was just teasing him. He smiled a bit awkwardly.

"Tell me everything," she said. Then, with a glance over her shoulder back at the house, "Afterward. Next time you visit. I must get back before I am missed."

"They will just think we are... doing something other than talking," he said, blushing fiercely. It didn't show up too well on his sun-darkened skin, but he could tell she saw it from her grin.

"Maybe it would not be so bad, then," she said. He dropped his eyes away from her, feeling the blush spread down his cheeks and neck. "Oh, come on," she said and took his hand when he would have turned away. "I just like to talk to someone who has been somewhere. I was born here. It is all I know."

"Were you?" he asked, curious. He knew that any questions he asked, she would be free with her answers. She held nothing back from him. And his hand felt strange in hers—the contact of skin on skin. Both of their palms were rough with calluses, but the friction of her fingers moving on his was something he had never felt before. He looked at their hands, entwined.

"My mother was brought over when she was young."

"So was I." He moved his thumb experimentally on her fingers and she smiled at him, a quick dart of her teeth visible before he was too embarrassed and had to look back at the ground. "It is better that you didn't have to face that," he said. "Hell's Descent."

"Even for freedom?" she asked wistfully.

He thought hard about it. Finally, he said, "Even for that."

CHAPTER 21

It was the first of many conversations over the next year. His time was his own, after his chores and lessons from Onas, and he often spent it at the farm with Mei every half-day the slaves had off. Onas smiled every time he saw Jiangxi heading along the path, but said nothing.

But they were not doing what everyone thought. At least, not much. They held hands and sat by the longhouse or escaped to the fields to hide under the tobacco plants, and dreamed. Her face became more familiar to him than his own, and he stopped seeing her individual features. She was simply Mei, and he realized one day as she looked up at him that he had never felt this close to another person, not since he was a very young child. The feel of her fingers in his no longer felt strange.

He had just told her about his idea of a community of freed slaves in the wide expanses of the north. She was saying something, and he was watching her mouth and the light of her eyes. Without thought, he pulled her towards him, standing up and bringing her to her feet also. Her words stopped mid-sentence and she looked up at him, a slight line appearing between her brows as he said nothing. He remembered his long-ago dream with the other girl, standing chest to chest, and he pulled her closer to him using only his hand in hers. When their bodies touched, she started abruptly before subsiding against him. Her eyes were wide and she breathed shallowly through her open mouth. He bent his head and touched his lips to hers.

Her hand left his and moved to his arms and he ran his palms up to her shoulders and then down again. She shivered slightly at his touch and he moved his mouth against hers.

When he drew back, her face was very solemn. He had grown used to seeing her smile and laugh, and he was afraid for one second that he had done something horribly wrong. Then, like the unfurling of petals in spring, her lips trembled and widened until she was grinning like a child.

With his arms casually looped about her, he smiled. Suddenly, anything seemed possible.

It took months of planning to reach the second step. Now he had an ally, it was only a matter of time. But he found himself oddly reluctant to risk Mei, although her opinion had hardened as time continued. The seasons were turning cold again and the guards relaxing. After all, who would want to run away when they had no shelter from the elements?

The boat on shore was packed with supplies. A family was chosen. A man, his wife, their two children. It would be a tight squeeze in the small boat, but they were warned on how to handle it. They left at night while the guards were gambling and dicing.

Onas said nothing to him the next day, nothing when the neighbors came. Jiangxi sat beside his master and stared the other men in the eye when they insinuated and even threatened. But nothing came of it and they went away again.

It wasn't until they sat down to their noon meal that Onas said briefly, "This is a dangerous game."

Jiangxi replied, "I play no game."

Onas nodded. "I know. But it is dangerous, nevertheless. And more so for the timing. A bad time for my people to be splitting their attention. There would be no mercy for one who helped slaves escape."

Jiangxi ate a bite of his meal, but it was tasteless and dry. He coughed before swallowing. "There is no mercy for slaves."

Onas suddenly stood and flung his bowl across the fire. Jiangxi paused, his spoon halfway to his open mouth. He had never seen Onas lose his temper, never heard him shout like he was now. "Have I not shown you mercy?" the *kuksui* roared. "Have I not turned my people against me to give you a chance? Do not tell me about a lack of heart. You are heartless, you who have been given every opportunity to begin to change. But the changes must be from the inside, as I am doing. You court disaster by doing this. They will find you and kill you, and all your planning will have been for nothing."

Jiangxi set down his bowl. But he did not stand—he simply looked up from his seat by the ground.

"If someone was a martyr—" he began softly.

"A martyr is a fool!" finished the *kuksui*. Defeated, he sank down again to the ground, seeming as old as when they made the trip on horseback over the hard ground of the mountains. His cheeks were sunken. "How do you measure your life, Jiangxi? How will you measure it when the executioner stands over you?"

When his apprentice opened his mouth, Onas held up a hand to stop him. "No, don't answer that," he said tiredly. "I don't need to know. There is no one so sure as the young." He stood up again, but it was slowly and with much stretching of his limbs, as if they were hard to control. He limped back into the hut.

Jiangxi cleaned up the remnants of their meal and continued with his chores. The two of them did not speak again for days.

Mei, though, was a comfort. When he worried about what they did—when he lost heart—she reassured him. Sometimes just with her simple presence. They had moved on to things other than kissing—she brought blankets now to ward off the chill of the ground and sky—but he worried about the consequences of their actions. She would laugh and kiss him, but he knew that a baby at this time could be used against him. Even his relationship with her was dangerous. But she calmed the rumbling in his chest, just as she soothed the twitches of his anger.

Another family was snuck from the farm. Another meeting of the neighbors with Onas. This time, the three men brought their overseers with them. Jiangxi, though unafraid, was aware of the nine men facing down the two of them. The frail old man at his side was all that stood between Jiangxi and what the neighbors wanted to do to him.

Onas appeared untroubled. The men left, and Onas disappeared back into his hut without another word to his apprentice.

Jiangxi spent most of that day by himself, sitting by the stream. It was cold, doubly so because of his proximity of the water. It seemed to dampen the very air above it, like a small rainstorm carrying the chill of winter. He sat and he looked into the heart of the water, and he listened to its tiny voice. But he found no answers there.

The next day was the slave half-day. Shortly before the midday meal, he ventured to the farm's longhouse. Somehow, he was unsurprised to find that Mei wasn't waiting for him.

"They took her in the night," said her mother. Her lips trembled and her eyes leaked tears, but her head was bowed beneath the weight of her helplessness. "The guards from the outside farms. I had warned her against you, but she was stupid and reckless."

The insult was half-hearted and Jiangxi didn't bother replying to it. "Which guards?"

"The fat one with bad teeth. And the one who is short."

Ah. The overseers of Hö:ga:k. He thanked Mei's mother absently, exited the farm, then took off running up the road. No one stopped him, no one called out, but the slaves followed his exodus with heavy eyes.

He was stopped at the gate to the neighbors' compound by two smirking guards. "What do you think you're doing, *slave?*" said one.

"I am no slave," he replied. "I am here as the apprentice of Onas. One of his people was stolen, and it was by Hö:ga:k's men. If she is not returned, he will go to the council."

Perhaps they could sense his lies or perhaps they had been given orders they wouldn't disobey, for they laughed at him. Jiangxi's chest was shaking with anger, but he had no weapons and no authority. "Go home, *hikTiSmin*," sneered the other guard.

He went. But he only walked a little way down the path, until he was out of sight of the walls. Then he leapt off the path and into the woods, circling back around. He found a likely pine tree, each branch like the rung of a ladder, and began to climb until he'd reached a suitable vantage point.

From the cover of the evergreen needles, he looked out over the wall of Hö:ga:k's slave compound.

The interior was similar to Onas's farm in terms of size and layout. Jiangxi could see in the distance where Hö:ga:k had erected an interior wall to separate his fields, and the fields of Yuure and Sirak also, from Onas's—a wall that had not been necessary or wanted when all the slaves lived in one compound. The new longhouse was near the juncture of the three remaining farms, not central, as it had been before.

He could see the figures in the rows of plants—aiding irrigation, clearing blockages, much as he had done when he had been sent to live in the compound for a year. Near the outer gate, where he had just been repulsed by the guards, he noticed they had a similar lean-to setup as on Onas's farm. It looked new, like the longhouse. He supposed that before the new wall and longhouse had been built, these men had also taken their meals together with Onas's guards. Now, they would gather here.

The likeliest place for them to keep Mei was either within reach, near where the guards spent most of their time, or at Hö:ga:k's home. Since there was no sign of her here, that left one more location.

Jiangxi bolted down from the pine and jogged in the direction of Hö:ga:k's house. All the owners' residences were built in a cluster on the far side of the fields, surrounded by their workers' homes, and relatively easy to distinguish from one another. Even though he had never had cause to enter it, he knew that Hö:ga:k's was closest to the main road. When Jiangxi reached the wall around Hö:ga:k's place, he found a similar tree as before to peer over the edge.

Built in the traditional Chinese style, Hö:ga:k's residence was surrounded by a stone border the height of a man. It was meant as a deterrent for wild creatures, but was less of a problem for a determined person to traverse. Jiangxi could see an outer courtyard filled mostly with small livestock, which would be for the household's personal use and not for trade. Inside was a two-story house with an inner courtyard from which a cooking fire let loose with a stream of grey smoke that rose above the roof. The smell of roasting meat drifted towards him with the breeze.

He could see no one in the house, only a glimpse of several distant heads in the inner courtyard through the open inner gate, but none of their individual faces. However, they looked like Amah Mutsun women based on their clothing and mannerisms, and he could guess that they were cooking the midday meal. The trees were cleared several lengths away from the outer wall, so there was no cover for him to approach it, but there didn't seem to be anyone watching for intruders in the back of the outer courtyard.

He broke away from the trees without thought and ran towards the wall. With a leap, he hooked his fingers on the edge of the stones, and his momentum carried him forward. Tucking his legs instinctively, he came down with a thud and a grunt on the other side and crouched there for a moment, silent.

No alarm. No one in sight.

They wouldn't be keeping her in the house, he guessed. One didn't take a kidnapped slave into one's home with grandparents, parents, wife, and children present. No, Hö:ga:k would have had her put away from his family, somewhere that could be guarded or that he would consider secure.

He glanced around. This outer courtyard ran around the house, but he hadn't scouted out the far side of it where the gated entrance was. He hadn't bothered to approach the gate; if the farm's guards wouldn't let him in, it was almost certain that the household workers wouldn't either. It was unlikely that Hö:ga:k would have warriors guarding his home, but probable that there were women who were employed, like most larger households, and generally the wives or families of the farm guards. The workers' own homes were in a cluster outside the walled houses of Yuure, Sirak, and Hö:ga:k, as he had seen when he had returned the horses after he and Onas had traveled to Aguasto that first time.

Jiangxi scuttled closer to the house. It looked like the building had been constructed several generations ago, before the outer wall was built, so it didn't have any windows on ground level. Unless someone looked down from a second-story window, he wouldn't be seen. He crept around the first corner, peeking around the edge to check that it was clear before he would go.

Unexpectedly, a creature casually wandered around the edge of the building and maaaed softly at him. He jumped at the sound. When he glanced at the goat, he saw his answer. The animals were allowed to mill around the courtyard, cropping the grasses and bushes, but penned in by the wall.

Jiangxi nudged the goat with his arm, and it trotted forward. He followed it, keeping low to the ground. Around the first corner—nothing. Just more empty courtyard. Then around the final and most dangerous corner—aha! There might be his answer: a storage shed built like a very small longhouse, separated from the main building and near the entrance to the courtyard. The courtyard gates were closed and secured from the inside with a crossbar. Near the entrance was a lean-to similar to the guards' structures on the farms, but it was empty now. He guessed anyone who had been set to keep watch might have carelessly departed to the inner courtyard for the midday meal, confident in the idea of a supposedly impassable gate.

He abandoned the curious goat and moved forward on his own, although the animal seemed to have grown attached to him and idly followed him. Instead of a loose blanket or other covering on the door of the mini-longhouse, a length of wood had been propped to cover it, with an added bar across to secure it. Further confirmation that it was being used to keep something in, rather than keep others out.

As quickly and quietly as he could, he scraped up the bar and leaned it against the side of the building. Then he moved the wooden covering enough to the side for him to slip through the opening.

The shed was not large, and it was only half-full of storage baskets and crates. It was not hard to see the figure crouched and bound to a central pole. She was naked and there were dark marks on her body—bruises and scrapes, some dried blood.

He must have made some involuntary sound, for she turned her head towards him blindly. A strip of cloth had been wound around and tied over her eyes, so she could see nothing. "Please," she whispered. "Please, no."

The horror of what they had done—and what more they might have done—froze him for one moment before he was able to gather himself enough to speak. "Mei," he whispered. Her body froze at the sound of his voice. "Shh," he said, coming closer. He felt as if he were moving in slow motion, the shock of seeing her like this, and his helpless rage—although he tried to move his lethargic limbs as fast as possible. He quickly stripped off her blindfold. At the sight of him, she made a quiet sound as she drew in her breath sharply. Tears flooded her eyes.

He worked at the ropes that held her. A quick search of the room revealed a lack of clothes, so he stripped off his own tunic and helped her into it. She was stiff as she stood up, and he tried to massage some life back into her extremities, but she flinched when he reached out too quickly to help her. At the gesture, he dropped his hands and looked away. The churn of emotions made him want to be sick.

When she was ready, he led her towards the door. The empty courtyard—except for the friendly goat—beckoned. He had the presence of mind to put the shed's wooden door and crosspiece back, to appear as if it had been undisturbed, before leading Mei to the back courtyard. But when they got to the outer wall, she shook her head.

"I can't," she said at first. With no time to convince her, Jiangxi started to open his mouth. But when she took one look at the panic on his face, she bit her lip and nodded instead of protesting more. He boosted her up, and she grunted with pain but managed to slip over the top of the wall and thud down on the other side. He performed the same maneuver as before to hoist himself over—running jump and roll. He stood up and put an arm around her despite her clear desire to remain untouched, and helped her into the shelter of the trees.

"There is no safe place for you here," he said grimly. "You must go." She nodded.

It wasn't until they were on the beach that she looked him in the eyes. "Come with me," she offered.

He looked into that familiar face and stroked it with his hand. She closed her eyes and he saw she suffered his touch. After what she had been through, she could only hurt. He didn't ask if it had been more than a beating. He couldn't, although he hoped that that was all she had endured.

"I love you," he said and his voice caught a little—only a little—on the words.

"Yes," she said softly. Then, when it was clear he had no other answer for her, she climbed into the tule boat by herself, still awkward with her scars of battle. He watched her paddle away, and it felt like she took an essential part of him with her.

CHAPTER 22

It was not hard to guess that Hö:ga:k would come. And he did.

Jiangxi was in the garden, having returned after sending Mei away. He was miserable with wanting, torn between ideals. What had made him refuse her request? Why was he still staying here?

"Boy," the voice cracked across his head like a whip. It was cold and hateful. He looked up to see Hö:ga:k standing at the entrance to Onas's hut. Behind him stood his two overseers, but he had come without the neighbors this time.

Onas was in town. Bad coincidence. Jiangxi stood to face them, but without much hope.

They left him alive, though they trampled the garden greens as they beat him. He remembered at one point laughing about the silliness of the observation. All that work he'd put into growing such beautiful plants, and they were beating the plants as much as they were him.

He faded in and out of consciousness, coming only fully awake when the old man returned and had to help bring him indoors, since he could not stand and walk on his own. Jiangxi remembered other

211

pains and other beatings as he puked blood and the old man bound up his cuts.

"Why?" asked Onas. And Jiangxi told him, at least some of it. Perhaps he revealed too much, for what he had done was considered a crime. But, "I see," the old man answered, and nothing more.

He was nursed back to health, but something had gone from him. Some motivation. He lay there listlessly even when he should have been well enough to stand and walk around. While Onas bathed him while he was helpless, the old man left off when he recovered. But Jiangxi did not go to bathe himself, and he stank with a lack of washing. Somehow, he didn't care.

Where was Mei now? Had she reached the shelter? Were any others there, waiting for her? Or had she given up and abandoned herself to the mercy of the ocean?

He wasn't sure. He tried to make himself not care.

Days passed—one handful, then two, then a third. Onas never spoke more to him than he had to, but on the morning of that fifteenth day, he came to stand over his apprentice where Jiangxi lay under his filthy rug. Jiangxi opened his eyes just as Onas reached down. The old man slapped him, hard, across the face. The sting of his hand threw Jiangxi's head to one side. He drew in his breath in a rush.

"Why?" he demanded angrily, sitting up.

"Wake up," said the old man before turning and walking through the door.

Jiangxi looked down at himself. Suddenly, he was disgusted. He pushed off his rug to stand, then thought better of it and took it with him to the stream to wash and beat it clean. It took him most of the morning to clear the stink out of Onas's house while the old man sat outside in the sun and stared off into the sky.

Next, he tackled the garden. Onas had done what he could, and some of the plants had recovered, but not all of them would last through the cold weather until spring returned. He tidied as best he could, then cooked the noon meal.

"You were right," he finally said once Onas and he had finished eating.

"It gives me no pleasure to be right," said the old man gently. "But I have seen more things pass in the time I have been here, and the spirits have helped me understand them. You cannot throw away the gifts of this life on a whim. Even a whim that is so strong."

Jiangxi wanted to argue, but he waited instead. The old man said, "Work within the system."

"But what does that mean?" he said fiercely. "I am outside the system. Outside any normal situation, for that matter. I am free, but I am not. I am your apprentice, but no one sees me as that. What can I do better than what I do now?"

"And is it working so well, your plans?" asked Onas reasonably. Jiangxi wanted to argue, but he shut his mouth when he could find no words to defend himself. "Buy them."

"Buy what?" he asked, still simmering.

"The slaves, you idiot boy."

The insult gave him pause, but not in a bad way. His brain, which had been asleep, as he had been this past month, stretched and yawned awake as he thought about what Onas had said. Finally, he asked, "How can I do that?"

"Through an intermediary," suggested Onas. "After we get approval from the council, we can proceed."

"Why?" he demanded. "Why would you suggest this? Why are you helping now?"

"Because I figured out the answer to our problems," the old man said calmly. "Both of them."

Jiangxi was sullen and didn't want to ask. Onas told him anyway. "They will be freed. Completely free, branded as you are. If they fight the Spanish, they can walk away once the Spanish are defeated and gone."

For once, words failed on Jiangxi's tongue. He moved his mouth, but nothing came out.

Onas laughed. "Thank you, *kuksui*," he prompted.

So, "Thank you, *kuksui*," Jiangxi admitted.

The approval from the council took many months of back-and-forth messages that stretched to nearly a year, but Onas, with Dá:snye't representing him from afar, was finally able to convince them. After that, it wasn't hard to find a third party in town who was willing to take a percentage of every slave bought. Harder was to find one who promised to keep his mouth shut—and then narrow down *that* number by separating out those who promised to stay quiet and those who actually would. After several private meetings with unsuitable individuals, they settled on Huupuspumsa, who agreed to talk one-on-two in a rented room above a *jiǔguǎn*, a wine shop. There was only one problem once they sat down to talk, resulting in another argument.

"Only men," said Onas firmly to Huupuspumsa when asked.

"What?" Although Jiangxi had agreed to keep his mouth closed during the meeting, the words sprang from his lips before he could hold them back. "What about the women? Children? What about families? Are you going to separate them?"

The old man turned to him and lowered his voice. "Our plan cannot work with women."

"*Our* plan? *Your* plan!"

"And how many people will you help when you break laws and join company with the spirits?"

214

Huupuspumsa looked nervously between them and deliberately cleared his throat. Jiangxi had quite forgotten about their hired broker, and he closed his mouth against additional arguments. A witness was only as loyal as the payment he was given. Jiangxi nodded his head without looking back at Onas.

As they walked out of town on an empty road, the older man spoke quietly to him. "They will only overnight at the barracks here, before they take ship for the south. Cosso's son will accompany them."

Jiangxi snorted. "And you trust him?"

The old man's black eyes were hard to read in the sunlight. "As much as I trust you."

At that, Jiangxi laughed, unfeigned for once. After a moment, Onas's face relaxed, although he didn't smile. At least, in this one regard, the male slaves would be safer with Cosso's son than if there had been women included.

"The women cannot go to war," Onas continued, his voice soft—like an apology. "Nor children."

"So, we leave them behind in the fields?" Jiangxi asked bitterly. His thoughts circled around a face he'd once thought plain, but now knew was filled with the beauty of animated joy. A joy that had been robbed from her the last time he had seen her. Mei, who was on a journey that did not include him anymore.

"We leave them," Onas agreed. He stopped on the road, and Jiangxi walked several steps forward before realizing it and turning back. "For now," the old man added, looking up.

Startled, Jiangxi held his old master's eyes. Perhaps there was a clue there, perhaps a promise. Perhaps it was only his imagination and hope that he wasn't alone in this battle. "For now," Jiangxi echoed. "But it can't be indefinitely. It can't be forever."

"Nothing lasts forever," Onas subsided to his usual inscrutableness as he began walking again.

Jiangxi snorted and fell in behind. "Especially not promises," he muttered to himself. Not his promises, at least. Not to Mei.

If Onas heard him, he did not reply.

Jiangxi sorely missed Mei, even over a year later—often when the slave's half-day came around, and he would sit by the stream, taking a moment to himself before heading to the slave barracks in his usual errand. A large part of his purpose had been taken from him. Jiangxi knew that not all of the slaves Onas had purchased would survive the coming combat with the Spanish, but they were earning their own freedom without any further help from him. And Onas had extracted a promise, however half-hearted and indirect, for Jiangxi to stop whatever clandestine activities he had been doing. In return, Onas would not pursue the matter further—the past would be left in the past. Jiangxi still wasn't sure if he would ignore his own promise to help the others escape. It seemed sort of pointless to him, now.

It wasn't just during the day that he missed Mei, but he would wake from vivid dreams and ache for her. He continued as an intermediary to Onas's slaves, but especially once the men were sent away, he wasn't as welcome as before. Mei's mother, who had been somewhat grateful for the news that her daughter had been rescued from a terrible fate, still looked at him with eyes that held the pain of the years that were going by without knowing what had happened to her daughter after leaving. Every time he saw her, and every time he saw the other slaves, he felt himself judged in the eyes of all the women, children, and elders left behind. When he used to be welcomed exuberantly, now he saw the empty places where the men used to be, and most especially the absence where Mei had brought him joy. He delivered his goods and left in as short amount of time as he could.

Even after all he had done for them, he felt less connection with the slaves than ever before. There was no continued gratitude from them for his previous actions, which had endangered him so much. And he felt only a weak compunction to continue in any more clandestine escapes, where he was unappreciated and the risks were higher than ever before.

He dreamed of Mei. Somehow, he knew that he would not see her again. And his heart hurt every time he woke up to see the blank, empty light of a new day.

Onas told him one day as he stirred the stewpot, "It is time for another trip."

"Why?" he asked without interest. Stir, stir.

"The training is going well," Onas said. "We buy new slaves every day. The Spanish are busy also—our spies have noticed new activity in their towns. We think they will finally strike in the better weather."

It was not quite spring, and the air was still cold enough at night that sometimes, away from the house and the cookfire, his breath came from his mouth in puffy clouds. It made sense to move soldiers during the warmer months, especially once the crops had been planted. They would be able to disrupt the summer and autumn harvest of their enemies and return home in time for the reaping of their own crops. Jiangxi, looking over the treetops, imagined burning fields, the haze of smoke reaching over the ocean. He blinked and the image disappeared.

The tribes practiced controlled burns of the underbrush regularly, to avoid larger forest fires that would take whole cities and communities with it. They would consult the *kuksui* and the Elders, and multiple tribes would come together to make sure the art of burning was practiced safely and efficiently. Still, on the occasions when the fires happened, the sunsets would flame with a fierce and colorful brilliance that crossed the spectrum of glorious colors, like a red-washed rainbow of shifting hues. It was beautiful, but knowing the cause, it was a beauty with a dangerous heart brought on by necessity. An uncontrolled fire sometimes sprang to life during one of the region's infrequent lightning storms, and the results could be disastrous.

"What about the... the Chinese allies?" he asked. For the first moment in a long time, he thought about his brother. While Onas seldom spoke about politics across the ocean, Jiangxi knew enough that his brother still held the Dragon Throne. Many slaves had been created to keep his brother in power, as there had been failed rebellions that provided fodder for the trade.

Odd thought that the brother who had created Jiangxi's lifetime misery might now be helping him indirectly. What would the Yonghuang Emperor think of freed slaves in the tribal Confederacy? Would he worry about their return to the mainland? Jiangxi had fixated so many years on revenge before giving it up that he was absolutely positive he couldn't be alone in hating the holder of the Dragon Throne, the man who had sent so many through Hell's Descent.

"They promised reinforcements years ago, but as you know, the grand council has been divided about the situation for a long time." Onas squinted into the pot that Jiangxi was still absently stirring, then threw in a handful of herbs. "They say a plan has been in place for years, but the Spanish threat has been looming for just as long. It didn't benefit the Chinese to bring troops to our shores if they would have been doing nothing but waiting for eventual battle. And we have always fought for our southern allies on our own terms.

"I have sent several messages through the ambassador asking for clarification, since the ambassador has promised action and told me that events are already progressing. I'm not sure what he meant, but it will still be two or three more turnings of the moon before troops would arrive here." He paused and shook his head. "*If* they have chosen to send men and there are no delays."

When Jiangxi said nothing, Onas continued, "The Spanish are at a disadvantage. They kill those who stand in their way, and also many who do not. They do not respect the natural world or the tribal ways." He gestured with one hand. "Many of our strengths can be used against their weaknesses. They squat on the land like a disease, spreading destruction wherever they touch." Onas picked up and handed the bowls to Jiangxi, who ladled up the meal and passed back Onas's portion. Jiangxi began to eat and didn't notice the older man simply holding his food and watching until Jiangxi glanced up from his meal.

"We have spent many years, many generations, rebuilding from the first diseases of foreign contact," Onas told him once he knew he had Jiangxi's attention again. He took a delicate bite, chewed, and swallowed. "We have a medicine to their types of illness that they will not be expecting."

"Medicine?" Jiangxi repeated. Onas, as always, spoke in riddles. Frustrating—sometimes, he could guess the surface meaning, and maybe even one or two of the top layers of what Onas was telling him, but there was always much more below the surface. And asking often brought more puzzles than solutions.

Onas nodded. Perhaps he could sense his apprentice's impatience, or perhaps he needed sense nothing, since Jiangxi's tone of voice was sharp. "We have many weapons in our arsenal—not just guns or allies or slaves. Disadvantages, too. But we are stronger for our differences." He gestured vaguely towards the nearby town. "Tell me, when you look at our homes, our cities, our people—what do you see?"

Jiangxi had no location to look at, since the town was too far away. Instead, he glanced over his shoulder at Onas's simple dwelling. "An Amah Mutsun home," he replied, knowing that the answer was wrong before he turned back to his food.

219

The old man shook his head. "Not just one house and one people," he said. "And not just one type of home. There are Amah Mutsun huts and Haudenosaunee longhouses and the Chinese *siheyuan* complexes where our neighbors live. We wear moccasins from across the Confederacy and *hanfu* from across the sea. We cook with soy and sesame, maize and acorns." He nodded as he chewed another mouthful. "Few of our tribes visit your homeland, but many of your people come here."

"In chains," Jiangxi muttered, but Onas seemed to hear, for he nodded again.

"We have gained much and lost some more with the coming together of our peoples—not just Chinese and the tribes, but the tribes themselves," he said. "It is hard for many to see, but easier perhaps for me, since I am between two worlds. I represent the farthest reaches of this Confederacy—the east and the west. And you would have done the same if you had been allowed to continue your natural path in Beijing."

Jiangxi's head snapped up from his food and his eyes bored into Onas. The *kuksui* had mentioned his background before, but it was still a sore spot. Especially now, after what had happened to Mei and his utter helplessness to prevent it. Beijing was a cruel joke, and he wanted to disavow his past as strongly as he wanted to free the slaves. Better he had been born here, like the others. Better he never had the connection to royalty, for it was a pretense to greatness that meant nothing.

He found his mouth opening, but no words came out. He had no real argument to present.

"It is why you were chosen," Onas continued. "Just as I was marked from birth, so were you. Your birth across the ocean. You span continents, as well."

"I span continents?" Jiangxi could feel a terrible response welling up in him, and he bit his cheeks to prevent himself from reacting.

220

The bubble in his gut might have been hysterical laughter at the absurdity of Onas's claims, or it might have been furious rage, a rage spurred by Onas's quiet voice, which revealed the depths of Jiangxi's bloody origins in plain and measured tones. He forgot to go along, forgot to pretend, and the words boiled out of him from the depths of his pain. "There is nothing I span. There is no mystical reason for me to be here."

Onas looked down at his lap, where his bowl of food rested, mostly untouched. Birds called in the distance for the taking of one breath, two, three. Then, "There is a story," he said in a sing-song tone and with a rhythmic cadence to his words. "You don't know this story, but it is a story of my father's people who have lived on this land since the last world was destroyed. Once—"

Jiangxi stood up abruptly, his forgotten bowl dropping to the ground with a thud. The mixed stew splashed out, sizzling when droplets and chunks hit the cooking fire.

"Your story means nothing to me," he said in a low, fierce voice. He glanced at the mess at his feet and felt a twinge, but didn't bother cleaning up. Instead, he turned and strode away into the woods.

He kept on waiting for Onas to call him back, but there was no voice to follow him. No footsteps, either. He resisted the urge to look back, feeling the itch across his shoulder blades that meant Onas's eyes were boring into his back. Judging him harshly for his temper.

Anger was a better emotion, though. Anger was fire and action. Anger gave him purpose.

Fear and guilt accomplished nothing.

CHAPTER 23

There was nowhere to go, not really. He found himself at his usual spot at the stream and growled in frustration that he had no better place to be. He could journey to the slave barracks, but he was unwelcome there too. He paced the dirt that had become shiny and hard with his constant footsteps over the years, and he muttered to himself, and his thoughts turned and returned to the same endless problems and the same lack of solutions.

Mei. He should have gone with her. He should have protected her, sheltered her, made sure that she survived her escape.

The amber-eyed girl, so long ago. He should have done the same. He should have been with her too.

Every opportunity, every *true* moment he'd had to make a personal sacrifice, take a chance to leap into the unknown—he had failed. He had helped others, who were braver than him. *They* had taken the leap. *They* had suffered and been able to look forward rather than linger on the same past that was holding him back. The past of his birthright that Onas had brought up just now, and that Jiangxi knew meant nothing to him anymore.

His time in the barracks, when he sulked and focused only on his own pains and problems… how had he not seen others had suffered much more than he had? He had withdrawn into his shell like a turtle and made no friends and kept himself too separate. No wonder they didn't trust him, not really. It wasn't just the difference of his situation or his birth. He was a part of the problem, part of the other class who sent them to the fields and never regarded that each slave was a person who had a story, a past, hopes, fears, desires. Each person had anger that moved them forward, just as it moved him forward.

His efforts to guide the other slaves to freedom had been a taunt to the masters, a pushing back against his helplessness. It had never been about them—about genuinely aiding others, about seeing others like him as deserving the freedom they desired. It had only been about him. It had been about his guilt with having a better life than they did, his desire to be better than them. His altruism was a front for pure selfishness. If he helped them, he could not *be* them.

He found himself suddenly running away through the woods, the stream at his back. His feet chose a path, and his mind followed in brief spurts of memory and recognition. Jiangxi wanted to escape these revelations whirling out of the darkest parts of his psyche, this reflection of his base motivations that made his actions monstrous rather than beneficial.

Even Mei, he thought. *Even Mei had been—*

He growled out his frustration as he ran and gripped his hands against his head, refusing to complete the thought. It attempted to squeeze out of his mind, to confront him with his own failure, but he couldn't. He wouldn't. He refused to look at that part of himself, even if he knew that it existed. Facing it would mean—

The trees thinned. Here, the bark was rough and weathered by the sea breezes. The hard dirt of the forest softened, sank below his feet. The sands were covered in a mess of colorful mosses and shrubs that petered out when he came to the beach and when he breathed in the wet spray of spuming water.

Jiangxi glared out at the waves, defensively putting up a palm to block the sun's sharp reflection on the far-off ocean. The gulls screamed at his intrusion into their sphere, scolding him as he sprinted across the wave-cooled sand. The water sloshed against his feet, then ankles, then calves, and he finally cupped his hands and dove below the surface into a foggy space of churning sand and scuttling creatures. His lungs burned as his arms scooped water and pushed against the currents, as his strong legs kicked like a misshapen frog and propelled him forward.

With a shout and a swallow of salted water, his head broke the surface. He bobbed up and down with the current, dunking his head in anticipation each time a forming wave would have submerged him again. He glanced back to shore—he wasn't too far out, but there were sometimes dangerous currents that could pull a person or boat out to sea unawares. He'd heard of fishermen lost occasionally to such a thing.

He fought and he battled against the indifferent sea, churning his feet and legs and hands and arms in an endless pugilist match. But it was a losing battle; the ocean would not tire, would not give up. The water was cold and merciless. It iced the blood in his body, cooled the heat in his head. Jiangxi's struggles slowed, until the leaden weight of his limbs spelled his defeat.

Reluctantly, he turned his face away from the victorious ocean and headed back to shore, letting the waves draw him to ground. When his feet hit the bottom, he slogged the rest of the way to the beach, his tunic sodden and dripping.

Through the guilty heat of his rage, he'd barely felt the cold on the run out to the waters, but now it cut across his wet body like a knife. Shivering and exhausted, he gathered together dry grasses from the dunes and age-dried sticks from the edge of the forest. Scooping a pit out from the sand, he rubbed the sticks together vigorously, patiently and tiredly blowing on the grasses until they caught alight. He fed twigs to the dancing flames, then larger sticks and eventually deadfall he gathered. The fire crackled pleasantly, and he stripped to the skin and propped his tunic over the fire with longer, crisscrossed branches so that it was out of immediate danger of getting burnt. Shivering, he rubbed sand on his torso and limbs to dry them, then warmed his naked body by the fire. Even though his back remained cold, the deep shivers from his ocean swim began to subside. He turned his tunic occasionally to dry both sides, and so it wouldn't scorch—if the heat ate holes in it, he would have to sew a new one and face Onas's disapproval as he did so. He'd already had to make this new one, after gifting his old one to Mei during her escape.

He didn't know how long he sat there, staring into the fire and feeding it as it burned down. His mind was blank as he watched the leap and flicker of the flames, the crumbling of the sticks as they were consumed and transformed to ash.

Something must have woken him from his trance, because he felt his senses spring back to life. Jiangxi glanced around, but all he saw was the sand blown by the wind, the waves crashing to shore, the sea birds lazily floating overhead on the vigorous breezes. He ran his palm over his tunic—dry. After pulling on his clothing and his body being pleasantly embraced by its fire-toasted warmth, he kicked sand over his impromptu blaze and turned inland.

The sun had drifted several handspans across the sky—he'd been gone a few hours at the very least. While he tried not to think about his realizations and how he could move forward from them, he wondered what Onas would say or do to him. He had no idea how an apprentice of a *kuksui* should act, except to know that what he had done wasn't it.

The walk back from the beach was much too quick. From a distance at the edge of the clearing leading to the hut, he could see Onas sitting by the cookfire, motionless and staring into the heart of the flames. Much as Jiangxi had done on the beach, it seemed the older man was lost in thought. Or anti-thought, the blank mind of true meditation.

Had he moved at all while Jiangxi was gone? Jiangxi walked closer and noticed details: his dropped stew bowl gone, the scattered food scooped away from the fire. The fire itself blazed brighter than would warrant if it had received no fuel in the interim.

Jiangxi dropped cross-legged to the ground opposite the older man. Onas's black eyes flickered over to him and he fought the urge to look away, to glance down, to fidget and twist like the boy he no longer was, and perhaps had never been allowed to be.

"There is a story," Onas said, as if Jiangxi had been gone for seconds rather than hours, and he was just picking up a conversation that had been paused. His musical tone was soothing, dropping into the quiet like a harmony after the natural cacophony of the beach. The rhythms of his words sounded like a seagull's cry, the crash of the waves, the sibilant hiss of drifting sand. For one moment, Jiangxi almost understood why this was so, could almost see the pattern of his life and Onas's, entwined and inseparable. Almost, he could see what his future would hold.

"It is a story from my father's tribe. They lived on this land since the last world was destroyed by the gods. Once, when we were all one nation, one world, and also one people—"

Jiangxi remembered the story from long ago that the *kuksui* had told around another fire. He remembered the girl who had not been content with simple things, who had been led astray by desire and betrayed. At the time, Jiangxi had thought he wanted to be the betrayer—he would work against the slaveowners like a snake in their midst.

He'd had some success in doing it. But just like the old man in the tale, just like Heno the Thunderer, Onas saw him for who he truly was. Onas saw Jiangxi as a snake, and acknowledged him as a snake. But instead of destroying him, Onas had freed him to be himself. Instead of killing Jiangxi's people, killing the slaves, he had given them an opportunity to seek their own freedom.

It made Jiangxi realize that when he had spoken, Onas had listened. While Jiangxi hadn't been able to see his fellow slaves as people, as individuals, Onas had seen *him* as a person, as an individual.

It did not bring forgiveness for what had come before in the older man's life, the things he had said and done, the slaves who had lived and died under his ownership. The past was as dark a shadow cast behind the old man as when the sun rose right in front of him.

But, at least, Onas's face was now turned towards the light.

Events accelerated. They returned a third time to Aguasto (their second journey had been after Jiangxi's vision quest, when he was fully accepted into the tribe as a man with a sacred name). They sailed upriver in a wooden *chuán*, since there was not enough time to travel overland, and met again with Dá:snye't and the Haudenosaunee Elders. After their private gathering, missives were carried throughout the city to the representatives of the other tribes, who sent ships up and down the coast and horses across the interior and to the south, bringing warning of an imminent conflict in the southwest.

What had been threatening before was becoming fact; Dá:snye't had received reports from scouts monitoring the Spanish. Troops were amassing under the direction of a religious leader who the northern tribes called *kaSsup-was iccin*, Mutsun for "The mosquito bit him." This man had an infected foot that had marked him for years, supposedly from an insect bite he had received after he came to these lands. The ongoing pain and suffering in their leader's infected foot was seen, at least by his followers, as part of his strong devotion.

kaSsup-was iccin had been born in a strange and foreign place across the eastern seas called Mallorca, but he had traveled to these lands to spread his religion of one god to the tribes. He claimed peace, but was followed by soldiers.

"It is said his Spanish name is Serra," Onas told Jiangxi. "And he travels with his people on ships and over the land to come here, where we do not want him."

"Only religious followers?" Jiangxi asked. He eyed Onas, thinking of a group of old men just like him. It wasn't really a frightening thought. He wondered how much trouble a group of Spanish *kuksui* could cause since, according to what was said about them, they didn't even have tribal magic like the Amah Mutsun.

"The fighters are separate, and have a leader named Portolá, or maybe it is Porvera," Onas replied. He shrugged and amended, "The reports speak of several groups of soldiers. I cannot remember all of them. Although they seem fairly small and disorganized, our scouts all say one thing: the fighters are pressing north in earnest, and they are imprisoning or killing the people of the Kumeyaay tribes who try to stop them. So far, they have burned a Kamia village to the ground and threatened to enslave the Tipai tribes they encounter. The Ipai are watching the sea and land, since runners have said that ships are being sent up the coast and soldiers over the scrublands to take their towns too."

"If they are so disorganized, won't they be easily defeated by the Kumeyaay? You've sent men from the fields too. Our guns are as good as their guns."

Onas shook his head. "We have grown comfortable in ignoring the threat because we are familiar with our eastern war, which is far from here and hasn't directly threatened us with violence. That is where we have gone wrong, for the Spanish have grown confident and multiplied like flies. But we must not lose to a known enemy who makes clear his intentions. If we close our eyes when a man attacks us, it does not make his attack go away. We will still be dead when he stabs us through the head."

Their conversation took place in one of the increasingly rare moments that they were alone. The lengthening days, as spring deepened and flowers began to bloom, were constantly filled by the tramp of many feet traveling to and from the nearby shipping town to consult with the *kuksui*. Messengers, supplies, sometimes even groups of slaves—Onas seemed the focal point of the entire war effort, at least to Jiangxi. He certainly had endless resources and contacts, plus a widening net of allies who turned to him for guidance.

Onas wasn't the only one who was returning to past relationships and strengthening them for these new and troubled times. After that day at the beach, after the revelations of his flight through the woods, Jiangxi spent the restless night that followed staring up into the darkness of the hut's roof and traveling in his mind down the paths of choices he could make. Onas's breathing was silent, and he felt as if he were all alone in the darkness of the hut, all alone to wrestle with the problems that faced him.

He imagined stepping foot on each route, each decision he could make, and tried to follow the choices through in his thoughts to see where they would lead him. Although he was free now, it was a freedom he had never had before, even when he was a child in the palace in Beijing. Now, he was a man. He had grown up trussed by slavery, but no longer; he could leave. There was nothing holding him here, not legally. Although it was harder for a freed slave to make their way anywhere, and he had no money or credit to his name, he could work as a scribe or other skilled or unskilled labor to earn enough to pay for ship's passage. Where, he was uncertain. Perhaps... perhaps even return to Beijing, if he could afford the trip.

Drawbacks: with no former master to vouch for him, he could be pressed back into slavery if he came across the wrong people. And there were plenty of "wrong people" who would turn him in as an "escaped slave" to collect a bounty. Many wouldn't care about his identity, or if his freedom was real or fake, or if he protested that he wasn't property; no slave's opinion was worth the breath it took to speak.

Other failure of this plan: if he left, would Onas still agree to free the slaves who fought for the Confederacy?

There was no guarantee, and no way to ask. But it seemed unlikely, since Onas's vision of the future included Jiangxi. With Jiangxi gone, his vision would become false, and he would have no reason to uphold the bargain.

A plan with endless risk and no reward. Jiangxi flopped over onto his stomach and breathed out a sigh as he pillowed his cheek against his arms and mentally cast the idea of that plan into the fire, like a discarded scrap of gristle.

New idea: he could stay here and help with the war effort.

Or, rather, not new at all. This was, essentially, to continue what he was doing.

This was a plan that already seemed to be working; Onas and Jiangxi had drafted multiple lists of "to be freed" slaves who had been purchased and sent south. They kept a triple set of these lists, one at Onas's home, one with their agent Huupuspumsa in the nearby town, and one that was updated each month and sent to Dá:snye't in the city, to be preserved in the tribal archives. Dá:snye't was a key ally, instrumental in procuring funds, slaves, and supplies and sending them to Onas, who directed them south to the war front.

However, Jiangxi's part in this plan wasn't enough for him. All the agency was Onas's, even though Jiangxi had been a key architect

231

involved in bringing it to pass. He was only indirectly taking part in leadership, much as a horse had no say in which direction it pulled the cart. While he was no longer the mindless cart that carried all the burdens, he wanted to be the driver—not the beast whose strength made the journey possible.

There was a group of people who needed a ride in the cart, though. A group he could help, even if he was denied helping them to their freedom. For a moment, he pictured them—smiling, clasping their hands in gratitude, bowing their heads in thanks.

The vision crumpled and blew away like ash from the fire. Jiangxi was not their savior, even if he aided them. And it was unlikely that their gratitude—if they even had any positive response for what he did—would manifest with uncomplicated joy. His fantasies from before, about leading the slaves to freedom one by one as the guards and slaveowners were too stupid to see what he did, had gone up in smoke. He shouldn't let his hidden craving for acknowledgement return him to blindness. What had happened to Mei in retaliation for his heedless actions had brought him to an awareness of his own inadequacy to carry out plans on his own.

At the same time, he cringed at the idea of facing the slaves' scorn and fear and mistrust, as he had so many times in the past. He knew the only way past that—the only way to prove his motivations, not only to them, but also to himself—was to reach out. He had to make a connection with them.

Not to make himself feel better, more secure, as he had been doing before. No, he had to do it for them. For Mei. For the girl with amber eyes. For the families he had helped escape.

And, in some small part, he did this for Onas. Because Onas had showed him that someone with nothing to gain by helping others could still learn how to change for the better, no matter if the cost was great. Even if the cost was so great as to change the very foundations of his life.

CHAPTER 24

First step, Jiangxi decided: make contact.

The next half-day of rest, he returned to the slave barracks. This time, he did so empty-handed.

When the children saw him walking up the path, the smallest ones pelted towards him, pulling to an abrupt halt in front and around him, patting his legs and waist with tiny and demanding hands. They looked around and behind him in a comical fashion—was the cart invisible? Was someone else bringing it later? Had he forgotten it today? They peppered him with questions in their little voices, high-pitched and excited like yipping canines. With no way to answer all the demands at once, he wordlessly held out his empty hands in a shrug. Unsatisfied, they went whirling off back to their mothers and grandmothers and the hidden corners of the longhouse that had birthed them.

One of the more outspoken women, who had been a nursing mother years before when he lived in the longhouse, walked up to him. Somehow, she had evolved as the spokesperson during these exchanges. Her name was Nuwa, although he knew nothing else about her. The baby from so long ago had become a toddler that had at first clung to her skirts, then disappeared into the group of other children; Jiangxi scanned the endlessly fluctuating movement of the kids—some were digging in the dirt, some helping at the fires, some running and laughing. Jiangxi couldn't spot Nuwa's son, and wouldn't know him even if he came out and introduced himself.

"Greetings, Mother," he said formally. Nuwa checked herself at Jiangxi's polite and quiet tone, her eyes narrowing in suspicion. Even though he usually tried to be polite, he was now trying to be humble when he spoke too. He didn't think he'd ever lorded it over his fellow slaves, but perhaps he had without knowing it. Nuwa's reaction certainly seemed to indicate so.

He felt a drop in the pit of his stomach—this wasn't going to work at all. They would never trust him or accept him. He was useless here.

But... he had to try. "I have a question," he said.

She squinted behind him in a more subtle survey than the children. "Yes?"

"Which one?" he asked awkwardly and gestured. "Which child is yours?"

Her suspicion deepened. "Why?"

Jiangxi sighed. "No reason. I just want to know."

Nuwa's stare deepened and her frown widened. After several moments staring up at him with a deep furrow between her eyebrows, she turned and looked behind her. In rapid *Guānhuà*, she barked out, "Hu, come here!"

A boy, who'd been squatting and scratching at the dirt with a stick, glanced up. Two other boys about the same age were with him, each with a stick of their own. What they were scratching seemed to be a pattern in the dirt—Chinese calligraphy? Or a game, perhaps?—but Jiangxi was too far away to tell.

At his mother's barked order, the boy stood and trotted over without protest. When he was close enough, Nuwa reached out and ran her hand through her son's loose hair, pulling him to her side.

"Hu?" Jiangxi inquired, and the boy tilted his head back to look up, nodding. Jiangxi couldn't think of anything to say, so he blurted out the first thing that came to mind. "A good name. I have a brother named that. Actually, I have a lot of brothers, but one of my older ones was called Hu."

Hu flipped his gaze to his mother without answering Jiangxi, obviously asking for her permission for something. She was still staring at Jiangxi and didn't notice. "Yes, sir," the boy finally said.

Jiangxi felt extremely awkward. "I'm not a sir. I'm just like you."

The boy put his finger into his mouth and chewed on the tip of it contemplatively. "No," he finally said. "You're taller than me."

Jiangxi's laughter came unexpectedly. It surprised even him. Nuwa seemed to relax at the sound. Or, at least, she seemed less tense when she glanced down at her son, who was grinning up at the two adults. "Yes, I am taller than you," Jiangxi finally managed to say when he stopped chuckling. "But I was once your size."

"I don't have any brothers," Hu continued, as if Jiangxi hadn't said anything. "I would like a brother."

The words flashed an image at Jiangxi, and it wasn't a pleasant one. It had been years since Jiangxi could associate the face of the new Emperor as his oldest brother, who had bent over him, sneering, before selling him into slavery. Even the cruel words he'd spoken had faded, leaving only a feeling of menace lingering whenever Jiangxi thought about the Emperor.

But Hu's mention of desire for a brother brought back a quick glimpse of the pain he had felt then, a memory of the betrayal and fear. "Brothers are more trouble than good," he said in a low voice. "Be thankful you are with your mother and will have no older brothers to put you through hell."

235

Nuwa drew in a breath sharply, but she said nothing. Jiangxi grabbed onto his rage and answered her unspoken question. "Yes, I had many brothers," he said. "Too high a number for me to count before I came here." He paused, trying to think what else to say. "I am from Beijing."

The boy flipped his gaze to his mother, but Nuwa was still looking at him. Her eyes roved over his face, and he was unsure if she liked what she found there because her suspicious expression seemed to deepen.

"Mother is from Beijing," the boy offered. His eyes flicked around. "Most of the grownups are from Beijing." He chewed on his finger again. "I'm from here."

"Yes," Jiangxi said, at a loss for words. The idea of this boy—all the children—born into slavery was a painful reminder of his personal mission to help them all to freedom. A mission they didn't know all the details about—couldn't know about, for fear of betrayal.

Betrayal from within the slave compound had happened to others before. Some bribed overseer sniffing around, carrying sly promises in exchange for information: a day free from work, extra rations, a luxurious treat from home... Some men and women would sell out their own ancestors for a moment of ease, the taste of a memory, especially in this lifetime lacking comfort. And this plan was too important to be halted before it began.

"You had many brothers?" Nuwa said abruptly. "Why? You come from a rich family?"

Jiangxi had thought that when he was given the nickname of *xiǎo huángdì*—little emperor—that someone would discover his past, would make the connection about his upbringing. But the affectionate nickname had never seemed to lead to more, although it had stuck with him and they still called him that today. It was an unspoken rule in the slave compound: ask no questions, except the basic ones of survival and the surface ones of existence. If someone offered the information, then that was different. But the asking of how someone became a slave—that was considered beyond rude, a shunning offense. Even Mei had no idea who he had once been—or, if she had guessed, had not asked—and he felt ashamed to talk about it.

Nuwa's brazenness in the question somehow didn't shock him, though. It fit in with her nature. She'd always been naturally forward and outspoken.

"Some might say it was a rich family," he hedged. "Are *you* from a rich family?"

She snorted. "I was a maid for one." Her gaze never wavered from his. "In the Forbidden Palace."

A strike of lightning coursed through his body. He lowered his voice, although only the three of them were close enough to matter. "Did you serve the imperial family?" he asked. When Nuwa just stared at him, he elaborated, "Did you—do you know who I am?"

"Now I do," she muttered. But he noticed she kept her voice low also, matching his. Amazingly, she offered more. "There were others from your family who survived Hell's Descent, but they're gone now. Sold away from here." She shrugged. "Not much news comes through. Most of them died. Too soft." Her eyes raked over him. "You—maybe you were young enough to adapt."

"No." He smiled ruefully. "I was fat. It saved me on the ship."

Nuwa laughed—a long, clean sound of amusement, with no overtones of sarcasm or anger. It was the first time he had heard her do so, and it startled him into laughing with her. "I think all the fat went to your head," she said in her sharp and abrupt tone, but he was coming to realize that it meant she was comfortable with him. At least, comfortable enough to show him a glimpse of who she really was.

This time, it took him less of a pause to recover from his surprise— the progress between the two of them, with her making an actual joke. "Probably," he agreed jovially. "Maybe it's still there."

A hand clapped his shoulder, and he jumped. The old woman who had tapped him was laughing. "Big strong boy, eh?" she said.

He glanced around, and saw that many of the women had come up to surround Nuwa and him. Their expressions were curious with the draw of something new.

"Nuwa," said a young mother carrying a sleeping baby. Her voice held a note of warning in it, as if she wanted to say more, but not in front of him.

"He's okay," Nuwa replied. "*Yăn ěr dào líng*. But he can't help it."

He wasn't familiar with the particular expression Nuwa had used: *cover your ears to steal a bell*. "What does that mean?" Jiangxi asked while the old ladies cackled, and even a few younger ones laughed too.

"Never heard the story, eh?" Nuwa shook her head. "You must have been too young. Or they didn't tell it where you were."

"What is the story?"

The same old woman—the one who had touched his shoulder— nodded her head and took over from Nuwa. "Once, long ago, there was a town that had a wealthy family named Fan. They had a beautiful and expensive bell that was the envy of the town. It was known that they would be leaving their home to go visit the wife's sick mother in the next village.

"While they were gone, a thief wanted to steal the bell, but it was too large for him to pick up. He decided to smash it into pieces so that he could carry it away.

"But when he hit the bell, the clang was very loud and the sound traveled far. His hands flew to his ears to block out the sound. There would be no way for him to continue to hit the bell and not alert the whole town.

"The thief had an idea. He went and took cloth and plugged up his ears. His foolish thought was that his hands had covered his ears to block out the sound, so cloth would do the same, only much better. He got to work smashing up that bell, but the Fan family's neighbors heard the noise he was making and caught the thief.

"The bell won't be silenced if you cover your ears. All things exist, with or without you. There are consequences to ignoring the facts right in front of you."

The story hit home to Jiangxi, much stronger than the thief had struck the bell. "Thank you for telling me." Jiangxi's eyes traveled over the old woman's face, realizing he had seen her that year he had spent in the fields, but never learned anything about her. She had sometimes worked with the others during planting and harvest when she could, but was often unable to—her back was bent with a hump, and her steps were slow and shuffling, as if she couldn't pick up her feet. Instead, she usually helped with the younger children and remained in the longhouse to do the cooking and washing.

"You might be right about me, Grandmother," Jiangxi said. "May I ask your name?"

She didn't hesitate. "I am Ah Kum."

"Do you have family here?"

She paused, then shook her head. He sensed there was more to the story, but obvious pain there too. "Is there anything I can get for you?" he asked instead.

Once again, she paused, eyeing him. Then shook her head.

"Please let me know if you need anything," he reiterated. He turned to Nuwa. "I've offered aid. But maybe, instead, you can help me."

"Us? Help you?" Nuwa snorted. "What do *we* have that you could possibly want?"

"Information." When the women leaned back from him, as if he had badmouthed their ancestors, he shook his head. "Information to help *you*," he emphasized. "I know what I've done—have helped happen—has made things harder. But there's a reason for it."

Nuwa stared at him for one long moment, then she slowly bent over and whispered something in her son's ear. He nodded gravely and began to run off. He shouted at the other children, and they abandoned their games and trailed after him. The group disappeared into the longhouse.

"We know your reasons," Nuwa said once the children were out of earshot. "But that doesn't mean they're *our* reasons. Or that they will help us. Or that they *do* help us."

"Not now," he agreed. "But once the war with the Spanish is over and the men have won their freedom, they can earn money. They can purchase you, free you."

His pronouncement was met with furrowed brows and silence.

Jiangxi blew his breath out in a sigh. "I can't do this by myself," he said. "I have limited resources and..." He didn't want to say he had made an agreement with Onas. It seemed like a betrayal, to ally with one of the masters. He knew they would see it as one, even though he knew—now—that Onas was different.

"And what?" Nuwa pressed.

"And... you're right. My reasons are not your reasons. My life has been different than yours. That's why I need to know how I can fill in the gaps. I need to get to know you. *All* of you. Then we can use your strengths to find the weaknesses in the system and figure out how to overcome them." An echo of Onas's words when he'd been speaking about the Spanish. But it could be true here, as well.

"Weaknesses?" Nuwa gestured at herself. "Our faces are our weakness, marking where we've come from. And if that weren't enough, the brands, which can never be erased." She tilted her head. "*Yǎn ěr dào líng*. You're blocking your ears again. *Away* is what most of us think about. But what happens once we're out of the fields? We have no homes to go back to, even if we're freed. Where will we go when we're no longer slaves?"

Therein lay the problem. When he was younger, Jiangxi had fixated on returning to Beijing. Going to the Forbidden Palace. Confronting his brother. But the reality was... he had been sold into slavery as a political prisoner. Slaves didn't go back to China—sold for profit, his fate could have easily been the harshest of the Five Punishments for committing a crime: death. Freedom in this new empire didn't mean freedom across the ocean. In all probability, it would mean execution if he ever returned to Beijing and the first time someone looked at the scars on his face.

Like these women, he had no home. Not outside of this land. There was no country to return to, no family or relatives, no wealth or power. The only things he had—the only life he had—was here.

His mind raced. If this was the only place left to them...

"Make a new home," he said the words slowly, as if feeling out the idea with his tongue as his thoughts struggled to keep up. "A place for freed slaves."

"Where would that be?" Nuwa's voice was full of scorn.

"I don't know." He squinted up at the sky, which was a radiant blue. Onas had told him to work within the system. Well... "A tribal land grant for freed slaves."

"Why would *they* give us land?"

"They wouldn't," he agreed jovially. At Nuwa's shocked expression at his light tone, and also probably because he had so easily contradicted his own point, he grinned. "But a system of taxation, like back home... back in Beijing... Let me see. Maybe a tithe on agriculture, so a percentage of the crops are paid to the councils. Perhaps the freed men continue to fight in the empire's wars in return for use-rights of the land." He ran a hand through his hair. "There are ways to make this work that would benefit everyone."

Nuwa wasn't nodding her head, but she was no longer shaking it either. She bit her lip.

"What about *these* lands? The owners won't just let us buy our freedom, all of us. Their farms would lie fallow and they would lose their wealth." This was another elderly woman from the back, her voice creaking with age.

Jiangxi turned to her and bowed. "They would if it profited them. I should know; I keep the books for Onas. If they could buy new slaves for less of an initial cost and sell their current slaves to freedmen for more money... they would make a profit. A freedman tax, perhaps, so they will see it as advantageous to trade out old labor for new. There will always be more slaves sent from Beijing."

The words sounded heartless, but they were true. China's rebellions and wars and political intrigues would never end. They would always have more slaves to sell.

And he would always have more slaves to rescue. But this... this could be the loophole he'd been looking for. A way to help *these* women and children en masse. Inspired by Nuwa's probing questions, the answers had emerged as a neatly packaged idea. A workable idea, at least, and a place to start.

Now, he just had to convince Onas. And the men, once they returned from war and faced the uphill climb of getting paid for labor or goods that they were now obliged to give away for free. And these women, some of whom still looked like the idea was about as palatable to them as drinking pickle juice. And the other slaveowners, who hated him anyway and would automatically try to reject anything he suggested, even if it could benefit them. And the council...

Despite the uphill climb facing him, his chest expanded with an ephemeral feeling of confidence that he'd finally found the right solution to the problem that had so entangled him. Jiangxi grinned, and was heartened when others smiled back at him. Tentatively, at first, but even Nuwa's eyes had an added shine, which had been missing when he'd walked up. Wistfully, he imagined that it meant he'd given her—given all of them—hope.

CHAPTER 25

Onas's first reaction was, "No." But Jiangxi had expected that.

The initial reason the *kuksui* gave: "There's no profit from selling experienced slaves and breaking in new ones, sick from the overseas trip and much more likely to die."

"True, there is always a chance they could not survive," Jiangxi said. "But if the women leave the farm one at a time—the freedmen won't be able to afford more than that once they're back here—the other women still in the longhouse can care and train for the new arrivals. After all, it's in their own best interests for this plan to work. Medicines are inexpensive compared to the profit to be made from sale and purchase." Jiangxi showed Onas the numbers, and how they added up quickly.

"Hmm," Onas said, eyeing the careful lists Jiangxi had labored over in his spare time since his visit to the fields. The *kuksui* reached out a hand and took the paper, continuing to study it.

Jiangxi added, "In a couple of years—maybe three or four—this would also make up the losses from freeing the men after their military service. It's profitable and self-perpetuating."

"Hmm," said Onas again, although his tone was a bit more considering.

Second argument against, when Jiangxi brought it up: Onas said, "Tribal Elders would never set aside land for a freedmen's town. Land is not a possession meant to be given away."

Jiangxi had a harder time with this one. Onas had the advantage to these discussions, since he would just claim knowledge about the Elders that Jiangxi clearly didn't have. But logic could once again win the day.

"Not a possession, but land can be shared by all," he said. "A centralized settlement is helpful in multiple ways. First, to have all the freed slaves together in one place. Where do you think escaped slaves would go? It would aid in their recapture, in the first place."

"Doubtful," Onas said. "But optimistic."

Jiangxi pressed on. "What if you created a job for freedmen to hunt slaves? More likely for recapture, and less likely for serious injury to the slaves."

"Hmm," Onas said.

"Also, easier to collect on land taxes. One place for tax collectors to travel. If ex-slaves are scattered throughout the lands, how to monitor that? Track them? Prevent them from illegal activities?"

"Hmm," Onas said, again with more consideration to his tone.

The first "hmm" was the bridge to acceptance, and this second one was the first step. Jiangxi pressed his lips together so he wouldn't smile and ruin the moment. "Not to mention that communities are more law-abiding. They help their own and govern their own, and wouldn't need much outside support. You'll have a self-sufficient group that will perpetuate itself."

"What about the children?"

Jiangxi raised his brows. "Of the freedmen?"

"Yes."

Greatly daring, Jiangxi suggested, "They would be free too." At Onas's opening mouth, Jiangxi quickly inserted, "But there can be a... birth tax. That will go to the tribe who gives the land grant. A payment for the children to stay free and unbranded."

Onas closed his mouth.

Jiangxi was sweating. His mouth formed words usually before his mind caught up, and the ideas that spewed out often seemed worse the more he thought about them. When he lay down at night, he couldn't rest. He would blink and blink endlessly, reviewing the conversations he'd had with Onas, and couldn't slow down his mind enough to actually shut his eyes and sleep.

But despite his lethargy the next day and the day after that, and despite the constant worry and stress, if he convinced Onas, and Onas convinced the council, and the council convinced their neighbors... it was a start in the right direction. A small start, but significant. Most of the Chinese slaves lived and died in the west, so any policy change here would affect the majority of them. While there were a few pockets of slaves that were owned by the Plains tribes, few slaves were taken much farther east. The overland trek was long and problematic, especially after the physical strain of Hell's Descent. Just the ocean trip alone killed off all but the strongest or the lucky.

Jiangxi wanted to believe that rules and laws could change, could be adjusted as time went on. The important thing was to find a path to freedom. He'd promised to work within the system, and Onas had promised to consider his ideas.

But it wasn't a fast process. And it didn't happen in a vacuum.

"Write these down," Onas said after days and days of back-and-forth arguments. "Everything you've said, and the reasons you've given. We'll send it to the council to discuss."

When the messenger was summoned to take the papers wrapped in Onas's wampum to the city of Aguasto, he also brought news that had traveled through town. A system of smoke signals had long ago been set up to communicate basic news up and down the coast, and the signals had been activated that morning. The tribal representative in town had sent the *kuksui* a message.

Onas's eyes had weakened over the past couple of years, and Jiangxi often was asked to translate the written notes into speech, since the old man was now unable to focus on the smaller characters. Jiangxi had tried to convince him to try Chinese eyeglasses, but so far Onas had resisted.

Once the messenger had gone, Jiangxi opened the folded missive and read aloud, "The troops of *kaSsup-was iccin* move into Tipai territory. They are a day's walk from the town of Kosa'aay."

"Take a mount from the farm and ride into town," Onas said. "Send back the message: *miSSimpiy puu Tey amSi yulke sottow*."

Jiangxi's brush flowed across the small paper, translating the spoken Mutsun to Chinese characters: "*Chuī hǎo huǒ cáinéng ránshāo qǐlái*." Once written, he ran up the road to the farm, passed the horse guards with a quick explanation, and then galloped into town.

Onas's message would be read by the town Elder, who would relay it to his men. Smoke signals and messengers would carry the words south. The warriors and perhaps-soon-to-be-ex-slaves would take up their weapons and ride from the town of Kosa'aay to engage the Spanish who aimed to come north, following the greed in their eyes and murder in their hearts.

The message said: *Blow well, so that the fire will burn.*

The fire burned.

Messages streamed in, sometimes multiple times a day. The Spanish had been defeated on land and killed to the last man, rejoice! But hold, another troop arrived from the southeast in a surprise attack. Retreated with casualties—regrouped, then attacked again. Another battle won—until ships arrived into the natural southern harbor and dropped anchor. Canon fire from land, returned fire from sea; two ships sank, but a brushfire raged on land that carried smoke far on the wind and interrupted the communications with the tribes' smoke signals and temporarily halted news traveling up the coast. As the fire died down, news resumed: in the interim, the Spanish ambushed and killed a group of Ipai-Kumeyaay who had come to aid the village of Kosa'aay and protect it from the wildfire.

"The Spanish planned to raze Kosa'aay and build a fort there," Jingxai revealed the latest message, which had been garnered from captured soldiers before the men were executed. "Our scouts have returned news: *kaSsup-was iccin* escaped our first attack. He is heading to their fort further south, but he sent messengers ahead of him to convince the Spanish they should retaliate. Perhaps it's just for added defense, but more of their troops are massing in the interior. Even if the Spanish march them over land, it will take some time to provision and send them against the Kumeyaay."

Onas sighed. "Another long war," he said calmly and a little tiredly. He was working wampum again, carefully and slowly placing each bead in order on the belt. Although Jiangxi knew the basics of wampum's importance to the Haudenosaunee in terms of currency, language, and power, Onas had never taught Jiangxi the intricacies of

247

his creations or their meaning. Only the Elders and their apprentices knew. It was a rare skill.

"Another long war," Jiangxi repeated. He watched Onas work the beads for a moment, the folded paper message sent from town dangling from his loose fingers. "What response?"

Onas rested his hands on his thighs and squinted up at Jiangxi. It was a warm day verging on hot. Cirrus clouds streaked the sky like unfinished Chinese characters.

The silence went on for a long time. Jiangxi could see the thoughts circling in Onas's eyes as he blinked and stretched his cramped fingers. Then, "*miSSimpiy puuTey amSi yulke sottow*," he finally said. *Blow well, so that the fire will burn.*

"You already sent that message," Jiangxi reminded him. "Before the start of the conflict."

The old man looked down at the belt on his lap, but didn't begin to work on it again. Instead, he gently picked it up to carry into the hut, along with the bag of beads that he used to form the complex and beautiful patterns on it.

"I know," he said over his shoulder.

"Send the message again?" Jiangxi confirmed.

"Send it again," Onas said, then he disappeared into his home.

Another day passed. The message had been received, and now the returning news turned darker. Fire—often useful, sometimes sacred, and a powerful tool used by many tribes—now it had become a weapon. They blew on the fire, and it became an inferno.

The warriors headed further south. The forts of the Spanish burned. More slaves had joined the battlegrounds, and they used fire to purify. But instead of the controlled burns that the tribes employed to keep the underbrush from taking over and creating wildfires, they forced the fire to cleanse the land of this invasion.

Canons. Rockets. Muskets. Fire. The never-ending details of battle relayed through message after message washed over Jiangxi each day, absorbed into his skin, crept into his dreams. He closed his eyes at night and was suddenly taking cover in a hummock on the ground, behind a gnarled tree, shooting and reloading his musket as men around him did the same. He woke to the boom of cannons and the acrid smell of gunpowder.

Jiangxi had nearly forgotten anything else, caught up in the stream of communications about war, but Onas had not. When a messenger arrived from the northeast, galloping in on a lathered horse, Jiangxi couldn't remember for a moment the missive sent to the council. It felt as if an infinite number of years had passed since the morning when he had handed the freedmen's town proposal to a messenger on his way to Aguasto. While they were nowhere near the war front, and the news of the war was distant and often delayed on its way to them—they might receive word of a battle from yesterday or from days before—still, it seemed terribly immediate every day. More guns came through, and he created tallies of slaves sent to the warfront, updating them as news came back of casualties.

It was unexpectedly cloudy for that summer day as Jiangxi tended to the garden. Onas had several maps of the south carefully stored in his baskets, which they brought down to look at when the messages came in, so they could follow troop movements. Jiangxi had drawn a primitive map of his own, marking the battles and camps of their warriors, plus what they knew of the enemy soldiers. He was letting his mind track over the movements of their warriors versus the soldiers still massing further south when the urgent drum of hoofbeats caught his attention.

It was the same messenger who had taken Jiangxi's list of rules and laws hashed out with Onas for the system of freeing slaves. When the messenger slowed and pulled up his mount in front of Jiangxi, his expression was distant. After Jiangxi's mind caught up to events and realized what news he might be carrying, the man had already handed him a wampum-wrapped package. "I'll be back tomorrow for the reply," he said, then wheeled his horse back onto the pass-through road and galloped off.

Jiangxi carried the wrapped package back to Onas, who was sitting cross-legged by the banked cookfire, working wampum again. He hadn't even glanced up when the messenger galloped up or, if he had, Jiangxi hadn't noticed. But now his eyes followed Jiangxi when he sat across the fire with the package resting on his lap.

"What do they say?"

Jiangxi unwrapped the bundle, handing the wampum belt to Onas. The *kuksui* took a long look at it—it contained a different pattern than the one he had originally sent—and set it aside. Jiangxi pulled out a handsewn book of papers about the size of his two spread hands. A loose, folded note was inside the book and dropped out when he opened the hardbound cover. He spread out the paper to read the note aloud.

"*Lǎo péngyǒu,*" it began. *Old friend.* "I commend your vision of the future. Since we were both young men, we have spoken on this issue many times. Like twittering birds, we can't stop until the sun has set. I do not know if now is the time for change, but I will trust your judgement, much as I have done before. I have been right to do so, much more often than you have been wrong. But with the southern conflict, be careful not to fight two battles at once—our Confederacy is strong only as long as we remain united against our enemies. *Yīqiè dōu zài biàn, wǒmen yě gēnzhe biàn.*" *All things change, and we change with them.*

"Hmm," said Onas.

Jiangxi turned to the book. It was a series of official documents—many of his suggestions changed into codified laws and rules, approved by not only the Haudenosaunee council, but the grand council also.

His mouth opened, but his throat closed. His vision blurred, and he blinked carefully so that the moisture didn't spill over and smudge the neat rows of characters in front of him. He kept his head bent over the book, but knew Onas was still watching him. Even faded with age, the old man's vision was sharp enough to see Jiangxi's reaction.

"Let us cook the meal early today," Onas suggested gently. "We will have time afterward for reflection and response."

Jiangxi nodded his head, still not trusting the tightness in his throat or the use of his tongue. One particular task had weighed heavily on him—going back to the women on the farm and telling them about the men lost in battle from the lists he tallied. Not many from their farm, but enough to cause grief and suffering. According to custom, slaves wouldn't be given proper Amah Mutsun funereal rites, since they were not from the tribe. However, it was believed ignoring the funereal customs could lead to their ghosts haunting the people who had owned them or overseen them, so it was considered the less said about the dead, the better.

But with this added news of a process to free the slaves still on the farm, he would be able to bring the women a visit that would be bittersweet. The yearning he had felt for so long—the desire to help in a meaningful way—might finally be here. No one was yet free except for him, but the seeds of success had been planted, and he was not alone in wanting them to grow.

Despite the past, despite where they had started, despite all the events of his early life, and despite what might happen next, this was not something he had accomplished on his own. Like the war, there was one person at the center of it all, one person he was indebted to, one person who held power in his hands like a gift.

Jiangxi still hadn't moved after Onas's words, hadn't closed the book on his lap or even brushed away the single tear that had disobeyed his control and escaped down the hot skin of his cheek. "Thank you," he finally managed to squeeze out.

Onas was silent for a moment, and Jiangxi darted his eyes upwards to see the *kuksui*'s reaction. Like usual, he carried no expression, but Jiangxi knew him well enough by now to understand what it meant when his lips tightened slightly, when he flexed his fingers together even when he wasn't working on the wampum. He was struggling with his emotions.

"There are many things I had forgotten as the years passed and I retreated to solitude before you were sent here," Onas finally said. "Or maybe they were things I never learned, despite being gifted with the wisdom of many great teachers in my lifetime. Perhaps, though," and Onas returned to working on the belt, although Jiangxi was sure he was invested in this conversation more than Jiangxi could guess, "perhaps when it comes to humanity, you have been the greatest teacher of them all."

The contrast was overwhelming. If there had been no words before, the ability to speak had been destroyed by Onas's observation. *I am no teacher*, he wanted to say. *I have learned it all from you.*

But he couldn't say it. Even if he had the ability, he had a hard time seeing those words crossing his lips, and an impossible time imagining how they would be received. They were not slave and master anymore, not since he'd been freed—and perhaps not before that, even though Jiangxi had thought so at the time. They had started out that way, but their relationship was more complicated than a simple power dynamic. Nor had they descended into some clichéd representation of father and son, for there was no blood they shared and sometimes even no affection between them. Suspicions? Often. Loyalty? Maybe. Lies? Definitely. Resentment? Probably on both sides, at one time or another.

Perhaps the most accurate definition would be back to the original one of teacher and apprentice. But Onas's words showed that it went both ways, that the master was also the student. Jiangxi had long questioned his own value, his worth, his purpose... but maybe this was where it lay. A—a partnership. A meeting of two travelers whose origins had been on opposite ends of the world, but who had a space, a moment, to meet here in the middle. And the opportunity to discover how, even though they were as different as a fish and a deer, they both had eyes to witness and a heart to power their actions.

After the meal had been cooked and eaten, Jiangxi read the law book to Onas. Some of the rules for this new town were taken verbatim from his original proposal. Some had been altered significantly in terms of the details of taxation or cost. One particular addition was especially galling to Jiangxi. While ex-slaves had to pay a childbirth tax, just as he had proposed, there was a harsh penalty if they couldn't afford it: their baby would be taken from them and branded and enslaved immediately.

When he read this, Jiangxi struggled not to shout in frustration. "This... this won't be accepted," he gritted out between teeth. "They would run from the tax collectors rather than have their children taken."

"A problem is only a problem if there is no solution," said Onas in his usual enigmatic way.

Jiangxi rubbed his forehead with ink-stained fingertips. They had been writing notes and a list of addendums that they would be sending back with their message to the council. When the men returned from the southern war and gained their freedom, Jiangxi and Onas wanted not only the rudimentary beginnings of the plan to be in place, but also the start of its implementation ready to be carried out. If they could prove the sustainability of their plan—if they could eliminate the obstacles before they appeared—they could show that this social experiment was worth doing.

"The problem: children returned to slavery will collapse the system," said Jiangxi. "Because one law broken will spiral into punishment and retribution."

Onas placed a black bead against a row of white beads on his belt and made a tuneless humming sound in the back of his throat, which Jiangxi knew was encouragement that he was heading in the right direction.

"Okay, so we must stop the children from being taken. Which means the tax will have to be paid, even if the parents can't afford to pay it." Jiangxi rubbed his forehead. "The important question is... *why* would they not be able to afford to pay it?" He paused. "Some families might not earn enough or produce enough yield on their farms to earn it. So... maybe the tax could be taken out as a credit against future earnings? Or military service?"

Shaking his head, Onas said, "That would be untenable. What if future earnings were projected, but the parent died? Or the child died? Or their crops failed? The tax would be owed and possibly forfeited with no one to pay it, yet also no one to benefit."

Jiangxi pushed down the resentment of Onas's mention of "no one to benefit," since what he really meant was that the slaveowners wouldn't benefit. The death of ex-slaves was terribly problematic to the ex-slaves in question, so question of "benefit" for them didn't really apply.

"Okay, that's a proposal with too much risk for the council. What about..." Jiangxi tapped the un-inked tip of the calligraphy brush against the blank paper. "What about a common fund? Let's say every adult put in a portion of their earnings into an emergency fund, so that if a family came up short, the fund would compensate them and prevent the children from being taken."

"Not everyone is inclined to help others."

They swatted ideas back and forth for several moments, but eventually Onas shook his head. "Perhaps there is a solution we will find in the future."

Jiangxi made a note. "The next point, about shared land use..."

In the end, they had a neat stack of papers to return to Aguasto for final council approval. However, the original book sent to them contained a map, with an encircled spot marked out for the proposed settlement. It was a no man's land about a quarter day's ride inland, northeast from the nearby town. It was just shy of the foothills to the north and south, but with a valley that stretched to the east and would lend itself to small scale farming once the lands were cleared.

The council had proposed the name *Zìyóu Zhèn*, which meant "Slave Town" in *Guānhuà*.

"That's terrible." Jiangxi frowned and glanced up, raising his brows in question.

"I have no objection to changing the name," said Onas.

Jiangxi flicked the calligraphy brush between his fingers in a spinning circle as his mind raced through alternatives. He straightened up with a small smirk curving his lips. "*Núlì Zhèn*," he amended, dipping the brush into the ink to write it.

"Freedom Town," Onas repeated. His slight smile echoed Jiangxi's. "With a name like that, it will certainly be noticed."

CHAPTER 26

"You've been gone a long time," Nuwa remarked when he next walked up to the longhouse. He had his usual wooden supply cart that he towed behind him to the slave compound, and the kids attacked it as soon as he dropped the handles. He often brought small treats for them when he could—honey candies and *àiwōwo*, snow-white glutinous rice balls with a sweet bean filling. "How did they punish you?"

"Punish me?" Jiangxi repeated, distracted. He waved to Hu and said hello by name. The boy scrunched up his face in greeting and rummaged in the containers with the other kids until they found the sweets. Then, in a tumbling and laughing group, they scurried off to enjoy their spoils.

The grandmothers and older women descended on the cart more leisurely, picking over the blankets and clothing and other necessities he had brought. He had found a traveling seller of used boots, and since it was several months until winter and Jiangxi could buy in quantity, he'd managed to bargain the man down to an amazing deal. The women oohed and ahhed over his find, scurrying away in

257

a manner similar to the children, carrying armfuls of goods. They would be stored and carefully doled out to the ones who needed them the most when the weather turned cold.

"Punished for your outrageous ideas," Nuwa said bluntly. "What you told us last time. Freedom for us." She made her voice both scornful and noncommittal—he felt he could take lessons from her in how to tell whole stories with the tone of a word or two.

Jiangxi glanced down at her, and she glared defiantly up at him. "I am sorry if you've been misled, Mother," he answered respectfully, trying to keep the amusement out of his words. "But I was not punished for my outrageous ideas."

"They ignored them, then? Unsurprising," she said. She fingered the rail of the cart, but it was clearly empty now. She could have shuffled her feet and conveyed the same idea of wanting to appear nonchalant, but unable to quite pull it off.

"No, they did not," he said, and this time was unable to keep the eagerness out of his words. "They accepted them."

Perhaps he expected more of a reaction. A cheer? A whoop of joy? But Nuwa simply turned her eyes to the ground. Her worn hands continued to fiddle with the edge of the cart. "Accepted them?" she repeated.

"Well... yes." He tried to match her casual tone and not let any disappointment at her blasé reaction spoil his excitement. He wasn't doing this for his own benefit, he had to remind himself. He was doing this for them. For her. For her son. And she was allowed to react how she wanted to react.

"Just like what you told us?" Nuwa asked. Her voice was low.

"Well... not exactly." He began to explain the idea of the township with the intricacies of tax laws and percentages, and though Nuwa kept her eyes trained on the ground, she didn't seem to react at all as he spoke. Eventually, he faltered and stopped talking. "It's the best I could do," he finished a bit defensively.

"Hmm." Her hum struck an odd echo with him, similar to Onas's response whenever he was met with an argument he was considering, but hadn't yet been convinced of. Perhaps she just needed more convincing.

So he spoke again. Told her of the plans to begin marking off the land grant area, getting rid of the brush that needed to be cleared, especially if the area hadn't undergone a controlled burn recently. Figuring out what trees in the area needed to be cut down to make space for longhouses, and which they could also then begin building the longhouses with.

"And you will be doing all of this? By yourself?"

"No," he replied. "I have arranged with *kuksui* Onas—two out of eight of your workdays will be devoted to this. And if you—any of you—would like added time spent on this project during your half-day, I can get a special concession to allow a group to the worksite. I have to arrange for accompanying guards, you see..."

Nuwa's eyes were still turned to the ground, and her shoulders trembled slightly. When liquid splattered on the ground and she wiped urgently at her face, Jiangxi realized that she was crying. He instinctively took a step forward and reached out an awkward hand, not sure about his ability to comfort her, but she jerked away from him when he would have cupped her shoulder.

"We must tell the others," she said.

"Are you...?" He ran a hand over his scalp. If she didn't want to acknowledge her tears, he would not confront her on them either. "Okay. There are some rules we must follow, though. Rules to help us pull this off. We can't discuss the details of it yet, especially with anyone outside the farm. The success of this endeavor depends on getting it up and running before anyone can object to it. If there's any conflict, and the council gets wind of it..." He held up his palms. "It will be over before we've begun. Can you—can *we*—do that?"

Nuwa's shoulders rose and fell with a deep and deliberate breath. She scrubbed at her face one final time before raising it to look at him. Her eyes were still a bit moist, but she blinked rapidly and cleared her throat before speaking. "Yes," she said fiercely, "we can."

Although it was not unusual for carts to be coming and going from Onas's, and it was not strange for the slaves on his farm to be working at road repair when not in the fields, the creation of a brand-new road brought unwelcome attention to what Onas referred to as simply "the project."

When the neighboring slave owners convened at Onas's hut and demanded answers for this new and dangerous precedent—there had been rumors of *freeing slaves*, and who would want to do something as silly as that?—Onas's calm demeanor never wavered.

"I am working on a project endorsed by the council," he would say. And that is all he would say.

But the rumors persisted. Perhaps it was because of spies among the women on Onas's farm—again, it would be hard for the enslaved to stay quiet when answering questions if "convinced" by the overseers, whether willing or no. Perhaps the breeze whispered in the ears of Onas's neighbors and brought their fears to light. Or maybe it was some other voice that said aloud what Jiangxi and Onas were trying, if not to hide, at least to muffle from the light of day until events were further along than just the planning stage.

However the knowledge spread, it did spread, and fears multiplied in the telling. These rumors, especially after sending slaves to the war in the south, spoke of great changes coming, and the upheaval of society as the community had known it for generations. Perhaps there had been no greater change since the Chinese ships had landed here over three hundred years ago and brought their marvelous technologies and trade, along with unexpected diseases that killed tribes too quickly for the people to even enjoy the marvels.

Although a number of people now recognized Jiangxi as connected to Onas, there were many ways in which he was also overlooked. With the old man's blessing, he spent some nights in town, drinking at tea shops and several of the taverns by the waterfront. Onas was still the *kuksui*, and respected, if not outright feared by some, so wagging tongues were not always free around him. But Jiangxi could blend into the shadows, slouch over his drink, and open his ears to the murmur and shout of voices around him.

"They're afraid," he reported back. He was not partial to the harder spirits, which left him dizzy and sometimes sick. But tea was another matter, and a comforting warmth that left him calm and collected even when he might have been apprehensive about being caught at his spying. Sometimes, he saw the other patrons eyeing him and his marked-over slave brands that declared him as free. The calculating flicker of their eyes told him all he needed to know.

"But what makes them afraid?"

When Jiangxi would have answered the question with a straight-forward response, he paused instead. It was not so simple a question, he realized, and he should never assume it was, especially not from Onas. "Not of the slaves," he said, but it was half a question. When Onas didn't react, he asked, "What, then, do they fear?"

"Themselves," Onas answered enigmatically.

He could have responded with the first thought in his head of: *That makes no sense.* But, instead, Jiangxi merely asked, "Why?"

"You have seen the world from the bottom," Onas replied. "You have been a slave in the fields. And you have seen it from the top, as a prince. Tell me, which one is better?"

Jiangxi paused. "That makes sense," he replied. "Take away a level at the bottom, and the entire hierarchy moves downwards."

"Our young men have always gone to war," Onas said. "At one point, we would fight our neighboring tribes. Our world was much smaller then, but the generations of conflict sustained our purpose. Now, our enemy is farther away and much different. And yet we have welcomed difference into our midst. We have made it our own. There is the fear—especially when we consider the ones like *kaSsup-was iccin*, who wishes all of us to become a part of *his* hierarchy, but as slaves—there is the fear that we cannot lose more of ourselves. There have been tradeoffs to what we have brought into our lives. Some of our older traditions have been lost, to make way for the new. There is the fear that more change will make us lose more of ourselves. If that is so, we will become a people who have no identity."

"But the Chinese have not always been here," Jiangxi argued, somewhat half-heartedly. "And it took years—a hundred, maybe more—before slaves were traded to the tribes. Before," he glanced down at the ground, "well, before, it was the Five Punishments for outcasts and lawbreakers in Beijing. More often for political prisoners such as me, it was the final punishment. Death."

Jiangxi shivered. There were events in his life that would scar him forever, much as the slave brands—and freedom brands—could never be erased from his face. But if history had been different, he wouldn't be here calmly discussing his fate and the fate of others like him who had been and currently were slaves. He would have been put to the sword when he was six, and never lived this life.

For a moment, he pictured an alternate tribal Confederacy where slavery didn't exist. Where Hell's Descent had never happened to his people. Where, perhaps, going back three hundred fifty-odd years—maybe Zheng He could have chosen to sail in a different direction, or perhaps no direction at all, and never made contact with the Amah Mutsun on this coast. Perhaps Zheng He would have never helped overthrow the Jianwen Emperor, perhaps he would have decided to stay at home instead of taking that fateful walk as a child that put him in the path of the Ming armies.

Of course, in that scenario, perhaps Jiangxi would not have been born a prince. Or... never been born at all.

"Fearing yourself is the hardest fear of all," Onas softly interrupted his wandering thoughts. "Because it is the one fear that will always be with you as long as you're alive."

Jiangxi shook his head. Onas was an expert at riddles and riddled speech, but it could lead Jiangxi around in circles until he was dizzy. "That doesn't help us with this problem," he said brusquely. "How do we make them unafraid?"

"A problem is only a problem—"

"—If there is no solution," Jiangxi finished impatiently. "But that's what I'm saying. There is no solution to this." He held out his open palms. "I cannot make them unafraid of a fear I have no control over. And I cannot make the slaves less of a threat to that fear, especially if they are freed. What can I do?"

Onas laced his fingers together and held them in front of his belly. "If a fear cannot be outrun and it cannot be overcome, then use that fear to lead the person where you want him to go," he replied. "Find a way to transfer that fear to something or someone else."

Jiangxi's eyes widened. "The war."

Onas nodded. "The southern war. Without it, I don't think our actions would have been accepted. And there are some who will still see this as a more immediate threat than the Spanish, just as they argued that Chinese troops on our lands, even as allies, is a bad precedent. But the gods have provided an opportunity—and a vessel." He gestured to Jiangxi.

He felt like a small boy again, forced to strip to his skin and stand on a platform naked while he was judged and found wanting. Embarrassment surged through him at Onas's belief, followed by scorn and guilt. Jiangxi couldn't believe himself worthy of Onas's praise, but at the same time, he *wanted* to have that confidence in himself. In some small inner way, he *did* believe in his own ideas and how much he could do to help others.

But he also knew, in the darkest and most angry part of his soul, that what Onas thought about him wasn't true. He wasn't special. He was certainly no hero. He was just as much spurred by fear as the owners who sought to keep slaves subjugated to bamboo whips and chains. His fear to be like them—and to be powerless *to* them—spurred him to try and take their power away. If they lost their slaves—if they were forced to see slaves like him as people and not as beasts—then he would have conquered his own fear.

Because he was afraid. Deeply so, just like them.

So, "Thank you, *kuksui* Onas," he said. A noncommittal message, neither confirming nor denying what had been said.

It was enough to end the conversation. But, like before, Jiangxi spent that night—and many nights afterward—tossing the conversation over and over in his mind, just as he tossed and turned, unable to sleep. Knowing that his successes, whatever they might be in the future, would not be enough to outweigh his very real and present failures.

He was a coward. And a liar. And not a man who anyone, least of all Onas or the slaves, should believe in. Because he didn't even believe in himself.

CHAPTER 27

As the summer bloomed and then began to wither, Jiangxi's days took on a new routine. After packing in his usual tasks—gardening, cooking, scribe work, loading and unloading carts, various errands in town, reading and dispensing of messages about the war effort and other *kuksui* business—he would ride northeast on one of several newly purchased horses, to where the road to the new town was being constructed. He'd initially marked out where the road would go by slashing a simple symbol into the trees that would be lining it. It had to be long enough that the village would be at a remove from the main road. The map Onas had shown him of the area revealed a small lake and several streams running through the land. Although they didn't want to build too close to the waters in case of flooding during rainy winters, the lake would be close enough for all other necessities.

After marking the road, he paced out the perimeter where Onas and he had discussed placing the initial longhouses. As he or the work crews cut trees to construct the road, they could simultaneously begin construction of the basic framework for the structures. Green wood was needed for building, since it was flexible and could be bent without breaking to form the curve of the roof. The poles couldn't be too thick or they wouldn't bend, so the best were young trees with layered and flexible bark. Jiangxi kept an eye out and marked ideal candidates for construction: red alder, dogwood, and maples.

The two days out of eight that the women from the farm were carted in to help, he set half the crew to working on the road—clearing the brush and trees, leveling it out for carts, removing stones and filling in gaps, then tamping down and hardening the dirt with tools borrowed from their field work. Later on, they could put down stones or other pavers, but this would allow for carts to bring in goods for building and, eventually, trade.

The other half of the group were on longhouse construction. The marked trees were cut one at a time, stripped of their bark, and placed into regularly spaced holes dug into the ground for this purpose. The good bark was separated into inner and outer bark. The inner bark was soaked in water for several days until it separated and could be braided into cordage that would be used to lash the poles together. The tough, outer bark was also used as a fastener to join the poles as they crisscrossed wherever the walls, built-in platforms for beds and storage, and roof would be. It would be cut into strips and wound tightly around the joins, shrinking and hardening as it dried in the sun and forming a strong bond. Any unused bark at the end of the day was weighted down in the water of the streams for storage, so it would stay supple enough to use the next morning.

It wasn't fast work, especially during the in-between days when Jiangxi was at the site by himself. There were no restrictions on access, so curious neighbors and townsfolk—some innocently so, some filled to the brim with rumors—would wander by. Each visit, one or two would ask questions of him, which he sometimes was able to answer; on occasion, he would simply look up from his labor and see a person or group of people standing nearby, watching him and not deigning to speak.

Each time, Jiangxi was glad these events ended with no true violence offered. He knew some of them were simmering with the potential for a fight, but while they might hit him with their angry questions and words, they didn't carry it further than that. His final response when he ran out of ways to evade their probing questions was, "Speak with the council."

Perhaps they followed his advice and spoke to the Elders, but perhaps they did not; some of the same people came again and again to observe his efforts and the work of the women from the farm. Their visits made the guards uneasy too—he witnessed the men keeping their hands away from their weapons, but a marked tension didn't leave their shoulders until the slaves were safely back behind the palisade. When the women weren't there, Jiangxi worked alone and with no guards.

Onas seldom came by the work site, but relied on Jiangxi to relay progress to him. The distance was too far to walk, and he tended to avoid riding on horseback or in carts. While he didn't complain out loud, it seemed clear that his joints ached when moisture filled the air, for a limp appeared in his step when the weather became humid or the clouds dropped rain.

Although progress continued slowly day by day, when the moon was whole again, the neighbors came again to confront Onas. Voices were raised. Jiangxi sat in the background, trying not to move and be noticed. He was more conscious than ever that between the two of them, they were an old man and an untrained youth. As a slave, he had never had occasion to be taught weaponry other than for hunting and fishing, and seldom even then.

Finally, weary, Onas suggested that he give the neighbors a tour of the grounds where they were building "the project." While many had already visited it on their own and seen that Jiangxi was building longhouses, they were amenable to the respect the *kuksui* was showing them.

After they left, Jiangxi asked somewhat sardonically, "Was that wise?"

Onas had looked tired during the confrontation, and Jiangxi was startled when he laughed aloud. It was rare to catch him even smiling. "Probably not," Onas said, a trace of amusement threading through his voice. "But I don't see what else would have been better at that point."

"Will you explain the whole plan to them?" Twilight had almost faded from the sky, and Jiangxi was as weary as Onas. He idly poked a stick at the cooking fire, which was settling down to coals. One tipi of flame flared to life briefly before it crumbled into ashes. Crickets sang their squeaky songs from the bushes and trees, and Jiangxi felt the knots in his back loosen. He had clenched his muscles so tightly in order to be completely still when the neighbors had been pacing and shouting that his back had twisted into cramped tangles.

Onas shrugged. "The matters are public record in Aguasto, if they are so inclined to travel there and look. I think at this point, it does more harm than good to keep it a mystery. They might scold me for a plan that they know, but they will truly fear a plan that is kept from them, since the unknown is insurmountable."

The next day proved him right. Hö:ga:k had many comments, some of them barbed ones, Sirak had many questions, some of them probing, and Yuure mostly remained silent. His one comment had to do with the nearby lake and fishing.

After the third or fourth time that Onas referred them to contact the council, Hö:ga:k said, "Oh, be assured that we will. They will be hearing from us about this... this..."

"Project," Onas inserted, as he had before. "A new business venture." He gestured. "When the slaves—ah, men—return from the south, I'm sure they will be eager to hire out their services for a cheap wage. When one is accustomed to worse, one can make do with little."

"Are you trying to buy their loyalty with these... trinkets?" Hö:ga:k asked, flicking a finger against a newly laid pole for the longhouse. "What are your intentions, *kuksui*?"

Onas threaded his fingers together and placed his joined hands across his stomach, as he did when carefully composing an answer. Before he opened his mouth, Jiangxi felt a twinge in the back of his neck, like someone had blown a breath across his nape, and turned his head. He glanced up the slight slope of the land. Endless greens and browns stretched out, a sea of rippling shadows and sun. But, over there... wasn't that a...?

He moved faster than his mind could catch up to his thoughts. For some reason, he knew the target. Hadn't he been thinking the same thing himself not too long ago, that there was one man who was the center of the momentous events happening right now?

One man, who was creating changes that upset the balance of status and power in this region. One man, who was highly visible and highly vulnerable. And, most importantly, one man far from his sacred place of power.

Jiangxi was on the ground, staring up at a canopy of leaves interspersed with the blue of afternoon, and didn't know how he'd gotten there. He blinked to clear his vision, which seemed blurry. Tears ran from the corners of his eyes and trickled down the edges of his face to pool in his ears. The liquid tickled and itched, and he tried to reach up his arm to brush it away.

Fire screamed along his shoulder, and he yelped and turned his head. Yuure knelt at his side and startled to jostle him, each movement sending waves of pain through his body. He gritted his teeth. "Wha—?" he started to ask.

"Be still," said Onas. Jiangxi creaked his neck to turn his head again, and encountered Onas's knees at eye level. The *kuksui* knelt on the other side of him, and in his hands, he had a length of the cordage the women had made yesterday. How he'd known where it was stored,

269

Jiangxi didn't know. "Yuure has removed the arrow while you were unconscious, but we must stop the bleeding."

Jiangxi nodded, not trusting himself to speak. As Onas started to tightly bind the wound in the front of his arm just below his shoulder, Jiangxi clenched his eyes shut and tried not to let the dizziness overwhelm him.

"Done," said Onas quietly. He'd tied the wrapping tight and sawed off the edge of the cordage with a sharp knife. "Now we wait."

"Wait for what?" Jiangxi matched Onas's quiet tone.

"For us," said a voice, and it wasn't soft at all. Hö:ga:k walked up in his usual swagger, but his footfalls were, at least, silent. "We didn't catch him—or even see him under the cover of the trees, damn him. He had a mount tied farther up, and we lost him once he started to ride." Hö:ga:k chuckled, but to Jiangxi, flat on his back and trying to stay conscious through the pain, nothing seemed funny about the situation. "I guess I answered my own question, there."

"What question?" Jiangxi asked. He was angry, and it showed in his tone. He didn't remember what had been said by Onas's neighbors before being distracted by the glint of light where no light should be. Before he'd leapt in front of Onas to take the arrow that was meant for the *kuksui*.

"Loyalty," Hö:ga:k replied. "Bought loyalty." One corner of his mouth was turned up in a lazy smirk, and Jiangxi couldn't tell if his humor was meant to be self-deprecating or if it was turned outwards. Either way, the humor wasn't meant to include him. "I guess it wasn't such a small trinket at all."

The arrowhead had narrowly avoided anything crucial, and while the force of it had been enough to spin him around and drop him to the ground, it had either been slowed down enough by the muscle to prevent bone damage, or had just been an incredibly lucky escape otherwise. In three days, Jiangxi's injury was more tender than painful, and he took care to refrain from extreme motion to avoid breaking open the wound. By the end of seven days, he felt only a lingering soreness, as if from a bad bruise.

Onas tended to him while he recovered, cooking the meals and otherwise taking on the tasks Jiangxi normally would have been doing. The initial exception was the reading and writing of messages, since his eyesight wasn't sharp enough anymore to focus on the details of the small characters. After the third day, when it was clear Jiangxi would make a full recovery, Onas disappeared to town for the better part of the day, and reappeared with a small wooden box about the size of his palm. When he opened the box, he took out a contraption of wire and glass that he unfolded and placed on his face: spectacles to sharpen his vision. After that, and until Jiangxi's full recovery, Onas wielded the ink and brushes with rudimentary accomplishment.

"I am out of the habit," he told Jiangxi on the seventh day, half-apologetically. Jiangxi repressed a smile and took up the brushes again while the *kuksui* sighed in relief. While cautious, Jiangxi resumed his household work and found himself only slightly more fatigued by the end of the day, although he was constantly hungry as well. "Food heals," said Onas, and served him an extra small meal each day until he was healed, like when he had been a boy freshly arrived from Hell's Descent.

There was one further change.

"I know you will be tempted to argue," Onas told Jiangxi on day eight of his recovery. So, when Jiangxi walked outside that morning, he was unsurprised to be confronted by the sight of two men who were sitting by the cookfire. They had muskets slung across their shoulder and a pistol strapped to their belt on one side, long knife on the other. They were dressed in a traditional Chinese *dàguà* long robe, with long, full sleeves and a hem that reached the ground. They seemed undisturbed by the heat of the summer sun or by his walking into their midst. They bowed to him from their sitting position, but said nothing.

Jiangxi immediately turned around and returned inside the hut to confront Onas, who was unperturbed. After Onas's answer to Jiangxi's question about the two men, Jiangxi asked, "What do you think I will argue about? It is good that you hired men to guard you."

"Only one," Onas replied. "The other is to go with you."

Then there was an argument, as Onas predicted. But, in the end, the *kuksui* won the battle.

So, for that moment forward, Jiangxi had a shadow. His bodyguard's name was Knöda:nöh and Onas's guard was Tijö:he'. Onas had requested guards from the city of Aguasto, based on recommendations by Dá:snye't, who had sent him these two. They were Haudenosaunee, so perhaps the thinking was they were less likely to be drawn into Amah Mutsun affairs; plus, with the worth of Dá:snye't's recommendation of their fidelity, they would hopefully be above being bribed to relax attention on their charges.

Jiangxi wasn't usually terribly gregarious, but under the watchful eye of his taciturn bodyguard, he found himself uncomfortably trying to fill in the silence. He felt like he did before, when he knew little about the other slaves' lives even though he had worked side by side with them for a year. Here was this new figure whose job it was to protect him, yet he knew nothing about the man. He found out pretty quickly why casual chatting was a bad idea.

"You were born in Aguasto?" he asked as they rode out to the work site the next day. Jiangxi flexed his shoulder in wincing remembrance. While he hadn't been the target the day he got shot, he very well could have been—or he could be the target tomorrow. Who knew who the would-be assassin was? The neighbors had supposedly sent out scouting parties with slave-tracking dogs, but the trail had ended abruptly at a stream, and they hadn't been able to follow it back to a source or a person. A dead end.

While Jiangxi had wanted to go chasing rumors in teashops and taverns again, Onas had strongly urged against it. For once, Jiangxi gave in with no feeling of resentment.

If he had been slightly misplaced with the accuracy of his jump in front of Onas, he wouldn't be here right now. Or if the assassin had accomplished his goal, who knew how he would have fared in the wake of Onas's death? How long would he have remained free without the protection of the *kuksui*? How long until the idea of freeing other slaves would have been abandoned when its strongest and most powerful tribal proponent was dead?

Aside from bringing home to him the fact that this new venture was dangerous in ways he hadn't considered until now—the danger had seemed more distant before—was the idea that it wasn't just his own mortality that was at stake. Or perhaps the new concept was that his own life had become inextricably entwined with the *kuksui*'s, and there was no way to separate them now without consequences.

To distract himself from these thoughts, which had circled and circled in his head as he recuperated from his arrow wound, he instead turned his attention to his bodyguard. Although it was hard for him to tell Knöda:nöh's age, he guessed it was similar to his own.

At Jiangxi's question about the location of his birthplace, his guard glanced at him, then back at the road. "Yes."

"You know Dá:snye't?" Jiangxi continued, somewhat awkwardly. He had no idea what questions would cross the line between polite inquiry and rudely invasive; the only Haudenosaunee he'd come across were from their visits to Aguasto, and those interactions had been limited and brief. Perhaps he would accidentally say something so rude that his own bodyguard would attack him in outrage.

"Yes," Knöda:nöh replied shortly. This time, he didn't even bother to turn his head.

"How do you know him? Were you on the—"

"Stop," Knöda:nöh interrupted him. "When you talk, I cannot listen. If you distract me with pleasantries, I will not be paying attention to dangers and cannot protect you." While his words were brusque, his tone was unemotional, as if he were commenting on a cloud passing over the sun.

"Oh." Jiangxi glanced to either side of them, as if an assassin would spring out now that he was freshly aware of the dangers. "Sure, that is fine. I can be quiet."

His bodyguard muttered something that was hard to hear over the thump of hoofbeats into the hardened dirt of the road. But it sounded suspiciously like, "I doubt it."

Jiangxi was unsure whether to be offended or amused. In the end, amusement won over and he laughed. Once he started, it seemed like he couldn't stop, and he laughed until his stomach started to cramp and his shoulder twinged in warning.

For the first time, there seemed to be a glimmer of humor as Knöda:nöh looked at him out of the corner of his eyes—or perhaps his expression just conveyed added exasperation. Either way, it was a reaction. "Are you finished?" he asked in the same emotionless tone as before.

Jiangxi leaned back his head and closed his eyes against the glare of the eastern sun. He was still smiling. "I doubt it," he said.

This time, it was Knöda:nöh who laughed.

CHAPTER 28

Another handful of days went by, and Jiangxi learned to hold his tongue—most of the time—when away from the *kuksui*'s home and when Knöda:nöh was actively protecting him while he continued his efforts at the worksite. However, once they returned to the hut and gathered around the fire in the evenings, the atmosphere was much more convivial. They would drink tea and talk about the events of the day, including the messages still being received from the southern war effort. Sometimes, Onas would be reminded of a story or historical tale that illuminated an argument or made clear an obscure reference. Often, they just sat in companionable silence.

Knöda:nöh and Tijö:he' slept outside by the cookfire for the first few nights as they constructed their lodgings. In the mornings before Jiangxi left for the worksite, they labored to put up their temporary dwelling opposite the path from Onas's more permanent structure. They'd cut willow saplings and laid them out in parallel rows against the edge of the forest. Then, from a nearby pond, they harvested tule and cattails and spread them out atop the willow. In the summer heat, it took barely a couple days for the tule and cattails to dry and shrink. They used wettened strands of the tule to weave together bundles of the dried material to create long mats. The willow saplings were taken up again, their thicker ends buried in the ground and weighted with stones, then fastened together at the top with braided rope to create a conical shape. The mats were attached in layers around the cone, woven and tied together so that they were secure and waterproof, with extra thatching around the doorway and a smoke hole at the top. When the walls were completed, they placed an elevated and rounded mat above the open hole, much like an inverted basket, to allow smoke to escape but also protect the interior when it rained.

Their dwelling looked like a smaller and shaggier cousin to Onas's home, which had stronger and more durable bark siding. The tule mats would last a season or two, perhaps a bit longer, but not endure past the end of the rainy season. If they stayed longer than that, they would have to burn it and construct a new one.

Jiangxi couldn't explain why he was restless again that night. The news from the south hadn't been particularly terrible, and he'd grown accustomed to creating the lists of casualty descriptions and reporting the names—when the names were even relayed to him, as some slave casualties were listed by their physical description or just as "slave"—back to the farm.

It was heartbreaking to be the deliverer of bad news, although it was a task he shouldered without complaint. To see the reality of the women who had lost a family member was a lesson in emotion. He had never had that close-knit bond with any blood relatives since coming here, and he'd never had it with his father at all. He'd had many brothers, but remembered none now but the cruelty of the Emperor when being sold into slavery. Feeling awkward and out of place while an old woman wept on his shoulder and he gently patted her back, or grasping the clammy hand of a woman whose father had died far away, or even simply being a fresh pair of ears to listen to stories about how a son took his first steps and it felt like yesterday... he did what he could, and at least hoped he was able to bring some comfort to them.

Of course, even worse was when he brought back a name or description of a man that received only shaking heads. A man who had died with no family to mourn him, no friends to cry, and only the half-puzzled frowns of the farm women to send him on his way. Jiangxi imagined if he were in the man's place—would he be mourned? Or would no one even pay much notice to his death?

The Amah Mutsun considered it beyond ill luck to speak of the dead, for there was the belief that naming the dead could bring their vengeful ghosts. To worship their ancestors, slaves had to do so clandestinely.

When these thoughts whirled behind his eyes at night, he often lay on his mat and stared into the darkness and let his mind spin like a wheel. But tonight, for some reason, he couldn't keep his limbs still. He sat up for a moment with his elbows on his thighs, considering, then got to his feet and quietly pushed past the hanging blankets and stepped outside.

He walked past the slumbering cookfire and wandered towards the edge of the clearing, his eyes drawn upwards. The sky was clear, as it often was during the summer, and the twinkling lights looked like the caps of waves breaking on a sandy shore—a long line of white foam jaggedly crossing the beach and leaving behind a smattering of popping bubbles, which were the stars. He breathed in the cooler night breezes and thought that he could almost smell the spray of the sea from here—a fresh and salty odor that was carried inland by the night winds.

It had been a long time since he'd gone to the beach where the boat was stored. Not since he'd helped Mei escape. He'd returned to the ocean to gather seaweed and mussels and fish, but not gone any farther up the coast.

Not for the first time, he wondered what had become of Mei. And the families he'd helped. Then, inevitably, his thoughts returned to the amber-eyed girl, the first person he'd shown his escape route to.

Had they escaped from the searchers? Had they found a way to live in freedom?

Would he ever find out?

A slight movement behind him, then the hiss of a voice, "You *hamaama*! I thought you were an assassin. I almost stabbed you in the dark."

He turned at the familiar growly voice of Knöda:nöh and smiled. There was no moon, and the starlight didn't bring Knöda:nöh's features into clarity. Jiangxi held up his palms in a shrug. "I couldn't sleep," he said simply.

"Hmph," was the grumpy reply. "Tea might help."

"Good idea. I'll stoke the fire..."

"I'll fetch the tea leaves."

The coals were glowing under the ash, and he piled on several mid-sized sticks and a handful of grasses. The fire caught in a moment, and he took the kettle to the stream to fill, returned, and placed it on the fire. He heard a footfall and looked up—then almost yelped at the sight that met his eyes in the flickering light of the growing flames.

Knöda:nöh sat down cross-legged on the other side of the fire. Having abandoned wearing the shapeless *dàguà* and stripped down to a tunic and short leggings that ended in a fringe at the knee, it was clear that Knöda:nöh was not what Jiangxi had thought.

"You're a woman," he hissed in surprise.

Knöda:nöh's eyes flickered up to him. Her expression was as inscrutable as it had been before, but perhaps a touch cooler at his blunt exclamation. "You have lived here many years and still remain ignorant of our society," she said dismissively and stared into the fire.

After an awkward pause, he said, "You're right. I am sorry." He judged the water to be just shy of boiling and removed it from the fire with a stick looped through the handle of the kettle. He held out a hand for the container of tea, and she passed it to him with a touch of reluctance. "I have been very isolated here," he tried to explain. "Mostly the *kuksui* and me. And the other sla—the women on the farm." He shrugged. "The *kuksui* has taught me some customs and traditions. Not all."

Her eyes flicked to his face, then back to the fire. "You would not know, then."

"I don't." He added a measured amount of the dried leaves to the pot to steep. "Are you..." He couldn't remember the term.

"Two Spirit," they finished for Jiangxi. "We live as part of the sacred realm, like the *kuksui*." They paused. "I was asked to guard your master."

"Asked to guard him?" he repeated inanely. "Then how...?"

"He refused," Knöda:nöh replied. "He said that you needed my protection more, since he had his own protections against evil."

Jiangxi blinked in surprise, not knowing how to respond. So, Onas had foregone the highest spiritual help, which had been sent specifically by the council, and asked them to protect his former slave?

He lowered his head and watched the flames. He didn't know how to feel about the revelation. Done without fuss, and even without his knowledge. It was obviously no great secret if Knöda:nöh felt free to speak of it, and yet...

"Thank you," he said. While the words were meant for them, he also meant to express his overall gratitude, some of which was for someone not there right now.

They shrugged their shoulders and reached for the kettle to pour the tea into the cups Jiangxi handed over. The teacups were imported from China, grey-green like impure jade, with a graceful painting on each side of a white crane spreading its wings to fly.

Jiangxi sipped his tea and stared into the flames, and Knöda:nöh did much the same. While he might normally ask them about their warrior training—it was rare to have this time to talk—he felt disinclined to break the contemplative silence. The hour was late, and he could feel the pressure of fatigue washing up on him. Tea finished, they parted ways with no more words.

CHAPTER 29

Perhaps the revelation of a Two Spirit warrior guarding him should have been more significant, but Jiangxi found, after a short period of reminding himself not to accidentally call Knöda:nöh "he," that there was no need to be more or less in awe of their skills and discipline. Both Knöda:nöh and Tijö:he' were focused on their tasks, and they brought an intensity with them that was hard to overlook. Onas had a bit of the same quality, but Jiangxi had grown up under his shadow and was not as cowed by his powers, through familiarity. Knöda:nöh and Tijö:he' were new, and more taciturn by nature.

The first longhouse for Freedom Town took form, and the road-work to the town was nearly finished. They would have to regularly repair the road as time went on, but it was flat enough and cleared to be able to accommodate carts and horses.

Now, he split the women's labor between work on the longhouse and erection of a palisade around the perimeter of the town. Especially with few residents to start out with, the wall would guard the people against dangerous animal attacks, such as bears, mountain lions, and coyotes.

In groups of two or more, they would dig holes in the ground to anchor the bark-stripped posts they'd cut down, then a team of them working together wove additional fresh-cut sapling and bark around and through the poles, like making a large and protective basket to guard the buildings within. Once the materials of the palisade dried and hardened, it would be a solid protection against animals and other threats. There would be room for many longhouses inside, plus a sweat lodge and other necessary buildings as the town grew.

Working side by side with the women and children had accomplished the original task he had set out to do, namely start a relationship of trust with them. Unlike in the fields, where the work was back-breaking but without hope or purpose of better, building the town gave promise to the future. Even the children seemed to move more quickly and accomplish more outside of the small learning moments of children; Hu was a leader like his mother, and helped organize the other kids into groups to help each section of workers. They would fetch water from the stream for thirsty workers, carry or drag away brush to clear the area once it had been cut down by the adults, and take turns rolling the stripped bark from the saplings into bundles for future use, when it was not too onerous or heavy for them to do so.

Knöda:nöh didn't hover like a shadow over him during this time, but kept enough of a distance to let him work. Sometimes, he forgot that they were even present, until he might glance up from a conversation or from pounding stakes in the ground or tying two poles together, and feel a presence. He'd immediately turn his gaze to Knöda:nöh and notice their eyes would be trained on him, casually and without the urgency of an imminent threat. Danger had seemed to recede into the past, and their protection seemed more symbolic than actual, although Jiangxi was without any doubts that Knöda:nöh would be a fearsome opponent if ever challenged to fight. There were no more assassination attempts against Onas, who had not visited the township site again.

Jiangxi had his own suspicions about the attack he had thwarted, and it was closer to home than some faceless enemy who wanted to target the *kuksui*. Onas's neighbors had been the only ones to know of his plans to visit the town site that day, and the most to lose with this venture, at least in their minds, if it turned out to be successful. Combined with their strong aversion to its success, it seemed clear to Jiangxi that one of them had made the extreme decision to take action, and found someone to attempt to stop Onas before he could complete "the project."

But the clear favor of the grand council showed in the arrival of Knöda:nöh and Tijö:he', and further action would be foolhardy. Not only would there be the possibility of getting caught in the act, but to declare opposition to the grand council's decrees would be reckless at best. Greater men than them had been executed for less.

Jiangxi was sure that Onas had his own suspicions, as perhaps did Knöda:nöh and Tijö:he' too. But it was one subject that, while not taboo, was not mentioned or discussed at the cookfire in the evening. Their conversations continued to center on war and town progress, and their silences remained easy.

His days returned to their normal routines, and Jiangxi laughed and joked with the women when they were there, sometimes gripping a shoulder in commiseration for one who had recently lost a loved one in the southern war. Building a place for freedom was a tough task when their future didn't include a family member now gone.

Without realizing when it had happened—during this summer of intense hope and pain, as the season moved into autumn—they had become like family to him. Perhaps not in a traditional sense of family, since they would never be blood relatives, and the power dynamics of his relationship with them was not as easy or natural as if they had been mothers and sisters and daughters and sons. But when they spoke, he listened—not as a way to wait out their concerns and move onto a more important task, but with both his head and his heart.

Even Nuwa, her prickly nature never far from the surface, was less confrontational when he was around. "I almost think you like me," he joked with her one day after she had asked for his assistance in bending a particularly recalcitrant sapling around two poles, which had been slightly too thick at its base to comfortably wedge into the weave without brute strength.

"And you would almost be right." She wiped the sweat from her forehead with the back of her hand. "Or maybe I just hate you less than this stupid tree," she said in her straightforward manner, but it was with a grin.

While there were many evergreens that flourished as the weather turned cooler and the season transitioned to the rainy winters that marked the coastal area, there were also many secondary growth saplings that the tribes particularly encouraged to grow. They nurtured the forest with controlled burns in the wintertime, and used these smaller trees in construction. Jiangxi had never accompanied Onas as part of his sacred duties to the land, similarly as he had been kept away from other tribal business, but the *kuksui* had told him that he would be welcomed this winter when they worked on the forests again. Jiangxi's days were full of the work on the town as well as his normal duties at home, and Onas seemed to realize this by not straining him with more lessons on top of everything else. "There is time enough," he would say.

As the leaves flushed into reds, oranges, and yellows with the lowering temperatures, they completed the exterior of the first longhouse. The frame had been finished during the summer, the outside covered in layers of bark, with spaced and covered holes in the roof to let out smoke from the cookfires. Inside, there was a double row of platforms on each wall—the lower for sleeping, the upper for storage. They'd built it large enough that it could accommodate all the families from Onas's farm; when the men returned, it would seem particularly empty without the women. They would rattle around inside like dried peas in a shell until they earned enough to liberate their families too. On each end was a doorway with a flat-roofed lean-to over it.

Now, the women started on the interior. They wove mats to hang on the inside walls and cover the platforms. Jiangxi went to the farm and brought back extra blankets to add to each sleeping platform, which were stored on the secondary platforms above the first. When the men returned to live here, Jiangxi would also cart over staple foods to last them for the wintertime to supplement what they could gather and hunt. In the spring, they could clear the land outside the compound and plant crops.

Each time he rode into the new township, with its half-finished wall and longhouse, cleared ground waiting for the spring, he felt a lifting in his chest as if he was taking a deep breath of fresh air off the ocean. It was invigorating to see the progress being made, the plans he had helped set in motion. It was as if all the moments of his life had led him here, to this spot, and the hope inherent in building a town for men and women who would soon be free.

Perhaps the Amah Mutsun would no longer call them *hikTiSmin*, the derogatory nickname for slaves based on their branded faces. Just as Jiangxi had renamed the town from "Slave" to "Freedom," perhaps they could become something new here, even if they could never discard the marks of their past.

That evening as Knöda:nöh was preparing tea to drink before they slept, the wind changed over as it usually did. During the hot day, the breeze blew inland from the ocean. At night, when the sun disappeared and the land cooled, the earth would exhale and the breezes would travel out to sea.

The smell of the breeze usually contained a mixture of forest and sometimes smoke from the town, if the wind was blowing from the southwest. However, the breezes today came from the northeast, and they were tinged by the urgency of fire and the taste of ash. Jiangxi raised his head and sniffed, feeling the tingle at the nape of his neck that alerted him to something wrong. He couldn't place what or why, and the elusiveness of being able to identify the problem scratched at his thoughts in an irritating fashion.

It was Knöda:nöh who first realized what was happening. They dropped the kettle next to the fire. It tipped over, loosing a stream of water that hissed as it hit the fire and turned to steam.

"Quickly!" they shouted and took off running towards the farm.

Jiangxi turned a puzzled glance to Tijö:he', who also seemed to understand what had caused Knöda:nöh's upset. "I will guard the *kuksui*," he said quickly. "Go with them."

So Jiangxi ran after Knöda:nöh. The two of them reached the farm, panting and out of breath, within a few moments. The guard let them through with no explanation needed when they caught sight of Knöda:nöh.

They wasted no time in adding accoutrements for riding, but flung themself onto a grey and brown mare, wound their hands into her mane, and took off at a gallop. Jiangxi, slightly behind, tried to follow suit. He'd ridden more this summer than he had for the entirety of his life, but while he felt reasonably comfortable on a horse, he'd never ridden bareback. A thrill of fear raced through him as he mounted and squeezed together his legs to set off after Knöda:nöh. He almost fell as his mare raced after the disappearing hindquarters of Knöda:nöh's, and was glad that there was enough of a moon out to provide fitful illumination on the hardened dirt road through the trees.

Because, as he followed Knöda:nöh, he suddenly became aware of where they were headed. And what had been niggling at the back of his head and causing an unnamed uneasiness was a dread that now had a name rooted in fear.

A fear that turned to horror as they approached the turnoff in the main road that led to Freedom Town. Even before they reached it, the billows of smoke made Jiangxi cough, and they could see the leaping flames through the trees.

The palisade had been inexpertly set on fire, but the burning seemed to have subsided. The arsonists had tried to burn the greenest part of the wood, and it didn't stay lit for long. They would have repair work to do, but it was mostly intact.

The longhouse, though—those flames reached for the sky. The green wood from its initial construction had weathered enough to be an easy burn. Or perhaps the arsonists had added something extra to fuel it, like oil. Either way, the structure was nearly consumed by the hungry inferno, and the heat was prohibitive from attempting any action to save it, especially with just the two of them.

Knöda:nöh had circled their snorting and panicking mount to the east side of the blaze, away from the smoke. Jiangxi attempted to coax his horse also, but without as much skill—the mare tossed her head, the whites of her eyes prominent, and pawed the ground when he tried to urge her forward. But she finally obeyed the commands of his legs and his fingers in her mane, skirted the burning building, and joined her companion at the far side of the conflagration.

"When will the men return?" Knöda:nöh asked calmly, as if asking what fish he had caught in a stream.

Jiangxi realized he was shaking only when he tried to unclench his fingers from the mare's mane, and had a hard time keeping his hands still when he rested them on his thighs. The fear and horror he had felt when first seeing the destruction had metastasized into something hard and deadly. He was angry—angry down to the center of his bones. The summer's work, the home he had built for the men who had fought for the Confederacy that had kept them in slavery—ruined. The men had battled the enemy with only the slim promise of freedom versus death, the promise of hope that had just begun to blossom—all of it had disappeared in ash and smoke, like the longhouse.

"They'll be here very soon," he said. "Half a lunar month, maybe slightly longer." After a brief reengagement, the Spanish troops had withdrawn to the south. While the warriors had pursued them for some distance and burned another mission to the ground, it was clear they were now retreating. The plan had been for warriors and the co-opted slaves to return north for the winter, and scouts from the Kumeyaay tribes to keep watch for any movement, keeping open the lines of communication in case of further attack.

It was strange they'd never received word about the Chinese troops that they'd been promised. Onas had speculated that perhaps they'd been delayed due to unrest on the mainland, but had no answers from the ambassador as the Amah Mutsun prepared their own men and slaves to return to the north.

The future war tax for the freed men would be for a period during each spring and summer, but only after the planting was done. A census would separate out half the male population each year to serve the Confederacy, with the other half sent on alternating years.

For now, though, they could return home. But with this fire, they would have no home to return to—just a pile of charcoal.

"We will rebuild," Jiangxi said.

"You'll want someone to guard the compound overnight until the men return," Knöda:nöh pointed out.

He nodded, then blinked. He flicked his eyes to Knöda:nöh. They were sitting very still on their mare, which seemed to transfer a type of calm to their mount. Jiangxi's horse was still snorting and pawing at the ground. "I will stay here," he announced. "Until the others arrive."

Knöda:nöh glanced at him. "Too dangerous." They tilted their neck at the flames. "Two attacks. Both here." They craned their neck around, but whatever they were looking for appeared to be absent. "Quick in-and-out."

"A neighbor," he voiced the thought that had plagued him since the arrow.

"Possibly." Knöda:nöh turned their horse with a knee and edged back around the fire. The crackle of flames became a whoosh as the roof caved in, a cascade of sparks flung into the air. Jiangxi's horse whinnied loudly and backed up when he would have tried to guide her to follow them.

"Damnit," he gritted out between his teeth, fastening his fists into the mare's mane to hold on. He gripped his legs on her sides. "Come on, you *èrbï*."

For a moment, he thought the mare would bolt. Possible away from the fire, but from the panicked roll of her eyes, maybe straight towards it. Finally, she began to respond to the commands of his knees and hands, and she skittered past the burning building. While still fierce and bright, with the collapse in on itself, the fire appeared to be using up the available fuel and settling down. There didn't seem to be a way for it to easily spread, for the first thing they'd done when they'd begun construction was clear the undergrowth.

Knöda:nöh had waited for him to get his horse under control, but turned their mare back to the road when seeing that he was following. "Wait!" he called out in frustration, and Knöda:nöh hushed him instantly.

"While it appears the people who did this are gone, we do not know for certain. Stay quiet, and stay alert."

"We have to sleep here tonight," he reiterated with urgency. "We've lost the longhouse. We can't lose the palisade too."

Knöda:nöh turned to look at him. Even with the moonlight, Jiangxi was partially night-blinded from staring at the fire, and couldn't read their expression. Although, considering it was Knöda:nöh, it was unlikely a discernable expression existed.

"Very well." They held up a hand when he would have had some sort of vocal, and probably loud, reaction. "Don't. We return to the *kuksui*'s and report what has happened, gather what we need, and then come back here. I want to be provisioned in case of added incidents." They pointed an accusing finger at him. "And you listen to me about *everything*."

He suppressed the grin he knew would drive Knöda:nöh over the edge and have them enact the very murder they were trying to prevent. "Understood."

The ride back was uneventful, the conversation once they returned less so. Onas simply nodded without added response to the news. "I am weary," he said. "I need to rest."

Knöda:nöh and Tijö:he' conferred privately for a moment in hushed tones, then Tijö:he' suggested that he sleep in Onas's hut to ward off any potential attack. The *kuksui* agreed.

Jiangxi bundled together a sleeping mat, blanket, hand ax, spare tea kettle and cups, and a few other items. It was the beginning of fall, so there would be plenty of foods to collect—acorns and pine nuts, cattails by the lake, crickets and fish, small and large game, seeds, berries and tubers. He only took what would make his work a bit easier: a couple of baskets for cooking and storage, a container of dried seaweed to flavor the food, plus a box of tea leaves.

Knöda:nöh appeared to have gathered only weapons. They had both bow and arrows, several large knives, a pistol, musket, and two pouches that rattled when they moved, which he guessed contained more ammunition. The only knife Jiangxi carried was for utility, rather than attack, and while he was passable enough with a bow to hunt, he'd had little opportunity. But he was more than enough of an expert at snares, slings, fishing, and gathering to be able to survive easily on his own even without access to more long-range weapons.

When they got back to the worksite, they set the horses loose in the palisade, and set up a temporary camp near the entrance, just inside the wall. It would afford them enough shelter should there be another arsonist or attacker, but keep them out of sight from prying eyes. The longhouse was just smoldering embers now, and he turned away from the sight of it, exhausted.

Knöda:nöh took the first watch while Jiangxi wrapped himself in his blankets and slept. They shook him awake after a few hours, and he yawned extensively and slapped at his cheeks to help his alertness, standing up and pacing around the charred remains of the longhouse and thinking about what would come next. The first step would be to rake out the embers and the coals so that they were completely cooled, then dig out the remnants of the posts and re-lay the framework. And then, they could...

If Jiangxi thought he'd worked hard before, it was nothing compared to the next handful of days. Knöda:nöh seemed to have a change of heart, also—they no longer held themselves aloof, but joined in the labor.

But they took security measures too. When out in the woods cutting saplings, they piled brush in the opening of the wall to pen in the horses, and never strayed very far out of sight from it. Side by side, the two of them cut and carried back the saplings they'd need to reconstruct the longhouse.

When the women arrived from the farm the next day, there was a mass exclamation of shock and anger. Nuwa's lips were as thin as a knife as she pressed them together, her brow furrowed and her eyes as hot as the fire that had burned down the longhouse.

After a long look at the empty space, it seemed like she had seen enough, because she turned to Jiangxi. He had taken a moment of rest to stand next to her and offer her and the others comfort, if need be. But while one or two had wet cheeks or had trained their eyes on the ground, the majority of them reflected what he saw in Nuwa's expression. Probably how his own face had looked when he'd first seen the destruction the fire had wreaked.

"We will not let them stop us," Nuwa said, her voice low and furious. The other women echoed her, a chorus of shouts and yells filled with all the rage contained from years of servitude and pain. "They will not stop us!" she screamed at the top of her lungs, clenching her fists at her sides and half-bent over with the force of her exclamation.

Jiangxi flicked his eyes to the guards who had accompanied them from the farm as the women yelled and stomped and beat their hands together. The three men milled by the entrance of the palisade, looking uneasily one way and then another. Jiangxi's eyes moved to Knöda:nöh next, who, as usual, had no expression that showed on their lips or in their gaze. The only betrayal of what they were feeling was a slight beetling of their brow, a line in between their eyes that marked a reaction to the anger of the slaves.

Before they were completely finished, Jiangxi held up his palms and raised his voice. "We will rebuild," he said, and the women turned to look at him. "We will do it, and there will be a home waiting for the men when they return."

Nuwa was the first to nod, but not the last. He saw something in her face that he'd stopped hoping for a while ago. Something he'd only seen in one person's face, which Jiangxi had never felt he deserved.

Belief. Belief in him, belief in this project, and belief in what he continued to promise for the future. Perhaps the emotion was not belonging, and it was definitely not familial love, but belief was more valuable than any possession he owned. It gave him hope that his fierce drive to do this was not in vain, and that he would be able to pull it off despite everything that had happened so far and all the doubts he carried with him. He hadn't believed in himself, but maybe he didn't have to. Maybe their belief in him would show everyone that what he dreamed for their future was worth it.

CHAPTER 30

It was almost a full lunar month. That is how long it took them to rebuild and restock the longhouse to the best of their ability, and how long it took for the men to return north and receive their new brands of freedom from the hands of Onas and Cosso.

Huupuspumsa acted as one witness and Jiangxi as another. It was agonizing for him to watch the branding happen to someone else. Each time the heated metal touched skin, he couldn't help but wince. Some of the men tolerated it better than others, but the hiss and smell of burned flesh, happening over and over again, gave Jiangxi more than one restless night afterward as he remembered his own ordeal. He would be woken from dreams where he was being held down and watching the brand approach his face, feeling the heat on his forehead, surrounded by a leering group of men who were indifferent to the pain they were about to inflict. When he jerked awake, he would be covered in a thin film of sweat, like from a fever dream. He would lie awake a long time, struggling to overcome the images.

Of the hundred or so who had ventured south, twenty-six had not returned. Not all of them had been from Onas's fields—some had been brought or bought from other places, including the slave market. But none had been fresh off the boat, and all of them had a reason to make Freedom Town become a reality, even if not all of them had the abilities to do so.

Once the brands had been given, Jiangxi traveled with them to their new home. The longhouse would be a tight squeeze until they were able to build another, and they would have to share space for sleeping, but it was not more crowded than the slave quarters had been.

The interior was fairly spartan and bare at this point, since there hadn't yet been time to weave many additional mats to hang in the interior, and the blankets and mats from the first longhouse had burned. There were fewer supplies than Jiangxi could have hoped for, but it was not yet the harshest cold of winter, and the autumn had so far been fairly mild.

"There's still much work to be done," Jiangxi said apologetically once he came to the end of the tour. "There are tools, but not enough for everyone—more will have to be made. I'll be here to help as much as I'm able."

There was some muttering at this, and a man stepped forward. He was slightly younger than Jiangxi, but looked harder, as if he had been pounded out of clay. His accent was strange to Jiangxi, almost as if he swallowed the ends of each word as he said them. With concentration, Jiangxi could understand him. "You are overseer here?"

Jiangxi raised his brows in surprise. "What? No, no. I am no overseer."

"You—" The man shook his head, as if searching for the word. "Not overseer. Magistrate?"

Jiangxi considered the title. Magistrates in China were the local officials who administered the laws and set the standards for collecting taxes from town to town. There was no political equivalent here, since most tribes had Elders, chieftains, and spiritual leaders like the *kuksui*. Since he had no official designation, it seemed fitting. "Yes," he said, but his voice cracked with nervousness as he said it. Then, "Yes," he said more strongly. "I will be acting magistrate to help you."

"Good. You—you go to... you go to..." One of the other men whispered the word in his ear. "To the farm?" he asked.

"Yes, I help out at the farm," he replied cautiously.

"My wife. You talk?" He shook his head in frustration as he tried to convert the words. "From me."

Jiangxi darted a quick look at Knöda:nöh. They were standing some distance away at the longhouse door, arms crossed, casually looking outside. So far, he had only spoken to them in Haudenosaunee and Mutsun. He wondered if they understood the quick patter of *Guānhuà* or if they had never bothered to learn it. Not many members of the tribes took an interest in it, although he'd heard from Onas that even fewer knew the language once one traveled away from the coast and the Chinese-allied trading towns and cities.

"I can take messages from you. From all of you," Jiangxi expanded the offer.

There was a sudden clamor as the men crowded around him, many calling out over the voices of others. "Hold on," he said. Then, when it caused no cessation of noise, "Hold on! I can't hear you all at once." The babbling died down. "Okay, how many of you have a message—wait! I didn't say to tell it to me." There were too many hands outstretched. While it wasn't all the men, quite a few were eager to make contact with the slaves who had been left behind.

"I'm sorry, but I won't be able to remember that many messages," Jiangxi apologized. "I have no paper with me now, but I will return tomorrow and transcribe what you've told me and bring it to the farm. Good?"

A murmur of thanks and gratitude.

"Last, there's something we need to discuss." Jiangxi told them of the recent attacks—both the arrow (he left out the detail that Onas had been the actual target, as few of these men had any love lost for the *kuksui*) and the fire. "I would suggest," he added, "that you form a watch for both day and night. Go everywhere in pairs for protection." He ascertained afterward that there were enough capable hands for fishing in the lakes and gathering foods around the compound before he left.

"I'll return tomorrow," he said, squinting up at the twilit sky.

Knöda:nöh and he brought the cart and horses back to the farm and then walked to Onas's hut. Tijö:he' had already brewed the tea, which all four of them drank in silence.

That night, Jiangxi had no dreams, good or ill. He closed his eyes and slept, the nights of worry and stress and pain and fear melting away. Perhaps it was only temporary, but he didn't twitch or roll or have a restless night—or perhaps even move—until the birds scornfully called him awake in the morning.

Messages flew between the new town and the farm via Jiangxi. The men worked hard, building a new longhouse, setting up winter food storage, collecting, hunting, fishing. Fall was not a time of growing things, but the prelude to winter, and there were many mouths to feed.

Knöda:nöh was especially helpful, although when Jiangxi had first asked for their help, he had been met with a long and unreadable stare. "Very well," they finally said, and they went on to educate the men about hunting and the crafting of weapons for this purpose. While most slaves became familiar with the sling or fishing spear for small kills, as Jiangxi was, almost none had ever used a bow and arrows, let alone crafted them. There were a couple who were more skilled at woodworking who were most eager to learn from Knöda:nöh, and these were the ones they taught.

The men completed the palisade, then added a platform running around the interior for patrol purposes. By the time the first frost hit the ground, the town was starting to look like... a town. Cookfires, smoked meat, acorn storage, people coming and going, laughter and shouting and occasional singing—the mishmash of inhabitants who did not always get along and might have very little that they could call their own—but they were free, and that was enough.

Jiangxi came by nearly every day when he could. He felt proud, as if he had been a father to these men, and then wallowed in guilt and scorn at taking credit for what they were building. He could take credit for setting this in motion, but they were far beyond anything he could point to as accomplishing solely because of him or his actions.

Knöda:nöh continued to follow him wherever he traveled, just as Tijö:he' shadowed Onas. However, when the first frost arrived, they prepared to depart.

"The danger has passed," Knöda:nöh explained. The two of them had led their mares from the farm and packed the few belongings they would bring back with them to Aguasto—one being a packet of tea that Jiangxi had gifted to Knöda:nöh. It was more fragrant than the tea they had brought with them, and which had long since been drunk by the four of them when sitting around the cookfire in the evenings. This tea was a Chinese import that he had discovered when making some other small purchases in town for Onas, and he guessed that they would like it.

"Thank you," Jiangxi told Knöda:nöh softly. "You have protected me and the town, and every single man who lives there owes you greatly for your duty." After an ambivalent pause, "Will you return this way at some point?"

Their inscrutable expression was spoiled by a small quirk of their lips. "I doubt it," they said. When Jiangxi was taken aback by the words, they added, "But at least you shut up after a while."

He laughed, remembering back to the first encounter between the two of them, before he had even known who they were. It seemed so long ago, but it had been barely a blink of a season. "Well, perhaps I will meet you someday in Aguasto."

"Perhaps."

With that, Knöda:nöh and Tijö:he' were gone. Onas glanced over at Jiangxi, who stood staring after the two of them as they trotted around a bend of the road and out of sight. "You have done well," he said.

Jiangxi smiled. But, for once, he had nothing more to say.

The next morning when he rode towards Freedom Town, he felt as if he were naked without Knöda:nöh by his side. Although they had done nothing to protect him other than with their presence, he felt as if any moment an arrow would come sailing out of nowhere now that the powers of a Two Spirit had been withdrawn from his sphere.

Jiangxi was concentrating so intently on trying to suppress this strange and irrational fear that he almost missed the actual strange occurrence when he turned the final curve in the road before the path leading to Freedom Town. Someone stepped out from the cover of the trees and gestured to him at the side of the road.

No, not just someone. It was a woman. He wasn't sure quite how he knew, since the air was cold and she wore a plain *hanfu* with a hood that cast her features in shadow. She seemed tall for a woman, perhaps as tall as he was.

He sat back on his mount, and the beast slowed and stopped. "Can I help you?" he asked politely, but there was that itch at the nape of his neck again that was a strong warning he wouldn't ignore. He had no weaponry on him except for his usual knife, and he wished now that he had brought something—anything—for protection. While he had never fired a musket, at least it would *look* threatening if he carried it.

"I've watched you," the figure said. Her voice was clear as a bell, vindicating his guess of a female interloper.

"I am expected in Freedom Town," Jiangxi said a tad nervously. "They will look for me if I don't arrive."

Not quite a lie. But certainly not the truth. They expected him, insofar as he had shown up every day to help out. However, no one would be coming to look for him, or at least not for days. The men of the town were focused on their own work and probably would consider his absence as an indication he was attending to other work with Onas.

"*Núli Zhèn*," she repeated his name for the town. Then she drew back her hood.

It had been years. Many, many years. But he had often thought of her, and he had never forgotten her amber eyes. She was different than before, of course—older, like him. She looked healthy, though. A lot better than when he had last seen her.

"Hello, Jiangxi," she said, and he didn't even question how she knew his name. He had never given it to her, nor asked her hers on that long ago day. She smiled, and the slave brand he had thought so ugly when she was a young teenage girl still struck him as a monstrous injustice on her otherwise beautiful face. It reminded him of the ugliness of the burned longhouse—something so lovingly created, only to be maliciously corrupted on a whim.

"What...?" he began, but paused when a new sound caught his attention. He turned his head to listen and, yes, there was the distant drumming of hoofbeats on the road. Someone was approaching in a hurry.

She must have heard it too, for she flipped up the hood again and backed quickly into the trees. "Meet me at the beach where we escaped into the sea. Tonight, when the moon is over the trees." She turned and ran, disappearing in a matter of heartbeats.

Before the other rider could catch up to him, he roughly kneed his mount and continued on his way at a gallop. If the other rider came around the bend in the road, there would be no evidence this meeting had taken place. In some ways, Jiangxi almost didn't believe it himself. He felt as if he were suddenly dreaming.

Her.

Her.

Her.

The rest of the day passed in a blur. Jiangxi found himself staring off into space more than once, his hands lying idle as his mind twirled in repeat. At the cookfire that night, he gulped his tea, burning his tongue. Onas's eyes felt like dagger points as they regarded him, but although Jiangxi noticed the observation, he felt too agitated to do more to hide his eagerness.

When Onas retired for the night, Jiangxi poured another cup of tea and raised it in explanation. The *kuksui* nodded and went inside the hut.

He didn't think about assassins or attackers as he set off an eternity later. Somehow, he knew neither one would bother him tonight.

A couple times, he tripped going through the woods—the moon was waning although still bright, but the shadows cast by the trees were absolute. It had been so long since he had been to that beach in particular, but he still found the deer trails through the forest to guide his feet. Eventually, he needed no guide, for the breaks between the trees grew wider and their branches stunted and warped from the salty breath of the sea. The dunes opened up, and he trudged through the sandy expanse until he topped a rise and saw the ocean sparkling under the beaming light of the moon.

Jiangxi couldn't see her anywhere nearby, but he guessed he was also probably too early, much earlier than her stated time. The moon yawned far above and would take at least an hour to make its way towards the horizon. He walked slightly up the coast and tried to find the spot where he had hidden her so many years ago while he went to fetch the boat. It hadn't been a direct route from Onas's hut that day, since he had been nearly to the slave fields. If he was correct, that would be right about here...

He sat in a hollow in the sand and stared out at the ocean. The sea breezes swirled around him, and he shivered. It was colder right at the juncture of land and sea, since the winds were always active, and it was the beginning of the winter months. Although he was wearing a long-sleeved jacket, it was thin and not much protection against the knives of the breezes. But it could've been worse, he considered—he was lucky it wasn't raining.

The sand hissed at his back and he spun around on one knee. It was too early for the girl—woman—to be here. But just as he had arrived far in advance of their meeting, so had she. The hood of her *hanfu* billowed back in the wind, but even with the moon over her shoulder casting her features in shadow, it was unmistakably her.

"Hello," he offered as she made her way towards him.

She glanced behind them and up and down the beach in what looked like a practiced scan of her surroundings before she echoed his, "Hello."

He settled back in the sand and she kneeled beside him to sit with her legs folded under her, arranging the folds of her *hanfu* around her. When she turned to face him, the moonlight washed out the scars on her face so that her features shone through clearly. There was so much tumbling through his mind that he wasn't sure where to start. He opened and closed his mouth several times without saying anything, like a fish.

She must have seen his reaction, for she laughed—low and quietly, as if she were familiar with the constant need to remain hidden. "Let me introduce myself, first. I am Daiyu." She paused and turned her

301

eyes out over the waters. "There were... I was very afraid when I met you. A lot of bad things had happened. I am thankful that you were there. Without you—well, I would not have lived."

They were the words he had always wanted to hear—gratitude from this woman he had rescued, the idea that his sacrifice and the punishment that followed had been worth the pain. But somehow, her thanks sounded hollow. Not because of the words—they were sincere. Perhaps because too much time had passed for him to connect himself now to the boy he had been. Or perhaps he had simply grown up, and the desires he'd had as a boy for some sort of acknowledgement for his sacrifice were no longer important. The act he'd taken to offer her aid had itself been important, but her gratefulness for his part in the act was no longer necessary.

He awkwardly waved his hand. "It was... I would have done the same for anyone in your situation." He bit his lip, irritated that his words sounded too casual and dismissive. He didn't want to discount the struggles and pain she had gone through, but wasn't sure how to bring up an apology without diving too deeply into her privacy. Before he made things worse, he tried to quickly move forward. "Um, but I am glad that you are okay. I've thought about you a lot... wondered where you went and if you surv—um, if you were okay."

Her grin was mischievous. "Yes, I surv—was okay," she echoed him deliberately. His lips turned up in a responding smile at her teasing. It was the surest sign that she was, really, better now. She glanced down at her folded hands, then back at him. "It wasn't easy, not at first. I stayed at that campsite for a while, but a lot of fishermen would go by on the waters, and I worried about being caught. It was still too close to the farm, and I was afraid I could be brought back."

"Where did you go?" he asked when she paused.

She shrugged, as if casting off memories she'd rather not dredge up. "Northeast. I kept near the coast for a while, but there were too many villages. I was nearly captured a dozen times before I decided it was too dangerous to continue traveling near the beach. Finally, I picked the next river I came to and followed it inland. Pretty soon, the ground became steeper, and the water led me into the mountains." The pause this time was longer, but Jiangxi didn't attempt to prompt her to continue. "I don't know what made me follow that particular river—or what guided my steps in choosing the right path each time it split and I had to make a decision about which direction to go. But whatever led my feet, it turned out to be a good spirit who brought me luck."

"You lived in the mountains all these years?"

She nodded. "Yes, but there's more to the story. As I followed the river, it grew smaller as it split, until eventually, it was only a stream. It took a long time, but once I moved away from the coast, I ran across very few people. An odd settlement, a wandering tribe, but none who came close to discovering me. And it gave me a purpose to follow the water. I had no idea where to go otherwise."

Daiyu unlinked her hands and placed them in her sleeves; while the wind hadn't become fierce while they sat and talked, the act of sitting and not being active made it feel colder. As the chill breeze cut into his back, Jiangxi wished he had his winter coat.

"I was so familiar with being on my own and away from people that I made a mistake. It was midday, and I was following the stream as it ran around a boulder. I was rushing a bit because I was hoping to find a place where I could have a fire to cook a turtle I had caught along the way.

"Around the bend was an area hidden in the trees, and I..." she took a long breath, "I had grown careless. I sped around the boulder and was suddenly out in the open. In the space of a second, I was standing in the midst of dozens of people. I had stepped right into the outskirts of a settlement and was instantly surrounded."

CHAPTER 31

Jiangxi's breath hissed in through his teeth. His reaction wasn't governed by what had happened to her afterward, for it was obvious that Daiyu was fine. She was here, and healthy, and seemed not unhappy.

However, his reaction wasn't met by the same in her. She laughed again. "The settlement was hidden in uncleared land for a reason. It was because it was a settlement of people like me." When Jiangxi just blinked without saying anything, she added, "Escaped slaves. They had come from all over. Many had traveled much farther than me, from farms in the north. What they said about their treatment there..." She shuddered. "Much worse than here. Many times so."

Her eyes drifted back to the moon's light glittering on the sea. "But we all had a reason to be there. There are many women, a few men. Some families, some children." She shrugged her shoulders, but it was as if she were giddy with the memories, for she was smiling wistfully. "It is a good place, a healing place."

She turned her eyes towards him. "I was happy there. But things were left unfinished in my life, and they ate at my thoughts. I was free, but so many were not. And while I had stumbled upon the hidden village, how many other slaves who escaped would not be so lucky?

"I spoke with the others there. Many just wanted to live out their days and not help. The threat of recapture was too great. And, as I said, they came from worse. Much worse.

"But others felt like I did. They wanted to do what they could. Which led us to come up with ideas on how to save others.

"Helping the ones trapped in compounds was too hard, even for us. The guards—the dogs. But we could find other slaves like us, the ones who had already made it out, and bring them to our home."

Wow, Jiangxi wanted to say. His heart was racing during the telling of her story. He couldn't take his eyes off of her face, at the passion and strength he saw there. It humbled him—she had been through so much and still wanted to give more of herself. She had been brutalized by her fears, faced them head-on, and been able to overcome them. By contrast, he had been held back by his fear and anger for years, even though he had suffered so much less than she. He felt ashamed that he had only recently followed in her footsteps, unknowingly.

He also was struggling with something else. The more she spoke, the more he felt drawn to her. Not as he had been drawn to Mei, who was friendly and sweet and had made him feel welcome and important. Their relationship had been the comfort of friends, and his own weaknesses and faults had brought an undeserved retribution against her, instead. He would carry the pain he had caused her with him until he reached the end of his life.

No, Daiyu created a lightning attraction in him, a physical and visceral response. If he were honest with himself, he had felt it from the beginning. Even when he had been too young to give it a name, he had been fascinated with her. But he was not too young now, and this feeling that she stirred in him had a name.

She paused in her tale once again and stared out to sea. His eyes played over her features, content with the idea of simply watching her. It still felt not quite real to be sitting on this beach with her at his side, finally knowing her name and learning her story. Perhaps he would open his eyes in a moment to see the roof of Onas's hut above him and find out that this was only a dream, similar to many dreams he'd had before.

To keep the dream going, he asked, "What happened?"

"It worked," she said. The moon had advanced, and when she turned back to him, half of her face was illuminated. But the colors of her features were washed out in the light, so he couldn't see the amber of her eyes that he had kept nestled in his memory all these years. The one eye lit by the moon looked luminous, but a pale shade of grey. "We found more stragglers—ones who had somehow escaped pursuit and been surviving by themselves since then. Some were good people to welcome. Some—" her voice hitched for a second and she bit her lip. "Some were not."

Another story there. Without thinking, he reached out a hand and held it, palm up, in front of her. They were distant enough that he had to edge closer to do so.

Her eyes dropped to his offer of comfort. He thought for a moment that he had made a mistake, offended her somehow, and he tensed his shoulders for her rejection.

But she withdrew her right hand from her sleeve placed it in his. Her fingers were like the icy waters of the ocean, and he gripped her hand firmly. After a second, he turned more fully towards her and brought his second hand around to join the first, gently chafing her palm between the two of his in order to bring some life back to it. She offered her other hand as well, and he curved his hands around them to provide additional warmth.

"We have been doing this for only a couple of years—it took me a long time to work up the courage to leave the village, and a longer time to convince others to be a part of it. But our network has grown during that time. There have been—there have been some casualties along the way." Her voice shook for a moment, and she bit her lip until she regained control. "I have lost friends. But none have betrayed our mission or our home."

"But how did that bring you here?" Jiangxi asked.

A slight smile creased her lips. "It started with rumors. Some of the escaped slaves talked about a crazy *kuksui* who was freeing his slaves. When I heard that, and the name Onas, I knew I had to come." She shrugged carefully, since her hands were still gripped by his. "And then I heard about the *kuksui*'s apprentice. A man who worked with the slaves, who helped them and brought them comfort. A man who was once a slave himself, but convinced his master to free him. A man who wanted to lead his people to freedom. *Xiǎo huángdì.*"

Jiangxi could feel his cheeks flushing when she spoke his nickname aloud, because it sounded silly. He was thankful for the fitful illumination. If he could see no color underneath the silvery light, it was unlikely she would be able to notice his embarrassment so easily either. "You make me sound like a... like a..."

"Like a hero," she said. Her tone was light, but without the joking note of before.

"I'm *not* a hero," he said fiercely, then regretted it when she instantly drew back from him at his hard words, reclaiming her hands into her sleeves. He quickly apologized, but the wariness of her expression didn't wane. "I've made a lot of mistakes," he admitted. "People expect so much of me, but I've—I've gotten them hurt because of my stupidity. Maybe killed." He shook his head. "I might never know."

At his confession, her expression changed. "I've made mistakes too," she replied acerbically. She rolled her eyes. "*Everyone* makes mistakes, you *èrbǐ.*" This time, she reached out to him and placed her hand on the knee of his breeches. "Even the gods aren't perfect. It is what you do after making those mistakes that matters. You have accomplished amazing things."

Greatly daring, he captured her hand again with his. This time, she did not pull away. "Thank you," he said. And he meant it.

She squeezed his hand. "That is the reason why I came."

He was distracted by the feeling of her fingers in his. Although her hands were small, they were not soft hands, like a noble lady, but rough and calloused. Like his hands, tough. "Why?"

"I heard the rumors, but I wanted to know the facts. How the slaves are being freed, and how we can make this part of a larger effort. I know you are starting small right now, but there are thousands— thousands of us. And so many of them are suffering and dying every day." She took a deep breath. "I came here to thank you. But, more than that, to convince you."

"Convince me?" He couldn't think what she was saying. "I'm not the one to convince—there's a lot of opposition to what Onas and I are doing. It's all I can do to carry out our plans. There have been—well. There have been attacks against us."

Her expression softened. "There's more than one way to do this," Daiyu said. She leaned forward, and he was distracted by the thrilling touch of her hands and the intensity of her eyes. He was tempted to cross the last space between them and kiss her, but he was certain that if he did that, she would take offense and disappear, and he would never see her again. But he had to grit his teeth to prevent from following through on the action, to prevent himself from reaching out to touch more than her hands. He wanted to brush his thumbs against the skin of her cheeks, which would be rough from her scars. He wanted to feel the heavy weight of her hair in his palms.

His voice sounded strangled when he spoke through his clenched jaw. "What way? How do we do this?"

Her joy shone through in her smile when he said "we," and it pierced his heart. At that moment, he would've probably agreed to anything that she would suggest, no matter the cost.

"*We,*" she emphasized, "can accomplish anything if we join our efforts. With both of us working together, we can do more than help one or two slaves find freedom." She paused and leaned forward. Her eyes roamed over his face as if she, too, were compelled by his presence, and his breath caught in his throat as his heart thundered.

"Jiangxi," she said breathlessly. "Let's free them all."

CHAPTER 32

The sky was lightening by the time he returned to the clearing. He knew he would wake Onas if he tried to enter the hut, so he instead rekindled the cookfire and lay down next to the warmth of it. He was still giddy and didn't think he would sleep, but it was full morning when Onas shook him awake and asked if he would be going to Freedom Town that day.

Jiangxi and Daiyu had spoken for most of the night. He had asked at one point, since her shivering was obvious when her chattering teeth started sounding like pebbles falling onto a dry riverbed, if he should kindle a fire. "No," she said. "A light will be seen."

They had still been holding hands then. Greatly daring, he pulled her against him and the warmth of his body, wrapping his arms around her elbows but giving her no other physical contact except the heat of his chest against her back. He held himself very still and kept his hands loosely resting near her forearms. He could feel the rigid stiffness of her body, which was not just from the cold. But, eventually, the combined heat of their bodies gradually eased both of

311

their shivering. Daiyu seemed to relax, the tension easing out of her muscle by muscle, until she was a limp weight pressing against him.

She didn't pull away until a bird trilled in the distance, even though the sky over the ocean was still black. The moon had long since set over the trees, and so the night was darker than before. Yet the bird would not be wrong about the advent of the sun.

"Where are you staying?" he asked when she regained her feet. He followed suit and they stood eye to eye, nearly the same height. When she tilted her head at him, he realized how much he was suggesting she trust him with his question. The place where she was hiding from the law—and where she could be caught. He amended it to, "Is it safe?"

"As safe as possible," she answered. He saw the whiter flash of her teeth in the semi-darkness, and knew that she was smiling.

"When can we meet again?" he asked.

He felt a whisper of astonishment when she raised a hand to his cheek and rested it there in a gesture that was both affectionate and deeply intimate. "Nighttime here on the beach is safe," she said. "But there are some things I must take care of, and quickly. Three nights from now?"

He swallowed audibly. "Yes," he said.

She took back her hand and turned north. He watched her walk up the beach and slightly inland, until she disappeared over a dune. The energy that had sustained him through the night abruptly disappeared once she was gone from sight. Exhausted, he headed back to Onas's hut to catch his few hours of sleep.

Work was both slow and quick that day. His mind wandered, partly from exhaustion and partly because it had wonderful daydreams where it wanted to escape. He was particularly accident-prone, also. He nearly cut his leg with the hand axe when he was chopping saplings, which were for another longhouse. He did slice open his palm when peeling the bark from the wood, although the cut was shallow.

Several times, people came up to talk to him, but he was so lost in his thoughts that they had to repeat themselves.

It was the man who'd spoken in broken *Guānhuà* that first day the ex-slaves had arrived in town who made the connection between Jiangxi's erratic behavior and the cause. Jiangxi knew the man well now, knew his name was Zixen, and his wife and daughter were still in the compound.

After Zixen failed to gain Jiangxi's attention for the second time that day, he grinned and made an exaggerated batting of his eyes. "You," he said and laughed. "Love."

Despite his sun-darkened skin, Jiangxi's reddening cheeks caught the men's eyes. Zixen laughed. "True—it is true!"

What could he do but laugh with him? And he did, but offered no more information, even when Zixen and the other men tried to pry. They teased him a bit, but when he reacted with only more laughter, they let him be.

It wasn't until Onas also commented that night about his apprentice's distraction that Jiangxi realized he had to hide it better. But it was hard—three entire days to wait to see her again.

The time ran like a hare and also dripped slowly, like melting ice. But it was suddenly the night they were supposed to meet, and he was on the beach again. This time, he had prepared a bundle to bring with him. When Daiyu arrived and knelt down next to him, he handed her a fur and hide cloak that he had sewn several seasons before. "This is for you."

She ran her hand over the soft rabbit pelts, breathing out a contented sigh. "This is beautiful," she said, meeting his eyes and smiling. "Thank you."

He stammered out the appropriate response, taking back the cloak from her hands and shaking it open, then wrapping it around her shoulders. She pulled it tight around her and did not shiver once that night. But he missed holding her and almost wished he had not brought the gift, if it meant he had to forgo that pleasure.

Perhaps she sensed his disappointment—or perhaps she was as disappointed as he was. Because when she was preparing to leave, she placed her hands against his chest, leaned forward, and kissed him.

That was all. A brief brush of her lips against his, cold from the sea wind and tasting like the salt of the water's spray. But the moment was electrifying. He couldn't remember a more perfect event in his life than that one brief kiss.

He held it close to his thoughts like a treasure, taking that darkened second out from his memories to examine it many times in the bright light of day. But there was something clandestine about these night meetings that carried beyond the simple act of secrecy required to protect Daiyu's freedom; it was an isolated bubble separate from other people and their expectations, a place where they could talk about dreams, hopes, desires, and the future. No one judged; no one knew. No one except the two of them.

And Onas. Perceptive as always, he seemed to know also.

"Is she from the farm?" the *kuksui* asked one day as they ate at the cookfire.

Jiangxi froze as he tried to formulate an answer. Mid-bite of his meal, he chewed and swallowed. "Yes," he answered truthfully. She had been from the farm, although no longer there.

"That is good," Onas said. His eyes flicked to the woods in the direction of the farm, then back to Jiangxi. "There could be... you could buy her freedom. Take her to wife."

Jiangxi had no purchasing power of his own—everything he bought from town was done on Onas's credit with his wampum, and only done with Onas's approval. Little had changed since he was a slave in terms of his work, except that he had more freedom of direction and didn't need to ask permission, although he still found himself falling back into certain habits at times.

Now, he didn't know how to extricate himself from the situation. He trusted Onas more than almost anyone else at this point. The *kuksui* had shown time and again that he was different than before, that he would put his reputation and his wealth and power on the line in order to help Jiangxi. But there were limits to what would be acceptable, Jiangxi guessed. And one of those limits might be Daiyu.

The next time Jiangxi met her on the beach, he brought up the subject. He blundered into his explanation, suggesting that she return to Onas and his overseer, and then Jiangxi would purchase her freedom.

She rocked back from him as if he had struck her, leaping to her feet and backing away from him. "*What?*" she hissed.

The word was full of all the rage and betrayal he'd felt towards Onas when he was younger and still a slave. The fact that Daiyu turned that tone on him stunned him. "He wouldn't punish you—he *wouldn't!* And then you would be free, and not have to hide anymore. We could carry out our plans in the open, together. Like I am doing now. And we could—" Here, he felt embarrassed again. His plan seemed infantile, now that he had said it aloud. Now that he had seen her reaction. Would she even *want* to be with him? To... to marry him?

From her glare, he doubted it. "We will do *nothing*," she growled. "You cannot *ever* tell him about me. You want me back in slavery? You want me back on the farm, so you can control me?" Her voice had started to get louder with each word, and he glanced around frantically, worried that now would be the time when they were caught.

"Sound travels over water," he reminded her in a low voice. He moved forward to grasp her arms, but she backed away from him again and wouldn't let him touch her.

"You are not the man I thought you were," she told him coldly.

"Daiyu, I love you," he said desperately. He knew the timing was wrong to say this, but he couldn't help it. After their few perfect moments together over the past few days, when they had seemed to be linked in everything that mattered, he was going to lose her.

Perhaps... perhaps he never really even had her.

Daiyu didn't answer him. Just gave him a long, intense look, her eyes searching the contours of his face, searching for... something. But when she didn't seem to find it, her shoulders fell and she turned away. She made a wide berth around him and began walking up the beach.

Jiangxi could have gone after her. He could have pleaded with her, argued for his reasoning, apologized. Maybe after her temper cooled, she would know that he meant well, even if the execution of his idea was untenable to her.

He didn't do any of these things. It took a thousand years to return to Onas's hut. Each step he took was as slow as a season passing, and as heavy and crushing as an ocean wave. He lay down on his sleeping mat and pulled the blanket over his body.

Jiangxi stared into the black air around him, a darkness that matched the emptiness inside. Nothing he had done with his life seemed to matter. Darkness was the only presence that he felt would ever embrace him.

CHAPTER 33

A day passed. Two. He worked. Came back to the hut. Kept his eyes open through the night as sleep eluded him.

The third day, a messenger came galloping up from Wacharon. Jiangxi took the message and handed the wampum wrapped around it to Onas. The *kuksui* took one look at it and his voice was grim as he said, "Read it."

The missive was brief, but it didn't need to be long. The ambassador simply detailed that the Chinese ships had arrived. Not just for support, but in force. The news was twofold: when word had originally been delivered to the Yonghuang Emperor about the Spanish threat, one of his fleets had been sent two years ago to navigate around the African coast and attack the Spanish trade at the source. The ambassador didn't know if they had yet engaged in battle, but the last word of their progress was good; they had lost only a few ships to storms and were within a month or so of their destination.

At the same time, a second fleet had recently landed on the southwest coast of the Viceroyalty of New Spain. The Chinese troops were currently marching inland, leaving swathes of destruction in their wake, and taking the settlers completely by surprise.

Onas seemed dazed at the news, as surprised as the Spanish must be at this development. His hands shook around the wampum and he slowly sat down. "And we invited them in," he murmured to himself. He stared off into the distance and said nothing else, but he seemed terribly old and burdened in that moment.

Jiangxi remembered the betrayal of his brother when he was six. The cruelty of him, even though the details of his brother's face and the words he'd said had faded from Jiangxi's memory. This didn't seem out of place for a man who had taken the palace by force, killed his own father, and sold his brothers into slavery.

But, at this moment, there was nothing he could do—either to comfort Onas or come up with a solution to the problem they might face. He did not have to voice the thoughts that must be at the top of Onas's mind, as they were in his: what would happen if the Spanish were defeated? Where would the Yonghuang Emperor's troops turn their attention next?

But they didn't talk about it all that day, nor that evening. Onas had sent no message back to town or the ambassador, but he spent some time in the sweat lodge, and some time making wampum. He appeared deep in thought, and Jiangxi could guess that he must be turning the problem over and over in his mind, trying to figure out where to go from here.

The next day, Cosso arrived when Jiangxi was pounding acorns for the meal. He spoke to Onas and then left. Jiangxi didn't bother trying to eavesdrop over the rhythmic thump of the pestle into the rock—the words seemed unimportant.

Until they weren't. Onas spoke from behind him. "She didn't die."

Jiangxi's head snapped around. He had been sitting cross-legged on a buried boulder that had seen many generations of use for grinding acorns. It was pockmarked by holes that had been worn into the rock over many years. Some of them Jiangxi had made himself. "*What?*"

"You remember, years ago. The slave girl who left the farm."

Jiangxi felt as if the air had disappeared from the clearing. He couldn't seem to breathe at all. "What happened?" he croaked.

Onas's shrewd eyes traveled over his apprentice's face. "She was caught cutting into the stockade at night. Apparently, she was trying to encourage the slaves to escape."

Jiangxi dropped the pestle that had been dangling from his fingers and leapt down from the rock. "*kuksui,*" he said in a low tone. Still, his voice wobbled with suppressed emotion. "Please. You must let her go."

"I must?" Onas asked, half to himself. Then he blinked. "Hmm. *This* is the girl."

Jiangxi didn't bother to answer. He didn't need to.

Onas sighed deeply. He looked tired, but with this on top of yesterday's news, it was to be expected. Also, he had been looking exhausted much more frequently. Ever since the news of the war with the Spanish. Or, perhaps earlier than that—ever since the trip to Aguasto, when Jiangxi had been freed. The journey had seemed to take a lot out of him then, and perhaps he had never fully recovered.

"I cannot," he said now. "There is too much at stake. I have gone to the limits of my influence, and pushed the boundaries almost to the breaking point. We have committed to this path. We cannot allow the slaves who break the laws to go free without consequence. We reward the ones who obey the laws, but must punish those who break it."

Jiangxi shook his head. "Then let her go, but do it quietly. There is no need for word to spread about it." He hesitated, but plunged forward regardless. "Have the guards look away. Give them a bribe. There must be some way to make this—"

"I said *no!*" Onas shouted.

319

Jiangxi was shocked into speechlessness. He couldn't remember another time when Onas had yelled, not only at him, but at anyone. He was always completely calm and completely measured.

The shout seemed to wither him, though, and his shoulders hunched. More quietly, he said, "I have indulged you too much for an apprentice. Too much for who you are. I have been lenient with you because of what I have known from the spirits. But this—this, I cannot do." He shook his head. "She will be punished and return to the fields."

He paused, and his eyes softened. "Jiangxi," he said. It was one of the few times that Onas had ever spoken his name, since even though he was only half Amah Mutsun, he tended to follow the customs and avoid names to avert evil spirits. "I do not have many years left to me. Our plan—your plan—is working. But it is still too soon to challenge it.

"Wait to do more," he added. "When I am gone, the farm will be yours. You can do with the slaves what you will."

Jiangxi raised his chin and glared at Onas. After all this time, after everything that had happened, it had come to this. "Will you reconsider?" he asked softly.

"No," said Onas. His tone was final.

Before speaking, Jiangxi moderated his tone to calm. He lowered his head so his eyes wouldn't betray him. He said, "Very well." He did not look up again as Onas walked away.

Jiangxi waited until the dew was forming on the grasses that night before he approached the farm. He knew where the two overnight guards would be—he knew their schedule, and guessed where they would keep a recaptured slave. They recognized him by sight and suspected nothing until their throats were slit and they choked on their own blood as they died. He was prepared for what they would have done to her because of what they had done to Mei, but the surprise of it was nothing more had happened to Daiyu except being trussed up and abandoned in the corner of the lean-to.

He untied her and led her out, past the two men he had killed, and past the slaughtered guard at the stockade entrance. Then he brought her through the forest, unspeaking, until they reached the beach.

"Go north," he told her. "Through the waves, so the dogs won't catch your scent. There is an abandoned hut there, which might have fallen to ruin. But the boat will probably be intact."

She eyed him—his bloodstained clothing and determination on his face. "You must come with me."

He shook his head. "Being with you now will put you in danger. I will grab some supplies from Onas's hut, and then lead them away from you. You've told me how to find your village, so go there. Wait for me. I will meet you when I can."

She closed her amber eyes and pressed her lips together to still them from trembling. Her cheeks were wet. "I am sorry," she said.

"No—no," he protested. "*I* did this. Not you." He stripped off his bloody coat and rinsed his hands in the sea before he dared to pull her towards him. She raised her arms to place them around him and he kissed her. Her lips tasted salty like the sea. "I will see you again," he promised.

She nodded and let go. He watched her run north in the moonlight, the hood of her *hanfu* floating behind her like a ghost.

EPILOGUE

Jiangxi was furiously buttoning his jacket when a familiar voice from the doorway stilled his fingers.

"Leave be. They have come here for you." After a pause, "You could not have waited for me to die?"

The tone of the words was lethargic. His master was an old man when Jiangxi had come to him and an even older man now, but his deep voice was slowed by sorrow, not age. The shadows of the room seemed to darken, despite the sliver of moonlight streaming in from the next room and the passage leading outside. The passage that should have led to freedom.

Jiangxi made no reply, but raised his head high. He stepped forward to face the stooped man waiting in the doorway. He met Onas's eyes, which were weighed down with the burden of mortality. There were a thousand answers Jiangxi could have given his master, but he made none of them.

Instead, Jiangxi asked a question with his eyes. *Will Freedom Town live on?*

Onas sighed. Nodded his head once—and then again. Answering the unspoken second question too: *Will you take care of them for me?*

After a moment more, regretting he would not be able to keep his promise to Daiyu, Jiagxi stepped past him.

A public execution would solve the problem. He pictured it: the slave market platform in town. A cheering crowd. All of their fears, which had converged in him, dissipating with his death.

At least Daiyu was safe. Although he knew she would eventually come down from the mountain and learn that he had died. She would carry on her work, and maybe his, too. When she told others about his sacrifice for her, he was sure the tale would grow in the telling.

Others might have stories about him too. Perhaps Zixen would speak about the magistrate who had created Freedom Town. And Nuwa could talk about the little emperor who had become a man. A man who listened to their hopes when no one else would. A man who began the process of making their dreams a reality.

Outside the door, he saw a row of rifles sticking into the air like the traditional spears of war. When the warriors saw his silhouette darken the doorway, they lowered their rifles and took aim. They were taking no chances, not after he had murdered the men who were there to guard against the terror of a freed slave—a freed slave like him.

Behind him, the old man sighed. Jiangxi walked towards the fate awaiting him.

They had come here to kill him. It was over.

Acknowledgments

There are so many people to thank, without whom this novel, these characters, and this story would not be here.

First of all, to the Pitch Week judges, coaches, and owners who helped make sure that this book is the best that it can be: Steve Eisner and his lovely bride, Barb Newman, Emma Irving, Amber Griffith, Peggy Moran, Ben Tanzer, Colin Hosten, and Marilyn Atlas. I appreciate everything you told me about how to carry this novel from start to finish, and I'm honored and thrilled that this story was awarded the Gold.

For my fellow Pitch Week contestants, who cheered me on as much as I was cheering for them: Rebecca Lowry Warchut, Amy Bleu, Shawn Samuelson Henry, and Julie Cadman—you gals are the best!

To the Fairfield Scribes: P.C. Keeler, P.M. Ray, Edward Ahern, Teresa Richards, Sarah Anderson, Michael Wiskind, Kevin Elias Kaye, E.J. Shoko, Leslie Burton-López, and Carolyn Matos. I'm so lucky to count such talented writers and editors as my friends.

To Henry Sullivan III and Suzanne Hayes, my writing pals who listened to my chapters and gave me thoughtful feedback on so much of this book—your advice was invaluable. All my love to you both.

To the members of the online writing group Shut Up & Write!, who so generously supported my efforts to write and edit this book—there are too many names to list, but you know who you are—I appreciate every single one of you. Special shoutout to the group leaders who constantly inspire writers around the world, including: Roger, Alan, Sid, Shawna, Theresa, Jeremy, Janet, Brennin, Ruth, Anne Marie, Marvin, Chris, Will & Jim, Bonnie, Cristina, Cecilie, Thea, Emily, Eugenia, and Céline.

Almost last, but certainly not least, to my good friends and fellow writers who've supported me on this journey: Gabi Coatsworth, Elizabeth Chatsworth, Mitzy Sky, Linda Polon, Beth P., Robert Tomaino,

Stephanie Bass, Sheryl Kayne, Joanne Dowdy, Ben Bisbee, Brian B. King, Mary Keating, and Jacqueline Masumian. If I've forgotten to list anyone here, I still appreciate you wholeheartedly, but I have terrible mom brain and must apologize for the lapse.

Finally, to a friend who has gone beyond writing her own words, but is deserving of all the kind words herself: Kora Sadler. You always led with your heart, and I'll remember you with mine.

Glossary of Non-English Words and Names

Amah Mutsun (Ohlone) Words & Names

Aguasto—A large coastal town; seat of tribal governments in the western part of the Confederacy.

Amah Mutsun—A group of tribes living from present-day San Francisco to Monterey, California.

Cosso—Overseer of Onas's farm. Translation: "burn with pain."

Kuksu—Religion of the Amah Mutsun.

kuksui—Leader/spirit of Kuksu religion.

Haayi!—Translation: "Come here!"

hahmestap—Slang for tribal men who have relationships with Chinese women; translation: "she was slept with in her sleep/to crawl over to the woman."

hamaama—Translation: "simple-minded/crazy person."

Hamatay—California goosefoot (plant).

hasseSte-k—Son of Cosso. Translation: "he's angry."

hikTiSmin—Slang name for Chinese slaves. Translation: "scarred."

Huupuspumsa—Merchant in the town of Wacharon who works with Onas and Jiangxi. Translation: "selling place."

kaSsup-was iccin—Amah Mutsun nickname for the missionary Junipero Serra. Translation: "the mosquito bit him."

kuutYiSmin rukka—Translation: "a small house/hut."

Maayit—Wise man of a nearby village between Wacharon and Aguasto. Translation: "laughter."

miSSimpiy puuTey amSi yulke sottow—Translation: "Blow well, so that the fire will burn."

Mutsun—Spoken language of the Amah Mutsun.

Porpor—Fremont cottonwood (tree).

Sirak—Onas's neighbor; lends horses to Onas for trip to Aguasto. Translation: "hazelnut."

Taacin—A kangaroo rat.

Wacharon—Town within walking distance to Onas's hut.

Yuure—Onas's neighbor. Translation: "hunts cottontail rabbits."

Haudenosaunee (Iroquois) Words & Names

Dá:snye't—Friend of Onas, who lives in Aguasto. Seneca, translation: "he spoke up."

Ëgadiyóhšö:'—Haudenosaunee councilwoman in Aguasto opposed to Chinese troops being sent to the south. Seneca, translation: "I'll fight against several people."

Gaëni:yo:h—Young man and Dá:snye't's grandson, member of the Haudenosaunee council in Aguasto. Seneca, translation: "good song."

Hö:ga:k—Onas's neighbor, bigger man. Seneca, translation: "goose."

Knöda:nöh—Jiangxi's Two Spirit warrior bodyguard. Seneca, translation: "I guard the town."

Níá'a:h—Son of someone Onas and Dá:snye't know, mentioned in passing. Seneca, translation: "he's small/small boy."

Onas—Both *kuksui*, an Amah Mutsun religious leader, and a Haude-nosaunee False Face religious leader of the Seneca tribe. Haudeno-saunee, translation: "quill, pen."

Onödowá'ga—Name for the Seneca tribe.

Tijö:he'—Onas's bodyguard. Seneca, translation: "we are just living."

Wampum—Small beads that are strung together into belts for cere-monial decoration and/or used as currency.

Chinese (Mandarin) Words & Names

Ah Kum—Older, enslaved woman. Translation: "good as gold."

Àiwōwo—Glutinous rice balls, a treat.

Ānchún—Translation: "quail."

Chuán—A mid-sized wooden cargo ship.

Chuī hǎo huǒ cáinéng ránshāo qǐlái—Translation: "Blow well, so that the fire will burn."

Dàguà—A long robe.

Daiyu—Amber-eyed girl who escapes from slavery.

Èrbï—Translation: "idiot."

Guānhuà—Mandarin language (a Chinese dialect).

Jiangxi—Enslaved boy from Beijing; son of the previous emperor.

Hanfu—A short robe/jacket.

Hu—Nuwa's son. Translation: "tiger."

Huǒchái—Translation: "matches."

Jiǔguǎn—Translation: "wine shop."

Lǎo péngyǒu— Translation: "old friend."

Li—Traditional Chinese unit of distance; about 550 yards.

Mei—An enslaved woman on Onas's plantation.
Translation: "beautiful/pretty."

Niskowŭkni ne'' Sadē'goshä—A week-long festival of thanksgiving.

Núlì Zhèn—Freedmen's town founded by Jiangxi and Onas. Translation: "freedom town."

Nuwa—Enslaved mother, who becomes the spokesperson for the slaves after the men are sent away to war. Translation: "mother goddess."

Pupai—A Chinese gambling game of double-sided tiles.

Siheyuan—A traditional Chinese housing compound.
Translation: "quadrangle."

Xiǎo huángdì—Nickname for Jiangxi. Translation: "little emperor."

Yǎn ěr dào líng—Chinese saying. Translation: "Cover your ears to steal a bell."

Yīqiè dōu zài biàn, wǒmen yě gēnzhe biàn—Chinese saying. Translation: "All things change, and we change with them."

Yonghuang Emperor—Current Emperor of China, Jiangxi's brother.

Zao—Type of Chinese boots.

Zheng He—Naval explorer and general who commanded the fleets of the Chinese emperor in the fifteenth century.

Zixen—Ex-slave who lives in Freedom Town.
Translation: "self-confidence."

Zìyóu Zhèn—Proposed new town name. Translation: "slave town."

Other Names & Locations

Kosa'aay—A town in Tipai territory; would have been located in present-day southern California near San Diego.

Kumeyaay—A tribe in present-day southern California, consisting of three groups: the Ipai (north), Tipai (farther south), and Kamia (inland desert).

Portolá—Spanish captain commanding the armies of Junipero Serra.

About the Author

Alison McBain is a Pushcart Prize-nominated author with over two hundred short stories, poems, and articles published worldwide. Her books have been honored with gold in the Literary Classics International Book Awards and When Words Count Pitch Week contest, as well as becoming finalists in The Wishing Shelf Book Awards and IAN Book of the Year. When not writing, she's the associate editor for the literary magazine *Scribes*MICRO*Fiction*, co-editor of *Morning Musings Magazine*, and pens an award-winning webcomic called *Toddler Times*. Alison lives in Fairfield, Connecticut.